Published by ECW Press
665 Gerrard Street East
Toronto, Ontario, Canada, M4M 1Y2
416-694-3348 / info@ecwpress.com

LIBRARY AND ARCHIVES CANADA
CATALOGUING IN PUBLICATION

Title: The Amber Garden / Cynthea Masson.

Names: Masson, Cynthea, 1965- author.

Description: Series statement: The Alchemists' Council ; book 3

Identifiers: Canadiana (print) 20190176377
Canadiana (ebook) 20190176385

ISBN 978-1-77041-275-0 (softcover)
ISBN 978-1-77305-462-9 (PDF)
ISBN 978-1-77305-461-2 (EPUB)

Classification: LCC PS8626.A7993 A86 2020
DDC C813/.6—dc23

Editor: Jen Hale
Cover design: Michel Vrana
Paper texture © Kamyshko/Shutterstock
Honeycomb © sauletas/Shutterstock

The publication of *The Amber Garden* has been generously supported by the Canada Council for the Arts which last year invested $153 million to bring the arts to Canadians throughout the country and is funded in part by the Government of Canada. *Nous remercions le Conseil des arts du Canada de son soutien. L'an dernier, le Conseil a investi 153 millions de dollars pour mettre de l'art dans la vie des Canadiennes et des Canadiens de tout le pays. Ce livre est financé en partie par le gouvernement du Canada.* We acknowledge the support of the Ontario Arts Council (OAC), an agency of the Government of Ontario, which last year funded 1,737 individual artists and 1,095 organizations in 223 communities across Ontario for a total of $52.1 million. We also acknowledge the contribution of the Government of Ontario through the Ontario Book Publishing Tax Credit, and through Ontario Creates for the marketing of this book.

PRINTED AND BOUND IN CANADA   PRINTING: MARQUIS   5   4   3   2   1

MIX
Paper from
responsible sources
FSC® C103567

THE ALCHEMISTS' COUNCIL
BOOK THREE

THE

AMBER

GARDEN

CYNTHEA MASSON

IN GRATITUDE AND DEDICATION
TO MY FAMILY:

ROD, MEL, KEN, VICKIE, KATHRYN, AND GREG

The outside world scribes implore you first to read Books One and Two.

Then choose for yourself whether or not to read Book Three.

Prima Materia

In the beginning, Aralia and Osmanthus shaped the Prima Materia of existence into two principal dimensions: the Alchemists' Council inhabited and maintained the one; the Rebel Branch, the other. As with all alchemy, Council and Flaw dimensions represent the binary opposition of Aralia and Osmanthus: the sulphur and the mercury, the sun and the moon, the light and the dark, the fire and the water, the one and the other. The salt of the earth — the outside world — binds the dimensions into a trinity of physical existence comprising time, space, and form.

Beginning with the Crystalline Wars, and continuing throughout the era of Eirenaeus, conflict raged between the two primary dimensions, and the people of the outside world suffered the consequences. Still, the alchemists and rebels persisted, fighting perpetual battles in their respective quests for victory: one over the other. But all remained relatively stable until, through an act of disobedience by a small group of insurgents, hell broke loose. And the dimensions began to dissolve. Now, only the words and actions of Prima Materia made manifest can initiate a new beginning.

PROLOGUE
Council Dimension — Dawn of the 5th Council

E buros stood on the Azothian dais, hands raised in the sacred gesture of Ab Uno, voice resonating through Council Chambers. "In the name of the Azoth Magen of the 4th Council of Alchemists, in accordance with the Codes of Law and the tradition of Azothian protocols, I hereby declare the dusk of the reign of Eburos and the dawn of the 5th Council. Thus, on this day, at this hour, in the presence of my Elders, I declare my intention to prepare for Final Ascension. Long live the Quintessence!"

"Long live the Alchemists' Council!" replied the Elders.

Makala lowered her head, not only to feign respect for the Azoth Magen but also to avoid the possibility that Corylus would see her grin. Now that Eburos had declared his official intention, Council's progression towards the Ritual of Succession would begin. Over the past few weeks, Rowan Savar had repeatedly warned Makala of Eburos's intention to delay the Ritual of Ascension for several months. The Azoth Magen had required an unprecedented length of time to decide which of the two Azoths would succeed him. Makala's faith in her ability to reign victorious over her brother remained unshaken. Soon, no matter Eburos's delay, she alone would be seated on the dais as Azoth Magen.

Makala had envisaged this moment for as long as her memory extended. Of course, she assumed Corylus harboured similar aspirations. At that very moment, he too was no doubt imagining himself taking pride of place within Azothian Chambers. Since entering the Initiate in the same quarto, Makala and Corylus had for centuries been in literal and figurative competition. With each conjunction, each ascension, each rotation, they had sparred to ascend within the Orders of Council before the other. But whether through coincidence or the alchemical formula of their bloodline, neither had managed to surpass the other long enough for the three nines to slay one or the other. Thus, Makala and Corylus had become Elders of the 4th Council within a week of one another. Now, both currently positioned as Azoths, they knew that only one of them could ascend to Azoth Magen; only one of the two would survive.

They were alchemical twins, after all; they embodied Aralia and Osmanthus's eternal conflict of opposition. *One must die so the other may live.* Such was the agreement made during the 1st Council of Alchemists between Rebel Branch High Azoth Deru and Alchemists' Council Azoth Magen Ashoka during veiled settlement negotiations made in the aftermath of the Crystalline Wars. *One must die so the other may live. The Creators will create them: one and the other, a conjunction of opposites, alchemy personified. Our battle will be their battle. In our stead, they will fight to the death. In their stead, we will survive eternally.*

But Makala knew that her conquest over Corylus would do more than mark the symbolic end of the Crystalline Wars. It would change the course of the worlds. She lifted her head, dark hair gleaming, and met his crystal-blue eyes.

Your days are numbered. She was holding her pendant, inset with a Dragonblood fragment that would allow him to read her thoughts.

Do not be so naïve. You should have died at birth, Corylus responded. *The 5th Council is mine for the taking. As are you.*

Meaningless threats. Only I have the corporeal power to carry the Seed, said Makala.

Yet you have no means to do so without me, replied Corylus.

Other than when Council business necessitated, Makala and Corylus did not speak during the eight weeks between the Declaration of Intention and the Ritual of Succession. Makala watched Corylus closely nonetheless, always wary that he would seek a means to cheat, attempt to outwit her and the promise she represented to their parents and to the dimensions throughout the timelines, both to her primordial ancestors and to her bloodline descendants. Eventually she grew apprehensive precisely *because* Corylus did nothing to warrant her suspicions. She refused to consider beyond the briefest of suppositions whether he had begun to relish the notion of becoming her Azothian consort.

On the appointed day in the ninth week, Makala and Corylus knelt, deceptively humble, on either side of Azoth Magen Eburos. Rowans Palash and Savar stood as honour guards, likewise anxiously awaiting the Azothian decision. Finally, when Eburos raised the Lapidarian sceptre and lowered it towards her shoulder, uttering the long-anticipated words *Long live Azoth Magen Makala*, Makala cried in joy and Corylus shuddered in agony.

Two weeks later, as Palash and Savar recited the requisite words from the *Nabatean Opus*, Makala readied herself for duty, raising the Sword of Elixir into position. When Eburos finally succumbed, when a mere skeletal trace of him remained, Makala charged forward, piercing his remains — Lapis-forged steel plunged into Azothian Quintessence for the good of All and One. Makala sank to her knees as the residual particles of Eburos rained down upon her. Now, with dust-drenched face, she would reign over all three dimensions. Now she could propagate the bloodline. Now her ancestral intentions could manifest.

"Long live the Alchemists' Council," the attendees chanted.

Knowing full well that no one would hear her beneath the din of collegial cheers, Makala finally uttered the words she had quelled within Council dimension for hundreds of years: *I live as the Flaw in the Stone*. To save or to destroy: the choice now belonged to her.

She watched Corylus shake his head in dismay. They both knew what must occur. Corylus had only one mission remaining to fulfill before his death. Once each day during the three nines, regardless of their distaste for one another, Corylus must perform his sacred duty and Makala must accept him.

Thus we have bred you. Thus you will breed.
Thus we have directed you. Thus you will enact.
Thus it shall be.

So when Corylus knocked on Makala's chamber door on her first official night as Azoth Magen, Makala invited him into her bed without hesitation. Experiencing no desire or arousal, Corylus struggled to prepare himself to enter her. *Think of someone else*, Makala suggested as she guided one of his hands down to rest between his thighs. To his own touch, he responded soon enough. He knelt between her legs, preparing himself until he could wait no longer. Of course, on that night, they had no means to judge the success of their efforts.

By the end of the first week, Makala wondered if she and Corylus had experienced an alchemical transmutation. Perhaps they had triggered a physical or psychological shift on the elemental level as their essences repeatedly conjoined in bodily union. As the days passed, they began to long for each other, barely able to wait for their nightly and mutual release. By the end of the second week, they had become more creative with techniques and positions, spending hours each night pleasuring each other. They got so little rest that they could only haphazardly perform their Council duties. Throughout the third week, they played and laughed and moaned and writhed in a perpetual state of ecstasy that neither of them would have dared imagine a month earlier. They both began to regret their years of mutual antagonism.

On the twenty-seventh day of the three nines, their hesitation emerged not from disdain but from sadness. They both understood that Corylus would never know the outcome of their intimacy beyond the immediacy of its pleasure.

"Hope will carry me to my grave, wherever that may be," Corylus said, before kissing Makala one final time.

Holding hands, they spent their few remaining hours walking through Council grounds, stopping on occasion to comment on the vibrant green of a tree, to admire the golden ripples of the channel waters, or to bathe in the orange-hued radiance of the evening sky. When Corylus stumbled, Makala reached out to him, putting an arm around his waist. But she could not support his weight. Moments later, they were both on the ground — Corylus, wordlessly gasping; Makala, caressing the fading warmth of his cheek.

Of course, corporeal death in and of itself was exceedingly rare among alchemists. The majority left Council dimension because of erasure or conjunction or Final Ascension. The few others who had succumbed to the three nines over the centuries had been transported to the outside world for burial. Thus, even by the dawn of the 5th Council, the dimension included neither a graveyard nor memorial markers. As Azoth Magen, Makala had no desire to honour the intention of her ancestors when it came to protocols for alchemical twins.

"He will be buried here," said Makala, nodding towards the ground where Corylus had collapsed at sunset. "We will build a walled garden with his Quintessence at its centre. Within it, we will mourn not only Corylus but all those we lose, by death or otherwise, throughout the generations hereafter. With those words, I declare my first edict as Azoth Magen of the 5th Council of Alchemists. Thus it shall be!"

"Thus it shall be!" replied the Elders at Makala's side.

The following day, as the sun began to set, the entire Council gathered at the burial grounds to perform the Song of Mourning. As Makala expected, her decision dismayed some of the alchemists; they feared the burial would disturb not only tradition but dimensional balance. She managed to assuage their concerns, convincing them that in death, as in birth, Corylus represented an exception to ancestrally established dimensional conventions. Those who initially doubted her were soon convinced otherwise. Evidence of Corylus's exceptionality literally sprang from the ground where his blood and bones rested. As their tears fell, the mourners watched spring-green shoots sprouting from the newly turned earth. The flora grew rapidly as sunlight gave way to moonlight. By the time the moon had reached its zenith, the shoots had completely enmeshed with one another to form a tall, solid stalk. By the time the Azadirian stonemasons had laid the foundation for the garden wall, a magnificent hazel tree stood strong and steady at the garden's centre. And by the time Makala confirmed her pregnancy, each of the tree's hazelnuts, one after the other, had transformed into glistening amber.

After Corylus's death, only one Council member remained whom Makala could trust: newly appointed Azoth Savar. Hundreds of years earlier, when merely a Senior Initiate, Savar had found and interpreted a prophecy in the primordial manuscript *Materia Liberi*. At the insistence of Junior Magistrate Palash, who saw unrivalled potential in his young apprentice, Savar had announced to the Elders that potential Initiates Makala and Corylus were to begin their Council tenure within one moon's cycle. At the time, Azoth Magen Carya had laughed, refusing to accept the declarations of a Senior Initiate as anything beyond inexperienced supposition. When Palash interceded, insisting that Savar be taken seriously, Carya had reminded them that Council currently had only one vacant seat awaiting a new arrival. *Another will unexpectedly open shortly*, Savar had asserted, humbly bowing to his Elder in Ab Uno.

As if on cue, Reader Vetasah permanently vacated Council, abandoning both pendant and Lapis, for a lover in the outside world. Abandonment of the Council by choice was unprecedented. Shock waves rippled through the dimensions. Azoth Magen Carya then convened a private session with Palash and Savar. Two weeks thereafter, as Savar had predicted, both Makala and Corylus had joined the Junior Initiate quarto of the 3rd Council of Alchemists.

Unbeknownst to anyone at the time, the manuscript passage Senior Initiate Savar had interpreted was a palimpsest comprising ancestral blood. To the untrained eye, the physical characteristics of the folio were indistinguishable from those inscribed with Lapidarian ink. But despite his relative youth,

Savar's alchemical skills were highly advanced. He could recognize variations of ink on an elemental level. One day, he noticed that the blood of Aralia had been used to inscribe Corylus and the blood of Osmanthus to inscribe Makala. Over the years, as Savar ascended through the Orders of Council, he honed both his alchemical powers and his interpretive skills. A few centuries later, newly appointed Novillian Scribe Savar felt ready to confront Azoth Makala.

"You and Corylus have been lying to us," Savar had asserted with bravado as they crossed the courtyard one evening. "Your mother was not an outside world scribe of the 3rd Council. You were created in an alembic by Aralia and Osmanthus."

Makala had stopped mid-stride, unable to vocalize a reasoned response or even to gesture in protest.

"As an alchemical child of the original ancestors," he had continued, "you were sent through the elemental fabric of the dimensions to a future point on the timeline, thus ensuring perpetuation and purity of the bloodline through the generations. *Where one matures, one is bound.*"

Makala recognized the words of her father: Savar had quoted from *Materia Liberi*.

"You matured in *this* time, so here you must remain," Savar had construed, illustrating his understanding of the text. "But your own children need not be limited. As a direct descendant of Aralia and Osmanthus, revisionary power literally flows through your veins."

In that moment, Makala jolted into comprehension: Savar desired to align himself with her and the potential that her future children represented. He had promised on that day to do all he could to assure her victory over Corylus, her ascension to Azoth Magen, her gestation of the Hallowed Seed, her preparation of the sacred alembic, her creation of alchemical children, and the placement of her children at a critical point in the timeline.

"What do you want in return for keeping my secret?" she had asked him.

"To conjoin — mutually — with you," he had replied. "To *be* you, Makala. To be Azoth Magen together in our conjunction. To ensure our edicts echo throughout the generations."

"We are not Aralia and Osmanthus. We cannot—"

"The inscriptions that Aralia and Osmanthus made within *Materia Liberi* were not limited to a single folio, Makala. The manuscript contains all we would need to succeed together as Azoth Magen, including the blood-alchemy formula for mutual conjunction."

"You know as well as I that the Elders outlawed blood alchemy after the First Rebellion."

"And you know as well as I that such ancestral prohibitions have served only to make such knowledge and power all the more tantalizing."

Makala glared.

"I offer my silence; I request your power. What say you?"

"Trade is troth," Makala had replied, sealing the agreement.

"Trade is troth," Savar had echoed in confirmation.

Through the multitude of years since that Vow of Agreement, Savar had kept his word on all accounts. On the final night of gestation, he knelt beside Azoth Magen Makala as she birthed the small Hallowed Seed that Corylus had implanted during the three nines. Together she and Savar then prepared the sacred alembic for the Seed's incubation. Together they awaited the ripening. Together they shattered the Sacred Vessel and welcomed the alchemical twins into their world. Though Makala knew that, eventually, one twin would live and the other would die, she nonetheless embraced them both, vowing to extend their lives for as long as possible. After covertly relocating the children to be raised in the outside world, she began to devise her plan to ensure their survival far into the future.

Trade is troth, Savar reminded her shortly after the twins' relocation. Three days thereafter, he and Makala had mutually conjoined. Together, they would reign as Azoth Magen of the 5th Council of Alchemists. Together, they would adjust requisite manuscripts to ensure that the Council admitted the children when they came of age. How could

Makala have known that within two hours of her conjunction with Savar, she would recognize and regret her seemingly irreparable mistake?

Once conjoined, Makala became invisible — literally. Only three of the remaining ninety-nine members of the Alchemists' Council could see and confirm her physical presence. Without Azoth Palash, Novillian Scribe Baccata, and Senior Magistrate Pyrus pledging confirmation of a visible and *mutual* pairing, the Alchemists' Council would have pronounced the conjunction standard and completed. In *that* scenario, the Elders would have deemed Savar victorious and Makala absorbed into his flesh and blood. The position of Azoth Magen would have opened and, given his absorption of Makala, Azoth Savar would certainly have succeeded over Azoth Palash as the candidate for ascension. The 5th Council of Alchemists would have been shorter, by hundreds of years, than all preceding Councils. Savar would have reigned as the 6th Council Azoth Magen, sole guardian of Makala's two children. And Makala would have remained trapped — conscious, unheard, and unheeded — within Savar for an eternity. Thus, she came to believe that Savar had purposely attempted to deceive her. If her conjecture were true, then she also had to consider that Savar had expected *no one* to be able to see her. Savar had expected uniformity on Council, whereas Makala knew difference always prevailed.

At first, the Elders could not determine why

only Palash, Baccata, and Pyrus could see Makala. They requested an inquiry with requisite and interminable assessments. What traits did these three alchemists share? What traits differentiated them from all the others? No notable similarities or variances readily appeared to the Council Elders. Not until a full four months had passed did Savar misstep, inadvertently gesturing towards a potential truth. One morning at Elder Council, he demanded further investigation into the allegiances of Magistrate Pyrus. *He admitted to me a desire to increase the Flaw in the Stone,* Savar announced. *Surely Magistrate Pyrus sympathizes with the Rebel Branch. Surely he is an insurgent whom we must erase.*

What if Savar's suspicion were true? What if Pyrus, Palash, and Baccata were *all* rebel sympathizers? Could all three see Makala's physical presence because her blood correlated not only to that of Aralia, Originator of the Alchemists' Council, but also — and most significantly in this case — to that of Osmanthus, Originator of the Rebel Branch?

Another two months passed before Makala could test her theory. Finally, of necessity, Savar began to spend extended periods resting in the shadows, thus restoring and rejuvenating his consciousness. Having first conducted benign trials, Makala became confident that these periods offered her a temporary means to both privacy and physical dominance. One night, certain that Savar slept deep within the shadows, she sought Azoth Palash and risked a direct request: *Escort me to Flaw dimension.* Within the hour, she had confirmed her theory. Not only could the rebels see her, they also highly revered her. Since she was a Child of Osmanthus, they deemed Makala inherently — without question or contention — a Rebel High Azoth.

When Savar awoke, Makala could sense that he seethed in anger. As long as their conjoined body resided in Flaw dimension, he would be rendered virtually powerless. Makala knew both the limits of her strength and the extent of his weakness, so she bargained with him. With the full support of the Rebel Branch, she agreed to move regularly between Flaw and Council dimensions, allowing Savar to rule Council as the Azoth Magen and Makala to advise the Rebel Branch alongside High Azoth Alon. Savar assumed good faith. But he had already betrayed Makala; thus, Makala had long since begun to plan vengeance against him. She plotted and she strategized. When certain Savar was asleep in the shadows, she consulted various rebels and all relevant manuscripts. Five decades later, long after Savar and the Council had dropped their guard, no longer expecting repercussions, Makala and her daughter — now a Rebel Branch Initiate — opened a breach that allowed the rebels to plunder Council treasures surreptitiously.

No one on Council detected their treachery until Makala, aided by Rebel Branch sympathizers, had confiscated thousands of manuscripts from Council dimension archives. During the Azothian trials held in the aftermath of this treason, which Council Scribes later dubbed the Second Rebellion, Makala claimed that wayward Rebel Branch Scribes had stolen the manuscripts via a dimensional breach without her knowledge. They had, moreover, secreted the manuscripts in innumerable locations throughout the outside world. Makala said she had permanently banished the Scribes from Flaw dimension as punishment. She had lied.

In truth, rebels had concealed only a mere fraction of the manuscripts in the outside world — as many as required to ensure Council members would find a hundred or so each decade and thereby believe Makala's story. Only Makala and a few trusted rebel advisors knew that ninety percent of the confiscated manuscripts now resided not in the outside world but in Flaw dimension. They were hidden in alchemically rendered archives, sealed into an elaborate series of obscured libraries. No one could break her blood-alchemy seal other than Makala herself and a prophesied chosen few. Thus had Makala regained both knowledge and power over Savar.

As Makala soon discovered, Savar doubted her integrity. Consequently, he attempted revenge during a rare and opportune occasion in which Makala fell, exhausted and unconscious, into the shadows. With the help of two Council Elders, he had recited the requisite words attained from

Materia Liberi and transported Makala's son through time.

"Fifteen fifty-five of the outside world's current era," Savar announced. "Such an appropriately *quintessential* year."

Makala seethed.

"Return the manuscripts to me, and I will return your son to you," he proclaimed.

Makala refused. Instead, at the first viable opportunity, she confiscated *Materia Liberi*, extracted what she needed from its blood-infused folios, and burned it immediately upon Savar's awakening from the shadows.

"You have destroyed the ancestral rituals!" he shouted. "I will never forgive you! You will never see your son again!"

"Just as he and I had planned and intended," she replied calmly.

Defeated, Savar recoiled into the shadows forever after. And their body became hers alone.

Makala and Corylus had spent their first five decades of existence with Aralia and Osmanthus. As children of the Prima Materia, they had learned the Law of Counterparts. In the Grafting of the Hallowed Seed, only one could implant; the other would gestate. In the Creation of the Alchemical Child, only one could live; the other would die. In

25

the Sacrament of Conjunction, only one could triumph; the other would fail. And so on, and so on. But parents and children alike also anticipated that evolution would necessarily breed exception, that ostensibly inexorable Primordial Laws would falter with replication, that divine design would fall victim to unforeseen contingencies. Thus, to mitigate annihilation of the bloodline, Aralia and Osmanthus had inscribed their blood and its alchemical properties into myriad manuscripts, thereafter sending their children and requisite manuscripts through dimensional time. Herself an evolutionary exception sent through time, Makala regularly sifted through the archives searching for the blood of her parents. With each new find, she would excise the blood, scraping it with a Blade of Precision, and combine it with her own blood into ink. With this conjunction of bloods, she inscribed new bloodline texts — manuscripts to perpetuate her powers throughout the generations. Her children would use one such text as both a primer for blood-alchemy lessons and an inheritance for their future.

"We will name this sacred volume *Chimera Veritas*," she announced to her daughter. "The formulas and accompanying depictions, which I illuminated using a blend of the most precious inks, should prove useful." She tapped her finger against one of the illuminations. "For now, the Champion of Dimensions is merely an illustration of a Lapidarian prophecy. But in your lifetime, of necessity, he may well become manifest."

Of course, like her father before her, Makala could not predict all complexities of the future, its exceptions, or the choices her children would make in her absence. She could merely attempt to fulfill her intention: to leave her mark on time.

"Am I to take *Chimera Veritas* with me, Mother?"

"Not in its physical form," responded Makala. "The manuscript must remain here, with me, in Flaw dimension. Use your remaining days with me wisely. Before venturing into the future, study its folios, contemplate its teachings. Its blood-alchemy laws will then be yours to follow or ignore. When you believe yourself prepared, you will hide the manuscript here — within my timeline. Then, in the future, within your new timeline, you will reveal its location to your brother when you deem him primed to receive its secrets."

"What do you envision for us?"

"That you will reign together in harmony over the dimensions, as Corylus and I should have done."

"But Aralia and Osmanthus—"

"Through Corylus and me, the blood of the original ancestors flows within the two of you. My hope is that, positioned together onto the future timeline, you will both be privy to the sealed procla-mations of Aralia and Osmanthus — proclamations that even I have been unable to access. My hope

27

is that evolution will breed exception, that both my children will survive the three nines, and that a grandchild of mine will become the prophesied one born of three — the one who, during the 17th Council of Alchemists, will enliven the *Osmanthian Codex*."

Two years later, Makala's daughter stepped into the circle within the square within the triangle to be transported, like her parents and brother before her, into the future.

"Thus it shall be. You have taught me well. Goodbye, my dear mother."

"Goodbye, Ravenea."

I

London, Waterloo Bridge Station — August 1848

Ravenea stood on the platform surveying the unfamiliar surroundings and glancing anxiously at the outside world folk hurriedly walking by. Was her clothing appropriate? Would she pass among these people unnoticed? She could not decide whether she was being overly anxious or respectably cautious. Perhaps if she were here on official Council business, or perhaps if this unconventional location were a crossing point at which she intended to greet a potential Initiate, her usual calm professionalism would prevail. Instead, much too late to change her mind, she repeatedly second-guessed her choice. What could possibly be worth this risk?

"Good afternoon," said Fraxinus. Ravenea flinched. Despite his flowing white hair and voluminous robes — highly unorthodox amidst the station's occupants — she had not seen him approach. "Our time here is limited. I will be boarding a train within minutes."

"Am I to join you?"

"Of course not!" His ice-blue eyes blazed at her, punctuating his words. "What excuse could you possibly offer the Alchemists' Council if Azoth Magen Quercus learned you had embarked on an outside world train journey with a Rebel Branch Azoth?"

"What excuse am I to offer even for leaving the London protectorate for this station?" she asked. She glanced around once again at the passersby, worriedly scanning for a familiar face.

"Simple curiosity. Is this station not an architectural marvel of the modern world?" He gestured up and outward. For the benefit of onlookers, she smiled and nodded.

"And for what reason, other than mutual observation of this outside world spectacle, have you requested a meeting?"

"To relay information that may affect your future." He paused.

She waited, hands clenched.

"Let me rephrase," he continued. "To relay information that may profoundly affect the future of all three dimensions."

Ravenea shivered despite the summer heat. "Yes?" Her impatience grew.

"The *Osmanthian Codex* has been activated. If memory serves, the manuscript will mature fully within thirty years. The Rebel Azoths will then, once again, possess the knowledge to create an alchemical child."

Ravenea froze, momentarily stunned. Her thoughts raced. "But the bloodlocks! Osmanthus himself sealed the *Codex* with his primordial blood. And Makala sealed the secreted libraries from intruders after the Second Rebellion."

A smartly dressed man within hearing range turned immediately to frown at her. She did not recognize him. He must merely have found her words vulgar.

"The ancestors intended worthy descendants to open the bloodlocks on both the Osmanthian and Aralian manuscripts," said Fraxinus. "And Makala followed their lead."

"Who is responsible?" she asked him. "A Rebel Branch Elder?"

"An Elder? Really, Ravenea, if an Elder both carried the bloodline *and* met the required prophetic conditions, one of us would have enlivened the manuscript centuries ago."

"Then who?

"An outside world scribe," he responded.

"That cannot be. Makala would not have allowed—"

"Yet here we are. And we have you to thank for this evolutionary exception."

Another chill coursed through Ravenea. "In what sense?"

"Our scribe was born in the outside world to exiled alchemists."

"Alchemists cannot—"

She stopped. He smiled. She understood. She caught her breath.

Ilex and Melia.

Fraxinus turned, walked along a nearby platform, and disappeared into a train. Engines bellowed. People shouted. Wheels shrieked. Ravenea could not move.

Nearly half a century ago, Ravenea had revealed the location of *Chimera Veritas* to Fraxinus knowing that Melia, desperate to save Ilex, would seek assistance from the Rebel Branch. Ravenea's intention had been honourable. She had desired only to save a friend from heartbreak. But Fraxinus must have had knowledge unknown and unshared about Ilex and Melia. Perhaps he had foreseen the outcome of their conjunction: conception.

Fraxinus had been the one to suggest that Ravenea ensure Ilex and Melia's removal from Council dimension. He must have predicted a child. He must have wanted the child born in the outside world. He had provided the alchemical chant and the carrier bees himself. He had advised her to forbid further contact with them. He had convinced her that kinship trumped friendship. He had lied. She had believed him. And now the fate of the worlds was upon her solely because, as Makala had hoped, Ravenea had kept faith in her brother.

With her head bowed and hands in the second position of Ab Uno, Ravenea stood, calm and silent, during the Announcement of Concurrence. Despite decades serving with him on the Council, she knew relatively little about her proposed partner for conjunction, Erez. Certainly, she had worked with him, having for decades carried out various scribal duties together. But she had shared neither physical nor emotional intimacy with him. All conversations had revolved around work or had been the mere trivialities of jovial chatter exchanged in the aftermath of rituals or during celebratory dinners. The casualness was for the best, she supposed now. She would carry no guilt if victorious within the conjunction.

Prior to the Announcement of Concurrence, Ravenea had hoped for several weeks to pass between the stages of the ritual process, as was traditionally the case. News to the contrary disappointed her: Azoth Magen Quercus had already determined precise dates and times for both the Sealing of Concurrence and the Sacrament of Conjunction. Ravenea would have only two days before the Sealing and only three weeks before the Conjunction. Though she had repeatedly been the bearer of news about impending conjunctions to other alchemists, she had never borne the weight of her own potential demise. She had never had to consider the possibility that Makala's creation and relocation of her had been for naught.

As Ravenea progressed along the channel path towards residence chambers, each step felt effortful. She stopped beside Lochan Pond — the Wishing Well — and sat on the nearby bench in the shade of the willow tree. Whenever seated on this bench, she inevitably thought of Melia, of the fractured expression Melia had donned upon hearing of her own impending conjunction with Ilex. Melia could bear neither the possibility of losing Ilex nor the prospect of him living without her. Ravenea, by contrast, had no such excuse for her current anguish. She had neither a lover in whom to seek solace now nor a beloved to leave behind to mourn her. A few of her close friends might shed a tear in the Amber Garden in the immediate aftermath of her defeat in conjunction. Saule would be saddened. But would her absence affect anyone *profoundly*? Would anyone *truly* miss her as the years progressed?

Standing up and leaning forward to contemplate her reflection in the pond, Ravenea concluded *no*. Throughout the dimensions, she had no one who considered her a cherished companion. Worse, at least one Rebel Elder — Fraxinus — might well champion her demise. The potentially eternal life that Makala and the Alchemists' Council had granted to her appeared to have amounted to nothing at its end. Here, in this very spot beside the Wishing Well fifty-five years earlier, Ravenea had insisted to Melia, *I am not lonely!* In that moment, Ravenea had uttered the truth; she had no need to seek intimacy because she truly had not felt the need to do so. She had for centuries focused her energies — alchemical, sexual, emotional — on fulfilling her Council duties and ascending the Orders towards her goal of reaching Azothian status. She had indeed never known loneliness; she had never felt alone — until now.

A noise distracted her. She turned. A young woman with long dark hair braided into a thick immaculate strand watched her. Ravenea recognized her as one of the dozen outside world scribes sent here to work with the Lapidarians in preparation for Azoth-administered examinations.

"My apologies, Scribe Ravenea." The woman bowed her head, moving her clutched hands to her chest rather than into the requisite Ab Uno position. "I mean no disrespect."

Ravenea wanted to address her by name, but she couldn't recall it in that fraught moment. "Coins are more accurately tossed from this position," Ravenea said, tapping the bench as she repositioned herself at its far end.

The woman looked at her, clearly taken aback. She then lowered her eyes once again but smiled pleasantly as she moved towards Ravenea. Seated, she continued to hold one closed fist against her chest.

"Worry not," said Ravenea. "I have no plans to report you to Azoth Magen Quercus. How would I know, upon witnessing a mere toss of a coin, whether you are making an illicit wish or simply practising manual dexterity for your official scribal duties?"

The woman moved her hand away from her chest, closed her eyes, held her coin between her fingers, and kissed it gently. She then tossed it, metal glinting in the sunlight, into the pool.

"May your wish come to fruition."

"Thank you, Scribe Ravenea. But I do not deserve such generosity."

"You surely do. As do we all, on occasion."

"Not this time."

The woman stood and faced Ravenea. With newly unencumbered hands, she assumed Ab Uno position, nodded quickly, and then hurried away along the channel path. Not until the young scribe had rounded a corner and left her sight did Ravenea remember her tree name: *Yinxing*.

Several months earlier, Elder Council had assigned Erez to be Yinxing's scribal tutor. Within a few weeks of this mentorship, Erez had spoken highly of her creative independence. Remembering that detail, Ravenea's confusion vanished. No wonder Yinxing had thought Ravenea generous. Tossing the coin through the air, the outside world scribe had certainly wished for Erez's victory in the Sacrament of Conjunction. Ravenea had, in effect, endorsed a wish for her own demise.

She moved the short distance from the bench to the edge of the pool. But now, instead of contemplating her reflection, she looked past it. Scanning the shallow water, she eventually spied the coin — small, shiny, and plainly out of reach. In that moment of contemplation, she remembered Melia's fondness for coins. How often had Melia ventured into this pool on a quest for a treasure to add to her collection? Perhaps Melia's elemental connection to water had afforded her some sort of alchemical advantage. Regrettably, she had never thought to ask.

Glancing first in each direction and seeing no one, Ravenea slid out of her shoes, hoisted up her robes, and stepped into the water. Though one of her sleeves fell prey to a plunge, she soon recovered the coin and returned to the bench. As her bare feet dried in the sun, she turned the coin over and over in her hands, contemplating both the wish and the implications of its removal. Even though Ravenea had witnessed not only Melia's wish to remain with Ilex but also their subsequent mutual conjunction, she did not believe in the pool's magic. Like Quercus, she thought the Wishing Well to be folkloric nonsense, devoid of orthodox elemental alchemy despite its continued presence within Council dimension's courtyard.

Nonetheless, she wanted to keep the coin as a tangible reminder of her current situation. She had already realized no one would truly mourn her demise; she now knew that someone had actively wished for it. She would carry the coin in her pocket to the Sealing of Concurrence. She would hold it in her hand at the Sacrament of Conjunction. And if victorious, she would treasure it forever after as a symbol of the vulnerability she had felt on this day — vulnerability eternally present at conjunction in both the lonely and the loved.

If victorious, she would endeavour to experience for herself the intensity of emotion she had witnessed long ago in Melia. She smiled, thinking again of her old friend. Melia could not have known, any more than Ravenea herself, what the choice to escape Council would mean for the dimensions. If she were still residing here, Melia would have admired this coin: a small copper signet with a crown on one side and an exquisitely carved bee on the other.

Later that evening, from the balcony of her residence chambers, Ravenea watched as Azoth Magen Quercus, Azoth Ailanthus, and Novillian Scribe Esche chanted a reconfiguration ritual at the edge of Lochan Pond. Ailanthus and Esche scattered Lapidarian dust onto the waters. Quercus then lit the dust aflame with a spark from the Azothian sceptre. Within ten minutes, the water of the Wishing Well alchemically transformed, segment by segment, into a moss-laden knoll — its wishes, its coins, its folklore consumed. Ravenea marvelled at the relative ease with which the Elders could permanently dissolve a segment of Council dimension.

"Regardless of Council prohibitions, outside world scribes will inevitably perpetuate its heretical use the moment they hear of the well granting even a single wish," Ravenea had complained earlier that day. "Yinxing was no exception."

"To the contrary. According to Erez, our coin-tossing scribe is quite the exception," Quercus had responded. "She shows unparalleled calligraphic abilities and exhibits no trepidation whatsoever during Azothian interrogations. Apparently, during one of Ailanthus's exams, she insisted on being addressed henceforth by her chosen secular name: Jinjing."

"Regardless of unorthodox nomenclature," Ravenea had retorted with an emphatic sigh, "sentimentality among outside world scribes is rampant and detrimental."

Quercus had nodded. "Judgment acknowledged, Ravenea. Have you a solution to proffer?"

Three hours after that meeting, Quercus, Ailanthus, and Esche walked away from the knoll, and Ravenea smiled down upon them.

"She has returned," reported Fraxinus.

Ravenea glanced up at the clock. Time unaccountably appeared both to stand still and progress rapidly during these infrequent and illicit meetings.

"Who has returned?"

"The breaker of bloodlocks — the one who activated the *Osmanthian Codex*. She has returned to Flaw dimension."

"You hadn't informed me that she had left. Why tell me now that she has returned? What is it you expect me to do with your haphazard morsels of information?"

"The rebels will soon braid her to an alchemical child — the first braiding in over three hundred years."

Ravenea paused to process the implications. Sixty-five years earlier, when Fraxinus had first informed her of the *Osmanthian Codex*'s activation, she feared only the improbability that the rebels would succeed at creating an alchemical child. Thirty years thereafter, when he informed her that the rebels had indeed created a pair of alchemical twins, she buried her qualms in the knowledge that the children would require at least three decades to mature and gain knowledge before they could pose a threat. Now her anxieties came rushing to the forefront. The news of braiding — an integral, unbreakable bond — implied that at least one child would choose to reside permanently within a primary dimension. Whether the child dwelt in Flaw dimension or inadvertently became initiated to Council, the risk to dimensional integrity would increase exponentially.

"Tell me their names — the names of both mother and braided child," she insisted.

"You know, as well as I, the boundaries outlined in the Treaty of Fair Warning. Though I am obligated to inform you of the existence of an alchemical child, I am under no obligation to reveal that child's name, physical features, or whereabouts. Your pleas cannot sway me to breach territory beyond that of my accorded duties. I have informed you that the child exists and soon will be braided. My obligation to you is fulfilled."

Ravenea seethed internally. She longed to scream. She longed to lash out not only here and now at Fraxinus but back through the ages at the Ancestral Elders who had composed the Treaty of Fair Warning. Why would the ancestors have placed limitations on matters of such critical importance? But she could not risk upsetting Fraxinus more than she had already. She still required as much additional information as he was graciously willing to provide. And if her fears of dimensional disintegration ever manifested, she would require his assistance.

"Has the child's twin survived?" she asked calmly.

"No. *One must die so the other may live,*" quoted Fraxinus.

"*Evolution breeds exception*," countered Ravenea.

"Exactly. Thousands of years have passed since Aralia and Osmanthus created Makala and Corylus, and hundreds since Makala and Corylus created us. These alchemical twins are mere evolutionary degradations of their bloodline ancestors."

"Then the child is not yours. If it were, the bloodline would be relatively pure."

"The child belongs to the High Azoth and the breaker of bloodlocks."

"In that case, the alchemical powers of the surviving twin are likewise degraded. Thank you for this particular nugget of information, Fraxinus. You have placated my concerns."

"Appeasing you was emphatically *not* my intention. I implied only that alchemical children no longer live or die by the ancestral time frame. You misinterpreted my point to conclude that early demise of one twin ensures alchemical deficiency in the other. Rest assured, Ravenea, all current evidence suggests that the bloodline powers of the surviving twin remain viable and potent — hence the braiding decision. Only the swift inevitability of the three nines indicates a shift from ancestral convention."

Ravenea glared. "What are you saying? For how many years did the twin survive?"

Fraxinus raised his eyes to the clock as if to calculate an answer but said nothing.

"Surely you can provide me with a specific time

frame without contravening the Treaty of Fair Warning!" exclaimed Ravenea.

"As made clear in the *Osmanthian Codex*, alchemical transmutation will shorten the time frame of the three nines with each generation."

"Fraxinus! The time frame!"

"Using a calculation chart embedded into the *Codex*, Dracaen and I determined that, within our current timeline, the three nines begin at birth."

"At what point in the process did you two make this determination?"

"Shortly before the chemical marriage."

"So . . . you knew. You and Dracaen both knew that the mother would have no means to prevent the inevitable death of one of her children." Ravenea shook her head. She felt compassion for both the naturally born mother and the alchemically created children. She had no sympathy for Fraxinus, who appeared delusional. "Do not fool yourself," she said. "Neither of us has eternally escaped the fate of alchemical children, despite Makala's precautions. Our three nines will begin someday, and one of us will die."

"Do not expect me to mourn for you."

"Nor I for you," she retorted.

"My work here is done. Good day, Ravenea."

"Wait! How am I to recognize the surviving twin should our paths cross in Council dimension? What if, as a Council member, this child's conjunction is prophesied and confirmed?"

"Perhaps you could convince Elder Council to ban the Sacrament of Conjunction for a few hundred years — or until your death, whichever comes first."

A wave of nausea overtook Ravenea. Had Fraxinus plotted this eventuality all along? Had he garnered the assistance of Dracaen with the tantalizing promise that a ban on conjunction would result in an increase to the Flaw in the Stone at the expense of the Alchemists' Council?

"Fraxinus, you must provide me a means to recognize the child! Even if I were Azoth Magen, I could not outlaw the Sacrament altogether. We must continue to replenish Lapidarian Quintessence for the sake of all dimensions. My only means to mitigate disaster is to manipulate Lapidarian manuscripts and ensure the child never conjoins in Council dimension."

"As I've already clarified, I have fulfilled my obligation under the treaty."

"What of your obligation to the Rebel Branch? What if the alchemical child should conjoin on Council but venture thereafter into Flaw dimension? What if allowing me a means of identification — a means to prevent the conjunction — should one day help not only the Alchemists' Council but simultaneously the Rebel Branch?"

Ravenea noticed a glimmer right then — a flicker of possibility that her makeshift logic had penetrated his resolve. But as quickly as it had appeared, it vanished.

"My commitment to the Treaty of Fair Warning is steadfast," he confirmed.

Ravenea sighed loudly and glanced again at the clock. Her own duties in Council dimension beckoned. Perhaps all concern would be utterly moot if Elder Council were successful at their recently agreed-upon intention to remove the Flaw in the Stone permanently.

"Of course," continued Fraxinus unexpectedly, "the Treaty does make allowances."

"Such as?"

"Though the Treaty prevents me from providing names, nothing within it prevents *you* from marking the child for future identification. Perhaps a strand of your Quintessence—"

"How am I to mark the child if you provide me no means for identification?"

"Use your creative ingenuity, Ravenea."

Her mind raced. Whatever act she committed, whatever statement she uttered, had to honour the restrictions of the Treaty. Ravenea needed to provide a recognizable mark without knowing or identifying or, indeed, without even mentioning the existence of an alchemical child. She noticed Fraxinus glance at the clock. She closed her eyes.

"Time is ticking," he warned. "Do not waste it on wishes."

"Wishes are as inconsequential as outside world prayers," she responded, eyes opened. But with the repetition of *wishes*, she thought of the Wishing

45

Well. She thought of Melia. She thought of Jinjing. She thought of the copper, bee-embossed coin that she had held firmly during her own conjunction. And she smiled as she retrieved the coin from the depth of an inner pocket.

"I understand Flaw dimension will soon host a braiding. A gift seems in order." She passed the coin to Fraxinus. "Of course, as you know, tradition permits the braiding participants to receive small tokens of congratulations from the outside world."

"You have given me but one coin. To whom should I present it?"

Ravenea smiled as she responded. "Please present it to the younger of the two."

London, Waterloo Station — 1973

Another sixty years had passed since Ravenea had relinquished the coin to Fraxinus. She had not seen it since. To the best of her knowledge, and despite her vigilance in screening Council Initiates, neither had she seen the child to whom she had bequeathed the coin. Nonetheless, in her quest for updates, Ravenea had entreated Fraxinus to meet with her once each decade. He acquiesced for the first two. On each occasion, he chatted briefly with her about outside world events before deigning to supply a minimal and seemingly insignificant detail about the alchemical child. Then, using the outside world war as his excuse, he refused to meet with her in 1943. On each attempt thereafter, Fraxinus would inevitably find a pretext to avoid seeing her. Ravenea submitted an open invitation as her final attempt to solicit his attention: she would await him at the same date and time each decade within sight of the station's main clock.

But Fraxinus never heeded her request. So she would spend her two allotted hours watching the hands on the clock move perpetually forward, admiring or rebuking the sartorial choices of passersby, imagining the stories of a chosen few — particularly those who were newborn or elderly. She would contemplate their lives and the way time moved them forward during the years she had spent in the relative timelessness of Council dimension. While she barely aged, these people would complete lifetimes. She imagined them boarding their trains, disappearing forever. More recently, she pictured herself doing the same — abandoning not only *the* station but also *her* station. She fantasized rescinding her Council obligations and all ancestral ties, including those she held with Fraxinus.

On this particular occasion, twenty minutes after contemplating her fantasy, she was walking along a platform, ticket in hand. She could have moved between any two cities within a few minutes by portal. But although her Quintessence remained as strong as always, she was tired. She was tired of being tormented. She was tired of being. Hundreds of years, and nothing ever changed — nothing of substance. She worked and worked to ensure stability of the dimensions, but nothing she did was ever enough. Nothing ended. She and her tasks and her vigilance existed in perpetuity. Today, she desired a journey with an end point. And given the available options at her point of decision, she chose Portsmouth. She stepped onto the train knowing that time would pass, that the train would reach a destination, finality.

For the first hour or so, she relaxed completely, watching the landscape move past, listening to the percussive rhythm of the wheels along the track. And then she saw him — Fraxinus — or so she thought. She would never know for certain because she passed him by so swiftly, because she was inside a train on a journey with a destination, because he stood outside in the landscape waiting to cross the tracks, oblivious to the train's passengers, its unreliable witnesses. By the time Ravenea stepped onto the platform at Portsmouth, she had convinced herself that the man she had seen could not possibly have been Fraxinus. After all, what reason would her brother have to be standing in that spot — miles upon miles from the nearest protectorate library — holding the hand of a child?

II
Coũncil Dimension — 2008

Ravenea could feel her hands shaking. One held the sheet of parchment. The other was poised to knock on Saule's door. She attempted to steady herself. Saule would neither welcome the news nor accept it as the dimensional necessity Ravenea would claim it to be. She knocked and waited impatiently. She pictured a line of dominoes; she pictured herself tapping the first one gently but firmly, with just enough pressure to cause the others to fall.

"Ravenea!" said Saule. "Come in."

They exchanged a few pleasantries. Ravenea aimed to maintain a demeanour of casual sincerity mixed with a hint of apprehension.

"Are you certain you're well, Ravenea? You appear out of sorts."

"I bear potentially distressing news. The Readers have found a scribal prophecy concerning you in *Arbre de cuivre 2089*."

Ravenea sat on the sofa and then gestured for Saule to sit beside her. She took one of Saule's hands into her own. "I did not want you to learn of this potentially upsetting news from anyone other than me," she continued. "I'm so sorry, my dear, but it appears you are marked for conjunction. I have not been so torn about a conjunction since that of Ilex and Melia."

Ravenea trusted that, with the mention of Ilex and Melia, Saule would infer the gravity of her despair. Ravenea had not spoken privately with her of the conjoined pair for years — not since she and Saule had helped them escape, thereafter vowing never to discuss the matter.

"Your sweetness is touching, Ravenea. But conjunction is a sacrament. We both knew this day would come."

"No, Saule, you do not understand. I did indeed know this day would come. It's the pairing itself that concerns me."

Ravenea held out the sheet of parchment. She watched Saule carefully as she silently read the single sentence of Lapidarian French that Ravenea had inscribed thereon. Though various translations and interpretations of this line were possible, Ravenea predicted the conclusion Saule would draw: *The willow will conjoin with the lotus*. To Saule, the line could mean only one thing — that she was destined to conjoin with her beloved Sadira.

"Your Quintessence is more mature, and your status is superior. You will certainly be victorious," Ravenea said reassuringly.

"Of course," replied Saule. "No doubt."

"Shall I stay? We can discuss—"

"No. No, thank you, Ravenea. I need time to contemplate this news alone."

"Yes, of course."

They moved towards the door. Ravenea embraced Saule and kissed her on the cheek.

"Goodnight," said Saule.

As Ravenea climbed the stairs to her own residence chambers, she reviewed the details of the conversation — words, gestures, facial expressions. Though Saule had appeared stalwart to the end, Ravenea knew the news had had its intended effect. Saule had certainly been a trustworthy ally throughout the years. But she knew too much. For one, she knew of the role Ravenea had played in assisting Ilex and Melia. Though, in the immediate aftermath, Ravenea had manipulated Saule's pendant to conceal accidental revelation of the illicit activity to the Elders, Saule herself still maintained knowledge not only of the escape but also of Ilex and Melia's child and, presumably, their alchemical grandchild.

As an Azoth during the dusk of the current Council, Ravenea could no longer take the risk that

Ailanthus or Ruis might learn of her involvement in the escape or its subsequent repercussions. To bury the knowledge, Saule had to conjoin. To be primed through blood alchemy for extraction of her knowledge if necessary, Saule would need to conjoin with an alchemist connected to both the Alchemists' Council and the Rebel Branch. Thanks to a chance comment made years earlier by Saule, the other alchemist Ravenea suspected of harbouring Rebel Branch ties was Cedar.

Cedar's failed attempt to conjoin with Ruis virtually ensured that she would be marked for conjunction again within the year. But the only way Ravenea could assure Saule and Cedar would conjoin, without more involvement than prudent on Ravenea's part, was to convince Saule that the prophecies had marked her to conjoin with Sadira. Saule would avoid doing so at all costs, including through the most likely means: manuscript revision via rebel assistance. If anyone discovered such unlawful revisions, if the Elders launched an investigation, Ravenea would be free of blame. After all, Ravenea herself had not committed treason; *she* had not falsified a manuscript. She had merely mistranscribed a line when she copied it onto the parchment sheet. She would feign innocence, knowing Elders tended to believe Azoths.

Yes, she had lied to Saule. But Ravenea felt no guilt. She had to mitigate all risks for the good of the dimensions. *Use your creative ingenuity*, Fraxinus had once said to her. She had done so then, and she had continued to do so ever since. Saule would simply and unfortunately be the first devoted friend to become a casualty of Ravenea's ambitions.

Council Dimension — 2013

Ravenea stared at Cedar, debating the intricacies of her reply. She recalled a moment from centuries earlier, sitting under the willow tree in the main courtyard, when Cedar swore to her that she would never lie to an Elder. *Not even by omission?* Ravenea had asked. *Of course not,* Cedar had replied. *Elder powers are potent. Any Elder would surely sense the slightest falsehood through pendant proximity.* Now, only a few years into her tenure as Novillian Scribe, Cedar appeared to be lying to an Azoth for reasons Ravenea did not yet fully comprehend. Did she believe her own status as Elder would protect her from thorough Azothian examination?

"On what do you base your suspicions?" Ravenea asked.

"Obeche has . . . convinced me."

"Obeche?" Ravenea crossed her arms and leaned back in her chair. "Obeche convincing you to agree with him on a lunch menu would be unprecedented. Yet you expect me to believe he has convinced *you* — a vocal proponent of maintaining the Flaw

53

— that an exceptionally bright Senior Initiate has ties to the Rebel Branch?"

"Ravenea, I advocate free will, not—"

"Free will comes at a price, Cedar. And that price is the Flaw in the Stone."

"Why would I report my suspicions of a potential rebel insurgent if I harboured my own rebel sympathies?"

"You have been walking a fine line for years, Cedar. Your views on the Flaw are no secret among the Elders. Frankly, I have no idea why Ruis maintained intimate relations with you for as long as he did. You would think political differences—"

"You know perfectly well the reason my intimacy with Ruis ended: I fell in love with Sadira. Politics of the Flaw held no sway, I assure you."

"And for that fortunate turn of events, you can thank—" Ravenea began. She had been about to say *me*, but shifted promptly to "your conjunction with Saule."

"What do my personal relationships or conjunction have to do with the topic at hand?"

"You are requesting Azothian support for an Initiate's erasure. You could have gone to Azoth Ruis or directly to the Azoth Magen. Instead, you have come to me. You have conjoined with Saule — who was not only Sadira's lover but one of my closest friends. If you want my help, I need the truth, Cedar. What are you hiding?"

Cedar breathed deeply before responding. Ravenea worried she had gone too far, that her accusation of deception had angered Cedar. She hoped nonetheless that her potency had compelled Cedar to provide more of the truth than she might have done otherwise.

"Obeche," began Cedar. "Obeche distrusts me. He needs to trust that you trust him."

Ravenea uncrossed her arms, placed both hands on her desk, and leaned forward towards Cedar. "Why?"

"Change is coming, Ravenea. My request is a move within the long game. One day — whether a few years or decades from now — the Azoth Magen will choose a successor. As you well know, Ailanthus is principled. When the time comes, he will seek advice from the Elders, including Obeche. Obeche has always aligned himself with Ruis. I need him to align himself with you. In the past, I too sided with Ruis. But now my sympathies lie elsewhere. Take that statement as you may, Ravenea. But I swear on the Lapis, I do not want Ruis to become the next Azoth Magen. I fear, as he did a century ago, he will once again attempt *Remota Macula*. I trust you will not."

Of all the possible admissions Ravenea had imagined, this revelation had not been one. Though she still could not know if Cedar had admitted the entire truth, Ravenea had to agree that Obeche's support could prove useful to her in the future.

Thus, for now, she saw no reason to deny Cedar's request to erase Senior Initiate Kalina.

Ravenea ran a hand along the edge of her golden velvet robes. They shone in the bright morning sunlight streaming through the corridor window. Standing outside Obeche's office, she was once again uncharacteristically nervous. With time progressing swiftly towards Kalina's conjunction with Tesu, stakes were substantially higher than even a week before. How many more glitches would Ravenea need to resolve before she could move forward without obstacle?

"Enter!" said Obeche.

Seeing her, he stood swiftly, moved to the other side of his desk, and raised his hands into Ab Uno. "Azoth Ravenea! To what do I owe this unexpected visit?"

"I request a favour," she said.

"A favour?" He smiled and gestured for her to take a seat.

She had anticipated her phrasing would both intrigue and delight Obeche. After all, a favour he fulfilled now could be a favour she granted to him in the future. *Trade is troth*, as the saying went. Ravenea crossed the room and lowered herself into one of the large and elaborately carved wooden chairs by the window. These must be the monstrosities Ruis had mentioned last week — Obeche's latest outside world imports.

"New chairs?" she asked.

"Yes!" He responded so enthusiastically that he startled her. "I spotted them in an antique shop in New York City a few months back. I had them delivered to the lobby of the Manhattan protectorate. Late-nineteenth-century R.J. Horner originals. Can you imagine?"

"No," she replied, feigning awe. She honestly would never have imagined any aspect of this scenario before today. Though she had known Obeche longer, by more than two centuries, than the chairs had existed, she had never heard him express such passion for anything beyond Council business — not even for Jinjing. If the mere request for a favour from an Azoth could lead him to be more personable with her, perhaps outright flattery would work inconceivable wonders.

"My current Azothian duties require me to take a Novillian Scribe into my confidence," Ravenea said with both predictable formality and atypical graciousness. "I seek someone who is both trustworthy and determined, someone with enough ambition to aspire to Azothian status. Can you picture yourself as Azoth alongside Ruis?"

"Alongside Ruis?"

"Think ahead, Obeche. Today you are seated in a nineteenth-century chair during the twilight of the 18th Council. Where will you be seated by the end of the first century of the 19th Council? I picture you in a gem-encrusted chair on the Azothian dais next to me — Azoth Ruis to my right, Azoth Obeche to my left. What do you think?"

"Your aspirations are admirable," he replied.

For years, Obeche had aligned himself with Ruis, most likely having assumed that he, not Ravenea, would be Ailanthus's chosen successor as Azoth Magen. She knew Obeche may well confide in Ruis the details of their meeting today. But Ravenea had calculated the risks and deemed them necessary to win his confidence. Obeche may always have been philosophically allied with Ruis on matters of the Flaw and other Council business, but the Elders had also repeatedly inhibited him from ascension for one infraction or another. Thus, Ruis — one of Obeche's own Initiates — had gradually overtaken him in the Council hierarchy. Would he not rather picture himself as Ruis's equal than his inferior? Would he not rather take Ravenea's hypothetical scenario one step further and imagine himself as the Azoth Magen of the 20th Council — reigning as the ultimate superior not just to Ruis but to the entire Council? If so, Ravenea would gain Obeche's support forevermore, even if the alliance was covert, even if Ruis and the other Elders failed to recognize it.

"At yesterday's Elder Council meeting, you agreed to monitor Magistrate Tesu and Initiate Kalina as we progress towards their conjunction.

Have you any specific reason to suspect one or both to have associations with the Rebel Branch?"

"Your timing is impeccable, Azoth," Obeche replied without hesitation. Clearly, she need not have worried about his reaction. "Just before you arrived, I had been preparing my findings with the intention of reporting them later this morning in Azothian Chambers."

"Then I have saved you a trip. What have you found?"

"Last night, I sought Initiate Kalina to review pre-conjunction security protocols — simply routine, I presumed. But I could not locate her. I looked everywhere. Finally, I posted myself outside the door to her residence chambers and waited. Cedar showed up and questioned my intent. As you might predict, I stood my ground. Kalina eventually arrived. She claimed to have been studying in the annex of the South Library. I implied that I believed her."

"But you knew she had lied to you. You had checked the annex beforehand."

"Precisely. As I said, I had looked everywhere. Of course, she would think I had sought her first in the most obvious place — her residence chambers. But, in fact, I left the obvious for last."

"Why not call her out on the lie? Interrogate her further? Read her pendant?"

"If Kalina is aligned with the rebels, her lies would merely multiply in response to additional questions. And the rebels may already have alchemically manipulated her pendant to hide certain facts. Instead, when she mentioned the South Library, I decided to feign acceptance. Rather than meeting her story with accusations of lying, I asked questions on the subject matter of her study session. My plan now is to continue to monitor her closely. If she thinks she can dupe me, her arrogance will get the better of her eventually, and I will contentedly bear witness to her treason."

"Someday, Kalina may indeed make an observable mistake," admitted Ravenea. "But for the foreseeable future, regardless of last evening's outcome, she will assume you to be watching her closely in Council dimension. That assumption alone may curtail her intended plans."

"Thus providing me even more time to gather evidence of her connections before she can inflict damage. After all, as a mere Senior Initiate, Kalina's powers are sufficiently restricted. She currently remains within our control."

"Your reasoning is sound, Obeche. Nevertheless, I would like you to consider an alternate plan — the favour I mentioned."

Obeche put a hand to his pendant and observed her intently.

"My request is nothing unseemly, Obeche. If Ailanthus or Ruis should read your pendant, they would note nothing beyond attentiveness and diligence. You did, after all, agree to monitor Kalina. And I am, after all, an Azoth."

"Indeed."

"For now, you need not bother Ailanthus or Ruis with your concerns about Kalina. Instead of reporting to Azothian Chambers today, I officially request that you report to the Vienna protectorate. From there, you will make your way to the Hotel Sacher and arrange a three-day visit for two of our sharpest Initiates."

Obeche's eyes widened slightly.

"One of these guests will be Kalina. The other will be Junior Initiate Laurel."

"Do you suspect Laurel—"

"No. Laurel is too dedicated to Council — well, to Initiate Cercis in particular — to risk erasure by aligning herself with the Rebel Branch. But she and Kalina do have one thing in common. Among other achievements, they earned gold in the Junior and Senior Initiate exams respectively. The trip to Vienna will be their well-earned reward. At leisure in the outside world thanks to a plausible reason, Kalina may neglect discretion."

"Alternatively, if your earlier supposition is correct, Kalina will expect me to observe her whether here or elsewhere. If I am stationed in Vienna—"

"By then, you will not be in Vienna. I will appoint Cedar as the accompanying Elder. Kalina will assume you have remained in Council dimension on official duties. Cedar is, after all, the one who first noticed Kalina's conjunctive potential with Tesu."

"Yes, Cedar surprised me when she presented the notation in *Philosophia Sacra 3490*. Something seemed amiss even then. Manuscript manipulation may be afoot."

"I agree."

Obeche nodded, smiled, but then frowned. "Forgive me, Azoth, but I fail to understand. If Cedar accompanies Kalina, how am I to observe her activities?"

Ravenea removed a small vial from a pocket of her inner robes. She held it up to the window where it glistened — vibrant fuchsia — against the light.

"Do you recognize this substance, Obeche?"

"Amrita! Of course! As a Senior Initiate, Kalina would as yet be unaware of its existence, let alone its alchemical properties. I can track her from the Scriptorium."

"Every move she makes."

A week later, Ravenea had difficulty repressing a smile as she listened to Obeche present his evidence against Kalina in Azothian Chambers. No one need know Ravenea herself had instigated the investigation on behalf of Cedar. She and Cedar willingly allowed Obeche to take the credit. He should take it. He had proven himself even more cunning than

Ravenea had anticipated. Alongside the tracing map inscribed through the Lapis and its concurrence with Amrita, Obeche had unexpectedly provided photographic evidence of Kalina's activities in Vienna. If ever she required outside world spies, Ravenea would know whom to ask.

Kalina sat perfectly still, seemingly steadfast, until Ravenea approached her and requested her pendant. Right then, Ravenea saw a momentary glimpse of concern cross Kalina's face. Obeche had observed Kalina not only entering a manuscript sector of the Vienna protectorate but also meeting with Rebel High Azoth Dracaen. Regardless of rebel allegiances and erasure techniques, Kalina would unlikely have had time to cleanse her pendant completely between those traitorous events and this tribunal.

Both Ailanthus and Ruis knew that if anyone could tease out Kalina's secrets and lies, Ravenea could. Her pendant-reading skills far exceeded those of everyone on Council, including the Azoth Magen himself. From her first pendant-reading assignment as a Senior Initiate onward, Ravenea had eclipsed her peers. So she had known even before approaching Obeche with her request that Ailanthus would later ask her, not Ruis, to confiscate and read Kalina's pendant upon her return from Vienna. Its chain dangling and unclasped from her hand, Ravenea moved the pendant to her forehead, closed her eyes, and inhaled deeply.

"The pendant's memory has been wiped," she proclaimed moments later. "Such treachery is surely the result of manipulation by one skilled with Dragon's Blood tonic."

"Recommendation?" Ailanthus asked immediately.

"Complete erasure," asserted Ravenea. "Once a rebel, always a rebel."

The Elders nodded and murmured their assent. Cedar appeared particularly content.

To all those observing the scenario, Ravenea had read the pendant and reached a logical conclusion swiftly yet diligently. Yet Ravenea had taken nowhere near the time she would need for a thorough examination of Kalina's pendant. She had anticipated complexities, including the requirement to leave the confiscated pendant with the Azoth Magen, so she had come prepared. Within those sixty seconds, Ravenea had not *read* the pendant as such; she had, in effect, *downloaded* it. Given the appreciative reactions of the Elders to her declaration, no one had noticed Ravenea's own pendant — removed earlier from its chain — cupped in the palm of her hand. Likewise, no one had noticed Ravenea pin Kalina's pendant between her own pendant and her forehead during the apparent reading. No one had noticed the spark of luminescence caused by the alchemically charged conduit Elixir she had earlier rubbed into the skin of both her hands and face. And, most certainly, no one noticed the utter astonishment she concealed as she walked out of Azothian Chambers, her right hand tucked into a pocket of her robes clutching copious downloaded pendant memories she never would have fathomed.

Safely ensconced once again in her residence chambers, Ravenea sat in the rocking chair on her balcony. She strung her pendant back onto its cord and began to rock slowly, clenching the pendant with both hands between her breasts. Though she had not yet brought it to her lips or forehead, spectacular vibrations had already begun to flood her senses. Ravenea knew that the memories she had extracted earlier from Kalina's confiscated pendant would exist within her own pendant for only three hours. Under normal circumstances, she would begin to read them immediately. But she needed her body to adjust to the physical sensations rushing through it before attempting the more cerebral act of detailed reading. So she rocked and she waited.

When Ravenea finally brought the pendant to her lips, a literal shock caused her to lurch backward so severely that she feared tipping the chair. She persevered, rocking steadily. Never in her hundreds of years of pendant reading, whether by illicit transfer or otherwise, had Ravenea ever encountered such extraordinary effects. At one point, completely unexpectedly, a wave of pain overcame her, and she dropped her pendant. She stopped rocking, utterly astounded. Kalina was only a Senior Initiate. As such, the Senior Magistrates would have subjected her pendant to monthly readings. *How*, Ravenea asked herself, *could Kalina have submitted her pendant month after month without someone noticing these forceful anomalies?*

Concerned about being overwhelmed again, she prepared herself by moving from the balcony into her room and onto her bed. She pulled on the pendant cord, held the pendant momentarily in her hand, and then brought it cautiously to her forehead. She need not have feared. The anticipated dramatic effects soon became relatively tranquil. Images — pictorial and emotional — drifted through her mind like memories of her own. Initially, they made no sense — myriad puzzle pieces that tried her patience. But as time progressed, connections formed. Gradually, meanings emerged. Two hours later, another piece of the complex puzzle manifested and then faded away with all the others: *Ilex and Melia.* At the very least, Kalina had met them; quite possibly she *knew* them intimately; potentially, she was their alchemical grandchild.

Could Kalina be not only a rebel infiltrator but also a physical manifestation of the mutually conjoined bloodline? She appeared extremely young, even for an alchemist. But who could say what effects ancestral blood of the current era might have on the maturation of an alembic-forged alchemical child? *Evolution breeds exception.*

Since that original meeting with Fraxinus at Waterloo Station — one hundred and sixty-five years ago — Ravenea had longed to know more, attempted to learn the name of Ilex and Melia's child, of the scribe powerful enough to break Makala's bloodlocks and reactivate the *Osmanthian Codex.* Fraxinus had purposely provided her only minimal information, and she had no one else to ask without risk of exposure. Even consulting with Saule about Ilex and Melia, let alone their child, could have had grievous repercussions along her path to Azoth.

And even if Fraxinus had agreed to reveal the name, what good would the revelation have done to help her in the long run? Names could be changed. Identities could be masked. Ravenea herself was evidence of extensive manuscript revision. What was she — *Ravenea rivularis* — upon her naming and renaming, other than a living, breathing palimpsest once conceived in an alembic, later sent through time, finally welcomed to Council dimension at an alternate point on the timeline through manipulation of amended texts? She had intended for no other being to suffer her fate, no other alchemist to spend an eternity hiding one's self and one's origins. Yet somewhere within the current timeline another alchemical child hid.

In that moment, amidst contemplation of the past, Ravenea understood her present. She realized with certainty that Kalina must indeed be the alchemical child, the granddaughter of Ilex and Melia, the one braided to her mother, the breaker of bloodlocks. No one on the Alchemists' Council had previously read the truth in Kalina's pendant because they were not bonded with Kalina. As Ravenea now suspected, only an alchemical child with whom a pre-established bond existed could effectively read another alchemical child's pendant. Years earlier, through the gift of the bee-embossed coin, Ravenea's Quintessence had marked Kalina. The instant Kalina accepted the gift — regardless of its subsequent fate — their essences had converged.

But Ravenea simultaneously understood a difficult truth. Yes, she had marked another alchemical child with her essence. Yes, she could read that alchemical child's pendant. Yes, she could excise her from the Alchemists' Council and, therefore, ensure she would never conjoin. In that sense, Ravenea had Cedar and Obeche to thank for unknowingly helping her to mitigate dimensional catastrophe. However, the braiding could prevent Kalina's complete erasure. Despite Ravenea's recommendation, despite Ailanthus's acceptance of the sanction, despite the Council's attempts and apparent success at erasure, despite alchemists of the lower orders forgetting the Initiate upon erasure, a trace of Kalina could remain. Thus, whether banished to the outside world or not, Kalina *could* decide to wreak havoc within Council dimension should she find a means to incise a breach. After all, if rebels had trained her and her mother's blood alchemy aided her, why would an alchemical child not take the opportunity to express her creative ingenuity across dimensional space and time?

Council Dimension — 2014

As she rounded the corner of the eastern passageway towards the stairwell, Ravenea sensed a slight but abrupt shift in the elemental balance of the building. At first, she assumed her unprecedented exhaustion had caused a spectral illusion. But after experiencing a longer vibration, she paused on the stairs to observe the alchemical interplay of her surroundings. Within seconds, she confirmed the sensation had not been a fatigue-induced illusion. The dimension's elemental balance was in flux. More concerning, the elemental shift could well be connected to the primary agenda item at each of the day's three meetings: the disappearing bees.

Like a few other Elders, Ravenea could not help but assume rebel involvement. Specifically, she suspected what no one else on Council would even think to consider: Ilex and Melia. Nearly two hundred years had passed since she and Saule had helped Ilex and Melia escape Council dimension on the wings of a bee. Linden's and Cedar's recent reports of vanishing bees had brought Ilex, Melia, Saule, and the blood-alchemy ritual to the forefront despite centuries of interceding events. Of course, Ravenea had no current means to confirm her suspicions. Nonetheless, if Ruis failed to determine a feasible plan for investigating the manuscript lacunae, Ravenea would begin her own inspection. For now, the flux having subsided, she longed for an evening of uninterrupted relaxation to regain her equilibrium. By the time she stepped over the threshold into her chambers, she had resolved to spend the remainder of the evening in her balcony's rocking chair sipping ruby liqueur.

The top floor of the residence building comprised only three suites: those of the Azoth Magen and the two Azoths. Therefore, unlike those of the lower orders, Azothian rooms and balconies were a grand and spacious refuge. If Ravenea sat in her rocking chair, she could contemplate the sky while enjoying complete privacy, positioned outside the sightlines of others. If she stood at her balcony's stone barrier, she could admire the beautifully landscaped grounds to the west, visible but generally unconcerned about who might spot her from the courtyard below. Tonight, her second glass of ruby liqueur in hand, she moved from the chair to the balcony railing to enjoy the luminosity of the Amber Garden. During the final half hour before sunset, its innumerable amber fragments lit up in a sun-drenched spectacle, an enchanted golden vision made manifest in the distance. Many an evening since becoming Azoth, Ravenea had surveyed Council grounds from this spot in awe and gratitude during these thirty amber-infused minutes.

But a knock at the door interrupted the night's picturesque relaxation. She expected Ailanthus, Ruis, or even Obeche to be the uninvited offender. Most probably, like Ravenea, one of them had sensed the elemental fluctuation and had come to consult on an immediate course of action. But instead, Magistrate Sadira greeted her.

"Apologies, Azoth, but I must speak with you privately."

The unorthodox situation intrigued Ravenea. Sadira had never visited her residence chambers. The matter must be more significant than a minor environmental disturbance. Perhaps Sadira sought guidance regarding her upcoming conjunction with Amur. As Ravenea gestured for her to take a seat, she thought again of Ilex and Melia. Sadira had been the Initiate who replaced the fugitive pair. Ravenea remembered the resulting fire that Sadira herself had extinguished. She could not help but conceive of her as a mere fragment of a much larger and increasingly complex design.

"A few hours ago," Sadira began by way of explanation, "I accompanied our newest Junior Initiate into Council dimension."

How could Ravenea have forgotten? The arrival of a new Initiate — not the machinations of Ilex and Melia — could explain the evening's environmental flux.

"Given the Meeting of Assembly," Sadira continued, "none of the Elders was present for opening introductions."

Was this all? Had Sadira interrupted Ravenea's otherwise pleasant evening of contemplation to request she return to Azothian Chambers to meet the newest recruit?

"Sadira, I admire your enthusiasm for protocol, but I am in no temperament for formal introductions tonight. Allow the new Initiate and Elders to rest until tomorrow."

"Apologies once again, Azoth. But I am not here to request an introduction. I am here to report an anomaly — well, a . . . variance of behaviour — that I noticed during my first meeting with the new Initiate at the outside world crossing point."

"Yes?"

"When I addressed him, he claimed to already know his tree name."

"And what is it — his tree name?"

"Arjan — a variation of Arjun or *Terminalia arjuna*."

"Arjan."

"Yes. He claims to have studied alchemy in the outside world. He said he read about *Terminalia arjuna* and knew his name was to be Arjan. Not only that, but he believes himself a potential prodigy within the Alchemists' Council."

"Well!" Ravenea laughed. "We could certainly use one."

Sadira smiled rather awkwardly. "Of course, Azoth." She stood to leave.

"Why did you come to me, Sadira?"

"As I said, I wanted to report the anomaly."

"But why come to *me*? Why not go to Ruis or any one of the Elders?"

"I consulted Cedar. She advised me to report to you."

"Did she? Well, thank you. I will report your concerns to Ailanthus in the morning."

"Yes, Azoth. Good night."

Sadira left, closing the door quietly behind her. Ravenea stood by the window, perplexed. Had Ailanthus approved Arjan's recommendation in consultation with Readers and Scribes without convening the Azoths? Why would he have made such an unusual move? Could this Initiate be *him*? Could Arjan be *the* one — the Champion of Dimensions, the redeemer that Makala had vividly inscribed into *Chimera Veritas*? Or was Arjan merely another alchemical child whom Fraxinus had neglected to name?

The Elder Council agreed that Arjan's effect on the dimensional Quintessence far exceeded that of most novice Initiates. His arrival had affected the entire Council, everyone having experienced or witnessed a manifestation of imbalance. Most had stumbled physically, but a few had faltered emotionally. Angry exchanges had echoed through the corridors two mornings in a row. Both Magistrates Linden and Sadira reported bouts of disruptive laughter by the Senior Initiates during iconography lessons. Meanwhile, Readers Wu Tong and Olivia had succumbed to crying during questioning about Arjan's recommendation and appointment.

"As always, extensive evidence convinced us," Wu Tong responded to justify his specific choice of potential Initiate Arjan over potential Initiate Ash. When Ailanthus reminded him that the choice of one meant the death of the other, Wu Tong could not control his tears. The dimensional flux was indeed overwhelming them all.

When Olivia fared even worse, weeping uncontrollably, Ruis moved that they consider the investigation complete. Obeche, angered, railed against Ruis for being irresponsible — a comment that reinforced Ravenea's confidence that Obeche's allegiance to Ruis had weakened. Elder Council bickering continued until Ravenea asked Ailanthus to make a unilateral decision, at which point he determined that Arjan was not only the correct choice of candidate but the optimal one. *His alchemical potential is strong. He will serve Council well*, decreed Ailanthus. And he officially closed the matter.

But Ravenea required proof. After meeting him, she suspected Arjan could indeed be the young man in Makala's portraits; he did, after all, share the physical characteristics visible in *Chimera Veritas*'s portrayals of both the sacred chimera and the Champion of Dimensions. Laughing to herself, Ravenea imagined requesting Arjan to dress in turquoise robes and visit Azothian Chambers wielding a gilded sceptre. But her more sombre thoughts painted Arjan as the next Kalina — another alembic-conceived threat. If allowed to remain on Council, if allowed to ascend through the Orders, he could be called to conjunction. Where would Ravenea be then? Where would any of the conjoined be? Granted, Ravenea and the Council were in no *immediate* danger of impending conjunction. But Arjan could already be positioned as the filament — the one string that, when pulled through time, would begin to unravel the fabric of Council dimension. That possibility, even if years away, was a risk Ravenea could not take.

Consequently, she ignored Ailanthus's official verdict. Instead, in hopes of learning more about Arjan, Ravenea observed him whenever able to do so without being too conspicuous. Over the month since his arrival, she had watched him at lessons in the Initiate classroom, studying in both the North and South libraries, consulting with Magistrate Sadira, dining and socializing with his peers, and regularly chatting with Initiate Jaden. Though he seemed more enthusiastic and less overwhelmed than most Junior Initiates adjusting to Council life, he otherwise did nothing particularly unusual, certainly nothing that would concern a casual observer, whether Magistrate or Elder. But none of Ravenea's observations had provided her with an opportunity to test her theory — not until she literally ran into Laurel, who was carrying a tray of spiced milk. The tray and its cups crashed to the stone floor, splashing the milk onto Ravenea's robes.

"Retire to your residence chambers for the day," Ravenea said to Laurel.

Though an onlooker of a higher order might have deemed the reprimand unnecessarily harsh, a Junior Initiate had little experience with Azothian penalty protocols. Only Laurel and Arjan had witnessed the incident, with Jaden and Cercis arriving on the scene shortly thereafter. For all these Initiates knew, colliding physically with an Azoth — even by accident — could indeed be a punishable offence. Laurel ran off in tears, an exaggerated response that the others would simply chalk up to lingering dimensional adjustments. Ravenea had no reason to believe anyone, including Arjan, would think her own behaviour out of character.

Jaden appeared distraught, as if the accident had ruined her entire day.

"Another time," said Arjan reassuringly.

"No need to linger," Ravenea said to both Jaden

and Cercis. "Your time would be better spent reviewing lessons before afternoon classes."

Jaden glanced at Arjan but departed swiftly with Cercis. Ravenea held the tray while Arjan picked up the broken shards of the cups.

"Be careful," she said. "Though we heal quickly, alchemists bleed easily."

"So I see," he responded. He stood up, deposited several jagged pieces onto the tray, and held up a hand to reveal a thin trickle of blood.

Ravenea smiled as Arjan knelt to collect the remaining shards. "Ingesting or applying a little Lapidarian honey directly to the wound should do the trick."

He stood again and looked directly into her eyes — the most unusual behaviour she had observed in him thus far. Both Senior and Junior Initiates were prone to lowering their heads in the presence of an Azoth.

"I have a jar in my office," she said to him, gesturing towards the nearby corridor with her head. "You are welcome to accompany me."

"Thank you, Azoth, but I am fine. I will ask one of the Magistrates for some balm after I return the tray to the kitchen."

"No need to trouble yourself," said Ravenea, holding the tray firmly. "The incident was my fault. I will return the tray and offer my apologies. Good day, Arjan."

Arjan met her eyes once again before assuming Ab Uno position and turning to walk away. Once he had moved out of sight, Ravenea carried the tray to her office. A drop of Arjan's blood was the only evidence she needed.

Over the following few weeks, with three blood-marked fragments of china hidden carefully away and the requisite alchemical formula gestating, Ravenea set about tasks that her colleagues might think somewhat eccentric but would ultimately deem to be business as usual. She held an impromptu meeting with Cedar, Obeche, and a few Lapidarian Scribes and Readers to indicate her concern — without Ruis to interject — about the bees. The meeting progressed even better than she could have hoped, with Cedar convincing the others to grant the Junior Initiates access to both the outside world and interim pendants. Should the blood-alchemy formula justify her suspicions about Arjan, Ravenea would have no trouble whatsoever getting herself to and from Santa Fe before the official Initiate pendant quest.

Next, she convinced Ailanthus to instigate a Ritual of Restoration. The Elders assumed she had based her suggestion in Council logic: a reasonable step towards restoring the bee-induced lacunae of *Ruach 2103*. But she had instead based her proposal in supposition. With their tactics threatened, with the lacunae about to be overwritten, the perpetrators responsible for the disappearing bees might retaliate. She feigned surprise when Kalina's voice rang out through the ruby haze.

Thereafter, Ravenea worked late into the night — alongside Kai, Cedar, and Tera — scouring manuscripts for signs of lacunae and Rebel Branch interference. With dawn a mere few hours away, Ailanthus entered the Azothian consultation room and encouraged them to relinquish their task and get some sleep.

"Once everyone is sufficiently rested, we will proceed with the Trance of the Nine."

After the others had retired from her office but before returning to her own residence chambers, Ravenea unlocked and peered into the cabinet containing the concealed formula. To her delight, it had finally turned intense azure, indicating its maturity. She cleared off the small triangular table beside the cabinet, laid a silver-lined Cloth of Quintessence on its surface, lit a Lapidarian candle, poured some of the azure liquid into a small copper dish, and retrieved one of the three fragments of china. Using small golden tongs, she set the fragment into the formula. Immediately it sizzled, bubbling up into a purple froth that ran over the sides of the dish.

As the blood-tinged froth seeped into the Cloth of Quintessence, Ravenea retrieved the Records of Essence from the official Council files.

Alchemical equivalents of genetic mapping, these Azothian records charted the essential particles of every alchemist who had resided for a year or more in Council dimension. One year in Lapidarian proximity was a necessity for an accurate reading by the usual — less covert — means. Ravenea needed to know if any current member of Council would match with Arjan at the central core of their essences; without a potential match, a conjunction could not proceed. In that case, even if Arjan were an alchemical child, he would not yet be a potential menace beyond the sort the Rebel Branch regularly imposed upon the Council.

Holding the cloth next to each alchemist's record, Ravenea compared Arjan's essence with every current member of the Council. She began with the lower Orders. Over an hour had passed before she reached the record that sent her reeling. She shook her head and rubbed her eyes before comparing the two mapped essences again. The record did not show a match per se — certainly not of the type required for conjunction. Instead of indicating a match of essence, it indicated a match of Quintessence, a phenomenon Ravenea had never before witnessed. Yet she knew precisely what it meant. She had proof beyond her expectations: not only was Arjan an alchemical child, but a member of the Alchemists' Council had conceived him.

Immediately, Ravenea locked all incriminating evidence into the concealed cabinet and rushed through the corridors to the Novillian wing of residence chambers. She knocked quietly, not wanting any of the nearby Scribes to hear her. She knocked again. Finally, the door opened.

"Azoth! Have you spotted another lacuna?"

Without invitation, Ravenea moved from the corridor into the room. "Close the door, Cedar. I need to read your pendant."

With Arjan and Jaden temporarily assigned to outside world duties in the Qingdao protectorate, Ravenea made her way to the North Library to speak with Coll. As current Keeper of the Book, Coll could supply her with a list of the manuscripts Arjan had accessed. If she were to ask for a Record of Retrieval for the entire Junior Initiate quarto, Coll would assume Ravenea merely required the information as part of a standard Initiate evaluation rather than suspect she intended to investigate only Arjan. Not that Coll's suspicions would matter. As Azoth, Ravenea could examine whatever or whomever she pleased, with no explanation necessary. Nonetheless, caution was prudent. *Dimensional walls have alchemical ears*, Ailanthus had often said to her in their early years on the Council. She smiled — those days seemed an eternity ago.

Over the century since Coll had arrived in Council dimension, Ravenea had found him quite amenable to her requests. His dedication and commitment to Council had proven admirable. Only his unusually advanced age and imperfect vision gave away his penchant for spending swaths of time in the outside world working on his poetry. This artistic inclination had ceased upon his "death" in the outside world, which he had faked in anticipation of the impending outside world war. Though she cared little for literary critique, Ravenea had admittedly wondered if she alone, while reading his outside world poetry, had pictured the beast slouching towards Bethlehem as alchemy's Green Lion, blood pouring from its mouth.

Ravenea had assumed her request for the Record of Retrieval would be met with Coll's usual smile and nod of agreement. But instead he set down the manuscript keys he had been sorting and stared at her over his spectacles.

"Is something wrong?" she asked.

He extracted a single piece of parchment from a folder and handed it to her. The list was divided into two columns. One was labelled *Terminalia arjuna*, the other *Crassula argentea*: Arjan and Jaden. Each column itemized manuscript names and the retrieval dates on which Initiates had requested them via the Emerald Tablet. Initiate residue signatures confirmed access to the listed manuscripts. Ravenea glanced down the columns. Nothing of note stood out — certainly nothing strikingly unusual.

"What of Initiates Laurel and Cercis?" Ravenea asked for good measure.

He shook his head and shrugged. Then he handed her a large manuscript — *Sapientiae Aeternae 1818*. From her days as a Magistrate, she recognized the volume as one featuring tree illuminations.

"I do not understand," she said.

"I assumed one Elder or another would come to me this week." He tapped a finger against *Sapientiae Aeternae 1818*. "Folio 16," he said. He then gestured towards a nearby table upon which she could open the manuscript and investigate.

"Your assistance would be appreciated," she said.

Not knowing what she would find on folio 16, Ravenea wanted Coll seated close enough to her that she could question him discreetly. The folio, verso and recto respectively, depicted summer and winter foliage of a shrub — red berries dotted the winter version. Beneath the summer depiction appeared the inexpertly inscribed words *Crassula argentea*. Ravenea quickly consulted the list Coll had provided. Jaden had recently retrieved *Sapientiae Aeternae 1818*. No wonder Coll had been preparing the list. He had anticipated a formal investigation by the Elders. Despite his impeccable work for the Council over the years, he would need to assure them that the manuscript defacement had not occurred as a result of his negligence.

Ravenea turned the pages to observe the illustrations and text on nearby folios. They all illustrated seasonal representation of trees or shrubs, and they all had the Latin name for each specimen written underneath. Clearly the image on folio 16 was *not* in fact *Crassula argentea*. Had Jaden erased the original name and replaced it with her own?

"Is this image not *Viburnum opulus*?" Ravenea asked Coll, pointing to the winter image on folio 16 verso.

"Yes," he replied.

She paused then, trying to remember. Not recognizing the name *Viburnum opulus* as associated with anyone on the current Council, she thought back through the decades, rotation after rotation, trying to recall anyone with a derivative name: *Vibur? Burnum? Opul? Opal?* Quickly, she realized her line of inquiry was pointless. Though Ravenea herself had opted for Latin, the once-fashionable custom had become rather antiquated over the years of her tenure. As an Azoth, she was familiar with hundreds of tree names in dozens of languages; yet, staring at this image in this moment, she simply could not recall any alternate names for *Viburnum opulus*. And even if Ravenea was correct in her assumption that Jaden had substituted her name for that of another Council member, that alchemist — like Jaden or Jinjing — may not have used any part of the official tree terminology as her preferred name.

Coll gave a slight cough beside her.

"Do you know?" she asked him.

"Do I know what, Azoth?"

"Names in other languages for *Viburnum opulus*."

"I know one," he said.

"Yes? What is it?" She failed to understand his hesitancy in responding. "Coll! What is the name?" She was growing increasingly and obviously frustrated.

"Kalina," he finally whispered.

"Kalina!" she shouted.

Coll glanced around the vicinity as if nervous about potential eavesdroppers. This precaution made no sense to Ravenea. Since her erasure, only Elders and Keepers of the Book could remember Senior Initiate Kalina. To any other alchemists listening, Ravenea would merely have overreacted to a tree name — an outburst they would undoubtedly attribute to Azothian enthusiasm for manuscript illuminations. She would have questioned Coll immediately about his knowledge of Kalina, if not for the violent shaking that overtook them within seconds of their exchange. They had to grip tightly onto the table to keep from falling out of their chairs.

"An earthquake!" Coll exclaimed the moment the shaking subsided.

"Technically, we are not on Earth," Ravenea managed to respond despite her astonishment.

"Then the dimensions have collided," Coll said, thus making a virtual impossibility seem like the only logical explanation.

Within an hour of the dimensional quake, Ravenea, Ruis, and a few diligent Readers had determined its cause to be an elemental disturbance originating in the Qingdao protectorate. Thereafter, throughout much of the subsequent Ritual of Restoration and Sacrament of Elixir, Ravenea pondered the involvement of not only Arjan and Jaden but also Jinjing. Since the Third Rebellion, Jinjing had worked alternately in the North Library and the Qingdao protectorate. Perhaps, like Coll, she knew more than Ravenea had assumed. Given their lack of Lapidarian pendants, Keepers of the Book maintained the ability to remember erased alchemists; generally, however, they followed strict protocols of discretion on such matters. Coll had sidestepped the protocol by naming Kalina. What protocols had Jinjing evaded?

Ravenea thought again of *Sapientiae Aeternae 1818*. Through her inscription, Jaden was connected to Kalina. Jaden's current presence in Qingdao connected her to Jinjing. Arjan and Kalina were both alchemical children. Ravenea wondered for the first time whether they all knew each other. If so, Cedar too must be considered suspect, despite Ravenea's reading of her pendant revealing nothing of Cedar's connection with Arjan — a glitch that continued to baffle her. Her

next step would be to investigate the other manuscripts on Coll's list, particularly the one neither
Arjan nor Jaden would have required for Initiate
lessons: *Serpens Chymicum 1414*.

As she pondered the various connections, Obeche,
Tera, and Arjan burst into Council Chambers
claiming that rebels had abducted Jaden. With official duties thereafter taking precedence, Ravenea had
little time for anything beyond Ailanthus's requests.
Along with the entire Elder Council, she necessarily
participated in conducting the Ritual of Return to
locate Jaden and alchemically wrench her home
through the portal. Ravenea could tell immediately
that the forced retrieval had left the young Initiate
nauseated and the Elders drained of Quintessence.
Detailed questioning regarding Jaden's and Arjan's
experiences in Qingdao would prove fruitless until
they had all had the opportunity to rest and recover.

As she lay in her bed that night, Ravenea contemplated the questions she would pose to both
Jaden and Arjan the next day in Azothian Chambers.
She imagined herself gathering bits of evidence,
snapping together fragments, one by one, until the
remaining pieces of the puzzle dropped readily into
place, and she could rest through eternity on the lau-
rels of her vigilance despite Fraxinus's perpetual lack
of cooperation and concern.

"Describe in precise detail your experiences and the sequence of events at the Qingdao protectorate," said Ravenea to Jaden.

The questioning of the Initiates thus began and at first progressed in precisely the manner Ravenea had imagined the previous night. Initially, the only detail Jaden unwittingly admitted was a physical attraction for Arjan. Not until she reported that she and Arjan had watched a young boy playing ball — a boy whom Arjan claimed to be *himself* as a child — did the investigation begin to veer unexpectedly off-course. The Elders became so animated in response that Ravenea had to mandate silence.

"Did you believe Arjan?" she asked Jaden. "Or did you understand him to be joking?"

"He wasn't joking. But I thought he might be wrong. *How could the boy actually be Arjan?* So I went outside to talk to him."

Though the events Jaden described thereafter were puzzling, Jaden's account of them seemed genuine. Despite the evident connection to Kalina inscribed into *Sapientiae Aeternae 1818*, Ravenea had no reason to suspect Jaden had purposely caused the disturbance in Qingdao. If she had played a role, it may well have been unwittingly.

Arjan, likewise, initially seemed an innocent bystander. Even when he spoke of remembering the event, of witnessing the interaction with Jaden years earlier as the young boy, Ravenea did nothing other than listen respectfully, her thoughts wandering first to Cedar's connection with him and then to his time-travelling potential. Even when he spoke of his grandparents and their skills at alchemical transmutation, she merely nodded, presuming them to be outside world charlatans commissioned with fostering an alchemical child away from prying eyes. Not until Arjan claimed his grandparents had succeeded at the transmutation of time did a chill run through Ravenea. She could barely breathe when Ailanthus bellowed the question all the Elders were wondering: *Who were your grandparents?* Ravenea knew the answer before Arjan uttered it: *Ilex and Melia.*

She rose from her seat immediately, but Obeche had already crossed the floor to Arjan in a few quick, broad paces.

"Obeche! Be seated!" she yelled.

But he ignored her. He seized Arjan's pendant, effectively draining its essence. Ravenea and Ruis both rushed forward, reaching out to support Arjan just before he collapsed to the floor. Obeche moved away, and Ailanthus took his place. He placed the Azothian sceptre against Arjan's forehead and held his pendant to his own. Though she knew that neither Obeche nor Ailanthus — being naturally rather than alchemically conceived — would read anything incriminating in Arjan's pendant, Ravenea trembled.

She had repeatedly suspected the involvement of Ilex and Melia in recent Council anomalies, but now she had confirmation. The certainty of their involvement in a time breach changed the terrain. Their alchemical powers were exceptionally remarkable, which was part of the reason she had agreed to help them to leave Council dimension long ago. But now, unless Arjan were to lead her to them — which, she assumed, he would not — she had no means to locate Ilex and Melia. As far as Ravenea knew, Saule had been the only person on Council to know their whereabouts, and she now resided within Cedar. Ravenea could hope only that Makala had trained her sufficiently in the blood-alchemy powers of conjunctive resurrection.

After reprimanding Obeche for his pendant assault on Arjan, and after Amur and Tera had taken Arjan to the catacombs for healing, Ailanthus informed Ravenea that he himself would enter a catacomb alembic for regenerative immersion. By the next morning, Ravenea decided to read the pendant for herself while both Arjan and Ailanthus regenerated in the alembics. Within the hour, she had made her way to the catacombs to attempt success where the others had failed. Now, having barely glanced at Ailanthus, who rested passively in suspended animation, Ravenea climbed the steps beside the alembic where Arjan lay and watched him for a few minutes.

Luminescent hues of red and orange flickered across the waters. Arjan looked peaceful, not at all like an alchemical child trained to infiltrate Council on behalf of the Rebel Branch. Of course, though a connection with the Rebel Branch seemed the most likely explanation for his presence, it remained pure speculation on her part. She wanted the truth, wanted to know precisely what Arjan was hiding — all the secrets she had been unable to attain reading Cedar's pendant, all the details neither Obeche nor Ailanthus had been able to attain reading Arjan's. After all, they had no reason to suspect Arjan to be an alchemical child. From the perspective of most Council members, alchemical children were an ancient mystery rather than a viable reality. Even the Elders had no cause to take precautions that might mitigate against ineffectual pendant readings. But Ravenea knew better.

Just as she moved her hand over the waters towards Arjan's pendant, Ravenea heard a noise in the distance. Someone was approaching. She could have repositioned herself to feign ritual concentration on the Azoth Magen, but she chose instead to crouch behind a dormant alembic from which she could remain hidden in the shadows but view much of the room. She assumed she could ascertain the interloper's true intention by covert spying rather than direct questioning. To say Ravenea was surprised to see Jaden enter the cavern would be an understatement. Was the crush she had perceived

Jaden to have for Arjan in fact loyalty bred in devotion? Little else would entice a Junior Initiate to navigate alone the depths and complexities of the catacomb passageways.

Though Ravenea could not see Ailanthus from her position, she had heard Jaden's startled reaction to finding him in the alembic. A Junior Initiate would have no reason to know that Azoths, including the Azoth Magen, occasionally required regeneration to rebalance their Quintessence. Once recovered, Jaden crossed the chamber towards the other active alembic. Ravenea silently repositioned herself to watch as Jaden carefully climbed the steps towards Arjan. Sitting on the step nearest Arjan's head, Jaden removed a small pouch from her robe and emptied its contents into the palm of her hand. With her empty hand, she reached into the alembic waters and retrieved Arjan's pendant. Hesitating momentarily, she then pressed the pendant against her other hand. This act produced a visible shockwave that jolted Jaden, causing her to release the pendant. Whatever she had emptied from the pouch into her hand had either fused with Arjan's pendant or fallen into the alembic waters. Seemingly unfazed, Jaden reached back into the waters, retrieved the pendant once again, and kissed it briefly. Given the brevity, she had no apparent intention to *read* the pendant; even trying to do so could be overwhelming for an untrained Initiate. Instead, she gently replaced it beneath the waters, descended the steps, and immediately left the alembic cavern for the catacomb corridors.

Ravenea waited a few minutes before emerging, crossing the cavern, climbing the steps, and reaching into the waters to retrieve Arjan's pendant. Given the powerful physical reaction she had experienced when first reading Kalina's pendant, she assumed the effect of reading Arjan's could be equally intense. Unlike with Kalina, Ravenea had not marked Arjan with a mere coin; instead, she had managed to mark his pendant. By alchemically manipulating its essence, Ravenea had ensured not only that Arjan would choose this pendant in Santa Fe but also that pendant proximity would irrevocably connect her to him. She braced herself against the edge of the alembic and gently placed the enhanced turquoise against her forehead.

Unexpectedly, the flow of images and emotions that began to move through her consciousness was remarkably calm and measured — more so than she had experienced reading any other pendant *ever*, including Kalina's. Within minutes, Ravenea realized that Arjan's pendant chain, like the pendant itself, was alchemically enhanced. Though she could not be certain, the combined enhancements seemed to filter the pendant's contents, presumably to mitigate the danger of overwhelming the reader. Someone must have suspected that another alchemical child would read the pendant, which in turn implied that someone — Ilex and Melia, she assumed — knew that multiple alchemical children existed.

The effect of the reading was so relaxing, so meditative, so sensuously comforting in its first half hour that Ravenea considered immersing herself into the waters beside Arjan for mutually restorative regeneration. Of course, communal immersion without mutual consent was forbidden even to the Azoths, but fear of repercussions or regret was not what stopped her from taking such an unforgivable misstep. Instead, one image brought her back to full awareness. Though it had emerged as serenely as all the images beforehand, it then remained in place, halting the steady flow of content and offering nothing further. She slowly lowered the pendant back into the waters and placed it gently against Arjan's chest. Not until she had descended the steps and walked a few paces away did she notice Ailanthus standing in the centre of the cavern.

"And?" he said.

She stared at him.

"What is the name of their child?" he asked.

She knew what he meant. The answer now resounded in her own mind — in the final frozen image from the pendant. But she remained silent.

"In the name of the Azoth Magen of the 18th Council, I command you to respond."

Ravenea pressed her lips together.

"Why do you think I entered the alembic?" he asked, taking a step towards her. "Do you presume

I needed healing? Regeneration? Balancing of Quintessence?"

Ravenea shook her head and shrugged. "I would not presume."

"Your feigned innocence is unbecoming, Ravenea."

"Your feigned ignorance is equally so," she replied.

"Touché!"

"I need to hear the oath," she said.

"I have made my decision. Though I chose to enter the catacombs only to see who visited Arjan, the alembic waters afforded me clarity of decision. The dusk of the 18th Council is upon us, and I have chosen my successor."

"I need to hear the oath," she repeated.

"Trade is troth, Ravenea. Answer my question and I will pledge my oath."

"Pledge your oath and I will answer your question."

He smiled and took another step towards her. He extended his hand, and she offered him her pendant. Clasping it tightly, he uttered the announcement she had been waiting centuries to hear: "I, *Ailanthus altissima*, Azoth Magen of the 18th Council of Alchemists, pledge to name you, *Ravenea rivularis*, as my successor. Long live Azoth Magen Ravenea!"

Still holding her pendant, not waiting for her to respond to his oath, he pulled against the chain and asked his question again. "Who was the child of Ilex and Melia?"

"Genevre."

"Fairly traded," he responded, letting her pendant fall back against her robes.

"Fairly traded."

"You will preside at the upcoming Sealing of Concurrence. Sadira and Amur must suspect nothing to be amiss prior to their conjunction. Everyone on Council must presume a full regeneration as the reason for my prolonged absence."

"Of course, Azoth Magen."

Ailanthus nodded and turned to leave.

"Where are you going?" Ravenea asked. "As your successor, am I not to be informed?"

Rather than face her directly, he merely glanced over his shoulder. "To bathe in Council dimension's light before extinguishing my own."

Ravenea and Ailanthus locked eyes as he uttered his final words: "Long live the Quintessence!" Years ago, at the Final Ascension of Azoth Magen Quercus, Ravenea had witnessed the spectacle of quintessential dissolution. Its horrific beauty had fascinated her. Today, watching Ailanthus age hundreds of years within minutes, knowing she herself would one day succumb to this demise, she shuddered. Tears stung as she thrust the Sword of Elixir into his skeletal ruins, which immediately fell as ash to the ground. Tears flowed as she gathered a handful of Ailanthus's remains and rubbed them onto her face, hands, and pendant. She stood aside to allow Ruis, Esche, and Kai to do the same.

"Having been chosen by Ailanthus as his successor," announced Ravenea, "I hereby accept my role and pledge my duty to the Council as Azoth Magen."

"And I, as Azoth," said Ruis, "pledge my allegiance to Azoth Magen Ravenea."

Applause filled the chambers. Her performance completed, Ravenea imagined taking a bow. Centuries had passed, but she had finally attained the pinnacle. Lost in her own thoughts, barely listening to those around her, she merely smiled and nodded in response to offers of congratulations. Not until Amur was writhing in agony on the floor was Ravenea shaken from her musings. Others had gathered around him — concerned and offering advice. They flew backward when Amur's body burst into flames. Someone screamed. Ravenea, in a gesture meant to quell the chaos, raised the Sword of Elixir. She almost dropped it in shock when she saw Kalina standing where Amur had just fallen.

How could this be? What had she missed? What had she neglected to understand? Ravenea stood, both fixated and dazed, attempting to compute the variables. Then the Sword of Elixir was gone — Cedar had plunged it into Kalina. At that moment, as Kalina stood proud and pierced and glowing, the truth overcame Ravenea.

"Rebels!" Ravenea shouted the moment she saw the first emerge from the radiant breach Kalina's victory had created.

Ruis signalled to her, and they rushed forward together to retrieve the Sword of Elixir and close the breach. But the damage had begun. The Fourth Rebellion was underway. In that moment, plunged into the fray, Ravenea fully and finally comprehended what no one could yet see — Amur had been a vessel for the mutual conjunction of Kalina and Sadira. Ravenea was no longer the only conjoined alchemical child in Council dimension. The prophetic riddles of the *Osmanthian Codex* had begun to manifest decades earlier than she had assumed they could.

Despite her efforts to curtail the predictions, to enact her precautions, Ravenea had failed. She had been Azoth Magen for less than an hour, and already her governance of the dimension was in jeopardy. Fraxinus had warned her about the *Osmanthian Codex*. Thirty years later, he had warned her not only about the alchemically created children but also of the enigmatic caveats he had gleaned from among its ancient doctrines.

Surely our Treaty of Fair Warning requires you to provide me not merely with a prophetic riddle but with a solution!

The solution remains yours to develop. Textual interpretation is all I can offer.

And what is your interpretation? she had asked.

Alchemical children are incompatible with the Sacrament of Conjunction.

Clearly a misinterpretation. My own conjunction with Erez succeeded without incident.

You are one child. The riddle specifies children — plural.

Regardless, failed conjunction is not the end of the world.

Success, not failure, will result in the prophesied discordancy. Provided my interpretation of a specific folio is valid, the conjunction of more than one alchemical child within a confined timeline of a primary dimension will mark the beginning of the end of that dimension. Not instantaneously, of course. Dimensional dissolution is painfully gradual — though apparently swifter if an alchemical child succeeds at mutual conjunction.

Painfully gradual — she had never forgotten those words. And now she had witnessed, horrified, the mutual conjunction of Kalina and Sadira within *this* dimension. Nightmares plagued her during the nights thereafter. In one, a raven-haired alchemical child pulled apart the tapestry of Council dimension fibre by fibre. At first, the alterations were barely noticeable — minor fraying on a well-worn carpet; by the end, in threadbare robes, Ravenea herself clasped the single remaining strand of the North Library and slipped into a wordless chasm. In another, a golden-haired child touched a pillar in the Scriptorium to reveal a holographic grid that sparked and sizzled, segment by segment until, in one loud short-circuited blast, all of Council dimension transformed into a blood-blackened void.

London, Waterloo Station — 2014

"I can no longer rely on your misleading interpretations. You must provide me access to the manuscript. I need to read and interpret the prophecies of the *Osmanthian Codex* for myself."

"I cannot," Fraxinus responded.

"No one would question a meeting between us now, Fraxinus! Out of necessity, Ailanthus regularly consulted with the Rebel Branch Elders within Flaw dimension, including with you!"

"Not in the deepest archives — and not without Dracaen."

"Fine, then take me to Dracaen."

"Dracaen is not . . . himself."

"Do not play rhetorical games with me. Alchemical children have conjoined. The prophecy regarding them is manifesting. Lives are at risk!"

"Even as Azoth Magen, you cannot prevent an Osmanthian prophecy."

"You know as well as I the strength of primordial blood alchemy. After thousands of years of dormancy, that manuscript required thirty years to mature. Alchemically programmed pages may well reveal additional inscriptions over the centuries.

The primary riddle regarding alchemical children and mutual conjunction may have offered up its own solution by now. I demand that you show me the folio in question!"

"I cannot."

Ravenea could no longer look at him. She turned away and, unintentionally, found herself staring at the clock as its minute hand moved. She choked back panic. How much time remained? How much time remained before this clock — before every clock in the outside world — stopped as a result of dimensional dissolution?

"If Council dimension unravels, the other dimensions will likewise be negatively affected. Yet you remain unwilling to show me even one folio."

"I am not unwilling. I am *unable*."

Ravenea gestured towards the daunting clock. "Time is of the essence!"

"Neither I nor Dracaen can show you the necessary folio, Ravenea. Long ago, the one who originally awakened it tore it from its bindings."

"The one who—" She stopped. She understood: Genevre.

"And even she is unaware of its location."

"The breaker of bloodlocks lost the folio?"

"No. For safekeeping, she asked a trusted colleague to hide it from everyone, including her. My assumption is that she intended to mitigate the possibility of an Elder forcibly extracting its location from her memory."

"So extract the name of the colleague and then extract the location!"

"We have recently learned the name of the colleague, but memory extraction is impossible. She was dissolved in conjunction almost six years ago. Thus, the folio is irrevocably lost."

Though to Fraxinus she revealed an expression of carefully forged regret, Ravenea inwardly nurtured a spark of elation. Genevre had alchemical powers beyond measure. She most certainly would not have risked irrevocable loss of the folio. She would have made certain that the conjunction of her "trusted colleague" would not result in complete dissolution. Genevre had been one step ahead of Ravenea all along: Saule could indeed be resurrected from Cedar.

III
Council Dimension — 2014

The aftermath of the Fourth Rebellion was manifesting in a series of events falling as surely and rapidly as stones in an avalanche. Soon Cedar herself would tumble. She had therefore been using her limited free time between meetings and Azothian interrogations to research mutual conjunctions. Specifically, she needed to understand the two pairings she and Jaden had witnessed at the edge of the redwood forest three days earlier. Now, as Jaden lay in a catacomb alembic healing from hundreds of bee stings — a process that, given the unusual severity of the wounds, could take weeks — Cedar sat in a private archival room contemplating two items. First was the note she had serendipitously found, which included a manuscript title: *Turba Philosophorum 1881, Qingdao protectorate, location marker 15.23.8.* Second was the manuscript itself, which Cedar had extracted from said location and brought back to Council dimension just over an hour earlier.

Protocols required alchemists of the lower orders to wear Azadirian gloves when working with pre-Eirenaeus manuscripts. Given her status as Elder, such restrictions did not limit Cedar. She slowly, almost sensually, ran a bare fingertip along the edge of the illumination on folio 16. The image depicted Makala, an Ancient Elder who had lived during the 4th and 5th Councils. From as far back as early Initiate history examinations, Cedar could recall reading accounts of Azoth Magen Makala. Among other overhauls to the Council's protocols and procedures, Makala had instigated the use of the alchemical dialect known subsequently as 5th Council script. To others, the scriptural language was innovative in its alchemical properties; to Makala, it was ancient — developed from the primordial manuscript inscriptions of Aralia and Osmanthus. Makala stood as one of the greatest alchemists of all time. However, as most real but quasi-mythical figures eventually do in the minds of subsequent historians, Azoth Magen Makala now occupied that strange liminal space between being revered and being forgotten.

Most inexplicably to Cedar, the script on the decorative ribbon surrounding this illumination alternated, thrice, between *Azoth Magen Makala* and *High Azoth Makala*. Could this Ancient Elder — whom Cedar had always known only as Azoth Magen — have been both Azoth Magen of the Alchemists' Council and High Azoth of the Rebel Branch? Before this week, Cedar would not have thought such an astonishing feat possible. However, having witnessed the impossible for herself with the mutual conjunctions of both Dracaen and Arjan *and* Kalina and Sadira, Cedar now wondered if Makala had been mutually conjoined of rebel and alchemist during a time of peace between dimensional factions: High Azoth Magen Makala.

But if so, why did she use only one tree name? Perhaps the name *Makala* was not her tree name at all; perhaps it represented two names, like *Meliex* — only, unlike with Melia and Ilex, Makala had officially adopted the hybrid nickname. Yet regardless of the nomenclature, why would such a spectacular accomplishment have previously been unknown to Cedar? She wondered briefly if some sort of erasure was at play. Then again, what had Cedar ever known about Makala? Beyond Initiate history lessons, she had had no reason to study her. Indeed, she had had no reason to study any of Council's ancient and enigmatic figures in detail until recently.

Cedar moved her attention to the note that had led her to *Turba Philosophorum 1881*. She had found it concealed within a parchment scroll Ravenea asked Cedar to store in her office. Ravenea had mentioned that Dracaen had brought her the scroll. Apparently, it comprised protocols for using the cliff face portal as a conduit between Council and Flaw dimensions. Concerned about more pressing matters, Cedar had haphazardly placed the scroll on an office shelf. But a few hours later, rethinking her brief exchange with Ravenea, she began to question her decision.

Cedar had then walked purposefully through the corridors and across the courtyard to her office, retrieved the scroll, and swiftly unrolled it. The small note inscribed with the manuscript name dropped onto the floor at her feet. Cedar wondered if Dracaen or Arjan had inserted it into the scroll for Ravenea. Or perhaps someone had correctly assumed Azoth Magen Ravenea would pass the scroll to her most trusted Novillian Scribe. In that case, the note rightly belonged to Cedar. Regardless, she should have followed protocol: she should have left for Azothian Chambers immediately, found Ravenea, and handed her the note. Instead, she had made her way surreptitiously to Qingdao, confiscated the manuscript, returned to Council dimension, and descended into the archives to search privately for answers — even if only an initial glimpse of explanation — to the numerous questions that haunted her regarding events of the past few days. To these questions, she added another at the moment she pulled the manuscript from its boxwood casing. How had an ancient

Rebel Branch manuscript found its way into the Alchemists' Council Qingdao protectorate?

Engravings along its spine clearly indicated that although the manuscript had originated in Council dimension, it had long been housed in Flaw dimension. Equally intriguing was its rarity: it hailed from generations ago. Even before reaching the illumination of Makala, the text's dialect and the illuminations' texture had confirmed Cedar's guess of 5th Council provenance. She recognized the gilding technique as one that both Rebel and Council Scribes had used prior to the era of Eirenaeus. Gold, silver, and bronze dominated the illumination's border. Flanking its margins were emerald palm fronds interwoven with spearheads shaped as ash leaves. Bright ruby and luminescent indigo created a subtle but mesmerizing lenticular pattern on Makala's robes. The fluctuating design prompted Cedar again to consider the possibility that Makala had been mutually conjoined. Above her head was a small alembic filled with multi-coloured circles — small stones perhaps — on a substantial slant, tipped over, spilling its contents onto Makala. As the circles of colour progressed over her head and shoulders, they gradually transformed to stripes, outlining Makala's body from her chest downward in a rainbow swath.

Years ago, a Lapidarian or Novillian Scribe — or perhaps Makala herself — had meant this manuscript to be read someday, had expected another alchemist or rebel to interpret it. *You spent years as a Reader,* Cedar thought. *Speak to me,* she pleaded aloud, not sure if she was addressing herself or the long-forgotten 5th Council Scribe of *Turba Philosophorum 1881.* She softly caressed the outline of the illumination once again.

Then, startled, Cedar felt something shift — a vibration beneath her fingertips. She moved her hand away quickly and peered at the page. The empty space directly beneath Makala's feet seemed to be moving. Was this phenomenon yet another example of dimensional fallout, of the unexpected after-effects of the recent mutual conjunctions within Council dimension? She watched as shadows began to flit over the page — they looked like narrow strands of ink dispersing in water. And then a word began to form, letter by letter: *R-a-v-e-n-e-a.* She sat transfixed. Never had Cedar experienced such a manuscript spectacle. Even the disappearance of Lapidarian bees from the manuscripts paled in comparison to the *appearance* of an inscription. How could such scribal alchemy be possible?

Cedar waited. Why would the name *Ravenea* appear on a manuscript folio featuring Makala? As the passing time became palpable, she wondered again if the message and manuscript had been meant for Ravenea. Perhaps someone had wanted the Azoth Magen to realize that Makala, like recent conjunctive pairings, had been a mutually con-joined alchemist and rebel. But what would such a revelation matter now, other than to illustrate — as Cedar had long suspected — that the Rebel Branch had always had its infiltrators in Council dimension and vice versa? At least such a disclosure would once and for all explain why Council had never been successful at permanently erasing the Flaw in the Stone.

Moments later, more characters appeared to form a complete sentence: *Ravenea is an alchemical child.*

An alchemical child? Cedar glanced again at the alembic and pebbles. Now she understood its relevance. Cedar herself had witnessed such a rainbow spectacle a century ago when she had peered into the sacred vessel housing the alchemical child she had conceived with Genevre. Out of shame and guilt, Cedar had willed herself to forget, suppressed the memories the moment even a fragment of recollection appeared, until she had eventually found peace. No wonder she had not initially recognized the symbolism surrounding Makala — she had trained herself to forget. But now the emotional turmoil of the past flooded her, surpassed her control. Guilt washed over her once again. If she had not peered into the alembic, perhaps the daughter she had created with Genevre would have lived. Perhaps together they would have been able to ensure the permanence of the Flaw in the Stone without Sadira and Arjan having to mutually conjoin. Together, Cedar, Genevre, and their daughter could have rebalanced the elements of the outside world and ensured its continuance thereafter. Cedar then silently but vehemently reprimanded herself for indulging once again in the fantasy she had for so long sought to forget.

A second sentence abruptly appeared: *Her twin also survived.* Her twin? Did alchemical children occasionally gestate as pairs? Was Ravenea's twin also an Elder of the Alchemists' Council?

Cedar waited several minutes, but no other names or words manifested. Disappointed and confused, yet intrigued, she began to turn the pages, scanning each folio for further explanation or revelation. But she found nothing on any of the remaining eighty-five folios. Remembering that this message may have been meant for Ravenea herself, Cedar began to question Ravenea's role not only in recent events but in everything she associated with both mutual conjunction and alchemical children. The message about Ravenea appearing beside an image of Makala suggested that the two were connected. Could Makala, a rebel alchemist, have alchemically created Ravenea? Perhaps Ravenea herself had no knowledge of her alchemical origins. Perhaps *that* shocking news was the message that the manuscript Scribe had intended for her. Either way, how could Ravenea be *that* old? How long did alchemical children live?

Clearly, the image and message had raised more questions than it had answered. But one phrase reverberated: *Her twin also survived.* Did alchemical children *generally* gestate in pairs? Did one child generally *not* survive?

And at that thought, Cedar shivered.

ſlaw Dimension — 2014

Upon conjoining with Dracaen, Arjan regained his temporarily distorted memories. In preparation for his entry into Council dimension as an Initiate, Genevre had used a blood-alchemy ritual to over-write specific memories that could compromise any of the insurgents. Unlike the way an alchemist's erasure can affect various alchemists' memories, carefully situated palimpsests had shifted Arjan's memory. But these temporary overlays had been scraped away completely at the point of his con-junction with Dracaen.

Arjan now remembered Ilex and Melia as more than his beloved grandparents. He remembered their stories: their reliance on Dracaen and the Rebel Branch to secure the Sephrim prior to their conjunction, their intimacy and ongoing friendship with Saule, their pregnancy. He remembered their daughter — his mother — Genevre. And Genevre's daughter — his sister — Kalina. He remembered learning of Genevre's wedding with Cedar, his second mother. He remembered meeting Dracaen years ago at Genevre's home. He remembered approving his memory alteration before Initiation to Council. Like Sadira and Kalina, he had agreed to conjoin. He had made his choice. And now he gripped the edge of the wardrobe to brace himself.

Arjan peered into a mirror of the wardrobe to face the consequences. Dracaen stared back at him, head tilted, moving towards and away from the mirror for varied perspective. Finally, Dracaen smiled and nodded. He appeared satisfied with himself and his decision.

"Come forth!" he demanded.

Hearing that utterance, Arjan realized that he had a distinct advantage over Dracaen. Thanks to Ilex and Melia, with whom he had lived for several decades, Arjan understood various intricacies of mutual conjunction that Dracaen could not have learned from manuscript study alone, no matter his status, age, or alchemical knowledge. Arjan knew, for example, that Dracaen could not force him to *come forth* by vocal command. Arjan must choose to manifest himself, to take control of their shared body the way any individual consciously chooses to make a specific physical movement: raising one's hand, sitting down, riding a bicycle. He merely had to concentrate and propel himself forward. For the shift to occur smoothly, Dracaen would have to give way, abandon the urge to resist. Of course, if Dracaen *chose* to resist, insisted on maintaining control of the body, Arjan would need to fight for dominance. They would struggle in an internal dance. On this occasion, however, no wrestling would be necessary. Arjan chose to *come forth* when Dracaen directed him to do so. He wanted Dracaen to believe that he, as High Azoth, still wielded power over the lowly Junior Initiate.

"Good day, High Azoth," said Arjan. He now looked at his own reflection in the mirror.

"No need to address me as High Azoth. After all, you are my child!" said Dracaen.

"No, I am not your child. I am the son of Genevre and Cedar."

"They created you, but you are conjoined with me. We are closer than father and son."

Arjan abhorred the comparison, but he simply nodded and then walked to a chair near the window. He did not want to watch the repeated shift of appearance during what would likely be an extended and troubling conversation.

"Need I remind you, Arjan, that you would not exist at all if not for the assistance I offered to Ilex and Melia years ago — the first successful mutual conjunction during the era of Eirenaeus? Given that chapter of the story, you are indeed one of my children. And now here we are, one of two nascent mutually conjoined pairs."

"Congratulations."

"When my intention manifests, mutual conjunction will become standard practice within a few generations. The barbaric self-sacrifice of our alchemical ancestors will become little more than a historical myth confined to the deepest archives. Through mutual conjunction between the Rebel Branch and the Alchemists' Council, we will be able to maintain both the Lapis and the Flaw while preserving the free will of *all* alchemists — not just those victorious in the Sacrament of Conjunction."

"Why did you lie about the bees?" asked Arjan.

"What does that have to do with the topic at hand?"

"You mentioned the mutual conjunction of Ilex and Melia. I want to discuss *that* topic. Jaden believed — indeed, *I* believed — that Ilex and Melia were erasing bees from Council manuscripts to increase negative space for the Flaw and remove Lapidarian bees from the main apiary. She believed the resulting absence of bees in the outside world would prevent the alchemical effect of wing vibration on free will — that the people of the outside world could then make their own decisions without Council interference. But you lied to her. I know for a fact that Ilex and Melia required the bees' Lapidarian Quintessence to sustain their conjunction."

"I did not *lie*. I simply refrained from disclosing the *entire* truth, as did you from the moment you stepped foot into Council dimension. Did you not purposely neglect to tell Jaden and others the entire truth about Kalina? About Ilex and Melia? About your origins?"

"My memories had been altered. I had agreed to carry out—"

"No matter! Jaden was not positioned to understand the complexities of mutual conjunction or the ultimate plan. She was merely supposed to make a choice — to align with either the Rebel Branch or the Alchemists' Council. As it happens, Jaden rejected my advice and chose instead to release all remaining bees into the world. She opted, in other words, to assist Council in maintaining control over the people of the outside world."

"Jaden released the bees to help Council maintain elemental balance — to heal the *environment* of the outside world and, thus, help its people."

"Yes — an unfortunate but harmless choice. The Rebel Branch will find a remedy."

"Now you are lying to me. Harm has been done. Harm will continue. The outside world is about to enter yet another era of political turmoil *because* the bees were *altered* before they were released. Their wing vibration currently has no effect — which means the Council's influence over the outside world has already begun to fail. You and Azoth Fraxinus manipulated this outcome in your quest to gain control over the Lapis and the dimensions."

"It appears you have been eavesdropping on my private conversations with Fraxinus."

"We are mutually conjoined, Dracaen. Privacy is a luxury of the past."

"I assumed you were . . . What is the term? *Asleep* . . . in the shadows."

"Occasional rest is required, certainly. But I suggest you stop making assumptions about my sleep schedule. They could lead to a false sense of confidence."

"Have you any other advice to offer your older and much more experienced Elder?"

"Yes, as a matter of fact. I suggest you permanently refrain from telling half-truths to the people who trust you. If Jaden had known the full truth about the bees, she may have made a different choice in the apiary. Lies may seem necessary or preferable in the moment, but they can lead to unforeseen circumstances. Jaden may never trust you again."

"Perhaps not. But regardless of her distrust of the Rebel Branch or of her affiliation with Council, she has aligned herself with *you* — an intended consequence that could yet prove useful to our cause. So, again, no harm done."

"Are you even capable of admitting the entire truth?"

"What is the *entire truth*, Arjan? The concept of unadulterated truth is a lie in itself. No one, including you, can ever be *entirely* truthful. Doing so is impossible given our inherent imperfections. We may be alchemists, but we remain human — most of us. Thanks to the Flaw, we *all* make choices. And each time we make a choice, we affect and manipulate everything and everyone. We lie to ourselves, and we lie to others. Faulty memory, political allegiances, self-indulgence, martyrdom, truths, lies, and muted versions of each affect all that was and all that will be. As mutually conjoined alchemists who can travel through time, we can alter both the truth and the lies until no one will comprehend the difference. Do you understand me, Arjan?"

"I understand, Dracaen. Therefore, I distrust you."

Council Dimension — 2014

Jaden writhed in pain. She struggled to free herself from her prison, but she found no relief. She felt caught in the quicksand of a nightmare. Darkness. Flashes of light. Splashing of water. Swelling. Her eyes would not open. Were they sewn shut? No. They were burning, inflamed. Sealed with the venom that she knew had invaded her — had enveloped her — when she and Cedar had released the Lapidarian bees into the outside world. She could sense the nightmare's presence pulsing, stretching, attempting to inhabit, convert, distort. She longed to scream. But she had no voice. She could not even breathe.

Where am I?

She understood then, intuited the answer for herself. She remembered. The bees had stung her when Cedar had removed her pendant. Now she was immersed, suspended in the curative waters of an alembic, deep within the Council catacombs.

So she must be alive. She must be breathing. She must, in fact, be healing. With that thought, the pain began to subside, returning thereafter only in short bursts rather than in all-encompassing waves. Perhaps the venom had not been as harmful to her as she had believed moments ago. Moments? Hours? She could not tell. Time blurred. Perhaps the bees had infused her with Lapidarian Elixir or Quintessence — much more powerful and invigorating than their honey.

Colours flashed rapidly. Blurred images began registering their subliminal messages like a high-speed slide show — messages she knew were important but that she could neither fully see nor comprehend.

Slow down, she pleaded.

And they did. Jaden had wanted to view the imposed images, and her intention had manifested. She watched them, one by one, rapid but visible. Some she understood; others she questioned. Arjan laughing, twisting his pendant chain around a finger. Cascading purple blossoms surrounding Ravenea. Ruis repressing a smile in the Initiate classroom. A man whose face she could not see, his back arched in the throes of ecstasy. A woman she did not recognize holding a newborn baby under a juniper tree. Kalina lying on the ground of an immense cavern, reaching for a hand extended to her. As the pictures multiplied, Jaden came to realize they were glimpses into the past.

But these are not my memories.

Though corporeally she remained in the cat-acombs, mentally Jaden realized she was moving through time. Picture after picture after picture. Memories from someone else's life crossing paths with her own. She separated from her self. She conjoined with another. She longed for both self and other.

Who are you? Who am I?

She was a speck in the universe. She was nothing. She was all. She withdrew. She expanded. She retreated. She encompassed. She was birthed. She gave birth. She bled. She wounded. She dis-solved. She embodied the dimensions. She was and was not herself.

The images returned, progressed, slowed even more. Still shots began to move. Film-like clips replaced the pictures. Jaden watched a thin blade emerge from a green velvet sleeve. An olive-toned hand, feminine, mature but not elderly, gripped the blade. An alchemist? A manuscript. The moving image skipped ahead, distorted. When clarity returned, a pen had replaced the blade. A word was being inscribed.

Cruentus. Vivid red ink. *Serpens Chymicum 1414.* Folio 44 verso.

The image pulsated. *Bloody, blood-thirsty, blood-red.*

Flash. North Library. Arjan: *Yes, someone can help us. Someone has led you here. Someone inscribed the reference to* Serpens Chymicum 1414. *Someone inscribed the word* cruentus *for you to find.*

Flash. Vancouver Art Gallery. Cedar: *You are Jaden, Junior Initiate of the Alchemists' Council. The Scribes have named you. The Readers have read you. The Word of the Book is the Word Eternal.*

Flash. Residence chambers. Sadira: *You heard two people. You saw only one body — one body shifting between two essences mutually conjoined.*

Ilex and Melia.

The blade extended. The hand gripped. Jaden watched again.

Rewind. Blade. Hand. Pen. Inscribe. Rewind. Blade. Hand. Pen. Inscribe. Rewind. Blade. Hand. Cut. Bleed. Pen. Inscribe.

Wait. Rewind.

Flash. Residence chambers. Sadira: *Do you recall being drawn to the word* cruentus *in* Serpens Chymicum 1414? *Kalina inscribed that single word with Dragonblood-infused ink.*

Yes. No. Sadira had been wrong. Or had Sadira lied? Intentionally? Unwittingly? *Cruentus* had not been inscribed in ink. It had been inscribed in blood — blood drawn not from the Dragonblood Stone but from the back of an alchemist's hand. Kalina's?

Cut. Bleed. Pen. Insert nib. Withdraw. Inscribe. *Cruentus.*

Rewind. Freeze image.

Jaden gazed at the hand holding the blade. She watched the hand cutting and the hand being cut. She winced as she watched the blood stream out.

"Now what?" asked Sadira.

"Magistrate?" an Initiate asked, tilting her head.

"Apologies . . . Laurel. I wasn't addressing you," Sadira said, flustered. "I was distracted — just speaking aloud to myself about Council matters."

Of course, Sadira had not been speaking to *herself* per se. Having noticed no one in the vicinity, Sadira had addressed the question to Kalina. As yet unaware of the protocols for mutually conjoined partnership, she had then come to a halting stop along a channel path in the main courtyard to listen for a response. Sadira had neither seen nor heard from Kalina since the previous night. Surely her rebel counterpart was not still asleep in the shadows? Too much remained for her to learn about this conjunction. Yet too much remained to be done throughout the dimensions for leisurely socializing.

"Magistrate?" said Laurel again.

Sadira now realized both Cercis and Laurel stood blocking her path. They seemed agitated. The fallout of the rebel breach and mutual conjunctions had affected everyone in Council dimension. The repercussions were manifesting like an exaggerated version of the elemental disturbances each new Initiate caused. These two Initiates were likely experiencing the anxiety-inducing effects. Sadira would endeavour to be more lenient.

"Yes? How may I help you?"

"We need to show you something," said Cercis.

Laurel nodded, gesturing to Cercis. He moved closer to Sadira and extended a closed hand.

"Are you expecting me to pry it open?" asked Sadira.

"No, Magistrate. I just . . . wanted you to be prepared."

"Cercis, as I'm sure you're aware, the repercussions of the Fourth Rebellion are innumerable. Council business needs attending. My time and patience are limited."

He opened his hand enough for her to see a small golden-brown sphere.

"Touch it," said Laurel. Sadira glanced at her, one eyebrow raised. "You won't understand its gravity unless you touch it, Magistrate."

"Its gravity? Does it float?"

"*The* gravity," clarified Cercis. "The *seriousness* of the situation."

Sadira prodded the substance with two fingers. It jiggled, gelatinous. Material they had retrieved from the hives of the apiary? An alchemical transmutation of honey or propolis? A new dessert anxious outside world cooks had contrived in the chaos? Given the profound distress emanating from both Cercis and Laurel, Sadira refrained from guessing aloud.

Cercis glanced back at Laurel.

"Do you know what it is, Magistrate?" asked Laurel.

"No, but don't worry. I am certain all will be—"

"It's amber," said Cercis.

"Amber? From where?"

"From the Amber Garden. The trees . . . in the garden. They're . . . melting."

Council Dimension — 2014

The inexplicable message regarding High Azoth Magen Makala and her alchemical twin had left Cedar reeling. She emerged from the dim archival hallways into the light of day with the intention of seeking assistance. She no longer knew whom to trust, but she had to start with someone as a potential ally, so she opted for Ravenea. Whether or not Ravenea was the intended recipient of the note and manuscript message, she was nevertheless Azoth Magen. As such, she would at least take the concerns of an Elder seriously. But Cedar's good intentions were waylaid when she literally ran into Sadira, who was rushing across the courtyard with Laurel and Cercis.

"Come with us!" she said to Cedar.

Sadira's tone implied such urgency that Cedar abandoned her plan to find Ravenea and, instead, heeded the command. As she quickened her pace to keep up, Cedar thought back to the short-lived exchange she had shared with Sadira a few days earlier. Regrettably, it had occurred in the presence of several Elders, not affording them requisite privacy. Cedar had initially longed to reach for her, ached to caress the lover she had assumed forever lost. But for the better part of the past three days, Ravenea had sequestered Sadira in Azothian Chambers — presumably to interrogate her regarding the conjunction and its fatal victory over Amur. Ruis, meanwhile, had detained and questioned Cedar incessantly on everything from her choice to release the bees to her opinion on who should ascend to Azoth. *You, of course, will be my recommendation*, Ruis had assured Cedar. *Given current circumstances, Ravenea would be wise to approve your direct ascension from Novillian to Azoth — a feat, as you know, which both Ravenea and I accomplished successfully. Besides, neither Rowan Kai nor Rowan Esche have Azothian aspirations. Imagine the influence we could wield as a team!* Cedar had smiled in response. She had no intention to ascend, let alone as Ruis's Azothian counterpart. After all, being a Novillian Scribe provided her all the privileges of being an Elder without Azothian responsibilities.

Admittedly, however, she had begun to wonder whether Kalina's presence within Sadira would cause her own emotional and physical affections to shift away from Sadira and towards Ruis once again.

Regardless, Cedar doubted she could embrace Sadira with abandon until she learned what secrets Sadira had kept from her prior to the rebel breach and mutual conjunctions. Despite the innumerable hours Cedar had spent in archival rooms consulting manuscripts, answers continued to elude her.

Obeche intercepted them just as they reached the entrance to the Amber Garden.

"Brace yourselves," he warned.

"For what?" asked Cedar.

With uncharacteristic disregard for status and protocols, Sadira pushed past Obeche and strode forcefully into the garden. Likewise unprecedented, Obeche refrained from the opportunity to reprimand an inferior. Instead, he stepped aside and gestured for Cedar and the others to enter. As Cedar looked back, watching Obeche following solemnly, she saw Ruis and Ravenea arriving in immediate succession. Something was clearly amiss.

They stood together — Azoth Magen Ravenea, Azoth Ruis, Novillian Scribes Obeche and Cedar, Senior Magistrate Sadira, Junior Initiates Laurel and Cercis — clustered, still and silent, mannequin representatives of the Alchemists' Council posed in tableau, awestruck yet horrified. The glistening amber that for thousands of years had sparkled brightly in the sun and rattled gently in the wind as an ever-evolving testament to hundreds of alchemists subsumed in conjunction or transformed through ascension, the solid and tangible manifestation of the pain and mourning endured by friends and colleagues, by lovers and dearly beloved, now oozed slowly into viscous puddles and pooled at the trunks of the trees.

You can mourn him in your precious Amber Garden, Cedar recalled a rebel taunting Jaden about Arjan. Had his gleeful gibe been even crueller than Cedar had realized? Had the Rebel Branch breached Council dimension purposely to wreak such devastation on their sacred spaces? *No!* That scenario simply could not be. If the rebels intentionally chose to destroy a memorial site, Cedar could no longer live with the choice she had made to maintain the Flaw in the Stone. She could no longer live. She clasped her pendant, longing through the Dragonblood fragment for an explanation that would free her from guilt, pleading through the Lapidarian fragment for a solution that would end the Council's anguish.

Cedar stepped forward, lowered herself to her knees beside one of the pools, and pulled at the golden substance. Rubber-like and dense, it rolled off her fingers and into a small sphere between her palms. As Cedar stood and turned to show the others, Cercis opened his hand once again. But instead of revealing a comparable sphere, he exposed a sticky mess that, within seconds, liquefied completely and ran between his fingers onto the ground.

That would have been enough — watching their treasured amber dissolve and disappear. The sight and touch had overwhelmed their senses immediately. But the sound began as an innocent whisper — as ordinary as a breeze moving through barren branches. A whimper then followed, causing Ravenea to turn her head towards the western wall of the garden. A cry — they all turned to observe the tree at the garden's centre. A gasp, a sob, a moan — one by one the sounds manifested and multiplied, gradually increasing in volume. Within minutes, a cacophony of weeping and wailing reverberated loudly off the garden walls. Cedar covered her ears with her hands, but it made no difference. Disembodied voices. Of the mourners? Of the mourned? Cedar could not tell. But the acoustic effect was chilling to the core — more unsettling than any sound she had heard in any dimension over her three hundred years of existence.

"Ravenea!" The name rang out, silencing the din of other voices. Everyone turned towards Obeche, assuming the voice to have been his. But he shook his head and shrugged, unnerved.

"Ravenea!" the same voice called into the silence again. They all turned towards Ravenea to find someone else standing in her place.

Laurel screamed. Cedar winced in recognition. Obeche took a step backward.

But as quickly as the apparition had appeared in Ravenea's stead, it disappeared once again, leaving only its tears on Ravenea's cheeks as evidence of its transitory existence.

"Who was that?" asked Cercis.

Only the Initiates, who had never known him, and Ravenea, who had not seen him, required explanation.

"Lapidarian Scribe Erez," replied Obeche.

"Erez?" said Laurel.

"On the final day of the Urizen Con of the 17th Council, I conjoined with Erez," Ravenea recited by rote.

Even the Initiates recognized his name in its context. Erez, the one over whom Ravenea had reigned victorious in conjunction, had somehow momentarily rematerialized.

Cedar surveyed the group. Laurel and Cercis clasped hands. Ravenea assumed Ab Uno position. Obeche trembled. Sadira fell to her knees.

Distraught, her call to Kalina left unanswered, Sadira struggled to restrain her tears as she walked with Ravenea, Cedar, and Obeche to Azothian Chambers. Her return to Council dimension after the apparently failed conjunction with Amur was unprecedented. Now, after fellow alchemists had mourned her in the Amber Garden, Sadira had returned mutually conjoined. Had her post-mourning resurrection instigated the garden's dissolution? Sadira's only hope for relief from simmering guilt was the prospect that the melting amber and reappearance of

Erez were extreme anomalies not repeatable outside the Amber Garden. But upon arrival at Azothian Chambers, they found Rowans Kai and Esche, along with Novillian Scribe Tera, anxious and distressed.

"Azoth Magen!" cried Tera. "The fallout from the Fourth Rebellion has become far more severe than we could have imagined."

"We need not imagine," said Obeche. He then succinctly relayed to Tera and the Rowans the events they had just witnessed in the Amber Garden.

In turn, Rowan Esche recounted that five other alchemists — one of whom was Tera herself — had already reported similar reappearances of conjoined partners. So Obeche's account of Erez's temporary presence was not as surprising to Tera or the Rowans as was his description of the state of the garden. If the amber was dissolving, the dimensional fabric might already be weakened beyond repair. Council dimension might be in impending jeopardy. Theories and fears abounded. Perhaps the conjoined were returning because Council members themselves were separating on an elemental level along with the dimension. If so, would they also begin to melt like the amber? Would they also finally liquefy and seep into the ground?

Sadira need not wait long for an answer.

Tera shook visibly. "Apologies," she said. "My body betrays me."

"Sit down," said Obeche. He pulled out a chair and reached for Tera's arm.

But the ramifications of conjunctive dissolution had begun. Tera fell to the floor, shaking so violently that she toppled the chair Obeche had offered. Her head hit the leg of a table. Though the thrashing prevented anyone from approaching or attempting to stabilize her, Ruis and Obeche worked to move other nearby furniture aside to mitigate injury. Ravenea wondered aloud to Sadira whether the catacomb alembics had already suffered the same tragic degradation as the Amber Garden. If so, Tera's injuries could become life-threatening.

The moment her seizure ceased, the wailing began — the single voice was as distressing as the myriad cries heard earlier. But unlike the loud but invisible vocal din witnessed in the Amber Garden, the source of this howl was clear: it emanated from Tera's partner in conjunction — Olea — who now lay, mouth open, where Tera had fallen. Olea sat up, screaming repeatedly for the torture to end. No one moved. No one knew what to do. Never had anyone on Council been so ignorant of procedure. All the lessons, all the readings, all the laws and protocols and rituals that had preserved both the dimension and the Council for generations now left Sadira and the others helpless in the face of the utterly unknown.

Then, without warning, Olea stood up and heaved his body onto the fires of the Azothian kiln. One final piercing scream echoed through the room. Olea became translucent momentarily and then burst, like a bubble, and vanished. In his stead, flames extinguished, lay Tera weeping — robe and gowns completely singed, naked skin seared raw.

IV
Council Dimension — 2014

Obeche had immediately summoned four Wardens and two Readers to transport Tera to the catacombs for healing. Ravenea and the Azoths thereafter agreed to postpone the official Elder Council meeting until Wu Tong returned with news of Tera and the state of the catacomb alembics. Now they awaited an update, stunned and silent, immersed in their frenzied thoughts.

Throughout her tenure with Council, Ravenea had toiled unceasingly to prevent what had nevertheless occurred: conjunctions of multiple alchemical children. No single point on the dimensional timeline could sustain the alchemical complexities of manifold Prima Materia Quintessence. In fabricating all from nothing, Aralia and Osmanthus had purposely imposed this law and other limitations meant to maintain order in the aftermath of the Crystalline Wars. Over the years, when hypothesizing possible outcomes of her labours, failure was one prospect Ravenea had repeatedly feared and acknowledged. But even on the occasions she had vividly imagined the direst of consequences, she had not anticipated the intensity of the physical horror she had witnessed on this day. What had she done? What had she been unable to prevent?

After an hour of such anxiety-laden musings, Ravenea was relieved to hear that Tera's healing had begun. "The catacombs appear stable," Wu Tong assured Ravenea. "We found no evidence of degradation."

The small amount of relief everyone felt upon hearing this update could not quell the worry that overwhelmed them all. As Ravenea glanced at the faces of everyone seated at the table, she understood their concerns mimicked her own. The catacombs *appeared* stable; no evidence of degradation *currently* existed. As Tera's experience illustrated, the Council could no longer predict with accuracy the future of the dimension or its alchemists. And even if the catacombs did remain stable indefinitely, the alembics therein were limited in number. What if all conjunctive partnerships began to dissolve? What if dozens of alchemists required alembic healing and the degrading infrastructure could not meet demand?

"Should we begin?" asked Ruis, jerking Ravenea out of her unsettling reverie.

"Yes, of course," she replied. "Let us proceed. Elder Council is now in session."

"One moment!" interjected Obeche. He turned to Sadira. "Leave us," he said abruptly.

Sadira raised her head, glanced at Ravenea, and then stood to leave.

"No, Sadira," said Ravenea quietly but firmly. "You must stay."

"With all due respect, Azoth Magen," said Obeche, "Sadira is not an Elder, thus she cannot attend Elder Council. Her original conjunction to Novillian Scribe Amur might have provided an exception under war measures. However, as we all witnessed, Amur perished. And as you informed Council yesterday, Sadira has mutually conjoined with Kalina, a formerly erased Senior Initiate with Rebel Branch affiliations. Sadira and Kalina have neither the knowledge nor experience to understand matters of this magnitude."

"With all due respect, Obeche, neither do we," replied Ravenea. "Sit down, Sadira."

Contrary to expectation, as Sadira took her seat, Obeche did not continue his protest. He merely glanced at Sadira and then back at Ravenea, as if awaiting an explanation. He appeared to understand — perhaps for the first time in his life — that his uninformed opinion held little sway. Like everyone on Council, including the Elders, he needed time to process the implications of the mutual conjunctions to both the Alchemists' Council and the Rebel Branch.

"Given recent events," said Ravenea, "we must all prepare ourselves for extensive meetings over the days to come. For now, however, we must proceed to a few particularly urgent matters." She glanced at the parchment where she had earlier recorded a tentative agenda for today's session and called upon Rowan Kai to make an opening statement.

"Word of these horrific anomalies will spread swiftly through Council dimension," said Kai. "Initiates Laurel and Cercis have likely already recounted their version of events in the Amber Garden to everyone they have encountered over the past few hours. News of Tera's ordeal will spread shortly if it hasn't already. Every member of the Alchemists' Council will be terrified, no matter their age or status. Elder Council must develop a feasible strategy to retain a semblance of order. More than ever before, the lower orders will look to the Elders for guidance. Individually, we each must endeavour to maintain composure no matter the circumstance."

As she listened to Kai, Ravenea surveyed the room. She recognized the visibly obvious. With the recent demise of both Ailanthus and Amur, and with Tera temporarily absent, Elder Council comprised only six of its nine required members; thus, even with Sadira currently included, two empty chairs remained at the table. They stood as a glaring reminder to everyone of the Council's recent losses.

"Beyond doubt, we have reached a crisis point," said Ravenea. "Yet before we can even begin to formulate a solution, we must first replenish the Elder Council so that we have a full contingent. Only then can we combine our Quintessential powers to perform the Trance of the Nine, our first step towards restored order."

"Agreed," said Ruis. "Azoth Magen, I humbly request that you first choose an Azoth from the Rowans or Novillians. We can later debate who will fill the remaining positions."

Ravenea stood. "Until circumstances once again allow leisure for traditional observance, I will refrain from the ceremonial portion of the Call to Azoth. Instead, let me simply announce my decision." She paused momentarily to raise her hands. "In the name of the Azoth Magen of the 19th Council of Alchemists, I hereby declare the installation of Azoth Kai."

Kai stood and bowed graciously to Ravenea. The others — including Rowan Esche, who showed no sign of disappointment — bowed their heads in Ab Uno saying, "Thus shall it be."

Kai sat down once again, but Ravenea remained standing.

"Azoth Magen?" said Ruis. Clearly, he expected her to sit for the first debate.

"In the name of the Azoth Magen of the 19th Council of Alchemists, I hereby declare the temporary installation of Rowan Obeche."

Obeche smiled and nodded in concurrence. "I accept with honour, Azoth Magen."

"I—" began Ruis. He then stopped, mouth open. Evidently, he was having an internal debate with himself in anticipation of protesting Ravenea's choice. Ravenea fully recognized that Ruis would have chosen Cedar to ascend. "Azoth Magen," said Ruis finally. "I do not understand your decision. Despite Tera's temporary incapacity, we must consider both Tera and Cedar for Rowan. Debates on Elder ascension are standard and essential protocol."

"I have considered the matter thoroughly, and Obeche is the only viable choice," said Ravenea. "Tera requires not only significant healing but also additional experience as a Novillian prior to ascension. And Cedar will not be residing here for the foreseeable future."

"What?" interjected Sadira.

"When she returns," continued Ravenea, glancing at Cedar, "Elder Council will proceed to debate and decide upon permanently installing either Obeche or Cedar as Rowan. With Cedar's departure imminent, you must agree upon three Lapidarian Scribes to ascend to Novillian status — two will eventually become permanent replacements, and one will be a temporary substitute during Cedar's absence. Meanwhile, you, Sadira, will ascend to Reader. We will adjust the remaining orders accordingly."

"Perhaps Reader Sadira can commence her tenure with a manuscript search for the required novice Initiates," suggested Obeche.

"No," replied Ravenea. "Until further notice, the only candidates the Elders will consider for the Junior Initiate are those who reach out to us. To that end, six Lapidarian Scribes are currently in the Scriptorium rendering an Initiate gateway manuscript." Ravenea paused and turned to address Ruis. "You will consult with Azoth Kai, Rowan Esche, and Rowan Obeche to develop a proposed rotation of orders to present to Elder Council by noon tomorrow."

Ruis stiffened, clearly stunned.

Cedar stood to ask the question they all must be thinking. "Where am I going?"

"Do not feign ignorance, Cedar. As I am sure you anticipated the moment you released the bees without sanction, you are to be erased and banished to the outside world."

"Silence!" called Ravenea, instantly quelling the vocal reaction to her decision. "Both the erasure and banishment are *temporary*. During Cedar's absence, we will confiscate her pendant; its Quintessence will remain intact. Consequently, her branch of the Alchemical Tree will not be affected beyond minor discomforts. *All will be well*, as the saying goes."

Cedar had indeed anticipated the possibility of severe reprimand, banishment to the outside world, even the possibility of permanent erasure.

All prospects would be reasonable repercussions considering her decision to release all the Lapidarian bees without Azothian approval — especially given her recruitment of Jaden, whom the Elders would deem innocent. After all, as a Junior Initiate, Jaden had merely obeyed the command of an Elder. Nonetheless, although Cedar had expected her remaining time in Council dimension to be limited, she had hoped for several days to investigate the mutual conjunctions. Given her discoveries about Makala, that hope had significantly intensified only to be vehemently quashed. At the very least, she needed time to speak with Ravenea alone rather than in front of the Elder Council.

"We will negotiate resettlement terms now," said Ruis.

"No! I must—" Cedar began.

"You are to come with me, Cedar," said Ravenea. "The terms of your resettlement negotiations will be agreed upon in private conference without Elder Council input."

"Azoth Magen!" protested Obeche. "Negotiations of erasure are the purview of Elder Council in its entirety! Though a breach of protocol, Cedar's release of the apiary bees does not warrant such extreme punishment, especially at this time of upheaval. She made a choice during a crisis to mitigate elemental unbalance of the outside world. I, for one, applaud her!"

Obeche applauds me? Cedar's expression disclosed visible shock.

"Obeche!" said Ravenea. "Need I remind you that you have ascended to Rowan, not Azoth. Disputing with the Azoth Magen immediately after ascension is unbecoming. It suggests you disrespect both my expertise and my authority."

Obeche raised his hands into Ab Uno and bowed his head. "Apologies, Azoth Magen," he began. "Since entering Council as an Initiate, its protocols have guided me at each step. Abandoning them is a challenge, to say the least. Evidently, I require time to adjust. But my respect for you has always been and certainly remains unparalleled."

"Do not mistake me, Obeche. We are not permanently abandoning protocols. We are temporarily adjusting our usual practices out of sheer and unprecedented necessity. By allowing for provisional modifications, I plan to return Council dimension to its pristine, eternal form — including its protocols — as soon as possible. But time is a factor we cannot currently deem boundless." Ravenea then turned from Obeche to address everyone. "We must all adjust our expectations and strategies quickly if we are to succeed."

"Of course, Azoth Magen," said Ruis.

Ravenea then adjourned the meeting, stood to leave, and gestured for Cedar to follow her.

Cedar's anxiety mounted during the short walk between Azothian Chambers and Ravenea's office.

Given the pending erasure, Cedar vacillated on how much of the earlier manuscript experience to reveal. Initially she said nothing, merely accepting Ravenea's offer of ruby liqueur. Not until she and Ravenea had commiserated for a few minutes about the disintegrating Amber Garden did Cedar decide she had nothing left to lose. If Ravenea did not trust that Cedar respected her, the temporary erasure could become permanent. Cedar therefore opted to explain the entire manuscript experience with all accompanying details. Now, having done so, she waited impatiently for Ravenea's response. At least ten seconds passed with little more than a concerned glance from Ravenea.

"I inserted the note myself," Ravenea finally responded. She refilled their crystal liqueur glasses. "Years ago — in 1939, shortly after the outbreak of the outside world war — I found another note instructing me when and where to leave you the note about the manuscript."

"You trusted a random note's instructions?"

"The note was written in my own handwriting. I assumed it had somehow been transmitted through time. But I have yet to find evidence of that hypothesis."

"And what about the manuscript itself? Did you inscribe *that* message?"

"No. I cannot yet fathom its origin or alchemy. But I trust, as time moves forward, we will come to understand."

"Is it true?" Cedar asked. "Are you an alchemical child?"

"Yes," she replied without hesitation.

"Am I the last of the Elders to know?"

Ravenea laughed. "Hardly! In fact, as far as I have been able to determine, Ailanthus was the only other Council member ever to have known. Not even Saule . . ."

"Not even Saule?" Cedar echoed, both her inflection and eyes questioning.

Ravenea observed her as if seeking confirmation of trustworthiness, or perhaps to ascertain if some semblance of Saule remained within Cedar. "I have come to suspect that Saule played a primary role in Genevre's . . . existence. That is, in her . . . procreation."

Ravenea's unexpected reference to Genevre, alongside her apparent struggle to find words, concerned Cedar. Perhaps the dimensional fallout had affected Ravenea more than Cedar had suspected. Or perhaps she was purposely choosing her words carefully, afraid to reveal too much to someone about to reside in the outside world.

"Saule knew more than she revealed to either of us," Ravenea continued with recovered pace and confidence. "Her knowledge — now hidden within you — is part of the reason you must be erased rather than simply sent on a mission to the outside world. You must be freed temporarily from Lapidarian influence."

"And from effects of dimensional fallout. We cannot risk Saule suffering Olea's fate."

"Exactly. Banished to the outside world, you may be able to access some of the knowledge Saule carried with her into conjunction. Though I doubt she suspected anything regarding my alchemical origins, I believe — through her connection with Ilex, Melia, and Genevre — that Saule knew of the existence of at least two alchemical children, including your own."

Cedar froze; the visceral sensation that instantaneously flooded her body immobilized her. She pictured herself, despite warnings against such interference, peering into the sacred alembic. She thought of Genevre cradling their daughter. Guilt for their daughter's death returned.

"You seem surprised. Did you not deduce my suspicion on the night I came to your room to read your pendant?"

Cedar shook her head. Almost a century had passed between her daughter's death and Ravenea's more recent impromptu pendant reading. Why should Cedar have concluded a connection between the two events? She thought back to their conversation on that night. Ravenea had spoken to her about Kalina and Arjan, not Genevre or their daughter. Given the extenuating circumstances of Kalina's renegade breech and Arjan's unorthodox behaviour, Cedar had understood the pendant reading as a routine precaution — or, at worst, Azothian posturing.

Neither Genevre nor their daughter had come to mind. And the incident itself had barely registered; she had not even thought about it again until now.

"Of course, I read nothing of the child in your pendant. I figured you had manipulated either its memory or your own. Pendant manipulation would have been difficult and risky — a punishable offence under the Law Codes — but certainly reasonable under the circumstances. After all, you were protecting your alchemical offspring from Council interference. However, in retrospect, I simply presume Genevre used blood alchemy at the time of your chemical marriage to mitigate pendant intrusion into your affairs."

"Azoth Magen, I don't understand. What are you saying?"

"Do not continue this act with me, Cedar. As I am sure you know, I have spoken at length with Sadira over the past few days. Surely she has told you—"

"I've barely seen Sadira, let alone exchanged more than a few words with her!"

"Regardless. I know that you and Genevre conceived a child. Do not pretend otherwise."

"Yes, Genevre and I conceived an alchemical child. But she died within hours of her birth. Almost a century has passed since that tragic day. Losing our child was the most difficult experience of my life. After a decade of grief, I chose to . . . repress the memories."

Ravenea stared, perplexed. She appeared as confused as Cedar felt.

"Yes, the one child died," said Ravenea. "But her twin survived."

Cedar jolted, knocking her crystal glass and its ruby contents onto the stone floor. Ravenea did not take her eyes from Cedar.

Her twin survived.

"Who?" Cedar whispered, visibly trembling.

"What?"

"Who is the twin? Who is my child?"

"Arjan."

"Arjan? Arjan. I . . . I didn't know."

Her twin survived.

Ravenea stood, her demeanour suddenly transformed. Avoiding the shattered crystal, she walked to Cedar, put a hand on her shoulder, and kissed her forehead. The gesture was endearing and comforting, despite the anger that had begun to seethe within Cedar.

"She didn't tell me. Genevre didn't tell me!" Cedar wept now, gripping Ravenea's hand. "How could she hide my own child from me?"

A few minutes later, Ravenea gently urged Cedar to move from the chair to the sofa. "Rest here until I return. Lie back against the cushions. Stay put. Do not do anything rash. I can help you. And you, in return, can help the Council. But I need to get a manuscript from the archives."

As soon as Ravenea left, Cedar's emotions

fluctuated among anger, astonishment, and joy. She could not fathom how, if ever, she could forgive Genevre for deceiving her — no matter the rationale Genevre would surely spout when confronted. But in the occasional moments that Cedar could set aside her anger for Genevre, she revelled in the idea that their child had survived, that she had a son. *A son!* She wondered how long Ravenea had known. She wondered whether Arjan himself knew and, if so, whether he had planned to tell her. She then remembered Sadira's notebooks and the notation: *Arjan has made his choice.* Had Sadira known of his origin, forced him to make a choice? Had their mutual conjunctions been made in Arjan's best interests? Questions abounded, their answers mere jumbled suppositions. But one revelation dominated all that occurred to Cedar: *My son survived!*

For the entire twenty minutes of Ravenea's absence, Cedar's thoughts raced. But they came to an abrupt halt when she realized that, if banished to the outside world, she may never see Arjan again. Ravenea walked back into the room just as Cedar had reached a seated position at the edge of the sofa — just as she was contemplating an escape to Flaw dimension.

"I need to see Arjan before I'm erased. We must make arrangements with Dracaen."

"No. I am sorry, Cedar. As I assured you earlier, your erasure will be temporary. As will your memory loss. By the time you return, all memories will have re-emerged."

"Memory loss?"

"What I have unintentionally revealed to you today, I must now overwrite. All other memories, save this one alone, will remain intact."

"No! Please, Ravenea, do not remove from me what I have only just found out! He is my son!"

"The adjustment to your memory—"

"No! You have no right to change my past to benefit your future!"

"Cedar, I'm merely proposing a blood-alchemy ritual, not a timeline adjustment!"

"If only you could send me back in time," said Cedar, her tone shifting from anger to longing. "If only I could see Arjan at his birth."

"Time travel has unexpected consequences, even for those capable of adjusting the timeline. We cannot risk travelling to the past when—" Ravenea stopped short. She paused long enough that Cedar wondered if a dimensional disturbance had interrupted her train of thought. Briefly, Cedar's fear for her own memory loss dissipated out of concern for her Azoth Magen and friend.

"Ravenea?" Cedar prompted.

"Um . . . yes . . . my apologies. We cannot risk travelling to the past when the future of the entire Alchemists' Council, as well as the world it sustains, is currently at stake. Both Council.

and Flaw dimensions — and everyone therein, including Arjan — are endangered. When your memory returns, you can reconnect as mother and son. For now, your conjunction with Saule must be our focus."

"And what of Saule's memories? What if my memory loss affects hers? Wouldn't that defeat the purpose of sending me to the outside world?"

"If your memories overlapped with Saule's, I would simply ask you to tell me what she knew. However, just as your memories do not affect hers, hers do not affect yours."

Cedar sought a counter-argument, but fatigue overwhelmed her.

"Duty calls, Cedar. Your alchemical child currently shares a body with the High Azoth of the Rebel Branch. To ensure the safety of both you and your son, I must repress your memory temporarily. Our goal is for Genevre to reconnect alchemically with Saule. If she suspects—"

"I've had no contact with Genevre for years. I certainly have no desire to see her now."

"Perhaps not, but *I* desire you to see her. Given the bond I believe Genevre had with Saule, your being with her may help bring forth Saule's memories. A few days from now, you will proceed to Genevre's residence in Santa Fe. In the meantime, you will retire to a catacomb alembic to rebalance your Quintessence. Your scribal powers will need to be at full strength since, in addition to recovering Saule's memories, you will be helping Genevre inscribe a manuscript intended to attract Initiates."

"You expect me to work with Genevre on a scribal endeavour after what she has done? She's been lying to me for years! I have only *just* discovered her betrayal — I am too angry to see her right now, much less collaborate with her."

"Hence the necessity of memory adjustment. Thanks to my blood alchemy, you will not be angry when you see her, since you will not know that she has lied to you."

Cedar grimaced. Ravenea moved to the main table and opened the manuscript she had retrieved from the archives. Watching her turn adeptly to the required page, Cedar realized that Ravenea was already intimately familiar with the manuscript. She wondered how many other minds Ravenea had altered in her past. Watching her move around her office to collect ritual ingredients and items, Cedar questioned whether trusting Ravenea had been wise. But second thoughts were futile now. Cedar had lived lifetimes of regret already. If she could no longer trust the Azoth Magen of the Alchemists' Council, she could never return willingly to Council dimension. And if Genevre's assistance was necessary for the good of the Council, the memory dampening was indeed a logical solution to Ravenea's misstep in telling Cedar about Arjan.

As Cedar watched Ravenea prepare, and as she thought about the erasure, her speculations moved from a place of theoretical hypotheses to one of empirical logic. Erasure of an individual from Council dimension affected the memories of alchemists of the lower orders by way, in part, of lacunae incised into relevant Lapidarian manuscripts. Once she was erased and exiled to the outside world, would Arjan forget her? Or would his conjunction with Dracaen and residence in Flaw dimension protect him? She was about to ask these questions aloud, but as Ravenea gestured for Cedar to move to a chair, a more pressing concern occurred to her.

"My mind is not a manuscript, Ravenea. How are you to expunge a single memory?"

"I am not going to wipe your memory. I am going to overwrite it, conceal it temporarily using the blood-alchemy equivalent of a palimpsest. The overlain script will guide you in your initial decisions and interactions regarding Genevre. Once you have played through the imposed script, your original memories will resurface gradually. Do not fear. Resurfacing memories — including the one in question — will not shock you. You will simply carry on thinking about Arjan and your relationship with him just as you otherwise would have done."

Cedar sat in the chair that Ravenea had placed, facing outward, at the end of the table. Ravenea stood beside her and mixed a dozen or so ingredients — only a few of which Cedar recognized — into a silver bowl. She manipulated the mixture with her hands rather than using the traditional pestle. Then, with a thin golden needle, she pricked two of her fingers and let several drops of blood fall into the bowl, gradually turning the paste ochre. Using her bloodstained fingers, Ravenea transferred some of the paste from the bowl to Cedar's forehead. As Ravenea rubbed it in, Cedar flinched from the burning sensation. After her forehead had cooled, Ravenea massaged a bit of paste into each of Cedar's hands. Then she recited a ritual chant in 5th Council dialect. Cedar wondered fleetingly whether Makala was an ancestor of Ravenea. She left this supposition unconfirmed. They did not speak. Ravenea merely guided Cedar to the sofa once again, where she swiftly drifted into a dreamless sleep.

Confident in the success of her blood-alchemy palimpsest, Ravenea left Cedar to rest while the ink set and the ritual effects settled. She needed to speak with both Sadira and Kalina before commencing the erasure process. Since the mutual conjunctions a few weeks ago, her conversations with Sadira had been stunningly enlightening. Fortunately, Sadira recognized the benefit of fostering comradeship with the Azoth Magen. She had therefore revealed the truth to Ravenea — or at least a plausible semblance of truth. She had not only acknowledged her mutual conjunction to Kalina but disclosed various events leading up to it. Nonetheless, Ravenea had yet to speak with Kalina directly. Sadira's rebel counterpart did not appear to share Sadira's trust.

"You would be unable to see her even if she were to agree to emerge," Sadira had explained a few days earlier. "For you to interact within Council dimension with a mutually conjoined alchemical child created in Flaw dimension, you would require a fragment of the Dragonblood Stone."

As a ruse — to avoid revealing her primordial bloodline ancestry for as long as possible — Ravenea had suggested that Sadira attain such a fragment from Flaw dimension for her to borrow. But Sadira had been affronted, informing Ravenea that Dragonblood fragments are not like library books.

"The Rebel Branch does not simply loan them out on request."

"Not even to the Azoth Magen?" Ravenea had asked.

"Not even then," Sadira had resolutely replied.

On that day, still unsure of Sadira's trustworthiness, Ravenea had refrained from explaining that she had made her heretical request for the fragment merely to maintain the illusion she had perpetrated for years. Ravenea did not *need* Dragonblood Stone — neither fragment nor tonic. The blood of Osmanthus coursed through her veins. As a direct descendant of the primordial bloodline, she was more attuned to Flaw dimension than even the Rebel High Azoth himself. But she had admitted nothing of the sort to Sadira. Instead, she had nodded acquiescence and suggested they discuss the matter another time. Now, that time had come. Ravenea's newly formulated hypothesis, combined with Cedar's impending departure and the time-limited stability of the blood-alchemy palimpsest, necessitated immediate disclosure.

When Ravenea arrived at residence chambers, Sadira invited her into her room without hesitation, where Ravenea progressed straight to the point.

"I need Saule to emerge from Cedar and to speak with Genevre."

"Saule?" Sadira replied, clearly perplexed. She crossed her arms defensively. Ravenea should have anticipated the residual feelings Sadira would hold for Saule.

"Saule knew Ilex and Melia intimately," Ravenea said. "Though I remain uncertain of the precise level of intimacy shared, I have long suspected Saule's involvement — whether physical or alchemical — in the conception of Genevre."

"What are you saying, Azoth Magen?" asked Sadira.

"Prior to her conjunction with Cedar, Saule had remained in contact with Ilex and Melia. And, as I assume you've already learned from Kalina, Genevre is their daughter. If allowed to speak together uninhibited, Saule and Genevre may be able to shed light on the intricacies of mutual conjunction — its strengths and weaknesses, its potential for survival and dissolution." Ravenea paused to assess the effect of these half-truths. Though Sadira was neither nodding nor smiling, she was listening attentively. "Saule and Genevre could engage in frank discussion not only with each other but with Ilex and Melia themselves. Together they could provide us with the solution we require. For the sake of the dimensions, for all the conjoined pairs, we must provide Saule and Genevre with this opportunity."

In a silent gesture of frustration, Sadira indicated her complete lack of comprehension. Ravenea sighed. If Sadira were to both understand and agree, Ravenea would have to explain even more than she had originally intended.

"Cedar and Saule both have ties to the Rebel Branch. As such, compared with conjunctions of other alchemists, alternate properties could bind theirs. I also suspect Genevre used blood alchemy to manipulate Saule's conjunctive adhesion. In other words, Saule allowed for the possibility that her conjunction with Cedar could be manipulated in the future. I believe Saule knew what she was doing and why she was doing it."

"So, you intend, using some sort of . . . what? . . . ancient and forbidden blood alchemy, to purposely bring Saule forth now? To promote her dissolution from Cedar? You intend for Cedar and Saule to suffer like Tera and Olea? I cannot abide—"

"No! As I said, I believe the conjunction between Cedar and Saule is different."

"You *believe*?"

"Be reasonable, Sadira! I cannot know the precise intricacies of their conjunction until Saule can speak for herself. But I have reason to believe that the conjunction between Cedar and Saule may be *mutual* — not of the sort you and Kalina or Ilex and Melia achieved, but one that would allow Saule to emerge from the shadows and maintain dominance temporarily."

"Ravenea, I have trusted you with details we've not yet revealed to Council. But I fail to see how you expect me to believe you now. If conjunction between alchemists with ties to the rebels or Genevre resulted in any form of mutual conjunction whatsoever, both the Rebel Branch and the Alchemists' Council would have discovered its secrets long before now."

"As powerful as your recent conjunction has made you and Kalina, neither of you currently holds Azothian privilege in either dimension. Even combined, the alchemical knowledge you and Kalina possess remains limited compared with my own."

Sadira reddened and lowered her head. Ravenea could not tell whether she was humbled and submitting or angry and strategizing.

"We must consider one additional factor," continued Ravenea. "Saule and Cedar share a connection with both Genevre and with me — one that may be difficult for you to fathom."

Sadira looked up, now intrigued rather than irritated.

"You likewise share this connection," said Ravenea. "Through your conjunction with Kalina, you are now connected to the primordial bloodline."

Sadira shook slightly, and Ravenea wondered if perhaps the statement had stirred Kalina.

"My connection with the bloodline began at conception," responded Sadira, "not conjunction with Kalina. Dracaen confirmed weeks ago that I am of the bloodline."

Given her ability to mutually conjoin with an alchemical child, Sadira must indeed be *of the bloodline*, but that blood was ancestral, not primordial. Moreover, she had been naturally, not alchemically, conceived. So Sadira's blood — its chemistry, its genetics — though *of the bloodline*, had necessarily been altered through the evolution of generational genetics. The powerful alchemical abilities of the ancestral bloodline inevitably paled in comparison with those of alchemical children created directly from the primordial blood of Osmanthus and Aralia. Only Genevre, for reasons Ravenea still had not uncovered, possessed blood-alchemy powers apparently superior to those of both Fraxinus and Ravenea. And Ravenea was not about to reveal *that* detail to Sadira.

"And now, with your bloodlines combined," said Ravenea, "you and Kalina are powerful. You can help me to help us all."

"What are you suggesting, Ravenea? Do you

expect Kalina and I to use our ancestral blood to bring forth Saule?"

"Yes, but not in the way you may imagine. If my hypothesis is correct, years ago Genevre already set in motion everything required for Saule's re-emergence. But I require Kalina's assistance to ensure that everything progresses as planned." With no response from Sadira, Ravenea continued, "A few days from now, Cedar will visit with Genevre. They will work on a manuscript together for several weeks. I need Kalina to take a journey on my behalf prior to the upcoming visit."

"Your hesitancy to provide specific details suggests uncertainty or, worse, deception," said Sadira. "What are you refusing to say?"

"Nothing. I will explain. But I need to speak directly with Kalina."

"Speak to me, Ravenea. Kalina will hear you."

"No. I need to see her first," Ravenea insisted.

"Why?"

"Evidence."

"Evidence? Are you implying that you don't believe we conjoined?"

"I believe you conjoined. But given recent events, I need proof Kalina has not dissolved or disappeared altogether."

"We are *mutually* conjoined. We're not like other conjoined couples. Kalina is not like Olea. She's not about to *re-emerge* and dissolve. She has not disappeared. She is here. She and I share this body equally — like Ilex and Melia. But I told you, Ravenea. To see her physically, you would require a Dragonblood fragment."

"Ilex and Melia could both be seen at will," Ravenea reminded her.

"Neither Ilex nor Melia was an alchemical child conceived within a primary dimension. Yes, they were mutually conjoined, but they were both born naturally in the outside world. Alchemical children do not adhere to the same elemental rules as other alchemists."

Ravenea thought then of Makala and Savar — of their problem with dimensional visibility after mutual conjunction. As with so many dilemmas of late, Ilex and Melia potentially held the solution to this one as well. But more pressing matters concerned her now. She could wait no longer. She needed to solidify the plan before Cedar awakened. Hiding her truths could no longer work in this swiftly changing world. *Something* had to change, and that transformation would begin here and now with Ravenea herself.

"Listen to me, Sadira. Listen carefully and choose wisely," said Ravenea. Slightly nervous, she concealed her hands beneath her robes. "Like Kalina, I am an alchemical child."

Sadira trembled once again.

"Under circumstances I cannot explain now but promise to describe when our time is less constrained, I am the alchemical daughter of 5th Council High Azoth Magen Makala who, in turn, is the alchemical daughter of Osmanthus and Aralia."

Sadira steadied herself against a chair.

"I am a direct heir, a manifestation of the primordial alchemical transmutation, a child of Makala and her consort twin Corylus. The blood of my grandparents, Osmanthus and Aralia, flows through my veins. I *am* alchemy. To witness inter-dimensional phenomena, I have never *required* a fragment — not of the Dragonblood Stone, not of the Lapis. As both an alchemical child of the pri-mordial bloodline *and* Azoth Magen of the 19th Council of Alchemists, I am more powerful even than High Azoth Dracaen. Yet as powerful as I am, I cannot heal the dimensions alone. I require your help. And I need Kalina to reveal herself to me — *now*."

Sadira had no chance to respond. Kalina instantly appeared in her stead. She smiled, pre-senting an air of confidence, but Ravenea could tell her revelation had had its desired effect. Kalina appeared both honoured and frightened. Neither she nor Sadira would have anticipated the strength of Ravenea's authority. Together, they had outma-noeuvred Novillian Scribe Amur and, in effect, the entire Elder Council to conjoin with one another. They had likely expected the Azoth Magen to be equally pliable. Now Kalina must realize that she had been wrong. Ravenea had become unpredict-able — to Sadira, to Kalina, to herself.

"What would you like us to do, Azoth Magen?"

"Manipulate the bloodline," replied Ravenea.

"I don't understand."

"Take this vessel," said Ravenea. She held out a small ampoule. "It contains my blood."

Kalina's eyes widened. She held out a hand.

"Yes, you could choose to abuse it," admitted Ravenea as she placed the ampoule into Kalina's palm. "The source of my power literally lies in your hands. You could use it to practise any of a dozen or so blood-alchemy rituals previously inacces-sible even to Genevre, let alone to you. But in the attempt, you would be wasting not only the blood but the opportunity."

"What opportunity?"

"I am testing you, Kalina. I need irrefutable evidence that I can trust you and Sadira. If you do what I request with this blood, rather than using it as you see fit, you will gain my trust. Keep the future in mind — my blood is currently abundant. And it is more powerful than yours. You may need an additional supply someday, and I may provide it to you. But you must take *this* blood — the blood in this ampoule — into the past."

"You expect me to open a breach in time?"

"No. I expect Genevre to open it. As you may or may not yet be aware, only a creator of an alchem-ical child can send that child through time. I expect you — with Sadira along for the ride — to travel through the breach."

"Ravenea! I've lived almost fourteen decades. I matured long ago. I am far too old for time travel!"

"Your interpretation of the timeline enigma is evidently flawed."

"What do you mean?"

"Maturity is not dependent on linear time. An alchemical child reaches maturity by *traversing* time, not by progressing through its chronological span. You will attain maturity only when you travel *through* a breach into the past or future. Thereafter, your time-travelling abilities become fixed."

"Fixed?"

"They will be limited within the linear timeline to the original point of breach."

"I don't understand," said Kalina.

"If you travel, as I propose, to 1814, you will reach maturity upon arrival. Thereafter, having traversed a breach between the present and 1814, your ability to traverse the timeline from any point in your future will be limited to 1814, give or take a few months on either side of your original entry point."

"If my time is limited — if my future time *travel* is limited — why should I allow you to make such a critical decision for me? Perhaps I would prefer to travel to 1380 or 1925 or—"

"If you refuse to take my blood to 1814, you will cease to exist."

Kalina tried but was unable to form words.

"Do not worry, Kalina. I am not threatening homicide. Besides, you obviously continue to exist as we speak. Therefore, timeline logic dictates that you will not refuse my request."

Kalina remained silent.

"The present already *is*," said Ravenea. "Paradoxically, you can change the present only if you *refuse* to return to the past. By carrying my blood to 1814, you will ensure the present continues to exist as is."

"Why would we want the present to continue to exist *as is*? The Amber Garden alone—"

"Yes, the Amber Garden has disintegrated. Yes, conjunctions are dissolving. Yes, it appears Council dimension is faltering beyond repair. Over the next few weeks — months, years — I suspect we will also hear of ripple-effect degradation occurring in both Flaw dimension and the outside world. But we must find solutions to our present circumstances in our *current* present, not in the *past*. Though your lack of existence might indeed quell the current dimensional furor, I suspect that without the birth of your mother, the primordial bloodline itself would be lost, followed shortly thereafter by the degeneration of the ancestral bloodline. In other words, not only Council dimension but the alchemical powers of all alchemists would irreparably erode."

"Ravenea, I—"

"We cannot transform the world without transforming ourselves," said Ravenea. "And we cannot begin to transform ourselves without consciously choosing to step out of our perception of the world as we currently know it. To do so, we need the world to be as it is, not as the entirely different place it would abruptly become without Genevre or you or Arjan."

Kalina moved the ampoule into her other hand and tucked it into a pocket of her robes.

"Therefore, I require you to take the ampoule to 1814," reiterated Ravenea. "You must find Saule. You must determine a means to inject her with my blood."

"What!"

"Of course, to do so, you will need to be both creative and discreet. You cannot risk Saule recognizing you in her future. As you know, your paths crossed in our current timeline — you entered Council dimension as an Initiate before Saule conjoined with Cedar."

"Saule and Cedar didn't conjoin until 2009! Why do I have to travel to 1814?"

"For its Quintessence to conjoin fully with her own, Saule must absorb my blood at least two years prior to the physical intimacy she shared with Ilex and Melia. Records indicate that Saule spent August 1814 in the Qingdao protectorate. In our current timeline, I presume Genevre is now in Qingdao awaiting word from you about your conjunction. Opening a breach between the two points in time within such close geographical proximity is relatively straightforward. Since you will be creating a time-limited bridge to the past — rather than one meant to open again in the distant future — you will require only a trinity of participants together rather than a physical triangle comprising people in three locations. You, Sadira, and Genevre will suffice."

"What is going on? What happened two years later? How are Ilex and Melia involved?"

"Think about it, Kalina. What happened in 1816? Surely your mother has told you something of her life."

"Genevre wasn't even born until 1818!"

"Precisely. Did she mention that Ilex and Melia's pregnancy lasted well over a year?"

Ravenea was certain the hairs on Kalina's arms and neck stood vertical amidst the goosebumps of realization.

"Ilex and Melia could not have conceived a child on their own," explained Ravenea. "Mutual conjunction in and of itself cannot account for such an anomaly. This discrepancy has bothered me for years. I have always suspected Saule's involvement. The rumours among alchemists at the time suggested she and Melia were lovers. I even confronted them once — and I knew they were lying to me. I just didn't know *precisely* what Saule had done or why her actions, even if sexual, would have had any effect whatsoever. After all, Saule is not of the bloodline *at all*, neither ancestral nor primordial. How then could she have contributed to the conception of a bloodline child — one so pure of blood as to enable activation of the *Osmanthian Codex?* Impossible, one would think. Or so I had assumed."

Kalina breathed heavily but said nothing.

"And then finally, just an hour ago while speaking with Cedar, I realized that the only way Saule could have contributed to the creation of a bloodline child — indeed, to the conception of any child — would be if someone had first given her a means to do so. Saule would have needed Osmanthian or Aralian blood. Not in an ampoule, as you now possess. She would require the blood to be part of her, con-joined — so to speak — with her own blood, her own bodily fluids, her own Quintessence. To create a child of the original Osmanthian bloodline with Ilex and Melia, Saule would require *my* blood."

Kalina was now visibly shaking. Ravenea could only imagine what Sadira experienced as she watched and listened from within a body currently outside her control.

"You, Kalina, with Genevre's assistance, are going to travel through a breach to 1814 to inject Saule with my blood. You are going to carry into the past the genetic material — my ancestral alchemical Quintessence — that will enable Saule to impreg-nate Ilex and Melia. Genevre is *my* child as much as she is Meliex and Saule's."

Kalina shook her head, as if in disbelief.

"Not only will the blood you carry into the past ensure Genevre's existence, it should also protect Saule from complete absorption into Cedar when they conjoin. Genevre — due to her connection with Saule through my primordial blood — should be able to draw her forth from Cedar."

"How?"

"Using her own blood and a blood-alchemy ritual, which I will provide before your departure. You will convince her to bring forth Saule for the good of the Alchemists' Council."

"Genevre will know you have been hiding your identity for centuries."

"We have all kept secrets. And we all had our reasons to do so. But today I am acknowledging the truth of my relationship with you. Both within and removed from Council dimension and its Hierarchy of Orders, I have been, I currently am, and I always will be your grandmother. You can trust me, Kalina. I would never harm one of my own."

Kalina returned to the chambers she now shared with Sadira and set the ampoule carefully upon the mantel. She felt no need to speak with Sadira regarding the primary issue of Saule and the bloodline. Kalina had already made that decision: they would indeed go to 1814. What choice did they have? But an agreed-upon plan of action was required, so Kalina stepped in front of the mirror and awaited Sadira.

"I'm worried," said Sadira. She had emerged suddenly, startling Kalina despite the anticipation of a conversation. "What if Cedar gets hurt? What if she suffers like Tera?"

"We have to do what the Azoth Magen requested," replied Kalina.

"Our conjunction has already done enough damage. What if we inadvertently make everything worse?"

Kalina stared intently into the mirror. She needed to *watch* Sadira. During Ravenea's revelations, Kalina had feared for herself. In its aftermath, on the walk back to residence chambers, she had feared for Arjan. She had not considered Sadira.

"Sadira, we didn't know what would happen. I don't think anyone did — not fully. I believed our conjunction was a means to an end, a means to conjoin alchemists and rebels, a means of protecting free will eternally throughout the dimensions. Under current circumstances, we cannot risk disobeying Ravenea. And we need to trust one another implicitly. Mutually conjoined, we cannot work at cross purposes."

"I agree. We are *one* now. We can debate with one another. But, in the end, out of necessity, our choices must coincide."

"Then let us plan. We need to present a united front to Genevre."

Thus, they strategized. They agreed to admit only the most relevant truths to Genevre. They would reveal Ravenea's origins. They would emphasize the significance of her powers. They would convince her that Ravenea's blood would inoculate Saule from permanent conjunction. They would instruct her on the blood-alchemy procedure to release Saule from Cedar. They would explain that Saule potentially holds information about mutual conjunction that could help save other conjoined pairs from dimensional dissolution. Genevre would surely open the breach if persuaded that Kalina's time travel could help save her conjoined children.

But, if possible, they would avoid telling her that Ravenea's blood was responsible for her conception by Ilex and Melia. What would that news do other than influence Genevre's understanding of — and communication with — Saule? Surely the Azoth Magen would want Genevre to interact with her mother without wondering how much of Saule was, in fact, Ravenea.

Qingdao — 2014

All progressed as anticipated in Qingdao. Though Genevre appeared stunned upon learning of Council dimension's disintegration and Ravenea's alchemical and bloodline origins, Kalina eventually persuaded her to open the breach. She saw no reason to refuse Kalina. After all, Genevre had no cause to suspect deception from her daughter. Her only question involved the date: *Why 1814?* Sadira claimed two hundred years were required for the blood to evolve fully. Genevre's face gave no indication as to whether she believed this lie; she merely nodded and suggested a wardrobe change before they crossed the breach.

Once in 1814 Qingdao, Kalina dominated their conjoined body — they could not risk Saule recognizing Sadira when she joined Council only two years later, whereas Kalina would not join Council until 2008. Presenting requisite papers, complete with Scribe Ravenea's signature, Kalina gained access to the Qingdao protectorate under the pretense of delivering some Elixir-infused cinnabar ink. *Flirt with her*, Sadira had earlier instructed Kalina. *Tell her you like her pendant.* The compliment garnered Kalina an invitation to lunch, during which she surreptitiously sprinkled an alchemical sedative into Saule's broth. Shortly thereafter, while Saule sat virtually frozen, Kalina injected her with Ravenea's blood. She felt Sadira flinch, clearly uncomfortable with this deception and its invasive procedure. *For the good of the Council*, Kalina whispered.

Not until they had returned through the breach and reviewed the method for releasing Saule from Cedar did Genevre make a revelation that neither Kalina nor Sadira had expected.

"I do find it fascinating that Saule was right all along."

"About what?" asked Kalina.

"Before she conjoined with Cedar, Saule told me

the day would come that I'd have to release her — that I *could* release her and unbury the knowledge she carried with her into the conjunction. Neither of us had any idea when that day would arrive. But I gave her my word that, if the time came, I would try."

"Did Saule say anything about the effect of the release on Cedar?" asked Sadira.

"Only to assure me that Cedar would be unlikely to suffer."

Sadira stood silently for several seconds, tears and anger brimming. "Yet again, we have neglected to think through the repercussions," she finally said. "Saule could not be certain of the outcome. If we've learned nothing else of late about our arrogance, we've learned that assurances mean little to nothing. Cedar *could* suffer. What right do we have to harm her?"

Genevre moved a hand to her head as if the idea caused her physical pain. "I don't want to hurt anyone, Sadira. But I believe, under the current dimensional circumstances, Cedar would want us to try."

"We believed our insurgence would save the dimensions, that our actions would lead to revolution for the betterment of all," continued Sadira through her tears. "Already, only a few days after our conjunction, Council dimension has blatantly illustrated we were wrong. At first, I did what Cedar wanted me to do. Later, I followed Dracaen's advice. More recently, I've followed Kalina's. And here we are — we've now agreed to a new plan because Ravenea has convinced us to believe her version of events. So, again, we adjust the narrative and continue."

"Yes, at each step, we have adjusted accordingly. We will continue to do so. And all will eventually be well," insisted Kalina. "Saule may offer a solution."

"Everyone believes they have the solution," rebutted Sadira. "Everyone believes they or their faction alone can save the world from the idiocy of everyone else. But they can't. They can't because we all weave tales — facts transmuted into fiction and then back into an elaborate illusion of facts. And we are no different. Each of us, throughout the dimensions, knows and tells only part of the story. And each one of us is an unreliable narrator."

V
Santa Fe — 2014

Within an hour of Kalina and Sadira returning to present-day Qingdao through the time breach, Genevre accompanied them via a series of rebel portals back to Santa Fe. Kalina and Sadira then returned to Council dimension through the Santa Fe protectorate portal, promising to return with an update as soon as possible. Genevre had walked back to her house feeling uncharacteristically lonely. Now three days had passed without word from anyone. Genevre could only presume the dimensional problems had worsened. Anxiety manifested — crawled under her skin, burned at its surface, and kept her awake at night.

Had her original interpretation of the *Osmanthian* folio been incorrect? She longed to see it again, to reinterpret, to remember that which she had forgotten. She knew the folio featured an image of an alchemical child — the homunculus — on its recto side, but she could no longer recall the verso text beyond a vague overview. She had no recollection of the word-for-word, line-by-line inscriptions. She could only assume some sort of primordial alchemy embedded in the manuscript had caused the memory loss. She should have suspected, years earlier, that lack of proximity to the folio would result in the demise of its words within her.

She likewise thought obsessively about Kalina and Sadira, about Arjan and Dracaen. She feared not only their conjunctive dissolutions but their deaths. Would her children meet the same end as her parents? In Qingdao, Kalina had been so preoccupied with reaching Saule that she had not even inquired after Ilex and Melia. Initially, Kalina's lack of concern for her grandparents concerned Genevre. Later, Genevre realized that news of their deaths would be better avoided until the dimensional chaos had been quelled. Why upset her daughter further when her world's existence was at stake?

Finally, in desperation for news, Genevre clasped her Dragonblood fragment and called out to Fraxinus. Though rationally she knew he could not hear her, emotionally she needed to believe he would sense her plea no matter their dimensional separation. When a loud knock startled her, she rushed to the door. Anticipating Kalina or Fraxinus, she instead found Jinjing. She embraced her friend, then escorted her into the main room.

"Are they still alive?" she asked. "Kalina and Arjan — are they still alive?"

"Yes. As far as I know, they are both alive."

"You're not certain?"

"I haven't seen Arjan. He and Dracaen left for Flaw dimension shortly after their conjunction. But I spoke with Sadira this morning. Her conjunction with Kalina remains intact. And I have heard nothing to the contrary regarding Arjan's well-being."

Genevre nodded, relieved. Tears welled. "Thank you! Thank you! Too much time has passed without news. I was beginning to fear the worst."

"I'm sorry, Genevre. I knew the silence would distress you. As soon as I learned Sadira and Kalina could not return, I requested a day's assignment in the Santa Fe protectorate."

"What's happened now? Why could they not leave?"

"The Council is in complete disarray — each day another alarming repercussion presents itself. Alongside Ravenea and the Elders, Kalina and Sadira are dealing with the fallout."

"Of course! Of course, they must remain where needed most — as must we all in such distressing times." She reached for Jinjing's hand. "Thank you for coming to me. Being here alone without news has been torturous."

"Where are Ilex and Melia?" Jinjing asked,

174

glancing towards the kitchen. "Did they stay in Qingdao as a precaution?"

"No," Genevre responded soberly. She had been dreading the inevitability of this moment. She would have to share the news — speak aloud the words. "They are gone."

"Gone? Where? Back into hiding? Do they fear—"

"No, Jinjing. They dissolved. Their conjunction dissolved. They're *gone*. They've died. They believed the release of apiary bees into the outside world caused their dissolution."

Jinjing shook her head, whispering *no*. Genevre could see Jinjing shaking. She wondered if, as she herself did, Jinjing felt culpable for her involvement — guilt for playing a role in events that had culminated in unanticipated death and devastation.

"Did they just . . . disappear?" Jinjing asked.

Genevre moved aside her shawl to reveal their honey-amber remains, which she had strung on a silver cord like an alchemist's pendant.

"They transformed . . . their elemental structure liquefied . . . and then crystallized."

"May I say goodbye?" Jinjing asked.

Genevre nodded, removed the chain and pendant, and passed it to Jinjing. Jinjing clasped it firmly between her hands, speaking inaudibly. After a minute or so, she kissed the amber gently before returning it to Genevre. Though neither Jinjing nor Genevre were pendant-bearing members of the

Alchemists' Council or Rebel Branch, they both understood the gravity of this moment. After the kiss, in that brief instant during which both Jinjing and Genevre held the pendant, they felt a surge of Quintessence — not their own but that of Ilex and Melia, permanently memorialized within the amber rather than restored to the Lapis.

"So should it be," said Jinjing.

"So should it be," confirmed Genevre.

Later, tears dried, Jinjing recounted her version of recent Council dimension events — the melting Amber Garden, the dissolving conjunctions, the disembodied cries. Though she had not witnessed it herself, she had heard enough about the dissolution of Tera and Olea to describe it in detail. Genevre listened, once again silent, attentive, and horrified.

"I didn't know," Genevre said.

"I thought Kalina and Sadira would have explained—"

"They did. I mean . . . I didn't know what would happen. I didn't anticipate the after-effects of the mutual conjunctions. No one told me about the dimensional fallout."

"Who would have told you?" asked Jinjing.

"Someone more knowledgeable about dimensional history. Dracaen and Fraxinus both extensively studied the *Osmanthian Codex* since its awakening, whereas I had relatively limited access. And their fluency with 5th Council script far surpasses mine. What if one or both of them purposely misled me? What if they deliberately provided me with inaccurate interpretations?"

"That makes no sense. As much as Dracaen craves power, he too expected the mutual conjunctions to unite the dimensions, to ensure the permanence of the Flaw within the Lapis — the permanence of *choice* throughout dimensions. If he had believed the conjunctions would wreak irrevocable dimensional havoc, he wouldn't have agreed to conjoin with Arjan — not even as a means to traverse time. And what would Fraxinus gain from concealing such information from either Dracaen or you? Where would either of them be without you as an ally? You are, after all, the one who enlivened the *Osmanthian Codex*."

"Exactly. My gravest mistake — an accident of circumstance that instigated the series of events that has led us here. I've brought us to destruction rather than . . . renewal."

"After all these years, I've finally reached an epiphany," replied Jinjing. "Whether rebel or alchemist, whether of the primary dimensions or the outside world, all each of us ever seems to do is make mistakes in the process of attempting to fix the mistakes of others — the paradox of good intentions. Your intentions have been worthy, Genevre. You chose to effect change for a better future, like all alchemists throughout the generations. None of us can know where we would be now if you had enacted different intentions."

"You're too kind to me, Jinjing. Yes, I intended to curtail Dracaen's tyranny and end generations of strife between the Rebel Branch and the Alchemists' Council. But instead I appear to have set in motion a means to destroy Council dimension. The rebels will celebrate if Council influence over the world's elemental balance terminates as a result of my good intentions."

"Oh, Genevre! The Scribes and Readers have confirmed reports filtering in from the protectorates. The people of the outside world are already headed towards disaster. Most are oblivious to the signs; worse, they are ignoring the dissenting voices of protestors. Meanwhile, Council appears powerless to intervene. That's ostensibly the reason for my trip — to obtain an update from the Santa Fe protectorate."

"So you've already spoken with Gad?"

"Yes. And he confirmed the world's elemental balance has already begun to fragment."

"But what about the bees? Ilex and Melia implied multitudes were released. The wing vibrations should have worked to maintain Council influence."

"The release of thousands of bees simultaneously *should* have placated populations and reinvigorated the environment, but they have not. Keepers of the Book have witnessed increased destruction and aggression throughout the outside world. And if the Readers are correct in their interpretations of recent

Novillian prophecies, the outside world will soon be awash in political turmoil and environmental degradation. Reports suggest the bees have been altered."

Jinjing's final sentence stunned Genevre. Was this revelation, after all they had sacrificed, the legacy of Ilex and Melia? They had made their choice *freely*. They had agreed to siphon the bees' Quintessence with the intention of saving themselves. They had agreed to continue erasing the bees with the intention of strengthening negative space and weakening Council influence over the world. They had agreed to allow the bees to feed on their blood with the intention of preserving the bloodline. Had this final decision damaged the bees, caused them to mutate? If so, their choice had inadvertently triggered not only their own demise but that of the outside world.

"I'm sorry to cut this conversation short at the height of its intensity," said Jinjing, tearing Genevre from her thoughts. "But my time in Santa Fe is limited. I need to report to the North Library upon my return, so that Coll may leave to collect news from the London and Dublin protectorates. I cannot make matters worse through my negligence."

"Of course not," said Genevre. "I understand."

They embraced once again and uttered brief but emotionally intense goodbyes. Genevre stood at the open door until Jinjing disappeared around a corner.

Seated at the table, Genevre thought about Jinjing and their days in Qingdao. She thought back to the time breach, to the fracturing of Ilex and Melia, to the idea for the bee-laden saving grace. *We'll inscribe an emblem of a queen bee in a manuscript of our own creation.* She had led Ilex and Melia and Saule to believe the idea was hers. She suggested blood alchemy to enhance the queen, *to attract bees from other Lapidarian manuscripts to her.* This suggestion — this innocent suggestion meant to heal her ailing parents — had marked the unintentional beginning of the end for them all. Ilex and Melia could not have suspected the danger. They trusted her; they trusted her powers with blood alchemy. She had, after all, enlivened the *Osmanthian Codex* and created two thriving alchemical children. Why would they not trust her and her ingenious proposal?

But the idea had never been hers. Fraxinus had proposed it. *She* had trusted *him. Put a drop here*, he had said that day in the archives. She had followed his instructions. Since her duties at the time included work in the North Library, she knew she could readily transport the manuscript to Council dimension without drawing suspicion. The Lapidarian bees would migrate. Ilex and Melia could then stabilize their conjunction through the bees' Quintessence, all the while creating negative space within Council manuscripts, sites for future rebel impact and manipulation. Genevre had thanked Fraxinus profusely. *Assisting your parents is the least I can do. The future is ours, Genevre*, he had promised. *We need merely wait for its unfolding.* But she had misunderstood him.

All will be well, she had inferred.

All will be destroyed, he had meant.

Council Dimension — 2014

Upon waking in the catacomb alembic, Cedar immediately recognized her whereabouts but felt unsettled. She remembered Ravenea escorting her here from Azothian Chambers, insisting that Cedar regenerate. But she had no recollection of time passing within the alembic. She presumed the requisite time had passed. Or perhaps the effects on the dimension since the conjunctions were interfering—

Cedar sat up, remembering Tera and Olea. Could Saule have cast her own conscious awareness into the shadows? She lifted her hands to her face to check if her physical features were still her own. Though by touch she appeared to be herself, she required proof. She climbed out of the alembic, smoothed her instantaneously dried robes, and then progressed as quickly as possible through the narrow skull-lined passageways of the catacombs to the main Council grounds. Hurrying across the field and through the main courtyard, she arrived breathless at her residence chambers, lit the lanterns on either side of her wardrobe, and stared into its mirror. She slowly tilted her head from one side to the other; she moved backward and forward. At one point, close enough that her breath became visible on the mirror's surface, she stared into the reflection of her eyes for several seconds.

"Where are you?" she asked aloud. She took a few steps back and surveyed her entire body before focusing again on her face.

Cedar had not examined her reflection this closely since her short tenure in Qingdao with Jinjing after the Third Rebellion. Was the fallout from every rebellion to necessitate such scrutiny of physical appearance? Unlike the mirror in Qingdao where she had scanned her face for signs of age, now she sought signs of her conjunctive partner. If Saule were to emerge and then dissolve as Olea had, would her eyes return to their pre-conjunction shade? Would Sadira be enamoured of those eyes? Or had her attraction for Cedar been integrally connected with Saule's conjoined Quintessence?

Of course, Cedar held one fear above others at the thought of Saule's re-emergence. During their conjunction, Saule may have sensed the presence of the Sephrim that Cedar had ingested. If Saule possessed the ability to speak aloud — as Erez had done in the Amber Garden — Saule might report the infraction to Ravenea or Ruis. As reprimand for such a severe violation, Cedar's temporary erasure would most certainly become permanent.

Cedar shook her head as if to remind herself not to let such thoughts overwhelm her logic. She had to believe, as both Ravenea and Obeche had suggested on the walk from the Amber Garden to Azothian Chambers, that the dimensions and its inhabitants were enmeshed in a flux of readjustment. She reassured herself that all abnormalities were *temporary*, including the return of conjunctive partners. Cedar's lapse in memory could just as likely be a result of dimensional flux and fatigue as the re-emergence of Saule. Other memories of her day remained clear — not just the tragedy of the Amber Garden but the message in *Turba Philosophorum 1881*. Feeling guilty once again, she wondered aloud if she should return to consult with Ravenea.

"No!" she said.

Only *she* had not said it.

Cedar immediately peered again into the mirror. This time she caught a glimpse of her other self. Saule had indeed begun to re-emerge. And she could speak.

Kalina is Genevre's daughter, Saule said.

Cedar thought immediately of Kalina's request for erasure and of her recent audible return to Council dimension. She thought of her own role in the Trance of the Nine and of her enduring faith in Dracaen's plan to increase the Flaw. Saule had proven useful rather than solely detrimental. She had just provided Cedar with a missing piece of the puzzle: Kalina was the alchemical child of Dracaen and Genevre. Since Cedar had protected their daughter repeatedly, perhaps Dracaen or Genevre would protect her during her upcoming erasure.

And Arjan is—

"And Arjan is—" Cedar repeated, waiting.

But she saw only her own reflection. Saule had disappeared. And Cedar's sole desire from that moment forth was to reunite with Genevre.

Santa Fe — 2014

The following night, still reeling from Jinjing's news of what could happen within the next few years, Genevre stood at her kitchen counter staring at the dishes in the sink: two plates, two mugs, some cutlery — so few altogether, yet the task overwhelmed her. She gripped the counter and stared. That action was all she could manage. She was unable to convince herself to turn on the water or reach for the soap. In that moment, the thought of abandoning everything she had known in Santa Fe — of moving to another country where no one could find her, of beginning her life anew in the floundering outside world, of buying new plates and mugs and cutlery — seemed eminently preferable to washing the dishes.

A knock at the door shook her from this dire fantasy and physical inertia. She rushed to the front of the house. As expected given Kalina's fore-warning, Cedar awaited her.

"I am here for sanctuary and for assistance with a manuscript."

Genevre did not respond. Once again, she stood motionless. She gazed at Cedar, uncertain. Like flashes on a screen came memories of Cedar, of Saule, of Saule's words, of the agreement made prior to their conjunction.

"For all intents and purposes," continued Cedar, "I have been erased from Council dimension."

With those words, Genevre's sympathies realigned. Cedar had nowhere else to turn. Genevre wanted to reach out to Cedar, take her into her arms, justify the half-truths she had perpetrated out of necessity for decades. Instead, consciously *not* touching her, Genevre invited her in, asked her to explain what had happened, guided her into the main room, and gestured towards the sofa. As it turned out, Cedar required a place to live temporarily.

"You are welcome here," Genevre offered. "You've always been welcome here."

As if no time had passed, a mixture of trepidation and longing to reunite flooded her. Then guilt followed on desire's heels. Within the first minute of their subsequent exchange, Cedar admitted to not knowing what to expect from Genevre. How could she, when Genevre now struggled with what to expect from herself? She extended useless words of consolation and then offered to make tea, at which point their conversation temporarily ceased.

Truly Genevre did welcome Cedar — if for nothing else than to snap her out of her stasis. Her invitation for Cedar to stay with her had been both honest and heartfelt. However, Genevre simultaneously felt twinges of guilt for her ongoing deception. Upon the birth of their twins, she had informed Cedar of the death of their daughter but not the life of their son. And now, upon welcoming her, Genevre proffered her willingness to offer sanctuary but not the plan to bring forth Saule.

Cedar's initial hesitancy had not surprised Genevre, but her admissions certainly did. Cedar knew of the mutual conjunctions — not only of Sadira and Kalina but also of Arjan and Dracaen. And, most unexpectedly, she claimed Saule had already emerged and spoken to her: *Kalina is Genevre's daughter. And Arjan is*— Genevre felt a rush of panic at the mention of Arjan. But then Cedar explained that Saule had left the second sentence incomplete. Not yet able or willing to tell Cedar the truth about their son, Genevre delayed the inevitable.

"How . . . how *odd*."

"Odd?" countered Cedar. "Is that all you have to say? Can you not at least tell me whether it's true or a figment of my imagination?"

"How am I to know whether Saule actually appeared to you?"

"No, Genevre! Is Kalina your daughter?"

"Yes. Yes, Cedar. Kalina is my daughter."

Genevre felt nauseated. Whereas less than an hour earlier Cedar had not known what to expect of Genevre, now their roles had reversed. Genevre had no idea what Cedar would say or do next. Outwardly, she remained calm as she responded to Cedar's anger. When Cedar accused her of hiding the truth, Genevre offered logic. Stumbling over her words, she asserted that decisions to maintain secrets must sometimes be made for the sake of those we love. Genevre at first felt relieved when Cedar agreed with this premise, yet she immediately wondered what secrets Cedar had been keeping from her. But she had no time to dwell on possibilities since their conversation swiftly shifted to the primary purpose of Cedar's visit: they were to construct a manuscript meant to attract potential Rebel Branch Initiates — one that Ravenea, not Dracaen, had requested after consultation with Kalina and Sadira. Kalina insisted that, to make an informed decision, potential Initiates needed to understand rebel history and philosophy from a perspective beyond that of Rebel Branch Elders.

Through the subsequent days, with little effort or tension, they fell quickly back into the rhythm and ease of working together. Though progress moved slowly, they drafted, edited, and inscribed the manuscript as efficiently and effectively as always. No matter the past secrets or current half-truths, no matter the lingering unspoken desires, they seemed of one mind in their scribal endeavours. As the days passed, as the manuscript progressed, and as their affection for one another once again amplified, Genevre found herself quite contented — happy even — spending time alone with Cedar. She attempted to quash persistent thoughts of Saule.

One night, setting their work aside to relax at sunset beneath the cottonwood tree, Genevre confessed the pleasure she felt working at Cedar's side but complained of the cramped workspace. She had never expected to transform her dining room into a manuscript scriptorium. "Tomorrow, we should go shopping for a larger table," Genevre suggested.

"What if someone should see us?" Cedar asked.

"See what? Two women out shopping for a table? Are you worried someone might assume we're . . . together?"

Cedar laughed. "I was referring to a protectorate alchemist or stronghold rebel. Rest assured, I am otherwise unconcerned."

"In that case," responded Genevre, "why should we limit ourselves to a dining room table? We should build a small scriptorium — a studio, as outside world architects would say."

"A studio!" exclaimed Cedar. "Imagine the possibilities!"

And they did. To break from their work, they proceeded to picture and suggest and negotiate the structure, furniture, and decor of their imaginary studio — everything from the square footage to the light fixtures and inkwells, from the window frames to the teapot and cups.

"We've not considered cost," said Genevre, one evening after an hour or so of detailed studio negotiations. "For this studio to happen, we'll need to turn a lot of lead into gold."

Cedar looked directly at her then, caught her eyes fleetingly. And Genevre realized too late what she had admitted in using that specific phrase. After all, they *were* alchemists. They *could* turn lead into gold. So, although the distance between their imagined studio and its physical manifestation was far too vast to contemplate traversing, Genevre had made an initial and unintentional step. With those words, she had inserted a fragment of reality into their otherwise impractical fantasy. And Cedar appeared to have noticed.

The next day, as they worked at the dining table, Cedar made additional suggestions for the studio. On each occasion, Genevre smiled but said nothing, focusing instead on the manuscript. Too much was at stake to engage in playful fantasy when sombre reality required her full attention. Eventually, Genevre's avoidance tactics worked, and Cedar refrained from mentioning either the studio or its contents. Genevre fluctuated repeatedly between relief and remorse.

The following week, hypothesizing methods to infuse a manuscript illumination with Elixir, Cedar proposed mixing her own blood with the Lapidarian ink. In that gesture — in that Quintessential self-sacrifice — Cedar had inadvertently presented Genevre with a means to an end. And with that revelation, the reality of their contented pleasure was immediately suspended, the fantasy of their studio utterly demolished. Genevre thought only of Saule. To bring her forth, she would need to inject her own blood into Cedar. *A single drop will suffice. A pinprick — that's all*, Kalina had explained when relaying Ravenea's blood-alchemy directives. *Easier said than done*, Genevre had responded. Yet here they were, a pinprick away from betrayal. Now all Genevre had to do was provide the needle.

When Cedar returned to clarity of consciousness from a barrage of pain-laced hallucinations, she was lying on a bed beside Genevre. She did not remember how or why she had ended up here. She looked at Genevre, smiled, and attempted to speak.

"Do not fear, Genevre. Cedar will be fine."

Cedar was startled. The voice had come from within her but was not her own.

"Where is she?" asked Genevre.

"Resting in the shadows."

Saule? Cedar was disoriented — even more than she had been when Saule had first spoken to her in front of the mirror.

"I'm here," said the voice.

That voice is most certainly Saule's.

"I'm here," repeated Saule.

"Are you all right?"

"Yes. I'm just . . . adjusting. I've waited so long."

Genevre nodded. "What if Cedar should choose to re-emerge?"

Has Saule re-emerged and forced me into the shadows?

"Cedar currently has no choice. The blood alchemy has confined her to the shadows. She's unconscious but safe — a state of being for which many a conjoined partner would be thankful, I can assure you."

No! Cedar attempted to cry. *I am not unconscious! I can hear you! I can see you!* But her efforts proved fruitless. She may be conscious, but she had been silenced and physically constrained. She had no idea how to regain the attention of either Saule or Genevre. *Help me!*

"Tell me of the night of my conception," Genevre requested.

Cedar calmed herself enough to listen. She too wanted to learn about the alchemical miracle that had led to Genevre's conception. Her face felt warm, and she realized that Saule must be blushing. How unusual for an alchemist! Perhaps Saule's period of dormancy had affected her personality. Or perhaps the blushing was not Saule's at all, but Cedar's own.

"Why?"

"I'm curious. I want to hear the story from your perspective while I can."

Saule glanced around the room, stretching her arms.

"Did you love them?" asked Genevre. "Ilex and Melia?"

"I loved Melia," said Saule. "As a friend initially. But eventually I became attracted to her. And then later, I wanted to help her . . . sexually, with Ilex. We shared a bed, just that one night. And somehow — alchemically — the three of us conceived you."

"But how could that happen, even alchemically?" asked Genevre.

"We never understood the alchemy ourselves. We could only assume the conception occurred spontaneously through a sexual conjunction of powerful ancestral bloodlines."

Genevre began to respond and then paused.

"What is it, my dear?" asked Saule.

"Nothing. Just . . . something Sadira and Kalina . . . did."

"How are they — my granddaughter and my beloved Sadira?"

"They're fine, for now," Genevre said. She then paused briefly before continuing her queries. "Do you think it could happen again? Pregnancy, I mean. What if mutually conjoined couples, unlike other alchemists, can become pregnant?"

"Ilex and Melia were of opposite biological sexes, unlike Sadira and Kalina."

"Perhaps mutually conjoined pairs of any biological sex could generate a corporeal alembic."

"Perhaps. Or, more likely, Ilex and Melia were the one and only evolutionary exception."

"If so, then I too am the exception — an enigma capable of creating alchemical children who, having mutually conjoined, appear to be the instigators of dimensional apocalypse."

As Genevre and Saule continued to discuss the physical, alchemical, and philosophical possibilities of sex, pregnancy, and impending disaster, Cedar's mind wandered elsewhere. She reran events of the past week: the message in the manuscript, the dissolving amber, the bone-chilling wails of the conjoined, the voice in the mirror, her erasure, her comfort at reconnecting with Genevre, the preparation of ink, the mixing of blood. What among these circumstances would account for her current condition? Blood alchemy seemed a viable explanation, but this and other suppositions only led Cedar to additional questions.

Why had Saule not reappeared only briefly like Erez had within Ravenea? Why had she not released an agonized howl, spoken her final words, and departed both body and dimension, as Tera had experienced with Olea? How were Cedar and Saule different from other conjoined pairs suffering the fallout of the mutual conjunctions within Council dimension? Then, recognition of a feasible cause overcame her: *the Sephrim.*

What if the shift from Cedar's victory to defeat was a result of ingesting Sephrim before the conjunction? Only a few weeks ago, she had feared Saule would reveal her use of the illicit substance to Elder Council. Now she feared Saule would say nothing at all — that she would simply return to Council dimension in Cedar's stead, and Cedar would be trapped indefinitely without a voice, tormented by the guilt of her imprudent decisions.

The last thing Cedar remembered feeling was overwhelming dread — her anxiety had heightened; she could not breathe; and she could do nothing to change her circumstances. She must have experienced the mutually conjoined equivalent of a panic attack. She had lost consciousness. Upon regaining it, Cedar found herself sitting on the living room sofa. How many hours had passed? How many days? Since Genevre wore different clothes, and the morning sun was shining into the room, Cedar assumed she had slept through at least one entire night.

"The bees had been consuming their blood for years," said Genevre.

Though Cedar did not understand what Genevre meant, she assumed the words were addressed to her, and she was momentarily relieved. Then Saule's voice confirmed Cedar's ongoing imprisonment. *No!*

"When Cedar left Council dimension, Jaden had not yet returned from the catacombs. Her wounds were severe. She may not have survived."

Cedar snapped to rapt attention. *Why did I not notice Jaden in the catacomb alembics? Why have I not thought about her at all until now?*

"The actions of my parents are connected to Jaden's suffering. The actions of my children are connected to Council dimension's demise. And these actions have one common denominator: me."

"No, Genevre. You cannot blame yourself. You alone are not responsible. Ilex and Melia made their own decision regarding the bees. And *I helped them leave Council dimension.* Jaden would not even be a member of the Alchemists' Council if not for me. *I* revised the manuscripts. And *I* offered to sacrifice myself in the conjunction with Cedar so that Jaden would be initiated and, as a result, be with Arjan in Qingdao at the appointed time."

Qingdao? But what of the Sephrim?

"Based on what we witnessed during the Qingdao incident," continued Saule, "I assumed I was doing the right thing. As did we all. If not for that day and that decision, Council would have welcomed potential Initiate Taimi instead of Jaden."

"No, Saule. We wouldn't have seen Jaden in Qingdao in 1939 if she were not meant to be in Qingdao again in 2014 as an Initiate of the Alchemists' Council."

"Yet the fact remains, Taimi died as an irrevocable consequence of my actions."

"*Our* actions. We did what we thought was right."

"Exactly. My point is that each of us took steps with sincere intentions — to repress Dracaen's power, to help the outside world, to ease the conflict between the Alchemists' Council and the Rebel Branch."

"I now doubt whether good intentions matter."

"They do, Genevre. We must maintain faith that they do. I desire nothing more than for all of us to succeed at our shared intention: for the Alchemists' Council to flourish alongside the Rebel Branch, for choice to prevail across the dimensions. None of us, including you, could have predicted the challenges we now face. We must use all available resources so that no other alchemist suffers years of silent torture."

Years of silent torture? Though Genevre appeared to ignore the phrase, it reverberated for Cedar as the conversation continued. *Imprisonment is torture for me here and now!* She felt unable to breathe. *Saule is breathing, Saule is breathing*, Cedar repeated to assure herself.

"Thank you, Saule," said Genevre, embracing her. "You're helping me regain hope — even if only a fragment to grasp. Your very presence suggests that at least part of my plan has progressed as I intended."

"Do you mean the vow I made to you?"

"Yes. The time has come. I need you to tell me where you hid the folio."

"What will happen to me thereafter?" asked Saule.

"You will return to the shadows and allow Cedar to emerge once again."

"Then let us wait briefly. Let us have a few final hours together."

Though indiscernible to Genevre and Saule, Cedar sighed in relief. Her agonizing confinement within Saule was temporary. Then Saule's words returned to her: *years of silent torture.* A chill of realization flooded her. Only one explanation of that statement made sense. Saule had been trapped — conscious — within Cedar since their conjunction. For more than five years, Saule had experienced the torment Cedar had barely been able to endure for a few waking hours. Having no means to control her intense and overwhelming emotional fluctuations, Cedar fell confused and guilt-ridden into the abyss for yet another immeasurable interval.

"Cedar still blames herself, doesn't she?" Genevre asked Saule. Genevre's voice was calm. She wore the same clothes as earlier, but the light in the room had shifted. At least a few hours must have passed. Having missed another segment of the conversation, Cedar once again felt disconcerted.

"She's not to blame."

Cedar grimaced. Ingesting Sephrim prior to their conjunction had violated the Law Codes and disadvantaged Saule. But Cedar was directly responsible neither for the dissolution of the Amber Garden nor for the re-emergence of other conjunctive partners.

Eyes narrowed, Genevre watched Saule intently. Perhaps she was looking for Cedar. "That's not what I meant," Genevre finally said. "Do you know if Cedar continues to believe herself responsible for the failure of the *Remota Macula* and for the death of our alchemical daughter?"

"I'm sorry, Genevre, but I don't know. She never said anything — aloud, I mean. And, of course, I can't read her mind. Not even Ilex and Melia could do that."

"No, of course not. Sorry. It's just . . . I thought . . . my ability to bring you forth meant you were never completely gone, that perhaps you would have, on occasion, overheard Cedar speaking with Ruis or Sadira."

"Cedar would never have admitted to Ruis the role she played in restoring the Flaw in the Stone. Nor would she confess to Sadira her marriage to you."

"I suppose not. Besides, an appropriate opportunity may not have presented itself. Five years is a mere blink of an eye within the lifespan of an alchemist."

"Unless you're an alchemist perpetually trapped within another," replied Saule. "Then each day is a long nightmare."

"Were the shadows a dream state?"

"No, Genevre. No part of my conjoined existence has been a *dream*. Until a few days ago, I was trapped, fully conscious, unable to move, within a body not my own."

Cedar recoiled, painfully discomforted. Her earlier suspicions had been correct. Had ingesting the Sephrim resulted in Saule's torture?

"To preserve my sanity," Saule continued, "I retreated whenever possible into the shadows, waiting to welcome a death that drew nowhere near. Most of the time, I observed Cedar's world in a haze. The only occasions on which I became fully present were those during which Cedar spoke with Sadira, Kalina, or Arjan. Seeing and hearing them provided me brief intervals of comfort or vicarious pleasure."

Arjan? So Saule was—

"So with Sadira, when they became lovers—"

Cedar flinched.

"Do not misunderstand, Genevre. I could not *feel* what Cedar experienced with Sadira — not in the way Ilex and Melia could be intimately present within one another, not in the way they were with me on the night of your conception. From my confined position, I could merely *observe* Cedar and Sadira, as one might observe characters in an erotic film of the outside world. My arousal was my own, inevitably left unfulfilled. I have been conscious within a body for years without ever being touched even for one fragment of time. Try to imagine that state, Genevre. Then imagine believing you might remain conjoined, alone, for ten years, for twenty, for hundreds. All I could do was retreat in despair."

Tears brimming, Genevre was visibly upset. "I'm sorry. I'm so sorry."

"I made the choice to conjoin. The decision was mine, not yours."

"But this time I am to blame. I opened the breach."

"In Qingdao?"

"No. I mean, yes, a breach to Qingdao, but not the one we opened together. I opened another one just the other day — a breach to allow Kalina to visit you in the past. She injected you with Ravenea's blood to ensure that you could be brought forth when required."

"You sent Kalina into the past with Ravenea's blood?"

"Yes. The idea was Ravenea's, but I followed through. I sent Kalina to 1814."

"Why then?"

"Apparently, the blood required two hundred years to evolve."

Saule remained silent for several seconds. "Two hundred years? I don't remember—"

"If I hadn't opened the breach, if you hadn't been injected with the blood, Cedar may have fully absorbed you at the conjunction. You would not have suffered."

No, Genevre! I ingested Sephrim! The fault is not yours!

"Do you understand what this means?" asked Saule. "The blood was Ravenea's. You wanted to bring me forth because of the folio. But Ravenea wanted something more."

"No. Saule."

"The alchemical blood responsible for your conception was Ravenea's, not mine. I am not the mother you supposed me to be."

This time, when Cedar regained consciousness, Genevre and Saule were sitting at the living room table. Again the shadows and light had changed somewhat. Another few hours must have passed.

"Do you ever imagine what would have happened if you had chosen differently?" asked Genevre. "Though an exercise in futility, hypothetical outcomes intrigue me. What would have happened if I had refused Dracaen's marriage proposal? What would have happened if I had discouraged his conjunction with Arjan?"

"What would have happened if I had not provided Jinjing with the Sephrim to give Cedar?" said Saule. "What would have happened if I had taken it myself to ensure my victory?"

Cedar bristled. *Saule provided the Sephrim?*

"Exactly," said Genevre.

"I often envisaged such scenarios, but after each imagining had run its course, I inevitably returned to being trapped within Cedar."

"When you agreed to the conjunction, what did you expect would happen?

"I had anticipated *rest*, which I desperately needed after hundreds of years on the Council. When I imagined what would become of me, I pictured myself in a suspended state — like a prolonged immersion in a catacomb alembic, not agony in a death-defying entombment. But as it turns out, alchemical death does not allow one to rest in peace — at least apparently not when conjunction is manipulated through Ravenea's blood alchemy. The conjunction forced me to writhe in prison. And all for naught. Back then, we couldn't risk my knowledge — of Ilex and Melia, of you, of Kalina or Arjan — being inadvertently exposed to the Council. Now, at the height of dimensional crisis, none of those secrets appears to matter. Time, with perspective along for the ride, has shifted our priorities. Cedar even knows of Arjan now."

"She doesn't know he's—"

"Ravenea, always the sleuth, uncovered their relationship," continued Saule. "She told Cedar outright — not realizing Cedar didn't already know — and then repressed the memory for Cedar's journey here. Ravenea did not want you to know that Cedar knew the truth about Arjan."

Truth about Arjan? Repressed the memory? Cedar felt both startled and betrayed.

"Like any Azoth Magen worth her weight in alchemical salts," said Saule, "Ravenea wanted additional information, which she assumed might be accessible through Cedar's relationship with each of us."

"Was she hoping for a loophole to the vow she made with you?" Genevre asked.

"We vowed not to speak of Ilex and Melia *for an eternity.* Would conjunctive resurrection cause an eternal dilemma or a temporal loophole?"

"Clearly, we have underestimated Ravenea's powers."

"I think she has underestimated yours," said Saule. "She may have suspected you had something to hide, but she made no reference to the *Osmanthian* folio."

Osmanthian folio? Cedar sighed in frustration. She felt lost. She knew of the *Osmanthian Codex* but not of a particular folio. Clearly, Genevre and Saule had shared secrets that neither had shared with her. Had they deemed her untrustworthy? She clenched her virtual fists and screamed forcefully in the imposed silence.

"Do you have a car?" asked Saule.

"Yes, why?"

"We need to immerse ourselves in water. Can you take us to a river or lake?"

"Yes. But again, why?"

"I will explain at the water."

Cedar had no idea what awaited her at the water, but she now feared for her life. What if they entered the water? What if she could no longer breathe? The agonizing voiceless existence against which she had been wrestling for untold hours had, when threatened, become her only treasure.

As Saule pulled the car door closed, Cedar cried out to Genevre for salvation.

During the first twenty minutes of the drive, Genevre repeatedly attempted to engage Saule in conversation. But even her attempts at small talk proved useless. Saule would respond with a word or two and then lapse again into silence. So Genevre's thoughts inevitably wandered as they progressed along the road towards the lake.

She worried that if Cedar re-emerged, she would accuse Genevre of recklessness for having brought forth Saule at the risk of losing Cedar permanently. *When*, she made the mental correction — *when*, not *if*, Cedar re-emerged. Genevre imagined herself explaining everything, including her arguments with Ruis. She thought about that day almost a century ago when Ruis confronted her in the Council archives. She had been careless not to recognize his suspicions as anything more than jealousy over her growing intimacy with Cedar. If she had known that Elders could do as they please under the auspices of war measures, including rifling through the personal belongings of subordinates, she would have left the *Osmanthian Codex* folio hidden in the San Miguel Mission, as she had done when living in Santa Fe between Flaw dimension tenures. But she had assumed it would be safe in Council dimension hidden amidst her multitude of books, ready to be moved along with her to whichever protectorate she was assigned.

To her dismay, Ruis had not only found but confiscated the folio. He accused her of manuscript mutilation, even though he had no evidence beyond the folio itself. *I would never deface a Council manuscript! I found the folio in an outside world library!* Of necessity, she had lied about the folio's origin. Though Ruis certainly would never have fathomed the truth, and though he failed to produce a defaced Council manuscript as proof of her crimes, Ruis could not risk treachery during such a volatile time. As she later learned, he therefore set about convincing the Elders to banish her from Council dimension until the end of the first outside world war.

During the two intervening years, Genevre presumed she would never see her treasured folio again. Then, when Cedar agreed to her marriage proposal and brought her back into Council dimension, she bided her time. After a few months spent proving her reliability, Genevre approached Ruis and requested the return of her *outside world souvenir.* He raised an eyebrow but did not protest. Evidently, he had deemed that a folio removed from its original source was useless to him.

Genevre hid the folio within an obscure Council manuscript of the North Library until circumstances necessitated a more secure hiding place. But in the aftermath of the Qingdao incident and the outbreak of a second world war, she feared another war-measures banishment. She then transferred the folio to a scroll cylinder and asked Saule to hide it in the outside world. *Do not reveal its whereabouts to anyone — not even to me,* Genevre had instructed, *until I request it of you.* Alongside her various other secrets, this one had thereafter been doubly secure: it resided within Saule, who later resided within Cedar. Genevre had had no need to retrieve it until now — now that the primordial blood of its inscription, whatever that inscription might be, could become her saving grace.

Abiquiu Lake, New Mexico — 2014

"Wait," said Saule, gently gripping Genevre's arm. "We need to talk before stepping in."

Standing a few inches from the water, Genevre moved her toes against some pebbles. They wore ill-fitting bathing suits that Genevre had bought years ago.

"Aren't you worried about privacy here?" asked Genevre, scanning the area for signs of outside world folk. Though no one lingered nearby — the temperature of the water too cold that day for people without alchemical enhancements — Genevre nonetheless felt exposed, vulnerable to the potential intrusion of passersby.

"Yes, we do need privacy. That's the reason I brought you here."

"I don't understand."

"Shortly after Cedar and Sadira first became intimate," began Saule, "they took an outside world trip to Hawaii. Even from my limited vantage point, I could appreciate the beauty — clear skies, bright sun, an expanse of soft sand. My jealousy of Cedar subsided. I relaxed into knowing that Sadira was happy. I could be content for a while. And then it happened."

"What?"

"They walked into the water."

"And?"

"At first, the effect was mild . . . a sort of static, like interference on an outside world screen. The static came and went as Cedar and Sadira walked over the sand towards the ocean. Several minutes passed before I recognized the pattern: each time Cedar stepped into a puddle or tidepool, the static increased. Whenever she stepped back onto the sand, all was well. But when they reached the ocean's edge and Cedar strode into the waves, the static gave way to a sharp pain. When the water reached her waist, I lost my ability to hear. And when she began to swim, when the water reached her shoulders, I lost my sight. Moments later, I could sense nothing at all. Even straining in the darkness, I could not perceive Cedar's heartbeat. For over an hour, I existed in that void — an absence that somehow sustained my existence but denied me all sensation. I was terrified."

"And then they walked out and your senses returned?"

"Yes — as they walked into shallower water and then back onto the sand. When I regained access to my regular prison, the relief was overwhelming. For a few days, I assumed the combination of salt and water had caused the sensory deprivation — some sort of elemental and alchemical disruption. But then they immersed themselves in a lake, and the effect remained the same. Over the years, it became clear that Cedar's immersion into any natural body of water would, for all intents and purposes, anaesthetize me."

"Saule, that sounds horrific."

"You cannot imagine."

Genevre's response moved from sympathy to dread. She realized why Saule had made the request that they walk into the lake.

"You told me Cedar was unconscious! But we're at the water so we can speak in private, aren't we? You believe Cedar is trapped but conscious inside you!"

"I did believe she was unconscious. But a few hours ago, I thought I detected something of her. So when you mentioned the folio, I decided we should take precautions."

"She must be terrified!" Genevre grabbed Saule by the shoulders and looked into her eyes. "Cedar? Cedar? Are you all right?"

"Even if she can hear you, she cannot respond."

"What do you mean *even if* she can hear me? Is she conscious or not?"

"My guess is that she has been moving in and out of consciousness. If Cedar's conscious right now, she will know what to expect as we enter the water."

"And if she's unconscious? What if she regains consciousness once we're immersed? She'll awaken amidst sensory deprivation! No, Saule, we cannot do that to her! She's my wife. I've hurt her too much already."

"Genevre, I must speak with you in private."

"Why? If Cedar was conscious earlier, then she's already heard everything."

"So far, we have said nothing that Cedar does not already know or will learn within the upcoming weeks. But the folio is yours alone, and I pledged to reveal its location only to you. We must speak privately."

Genevre realized, face to the sun and sky, that the water likewise provided her the opportunity to tell Saule what she had been avoiding.

"Okay. But we'll remain in shallow water, so

Cedar can maintain her sight and see her surroundings. I need her to know she's safe."

"That won't be deep enough—" Saule began, but then paused and turned towards the shore. "Fine," she continued. "Let's do that. We will sit in shallow water — waist deep, our shoulders exposed. Cedar will be able to see but not hear. But don't face me; we cannot risk Cedar reading our facial expressions or lips."

Once they found a suitable location, they were able to sit comfortably, their shoulders well above water. Immediately thereafter, Genevre admitted that Ilex and Melia had dissolved.

"No!" Saule cried, looking directly at Genevre. Tears began to well. She then completely immersed herself, head included. She remained under water until the need for air forced her to resurface. As Saule lay gasping, Genevre worried about Cedar. What was Saule doing? What must Cedar be thinking?

"How?" Saule finally asked, turning away from Genevre.

"I don't fully understand it myself. It involved the release of the bees and — I presume given the Council dissolutions — the fallout from the other mutual conjunctions."

"What happened? Did they suffer, like Tera and Olea?"

Genevre recalled Jinjing's disturbing account. "No," she assured Saule. Genevre described the dissolution of Ilex and Melia in as much detail as she could manage. Like Jinjing, Saule asked to hold the amber pendant. Unlike Jinjing, Saule held it to both her heart and her lips. Jinjing had admired Ilex and Melia as friends and colleagues, but Saule had clearly loved them. And Genevre had no means to console her.

Returning the pendant to Genevre, tears and lake water marking her face, Saule moved directly to the topic that had led her to request immersion in the lake. "I hid the folio among outside world archival materials that I assumed eventually would be relocated."

"Relocated to a location unknown even to you?"

"Yes."

"Please tell me you put a contingency plan in place."

"Of course, but to activate that plan, you will need to consult with Kalina."

Over the next fifteen minutes, Saule provided all the details Genevre would require. To Genevre's dismay, Saule had solicited Kalina's assistance to inscribe a blood-alchemy talisman onto the folio. When deemed necessary, an identical talisman could be released into the outside world that, in turn, would trigger a potential Initiate to unearth the folio. The two talismans together would then aid the potential Initiate in achieving contact with Council.

"I presume Kalina has already inscribed the talisman into the Council Book," said Saule. "Once I describe it to you, you can inscribe it into the Rebel

Book. With both books in the outside world, a potential Initiate of either the Alchemists' Council or the Rebel Branch will have the means to find the folio."

"You needn't have made the folio's retrieval so complex."

"You needn't have made my existence so complex."

Genevre nodded solemnly. She listened without further interruption to Saule's description of the talisman. All appeared settled in the immediate aftermath until Genevre suggested they return to Santa Fe to commence the ritual to reinstate Cedar. Saule patently refused. Genevre chastised herself for not predicting this outcome before departing for the lake. She had brought none of the alchemical supplies required to restore the original conjunction.

"Saule, you made your choice. You cannot leave Cedar trapped. You promised—"

"No, Genevre. You don't understand. I am asking you to free us both."

But when Saule explained, and when Genevre fully understood, she could not move. "No! Saule!" she cried.

"Yes. Cedar is required for the Renewal. I am not. The choice is logical."

"Logic is irrelevant!"

"Then hear my emotional plea! I *cannot* go back. Being trapped for years within Cedar traumatized me. If you refuse my request, you are condemning me to an eternity of torture. Could you live with that knowledge?"

"And if I agree, can I live with *that* knowledge?"

"Listen to me, Genevre. I have been immeasurably faithful to all of you — Ilex, Melia, Kalina, Arjan, Jinjing, Cedar, and you. Now *all of you* owe me the courtesy of fulfilling my one final request. You must bear the burden alone, Genevre, because you are the one here with me now. I have made my choice. I ask only that you respect it."

Genevre stood up and walked slowly towards deeper water. Saule followed. When the water was deep enough that, when sitting, it reached her shoulders, Genevre turned to Saule and embraced her. Finally letting go, she fought back tears.

"Ravenea may have supplied the blood, but you are the person who helped Ilex and Melia conceive me. You are one of my parents. You are my mother."

"Thank you, my love. Goodbye."

Saule fully submerged herself in the water. And Genevre held her beneath the surface, tears streaming down her face, until Saule's struggle finally ended.

When Cedar regained consciousness, she could feel waves lapping against her body. She quickly realized that, except for her shoulders and head, she was entirely immersed in water. The sensation felt cool and comforting. At first, she thought she was lying in a catacomb alembic. But when she opened her eyes, she could see a bright blue sky sprinkled with clouds. Someone was supporting her, holding her hand and keeping her head above the water.

"Where are we?" Cedar asked.

As she leaned forward, Cedar recognized Genevre, who seemed surprised by Cedar's question. Her wet hair brushed against Cedar's cheek as she examined her face. She stared into Cedar's eyes so attentively that Cedar wondered if they were about to kiss.

"It worked," said Genevre. She leaned back again, smiled, and then frowned.

"What did?" Cedar asked, struggling to sit up.

"Saule is gone."

"How can you tell?"

"Your eyes have changed colour."

"Where are we?" Cedar sat fully upright. She could see they were in a lake, several feet from land, well removed from a cluster of people walking along the shoreline.

"At a lake, about an hour's drive from Santa Fe."

"And where is Saule?"

"She . . . drowned," said Genevre. "The elemental water overcame her quintessential fire."

Cedar thought of the fire that had consumed Olea. "Yet I remain alive and disoriented."

"Losing a conjunctive partner must have physical repercussions. You'll need to regain your strength. We should go home. You can rest. The dissolution of Saule will have registered through the Lapidarian Quintessence of Council dimension. As soon as the Scribes and Readers interpret the resonance, the Azoth Magen will surely request your return."

At the thought of Ravenea, Cedar began to remember the hours leading up to erasure — the ruby liqueur, the shattering crystal, the blood-alchemy palimpsest. Anger overcame her.

"Arjan!" she exclaimed. Cedar moved swiftly away from Genevre, stood up, and glared down at her. "How could you have kept him from me?!"

Genevre lifted herself to her feet and stood facing Cedar. But before Genevre could utter even a sentence of explanation, Cedar had clasped Genevre's upper arms. She gripped firmly and struggled to push Genevre back into the water. Cedar needed to be the one in control, the one holding the power, the one demanding restitution. But Genevre fought back, and the dissolution of Saule had weakened Cedar. So they soon fell together into the water, writhing in struggle. Cedar finally collapsed, exhausted. She sat in the water, slouched forward, and sobbed. Genevre put an arm around Cedar's shoulder and pulled her close. Cedar jerked away.

"You lied to me!" she yelled. "You led me to believe our child had died!"

"She *had* died! Our daughter died in my arms,

Cedar! I needed to save our son! Saule convinced me that keeping our son a secret from everyone other than Ilex and Melia was the only means to keep him safe."

"Saule convinced you? Genevre, I was your *wife*. He was our *son*! I deserved more than half-truths and promises of a better world. I believed you! And you betrayed me. How do you expect me ever to trust you again?"

"I don't," said Genevre. "But right now, I'm the only one by your side — literally."

Genevre stood up again and held out a hand. Cedar paused before accepting. And she let go of Genevre the moment she was fully upright. On that day, in that moment, Cedar believed she could never forgive Genevre. Yet she followed her closely as they walked out of the water.

Santa Fe — 2014

"Why did you leave me?" asked Cedar, exasperated.

"I needed to release Saule. I didn't know you'd be conscious," said Genevre.

"No. I mean, why did you leave Council dimension at the end of the second outside world war? Did your guilt necessitate avoiding me?"

Genevre dipped a pen into the ink several times more than necessary. She held it over a sheet of parchment and let an indigo drop fall with an audible splash. If they were working together on an official Council manuscript, they would have swiftly excised the blemished page from the volume. Cedar could imagine Obeche reprimanding Genevre for her carelessness. But the aesthetics of the splotch inexplicably intrigued her, especially as Genevre added a series of words surrounding it in a spiral pattern.

"I could no longer work with you," Genevre finally responded.

"Why?" Cedar placed a hand on the manuscript, nearly touching the shimmering ink.

"My disdain for the Council and my . . . connection with you, and therefore my guilt over my lies, had escalated as the war progressed. Remaining in Council dimension under those conflicting circumstances would have been unbearably deceitful."

During the years between the outside world wars, Cedar had repeatedly questioned Genevre's intentions staying in Council dimension. But she had refocused her attention on her work and, of course, on her beloved Ruis. So the occasions on which she contemplated speaking with Genevre about the daughter they had lost together became increasingly rare as the years progressed. At the time, Cedar could not have guessed that Genevre's departure had anything to do with their son. And now her explanation seemed frustratingly inadequate.

Genevre set down her pen and reached for Cedar's hand.

"Don't touch me!" Cedar snapped, pulling away. "I don't care how you currently feel about me, Genevre. You lied to me for years! You let me believe I had killed our daughter. And you hid our son from me. And then you abandoned me!"

"I told you, I hid our son from everyone, Cedar. Saule convinced me! For the good of—"

"No excuses!" seethed Cedar.

Genevre sighed. "No excuses. You're right. Nothing I can say will suffice. But guilt has plagued me, Cedar. Guilt tinged every decision I made during those years with you. Whenever we worked together, I could sense your sorrow — the depth of it, beneath what you exposed to Council or even to yourself. I wanted to tell you—"

"Shut up!" Cedar screamed. She stood up, glaring at Genevre. "If you had truly wanted to tell me back then, you would have found a means to do so! And if you had cared about me at all, you would have told me the truth. But you did *nothing*! Nothing! Because after I had played my part, I was no longer scripted into your carefully laid plans."

"Cedar! No! That's not true! I wanted to tell you the truth. I *ached* to talk with you, to tell you we had a child together. But I could not endanger Arjan or, frankly, myself."

"I hardly think you were—"

"Ruis had always suspected I was aligned with the Rebel Branch. If I had stayed, if we had grown closer thanks to our son, Ruis would have found a way to discredit me to the Elders like he did at the beginning of the first outside world war!"

"And I would have defended you, if I had known I had something to defend," Cedar said quietly. She was tired. She had spent hours trapped inside Saule, moving in and out of consciousness, almost drowning. The last thing she wanted now was to hear Genevre describe what might have happened *if only. If only I hadn't lied to you. If only I had told you about our son.* Cedar wanted nothing more to do with Genevre. She longed for Sadira, but tears began to well at that thought.

"You took *her* from me too," said Cedar.

"Our daughter?"

"No — Sadira. I mourned her in the Amber Garden. Now she has returned."

"Yes, and you can return to her as soon as Ravenea calls you back to Council."

"No, Genevre. Because of you, I've lost her as well. Sadira has mutually conjoined with Kalina, a circumstance that I assume you permitted. She is no longer herself, no longer able to be alone with me in any sense. And I learned enough during my confinement within Saule to know that you also agreed to our conjunction. I had assumed myself victorious, believed Saule dissolved. But now we know differently — the entire time she was conscious inside me. How can I help but believe she influenced me in some way, that her presence — her still-viable Quintessence — might be the reason I became attracted to Sadira? So, you see? Because of you, I neither have hope for a future with Sadira nor faith in my past with you. I am done with your lies, Genevre! I am done with you!"

Genevre worked alone at the living room table. Since their argument two days earlier, Cedar had spoken with her only when necessary to complete the manuscript work. Then, a few hours ago, Cedar had put down her pen and walked out of the house without saying a word. Genevre assumed she would return shortly given Ravenea's message: she had directed Cedar to return to Council dimension as soon as possible. And since Genevre had only a few finishing touches to add to the manuscript, they both assumed Cedar's permanent departure would occur that night. Perhaps she had gone for a walk around Santa Fe before Council duties would once again demand all her time and attention.

Cedar's absence provided Genevre an unexpected opportunity to inscribe the blood-alchemy talisman onto five key pages. Like the Council Book, the Rebel Book's primary purpose was to illuminate the path towards Initiation for potential alchemists. But, thanks to the inscribed talismans, the book would provide additional instruction to one particular individual. *That* person — a yet-to-be-discovered individual of the ancestral bloodline

— would extract the *Osmanthian Codex* folio from its secreted location. Genevre herself had no means to locate the person. But the talismans would draw the Keeper of the Folio not only to the folio itself but also to the primary dimensions. Now that Genevre had set up the pieces, she need only wait to see who would make the next move.

VI
Council Dimension — 2014

"Long live the Quintessence!"

The call of the Azoth Magen reverberated through Council Chambers.

"Long live the Alchemists' Council!" responded everyone but Jaden.

She could not dutifully reply by rote. Shock had silenced her. Learning about the erasure of an Elder had been difficult enough to bear; realizing that the Elder could be the Novillian Scribe who had first accompanied her into Council dimension was horrifying. Jaden attempted but failed to focus on what Ravenea and the Azoths were saying. Repeatedly she called to mind her first contact. Who had met her at the Vancouver Art Gallery? She could no longer see the person's face or hear the voice. Only fragmented images remained. What else had she forgotten? She felt unbalanced. She longed to return to the catacombs or even the outside world, to remove herself from the Alchemists' Council and its perpetual chaos. If only the bee stings had killed her.

As the meeting progressed, as the disturbing details of the rebellion's fallout multiplied, Jaden's anxiety grew. Earlier, on the short walk between her residence chambers and the main Council building, Jaden had noticed nothing amiss. Indeed, she had admired the glistening channel waters, assuming Council dimension had healed from the breach during her weeks in the catacomb alembic. She realized now how wrong she had been. Worse, as an Initiate — even as a newly ascended *Senior* Initiate — she felt useless. She had no means to leave Council dimension, yet she had nothing to contribute to this world. She felt a sharp pain in her head. Perhaps she should have remained another day or two in the catacombs. Then she noticed Sadira momentarily move a hand to her own head. She remembered then that she and Sadira shared the same branch of the Alchemical Tree. Perhaps these pains were effects of the erasure that all members of the erased Elder's branch shared.

She watched the Scribes, seeking a familiar face. When Tera turned in Jaden's direction to hear a Reader's comment, she startled Jaden. Tera looked different. She looked substantially *older*. And the colour of her skin had changed to a lighter shade than it had been before. She also had a wound on her somewhat wrinkled forehead. Had the Fourth Rebellion caused Tera's injury? The battle might account for an unhealed wound, but the shifts in age and skin tone were inexplicable. Was Jaden misremembering? Or were the alchemists, like the dimension, changing because of the fallout? Perhaps everything she was currently witnessing was an elaborate catacomb-induced nightmare from which she had not yet emerged. To comfort herself, she reached for her pendant. Then she remembered she no longer wore one. Someone had removed it after she had released the bees.

The bees! Jaden's focus since emerging from the catacombs had been on the effects of their stings, not on the consequences of their release. What if the rebel breach had nothing to do with the dimensional fallout? What if her release of the bees had triggered the disintegration? Or what if Council dimension were unable to repair itself without the aid of its insect alchemists? Jaden shook her head, attempting not to cry.

During the final torturous hour of the meeting, Jaden learned the reason for Tera's physical changes — the dissolution of Olea, the one with whom Tera had conjoined. Thanks to eyewitness updates, she could also now vividly picture the melting of the Amber Garden. While others mingled to exchange concerns or departed to begin their assigned tasks, Jaden remained seated and immobile. Once Council Chambers had emptied, she lifted her head, staring into the rafters, watching the play of light and shadow on the ceiling, peering at the cloud-laden sky outside the upper windows that flanked the room. The silent tranquility belied the disorder both in her mind and beyond the walls. Something about that moment reminded Jaden of a synagogue she had visited years ago. She longed to remember the one erased, not outside world architecture.

"Come with me."

Jaden turned, startled, towards the voice behind her.

"Magistrate— I mean *Reader* Sadira, I—"

"Your presence has been requested elsewhere. Follow me. Do not ask questions."

Jaden had no will to protest. She felt confused, defeated, guilty. In silent submission, she followed Sadira along light-drenched hallways to the Salix portal. She wondered briefly if Sadira planned to accompany her back to Vancouver, if she could retreat into her old life again. But she soon abandoned speculation and steeled herself for the inevitable nausea of portal transport.

Santa Fe — 2014

Upon arrival at their destination, bright sunlight momentarily obstructed her vision. But once she turned her head towards the shadows, Jaden recognized the location. Sadira had brought her to Santa Fe. Quickly orienting herself in relation to the San Miguel Mission, Jaden took a few steps in the direction of La Fonda and Palace of the Governors.

"This way," Sadira called to her, heading in the opposite direction.

The journey into unfamiliar territory immediately thwarted Jaden's relief. Not until they crossed the yard of a small clay-hued house in the shade of a cottonwood tree did Sadira enlighten her on the journey's purpose.

"We have come here to retrieve your pendant."

Jaden stared in alarm at the person who had spoken. "Who are you? Where's Sadira? I don't—"

The woman sighed. "I'm Kalina. You will remember me soon enough. Come inside." Kalina walked along the narrow stone path leading to the door and knocked softly. Jaden quickly followed, standing behind and slightly to the left of Kalina as they waited. When had Sadira departed? When had Kalina arrived? Back in Council dimension, Jaden had assumed her lapses in memory were due to the erasure of the Elder. Now she had to admit the possibility that the bees had inflicted unhealable neurological damage.

Kalina knocked again with more force. Seconds later, a strikingly beautiful woman answered the door. Her long dark hair featured one narrow but distinct white strip.

"Hello Jaden," she said. "I'm Genevre, former outside world scribe."

"I am Jaden, Junior . . . no, Senior Initiate of the Alchemists' Council. I have carried my pendant . . . no. I've lost my pendant. I . . . never mind. Sorry. I'm just Jaden."

Genevre and Kalina both smiled.

"No need for a formal introduction," said Genevre.

"Have we met before?" Jaden asked. No longer able to rely on her memory, the direct approach seemed best.

"Not officially. Several years ago, we crossed paths in Qingdao, but we did not meet."

"Years ago? I've not—" she began, then quickly recast. "My only memory of being in Qingdao is relatively recent. I don't recall—"

"As you may have surmised by now," interjected Kalina, "the situation is complex."

Genevre ushered them into her front room. The space was bright and colourful, replete with eclectic furnishings. Books, parchment sheets, pens, and inks cluttered the main table. Kalina gestured for Jaden to sit on the sofa. She then left the room, returning shortly thereafter with two other women. One was Jinjing, Keeper of the Book of the Qingdao protectorate. Jaden did not recognize the other. In the bright sunlight streaming into the room, the woman's eyes seemed an intense bluish-green that discomforted Jaden.

"Do you remember me, Jaden?" the stranger asked.

The other women stood a few feet in front of Jaden, observing her intently.

"No," Jaden said. She sighed. "My memory has become . . . not fully functional."

"I believe this belongs to you," said the stranger. From the fingers of her left hand dangled a fissure-marred, turquoise pendant on a long silver chain.

"Yes!" said Jaden as the woman stepped close enough to slip the chain over Jaden's head.

"I had hidden it in the Santa Fe protectorate to retrieve for you."

The moment Jaden grasped her pendant, forgotten memories began swiftly to resurface. The rushing sensation made her dizzy. She leaned back against the sofa for a few seconds before jolting forward to cry, "Cedar!"

Cedar smiled and nodded.

"I don't understand. Sadira told me you . . . you had been erased. Shouldn't pendant proximity ensure that I *don't* remember you?"

"Your interim pendant was infused only with Lapidarian essence, not inlaid with a fragment of the Lapis itself," said Cedar. "More importantly, as you should recall shortly, it was fused with a fragment of Dragonblood Stone, which can restore alchemically erased memories."

Jaden nodded. "Yes. Of course." She glanced towards Kalina and then Jinjing. "The fragment you gave to me in Qingdao. The one Cedar later told me she had given to you."

"Yes," said Cedar. "The very one."

"I remember now. But I don't understand."

"You will," said Kalina. "You'll be staying here for the next few days to recover your memories and confer with Genevre and Jinjing. Meanwhile, Sadira and I will accompany Cedar back to Council dimension. The Azoth Magen awaits us."

With the mention of Sadira came the memory of the mutual conjunctions: Kalina with Sadira, Arjan with Dracaen. Jaden's earlier anxiety was immediately replaced with relief. She now understood the privilege of this moment. Though still only an Initiate, she held knowledge unknown to many Council alchemists. In releasing the bees, in confiscating and hiding the pendant, in being erased from Council and banished to the outside world, Cedar had ensured that Jaden would be able to regain her memories, see both members of each conjoined pair, and continue her role in the revolution. She then remembered the words Cedar had uttered before ripping away Jaden's pendant: *What I am about to do is for your own good.* The last thing she remembered before succumbing to the bee stings was the look of concern in Cedar's eyes.

"Wait!" Jaden called when she noticed Kalina had already left the house, and Cedar had one foot over the threshold. She stopped and turned towards Jaden. "Your eyes! They—"

"They reverted to their original colour after Saule departed," Cedar responded.

"Departed? You mean she dissolved? Like Tera's partner?"

"No, unlike Olea, Saule did not alchemically — dimensionally — disintegrate."

"What happened to her?"

"Genevre killed her," said Cedar, slamming the door shut.

Council Dimension — 2014

As upsetting as they were, the arguments with Genevre had offered one advantage: Cedar longed desperately to return to Council dimension, free from seeing Genevre indefinitely. The Rebel Book, as Genevre had dubbed the counterpart to the Council Book, had caused their final argument. Genevre had suggested Cedar deposit it nearby — in Albuquerque, if not in Santa Fe. But Cedar had refused. *Azoth Magen Ravenea requested that I bring the book to her*, Cedar had announced, thus bringing the argument to an inflexible end.

And so it was that Cedar, thanks to Sadira and Kalina's transport assistance, now found herself standing in the Salix portal anteroom holding the newly inscribed manuscript before both Azoth Magen Ravenea and High Azoth Dracaen.

"Quite the welcoming party," said Cedar. She stared at Dracaen, hoping for a glimmer of Arjan.

"Whom do you see?" asked Ravenea, taking the Rebel Book and gesturing towards the Rebel High Azoth.

"Dracaen," Cedar responded.

"Nothing of Arjan?" asked Ravenea.

"No. Where is he?"

"Interesting," said Dracaen. "I continue to find this conjunction confounding."

"The process of your *un*-erasure will take a few days," said Ravenea, shifting topics. "Its lack of precedent has left the Scribes and Readers a bit out of sorts. Sadira will escort you to your chambers, where you will remain until they have completed the revision process."

"Where is Arjan?" Cedar repeated.

"Unavailable," responded Dracaen. "Likely by choice."

Cedar experienced a visceral flashback to her confinement within Saule. She grabbed Dracaen by the arm and insisted on seeing Arjan.

"Protocol!" Ravenea commanded loudly, but Cedar did not release her grip on Dracaen.

"Do you forget who I am?" bellowed Dracaen.

"Do you forget who *I* am?" Cedar retorted.

"Do not presume the Fourth Rebellion fallout has resulted in instantaneous anarchy," seethed Dracaen. "Though conjoined with Arjan, I remain High Azoth of the Rebel Branch."

"And I am an Elder of the Alchemists' Council!" snapped Cedar. "You, High Azoth, are a visitor to this dimension."

"Dracaen is an honoured guest," said Ravenea. "At my invitation, he has come to Council dimension to consult with me. You, on the other hand, are here only to deliver the newly minted Rebel Book. Currently, you are *not* an Elder, Cedar. Indeed, you are not presently a member of the Council at all. Until the erasure's reversal, you remain in limbo. Thus you too are currently a guest to this dimension. And you will do as I tell you to do. Unhand Dracaen!"

Defeated, Cedar released her grip. She realized in that moment, aware of the pain in her fingers as she opened her hand, that without her Council pendant, she would remain powerless here. Her influence in Council dimension was only marginally better than it had been within Saule in the outside world. Her hundreds of years of alchemical training and experience meant nothing without Quintessence, without the conjoined fragments of Lapis and Dragonblood Stone embedded in her pendant. She looked towards Sadira, hoping to take comfort in her warm familiarity. But all she could see was Kalina who, inevitably, reminded her of Genevre.

Kalina accompanied Cedar to residence chambers. As Ravenea had advised just prior to departure, they walked in silence, heads down, so as not to draw attention from passersby. But when they reached the door to Cedar's room, Kalina asked to come in to talk. Though chatting with Genevre's daughter was the last thing Cedar wanted to do, she realized that she no longer had the will to object.

"Dracaen found it interesting, but I find it utterly astounding," said Kalina as soon as she had closed the door.

"What? Mutual conjunction?" asked Cedar.

"That you can see both Dracaen and me. Yet you cannot currently see Arjan or Sadira. In Council dimension, without your pendant and its Dragonblood fragment, you should be able to see *only* Arjan and Sadira. And yet here we are, plainly seeing and hearing each other. Why is it that you can see Dracaen and me outside Flaw dimension?"

Cedar balked. Kalina was right. Something was clearly amiss.

"Did she give you another Dragonblood fragment?" asked Kalina.

"Who?"

"Genevre."

"No," said Cedar. "At least not that I know." She checked her pockets. "Wait . . . she did inject me with her blood. Perhaps—"

"Ah! Your valiant protector," said Kalina.

"Protector? Her blood released Saule, imprisoned me, and is now preventing me from seeing both my son and my beloved."

"You'll be able to see them soon enough — as soon as the Elders return your Council pendant.

After that, while wearing a Lapidarian pendant fused with Dragonblood Stone, your blood fused with Genevre's, your alchemical powers will multiply exponentially. Even rebel manuscripts might reveal their secrets to you. Genevre didn't merely *inject* you; she inoculated you."

Everything Cedar thought she had understood shifted as if Kalina's interpretation of events had removed a veil. She opened the balcony doors, moved to the railing, and looked to her left towards the Amber Garden. The spectacle was shocking. During her weeks in Santa Fe, the trees of the Amber Garden had all dissolved, leaving behind a stagnant pool of amber-coloured sludge. She knew she could not yet forgive Genevre. She knew she would yet be awash in waves of anger. But neither could she completely abandon hope. Cedar inherently understood that, along the road towards healing the dimensions, she would inevitably cross paths again with her chemical spouse.

Santa Fe — 2014

Needing a moment to herself, Genevre had retreated to the kitchen after explaining the complexities of Saule's death to Jaden. Now Jinjing and Jaden sat on the living room sofa talking about Qingdao. Genevre could see and hear them through the kitchen doorway. Clutching a blue and gold cushion, Jaden asked questions. Jinjing provided answers.

"So, Cedar sent Arjan and me to Qingdao purposely? She knew about the time breach?"

"No. But we did — Genevre, Kalina, and I have known since 1939," said Jinjing. "We planned accordingly, adjusted manuscripts, influenced decisions. During her time with the Council, Kalina hid three Dragonblood fragments in Council dimension. When time and events aligned, when I received confirmation that you and Arjan would be working in the Qingdao protectorate, I sent word to Cedar. She brought me one of the fragments before you and Arjan arrived."

Genevre placed a tray of sugared cranberry biscuits on the table. She motioned for Jaden to help herself. But Jaden remained focused on Jinjing.

"Arjan told me that his grandparents had brought him to Qingdao as a child — that he was the child we saw. Were Ilex and Melia also with you in 1939?"

"Yes. Both in 1939 and in 2014, they were in Qingdao."

"Where are they now?"

Jinjing looked at Genevre.

"They died," said Genevre.

"What?" Jaden stared wide-eyed at Genevre. "What happened?"

Neither Genevre nor Jinjing responded. Genevre knew Jaden was struggling to assemble the pieces, and she feared overwhelming her completely.

"Please tell me the truth," said Jaden. "Is their death connected with my moving through time in Qingdao? Is that why I'm here? Am I partly to blame?"

"You couldn't have known," Jinjing reassured her.

"Known what?"

Genevre finally offered up the story bit by bit. She spoke of Ilex and Melia, of Saule and the pregnancy, of Dracaen and Kalina, of Cedar and Arjan, of the erasures, the manuscripts, the bees, the feeding, and, finally, of the primordial blood that now coursed through Jaden herself. Understandably, Jaden said nothing at first. She simply shook her head repeatedly, visibly distraught. Finally, she uttered not only a blunt summary but also a question that Genevre had been asking herself.

"So, my actions resulted in the deaths of Ilex and Melia. And now I thrive, infused with their blood. How can I live with that knowledge?"

"By choosing to remember what others could force you to forget," said Jinjing.

Council Dimension — 2014

Cedar stood at the edge of the Amber Garden surveying its remains. She had come here hoping for sanctuary to mourn Saule. But the tree under which Cedar had originally participated in Saule's Song of Mourning no longer existed. Both the tree and Saule were gone.

"Cedar?"

The voice startled her. She turned. "Arjan!"

"Dracaen has agreed to step into the shadows for an hour."

"Oh, Arjan!" She moved towards him, falling into his embrace.

To Cedar, he was no longer the clever new Initiate. Nor was he the conjoined partner of the High Azoth. He was her son. And she longed to get to know him as such.

"I need to assure you," he said as they walked together along the channel path, "that I hadn't remembered that you were my mother. Prior to my initiation to Council, I'd agreed to have my memories altered. I'd never met you, so I thought I had nothing to lose and everything to gain by masking parts of my history. I regret the pain my decision may have caused you. And now, knowing you as my Elder, I regret a lifetime of not knowing you as my mother."

"As do I," Cedar replied. "But we were both victims of others' decisions. And I understand that repressing your knowledge of me was merely a consequence of good intentions." She gestured towards a bench near the central fountain. They sat close to one another, listening to the water.

"We need to treasure these moments — every aspect," Cedar asserted gently. "Despite the Lapis, despite Quintessence, despite Elixir, I no longer hold faith in eternal life. Memories, people, this fountain with its sparkling water, the stones under our feet, the bodies with which we walk, all we know could disappear at any moment, regardless of the choices we make or intentions we hold. So, Arjan, my son, I need to assure you of only one thing: no matter the past, no matter the future, I am thankful for this time we have together here and now."

"Here and now," echoed Arjan, taking hold of Cedar's hand.

Santa Fe — 2014

Having agreed to meet with Genevre in Santa Fe, Arjan and Dracaen made their way through the streets between the Rebel Branch stronghold and Genevre's home. Arjan smiled, a habitual physical gesture of his that Dracaen typically attempted to suppress. That the High Azoth did not try to control their face or its expression during the walk made Arjan assume that he too anticipated their meeting with delight. Dracaen had, after all, admired Genevre for many years despite her betrayal on the day she tore the folio from the *Osmanthian Codex*. He had married her, he had conceived a child with her, and now he was mutually conjoined with her other child. Arjan assumed these bonds, like his own familial ties with Genevre, would inevitably pull at Dracaen's heartstrings. Of course, he remained uncertain whether the High Azoth had any such emotions.

"Remember," Arjan said aloud to Dracaen, "we agreed that I would be the one first visible to Genevre. You are to refrain from attempts to override me."

"Yes, Arjan. And you are to remember that after fifteen minutes, you are to surrender control to me for *my* fifteen minutes. Thereafter, Genevre's choice stands."

"You need not remind me of our agreement, Dracaen. I honour my word."

"As do I," declared Dracaen, "when circumstances justify doing so."

With Genevre's front gate mere steps away, Arjan refrained from response. Instead, he focused on maintaining control of their body and appearance. He needed Genevre to know she could trust his influence over Dracaen, to know that all remained well with the plan. When he knocked on her door, his hand felt and looked like his own.

"Arjan! Come in!" Genevre said.

She hugged him and gestured for him to sit. Arjan knew that Genevre would understand he could not speak openly. After all, Dracaen was not unconscious in the shadows; instead, fully but passively awake, he waited within and observed. He would both see and hear whatever communication passed between mother and son. Even physical gestures such as a roll of the eyes or a shrug would be physically discernible to Dracaen. They would necessarily engage in small talk. The meeting, after all, was a ruse — one meant to convince Dracaen that in agreeing to the mutual conjunction, he had made a wise decision.

"Has all been well?" Genevre asked. "Did the conjunction progress without incident?"

"Yes," Arjan responded. "The conjunction seems flawless — so to speak." He laughed and then relaxed into the conversation.

"How have you adjusted in these intervening weeks? Physically, I mean. How do you negotiate . . . everything?"

"Some actions come without effort — walking, for example. Others take active coordination — writing, eating, sex."

Genevre raised an eyebrow and smiled awkwardly. Perhaps she was thinking back to her marriage with Dracaen. Or to her wedding with Cedar. Or recognizing the peculiarity of the current situation: for all intents and purposes, her husband was now mutually conjoined with the son she had conceived with her wife.

Arjan regretted mentioning sex.

"Be careful," she advised. "Keep in mind that Ilex and Melia conceived me unexpectedly."

"So I've heard. Lesson learned," Arjan joked. They both laughed, but Arjan felt Dracaen shift in seeming discomfort.

"What are your intentions?" Genevre then asked, moving the conversation into a more serious arena. "For the foreseeable future, I mean."

Dracaen stirred again. His fifteen minutes of imposed passivity were evidently moving too slowly for the High Azoth.

"As I've told Dracaen," said Arjan, "I intend to refrain from proceeding rashly. Given the reports of fallout from Council dimension and the outside world, I've proposed several months of archival research and vigilant planning prior to taking an action we might otherwise regret."

"Sounds logical. Does Dracaen agree?"

"He disagrees with almost everything I suggest, even though I repeatedly remind him that we cannot yet know the complexities or long-term consequences of mutual conjunction on either of the primary dimensions, let alone in the outside world."

Arjan relished the remaining minutes of this conversation with his mother. Despite the lack of privacy, he nonetheless managed to convey to Genevre some of his frustrations with Dracaen.

"As experience has taught me," said Dracaen, suddenly taking control of their body and appearance, "unreasonable delays also have consequences." Arjan retreated as promised, wondering briefly and bitterly if Dracaen possessed some sort of alchemical stopwatch.

"Hello, Dracaen," Genevre said, her face betraying her attempt to mask her annoyance.

"We must proceed promptly with the plan for adjustments to the timeline," insisted Dracaen. "Ironically, we have no time to spare. We must ensure that the strength of the Rebel Branch continues far into the future. We must ensure the Flaw in the Stone remains permanently incised, that free will and mutual conjunction are assured not only for today but for eternity. We welcome your assistance with manuscript manipulation."

"Of course," replied Genevre. Arjan wondered if Dracaen could sense deception. "But my cautious nature leads me to side with Arjan. Acting in haste may prove detrimental."

"And all these years, I had assumed acting in haste was your forte!" Dracaen laughed.

"My prior tendency is precisely the reason I advise caution now."

"Fine," said Dracaen. "A compromise. I will agree to three months of research and planning. But thereafter we will proceed. In three months, you will report to Flaw dimension to assist us with preparing both the manuscripts and the ritual."

Three months was more time than Arjan had expected.

"The ritual? You said you wanted manuscript—" began Genevre.

"The blood-alchemy ritual to propel Arjan and me through time."

They now had three months to avoid revealing that, even with Genevre's assistance, Dracaen would not be able to propel their conjoined body through time in the manner he intended.

"Yes. Of course," said Genevre. "I apologize, Dracaen. These last few weeks have been trying. The dimensions themselves are changing, so I thought you might have adjusted your plan in consultation with Azoth Magen Ravenea. Perhaps you could provide me with an update on the specifics?"

Though Arjan remained silent, he flinched. Genevre's approach concerned him. They both needed Dracaen to believe the mutual conjunction would benefit the Rebel Branch at the expense of the Alchemists' Council. If Dracaen began to doubt Genevre's loyalty or willingness to help, he would distrust Arjan even more than he did already. Without trust, their conjunction would become unbearable — Dracaen would refuse to accept even Arjan's occasional counsel, let alone his physical dominance. Arjan and Genevre required the additional months to hone their influence over Dracaen and develop a plausible excuse for continued time travel failure.

"Once our Scribes have revised the manuscripts," Dracaen explained, "we will transport the texts into the past and future, at various advantageous points on the timeline, positioning them strategically through Council dimension archival libraries. As the current and future Council members reach out to the ancient sages for advice, inscribed candidates of our choosing will be deemed potential Council

Initiates. Gradually, Council Scribes and Readers will confirm entrenched Rebel Branch infiltrators as ideal partners for Council conjunctions. Within a few generations, the Alchemists' Council will comprise as many rebels as alchemists. And the Flaw in the Stone will strengthen. Meanwhile, we will proceed with reformulating Sephrim through blood alchemy to work towards mutual conjunction for all. To enhance the Quintessence of the Stone and its Flaw, the Sacrament of Conjunction will no longer require self-sacrifice. Choice will be a right that one and all inherently possess."

"My blood alchemy is powerful but limited," responded Genevre. "Certainly, opening a breach through time is possible. But adjusting the future via manuscript manipulation to match your whims is, at best, a speculative alchemical art."

Arjan could physically sense Dracaen's response — muscles tensed, nostrils flared.

"Azothian decisions are not made on a whim, Genevre. Neither are they solely my own. All Rebel Branch Elders will consult on the specifics — including Fraxinus, whom I know you respect and admire. As we have always done, as we now do: we strive through the Flaw to influence the dimensions for the benefit of all."

"As do the alchemists through the Lapis," replied Genevre. "They too believe they work towards eternity for all."

Dracaen stood, walked to the window, and

peered into the yard. "Yet they have consistently failed. The outside world has suffered excruciating consequences. As has Council dimension, long before their current chaos. My plan will bring an end to all suffering, allow the Flaw to expand, provide space for wounds to heal."

"Ointments and bandages are stop-gap solutions. A complete renaissance is required — destruction and resurrection."

Dracaen turned and smiled. "Perhaps I have underestimated you."

"Perhaps you have," said Genevre.

After a sizable pause, Dracaen returned to the table. Instead of aggressively toppling it and its contents, as Arjan feared he would, Dracaen collected a few dishes, moved them to the sideboard, took a seat, and gestured to the newly cleared expanse with open hands. "A pledge of your troth appears warranted," he announced formally. "I await your Tribute of Devotion."

Arjan understood by his words and gesture that Dracaen expected Genevre to place an object onto the table in front of him. Though any item she had possessed for more than a decade could be used, one of significant value — whether monetary or sentimental — was customary and preferable. After all, once accepted, the token would signify the bond of agreement between them. The item's return to Genevre would occur only after she had fulfilled all promises made during the formal pledge.

Genevre glanced around the room. Arjan assumed she sought an object valuable enough to satisfy Dracaen but insignificant enough to be disposable. She would need to choose carefully — otherwise Dracaen would deem her unfaithful. Finding nothing in sight, Genevre left the main room for a few minutes. When she returned, she held a decorated feather, which she placed directly into Dracaen's open hands. Though Arjan did not know the feather's significance, he could tell by Dracaen's reaction that it satisfied the requirement of the pledge. Thereafter, the agreement moved forward with Genevre promising to assist Dracaen and Arjan with both the manuscript revisions and time breaches. She requested only that Arjan be Keeper and Arbitrator of the Pledge.

"As my son and your conjunctive partner, he is the neutral party," she reasoned.

Dracaen and Arjan both agreed. Within the hour, they brought the preliminary meeting to a close. During the walk from Genevre's back to the rebel stronghold, Arjan contemplated the intricate beadwork on the feather. He learned that Dracaen had beaded it himself prior to presenting it to Genevre as a Gift of Proposal. In accepting it originally, Genevre had accepted Dracaen's proposal for a chemical wedding — the one that had resulted in the conception of Kalina. Arjan understood then that Genevre had presented the feather as a reminder to Arjan that his agreed-upon decisions would affect not only his mother and father but also his sister — the only other person he knew who could understand the challenges of being a mutually conjoined alchemical child upon whom rested the fate of all dimensions.

VII
Flaw Dimension — 2016

Dracaen and Arjan sat across from Fraxinus at a mahogany table in the centre of the sixth archival library. Books and manuscripts ran floor to ceiling along the surrounding walls, and wooden stacks full of archival materials filled the large room on either side of the centre table. When Arjan, within Dracaen, had first traversed the ancient archival libraries, awe had dazed him — each of the libraries, especially those in the sixth through ninth, appeared to house more manuscripts than all Council dimension's libraries put together. Not until weeks later had he learned the truth. The expanse of the secreted libraries was an alchemically enhanced illusion. The four largest of the libraries housed only a few thousand original manuscripts each, not the tens of thousands he had originally believed based on their extensive but deceptive appearance.

"How is this illusion maintained?" Arjan asked, gesturing outward.

"An elemental infinity spectre," explained Fraxinus, "manifested through blood-alchemy rituals implemented during the 5th Council by High Azoth Makala."

"To demonstrate her powers?" asked Arjan.

Fraxinus glared at him. "To hide treasured alchemical manuscripts from unwelcome intruders. High Azoth Makala had no need to perform parlour tricks to impress subordinates."

Arjan found Fraxinus exasperating. Hundreds of years as a Rebel Branch Elder gave him extensive knowledge but not the right to act as if he had known Makala. How much could any 19th Council Elder reasonably know about the motives of the 5th Council High Azoth? If Dracaen were any indication, High Azoths enjoyed their status, willingly flaunting their abilities over those of the lower Orders. *Choice is only as free as a dimension's dictator permits*, thought Arjan cynically.

"Is that still how you think of me, Azoth Fraxinus? Do I remain a subordinate despite my being conjoined with your High Azoth for two years?"

"You were a Junior Initiate of the Alchemists' Council. In that sense, yes, you are my subordinate. But you have mutually conjoined with High Azoth Dracaen. My respect for *him* has not changed despite

249

his conjunction with you. *He* officially remains my superior. *You* officially remain an outsider."

"If I am not fully aligned with both Dracaen and the Rebel Branch, how is it that you can see me — physically, I mean, here in Flaw dimension?" Arjan asked.

He could feel Dracaen smile, despite Arjan's efforts to keep a straight face on this occasion. Fraxinus's nostrils flared slightly.

"Though not yet High Azoth," said Fraxinus, "I have nonetheless attained Azothian status. My position within Rebel Branch hierarchy is a logical explanation for my ability to see you — especially in these disreputable, unorthodox times. Azothian authority must prevail."

"With all due respect, Azoth," said Arjan, "in these unorthodox times, I believe logic without evidence no longer suffices. Given the multitude of hours we have spent over the past few years searching archival manuscripts for solutions to the dimensional abnormalities and fallout with no success, I contend that all rebels and alchemists are currently ignorant *regardless* of status."

"I agree with your sentiment," Dracaen interjected, taking control of their conjoined body. "The time we have spent examining archival materials to aid in dimensional repair would have been better spent reviewing manuscript intricacies related to threading the fabric of time. Our numerous failed attempts at traversing the timeline are disgraceful and infuriatingly frustrating."

Arjan thought back to the accusations of incompetency Dracaen had levelled at Genevre. After the agreed-upon three-month research delay, she had returned to Flaw dimension as promised. Their lack of success at time travel had unnerved Dracaen; he blamed Genevre. But she feigned disappointment with truly admirable skill and, gradually, managed to convince Dracaen of her innocence. *Given elemental imbalance, a few years of research may be necessary*, she had advised.

"We must shift our focus," continued Dracaen. "Visual and dimensional irregularities will cease to matter once we sow our seeds across dimensional time."

"Sow our seeds?" asked Arjan.

"You object to an agricultural metaphor?" asked Fraxinus.

"If referring to people instead of crops, yes!"

Dracaen slammed the manuscript they were holding onto the table. "Arjan! My intent is to alter manuscripts throughout the timeline, not to create alchemical children," he asserted loudly. "And since you have thus far proven yourself a virtually useless alchemical child in regard to timeline travel, I suggest we stop talking and adjust our research priorities!"

Arjan refrained from an immediate reply. Instead, he grounded himself firmly and silently within

Dracaen. He still required additional practice on sensing when the High Azoth was lying. Currently, he felt nothing beyond a calm resolve from Dracaen. Arjan wondered if his Initiate status did indeed matter; perhaps it negatively affected his ability to intuit and manipulate the decisions of an Elder. After two years of being mutually conjoined, Arjan still remained uncertain of Dracaen's true interdimensional goals.

He knew only what Dracaen had admitted aloud of the grand plan when discussing it with him or Fraxinus or, on occasion, Genevre. Even then, Arjan could not determine if Dracaen's words were merely conciliatory half-truths spoken to appease an Initiate outsider from Council dimension. How could he possibly fathom what Dracaen had planned at the level of minutiae? What Arjan realized in the aftermath of this most recent conversation with Fraxinus and Dracaen was that he too needed to adjust *his* approach — to convince them both that to reach their own stated goals, they would have to adjust much more than merely their research focus.

"If we are to succeed at repeatedly traversing the timeline during a crisis in dimensional adhesion," said Arjan, "we need to be innovative. From all we have read in the historical records, complexities of the current magnitude have never occurred. Ancient documents, even the most prized Draconian and Lapidarian manuscripts, have offered us no guidance.

Our only remaining option is to find an alternative — a means to clear away the dust, so to speak."

"What dust?" asked Fraxinus. "Everything changed with the mutual conjunctions! We have already scattered the figurative dust to the winds."

"Alchemists perpetually write and interpret manuscripts based on ancient methodologies passed from generation to generation through the Orders," replied Arjan. "We must reconfigure our approach to repair the dimensions anew."

"Established methods have maintained the dimensions since the beginning of linear time," countered Fraxinus. "Rebalancing the elements and traversing the timeline will require adherence to tradition, not the haphazard experimentation of an Initiate!"

"As we have always done, as we now do," agreed Dracaen. His words evoked the Alchemical Law Codes rather than a personal penchant.

"Traditional methods have worked for millennia to maintain the status quo," admitted Arjan. "But the status quo is becoming less and less viable as the months progress. As you yourself said, Fraxinus, *everything changed* along with the mutual conjunctions. Dimensional laws themselves have shifted, and they continue to do so as we speak. Within these circumstances, outmoded methods cannot reliably yield results."

"*As above, so below,*" quoted Dracaen solemnly. "If—"

"Precisely!" responded Arjan before Dracaen could proffer traditional interpretations of the ancient proclamation. "*As above, so below* — the macrocosm and the microcosm. If we hope to change the one, we must begin by changing the other."

"*As we have always done* through the ancient manuscripts," insisted Fraxinus, gesturing to the multiple volumes spread across the table.

"You don't understand what I mean, Fraxinus. We *are* the microcosm. Through our scribal powers, alchemists have controlled the dimensions. But all our training and skills are now proving useless. To repair the worlds, we must write new texts rather than relying *only* on archival ones. At the very least, the old manuscripts require new interpretations."

"You would have us altogether abandon the manuscripts?" asked Dracaen.

"For generations, the Alchemists' Council and the Rebel Branch have maintained a hierarchy of Orders, struggling both within and between dimensions to maintain power *over* — over the *Calculus Macula*, over the outside world, over one another. The Rebel Branch promotes free will. But your own desires, the choices you have made in the past, and the plans you intend to enact in the future impose your will on others. Nothing has changed for millennia *until now*. Now we have an opportunity to change."

"I agreed to conjoin with an Initiate!" exclaimed Dracaen. "What further evidence do you require of my willingness to transform?"

"You agreed to conjoin because I am an alchemical child," said Arjan. "And you did so to gain an advantage over the timeline and thereby over others."

"Together our conjoined advantage will ensure the permanence of the Flaw itself — without which no one, including you, would be able to choose to utter your radical theories!"

"What good are innovative theories if ancient practices suppress them?" asked Arjan.

"We are alchemists!" cried Fraxinus. "Our very nature is to transform. Azoths make transformational decisions based on experience. Initiates suggest alternatives based on youthful impatience. Of course our pronouncements will repeatedly eclipse yours."

"As we concluded earlier, my Initiate status is moot now that I am conjoined."

"You have misunderstood," said Dracaen. "Your Initiate status means nothing to Fraxinus because he assumes you will follow my lead."

"Yes, I will heed your advice, Dracaen," said Arjan, "but I need you to consider my suggestions. Our respect must be mutual. Otherwise, arguing with one another will distract us from moving forward together."

"What specifically would you suggest we do, Arjan?" asked Dracaen.

"To start," replied Arjan, "I suggest inviting Azoth Magen Ravenea to help us form an official joint coalition of members from both the Rebel Branch and the Alchemists' Council, one that meets regularly, one that includes alchemists and rebels of all Orders. Perhaps then we can develop a workable approach on which we can all agree."

An hour and a heated debate later, Dracaen finally conceded. But Arjan was certain he had seen Fraxinus recoil.

Arjan stood under the stone archway of the small but functional consultation room. Three wooden benches were pushed against the left wall, one against the right. A metal trolley holding a few manuscripts rested near the back of the room. Ravenea stood at the quartz countertop that traversed the centre of the room. She was bent forward, peering at an unfurled scroll. A copper luminescence lantern glowed brightly above the scroll.

"I have finally found something interesting in my investigation of outside world materials," said Ravenea, glancing briefly over her shoulder towards Arjan.

"Are you openly acknowledging that outside world alchemists have produced something beyond useless drivel?" asked Arjan.

"Dracaen?"

"No. He's asleep — resting in the shadows, as Ilex and Melia would say," replied Arjan. "Or, as you might say, the tonic you supplied me has rendered him unconscious. Mercifully, he has not uttered a word for the last twenty minutes."

Ravenea closely scanned Arjan's face, apparently attempting to assess whether Dracaen had indeed moved into the shadows. "What do you plan to tell him when he awakens?"

"If he notices the missing time and demands an explanation, I'll claim — based on my experience with Ilex and Melia — that mental fatigue occasionally causes lapses in consciousness. I'll then suggest he purposely rest in the shadows an hour or so each day before conjunctive exhaustion renders him impotent."

"Clever," said Ravenea, nodding. "Pockets of time without him could prove useful."

"What have you found?" Arjan asked, turning his attention to the scroll on the table.

"A clue to the folio Genevre removed from the *Osmanthian Codex*."

"Really?" Arjan attempted to appear interested but not too apprehensive or enthusiastic. He did not want Ravenea to doubt his allegiance to her or to the Alchemists' Council on a matter connected to his mother's alleged manuscript treachery. "May I look?"

Ravenea nodded and turned back to the scroll. Arjan, now standing beside her and peering downward, was initially taken aback. The scroll was a ruse. Atop it lay a sheet of newsprint featuring a story by a journalist rather than a treatise by an outside world alchemist.

"I don't understand," said Arjan.

"Were you expecting a map?"

"No. But neither was I expecting an outside world newspaper — a relative rarity even in the outside world these days."

Ravenea read the headline aloud: *Ancient Alchemical Manuscript Leaf Unearthed — Origin Unknown.* "We must investigate this woman," she said as she tapped on the newspaper article's accompanying photograph.

Arjan picked up the page and read the article quickly. The story focused on a Canadian scholar — Virginia Albert — who had discovered the "ancient treasure" while doing archival research in a library at the University of North Alabama. Apparently, the manuscript page had been inexplicably housed alongside regional historical documents. Though a photograph accompanied the story, the text on the manuscript page itself appeared indecipherable to Arjan. He certainly would not have guessed it to be the page Genevre had extracted from the *Osmanthian Codex.* In fact, he found Ravenea's claim suspect and wondered briefly if he should doubt *her* allegiance to the Joint Coalition.

"North Alabama? Why would—"

"Both Kalina and Genevre activated manuscript talismans with the intention of leading a potential

Initiate to the folio. Virginia Albert may be that Initiate. Her location is irrelevant."

Arjan quickly lifted a finger as if to silence Ravenea. After a pause, he apologized. "I felt Dracaen stir for a moment, but he's fallen back into the shadows."

Ravenea nodded.

"We've already spent too much time over the last few years attempting to locate this one folio," reasoned Arjan, unexpectedly feeling resentful towards his mother. "If Genevre had kept the folio with her rather than engaging these complex tactics, we could have verified its utter uselessness to solving our current dilemma years ago."

Ravenea put her hands on her hips and stared at him. "First, if Genevre had kept the folio, any number of unforeseen circumstances could have resulted. Hiding it was her only viable choice at the time. Second, regardless of whether the content of the folio proves useful or useless to our present crisis, caution warrants its retrieval. For safekeeping, we must return its Osmanthian blood-infused inscriptions to the primary dimensions."

"Unless we transfer all Council and Rebel Branch manuscripts to the outside world, no outside world alchemist would recognize Osmanthian blood, let alone know how to access its inherent powers. The folio and its primordial blood-inks may well be safer there than here."

Ravenea looked at Arjan quizzically this time. "Interesting. I will keep that innovative notion in mind for future reference. For now, however — if we are to believe Genevre — this news story warrants our attention."

"If you are implying that Genevre is lying—"

"I am implying nothing of the sort, Arjan. But I do suggest adamantly that you investigate this woman." She tapped again on Virginia Albert's image.

"Why do we need Virginia herself? Would it not suffice for me to find a means of confiscating the folio for authentication?"

"Your inexperience betrays you, Arjan. You have missed the point entirely."

"Please enlighten me, Azoth Magen."

"The manuscript page depicted in the photograph is not the lost folio from the *Osmanthian Codex*. If it were, its sacred inks would not be visible at all. They would appear as negative space — like the Flaw itself from the perspective of Council dimension — when replicated using outside world technology. Though not easily readable in the photo, I can see that the calligraphy on the manuscript page is a forged transcription."

Arjan nodded. He thought of the day he had spilled Lapidarian ink in the Initiate classroom with Jaden and Cercis. Its sudden disappearance had astonished him. Months later, Jaden asked him if he had dropped it on purpose. *I assumed an intentional accident would yield swift and intriguing results*, he had reluctantly admitted. Though Cedar had reprimanded her for the mishap, Jaden had not reproached Arjan. *We must learn as much as we can*, she had responded to his admission. *Alchemy's power and the Council's future reside in its inks.*

"If the page is not the extracted folio, then what is prompting you to investigate?"

"Virginia Albert herself," Ravenea responded. "I recognize the calligraphy as a poor but passable imitation of either originary or 5th Council script. Someone — possibly Virginia — made this forgery to replicate a portion of the original text."

"Or the forgery itself could have lain amidst the historical documents for decades," suggested Arjan. "The article says she found the manuscript fragment in an archival box last accessed over forty years ago."

"Yes, that possibility occurred to me. But hiding a forgery makes no sense. What would be the point? More likely, Virginia found the original and then realized — perhaps after trying to photograph the folio herself — that the ink's image could not be reproduced. She purposely created the forgery for display and secreted away the original folio for safekeeping."

"If secreting the folio were her intention, why publicly display the forgery at all?"

"The alchemically rendered books — both the Council and Rebel Books — have been circulating in the outside world for almost two years. If she correctly interpreted even one of the books, the elements would respond accordingly to align her essence with ours in order to open a portal — a means for her message to reach us. Virginia Albert may be just the worthy Initiate we had hoped to find: one skilled at reading between the lines, understanding esoteric parables, analyzing rhetorical structures, and unfastening the dimensional locks between our worlds by inscribing her name into one of the Books."

Arjan glanced again at a specific phrase in the newspaper article: *Canadian doctoral candidate at the University of Edinburgh.* "What would a Canadian student studying at the University of Edinburgh be researching in the archives of the University of North Alabama?"

"Precisely — that incongruity adds evidence to support my hypothesis. Contact with Lapidarian or Dragonsblood inks of either the Council or Rebel Book would empower a potential Initiate. Such contact could have drawn Virginia Albert to an ancestral document in Edinburgh that, in turn, led her to the folio in Alabama thanks to the talismans. She intended for us to notice her."

He nodded, wondering briefly if Genevre had worked to manipulate this coincidence years earlier. He then added quietly, "Your theory sounds both plausible and improbable."

"You asked Dracaen and Fraxinus to consider unorthodox approaches. I am now asking you to do the same. We cannot simply ignore the possibility that Virginia is a future Scribe — one who might have the skills to repair the damage inflicted upon Council dimension."

"How do you plan to gain proof of her alchemical abilities?"

"You will accompany her to Flaw dimension. With a few simple questions, we can then determine in which of the primary dimensions we will hold her tribunal."

"What am I to tell Dracaen?"

"The truth: that she has discovered an alchemical manuscript folio, that you suspect she read one of the Books, and that she may be the next Council or Rebel Branch Initiate."

"Would you prefer I imply she's a descendant of the ancestral bloodline or a malleable youngster who would do the bidding of his nascent regime?"

Ravenea smiled. "You clearly are an alchemical child, Arjan. Tell Dracaen whatever you must to convince him to investigate."

"Why don't you investigate Virginia and her folio yourself?"

"The *Osmanthian Codex* resides in Flaw dimension. Dracaen studied it for years. He is more capable than I am of ascertaining whether the missing folio was the model for the forgery. Or so I would have him believe."

"And if it is? Will you inform Genevre?"

"Of course. But first you will escort the folio *and*

Virginia Albert to Flaw dimension. We need this woman to reside where we can keep her in unobstructed sight."

🐝

ff[lorence, Alabama — 2016

Dracaen and Arjan stood beside a statue of a lion who, poised upright, held a book in its paws: *Knowledge*.

"Let's walk over to the enclosure and see if the actual lions are awake," suggested Arjan.

"Stop speaking to me in public," whispered Dracaen fiercely. "Onlookers will assume you are talking to yourself."

"No. They will assume I'm talking to the statue." He smiled and patted its unencumbered paw. "I can relate to him — a creature artistically rendered from the elements." He could feel Dracaen grimace as he attempted to wrest control of their body from Arjan.

"You are drawing unwanted attention!" Dracaen said gruffly.

"Unwanted to you alone," replied Arjan.

Though he assumed Dracaen longed to bellow for Arjan's submission, he likewise supposed that Dracaen restrained himself for the sake of *professionalism* — a word the High Azoth had oft repeated of late. Intentional unsettling of Dracaen had been part of Genevre's plan from the beginning; in the end, Dracaen would be uprooted and toppled, and Arjan needed to set the stage for that future day. But he had not expected Dracaen to be such an aggravating companion in the meantime. Since the argument in the archival library a few weeks earlier with Fraxinus and Dracaen, Arjan could barely stand the sound of Dracaen's voice. He could not fathom how Ilex and Melia had been able to tolerate one another for even a decade, let alone two centuries. He found himself wishing yet again that the ancestral alchemists had incorporated mandatory retirement into their hierarchy of Orders. A sudden physical wrenching refocused Arjan's attention.

"Virginia Albert!" called Dracaen, waving.

Damn!

Arjan attempted but failed to protest. His meandering thoughts and Dracaen's willpower had thwarted his hope to be the one in control of their body during their first conversation with Virginia. She had already seen Dracaen; thus, Arjan must necessarily remain hidden until they retreated from the outside world.

Lack of professionalism, he imagined Dracaen thinking, *will be your undoing*. But really, the High Azoth himself was the problem. If not for Dracaen's privileged Azothian obstinance, Arjan could have remained focused on his task.

"Hello!" Virginia said as she held out her hand.

Her dark hair drifted backward in the breeze; tiny amber flecks glistened in her deep brown eyes. She wore jeans with a green suede jacket over a blue cotton shirt. When Dracaen clasped her hand, Arjan felt a slight spark — like a static-induced electric shock in the outside world. Could Virginia be naturally born of the bloodline? Dracaen did not appear to notice. For all his bloodline talk, he seemed unskilled in its detection.

"Shall we look at the manuscript folio?" proposed Dracaen.

"A cafeteria table would do for an initial viewing," she responded, gesturing for him to follow her along the pathway. "It won't be busy at this time of day, and the tables are clean."

Dracaen would have preferred to meet with Virginia in a private room — *We could rent a hotel suite*, he had suggested — but Arjan had convinced him that she would reject such a request outright. At least on this point, Dracaen had acquiesced.

Upon settling into their seats, Virginia unlatched the flap of the narrow bag she carried. Based on the bag's size and fabric, Arjan expected her to extract a computer. He feared in that moment that she planned to reveal only digital images of the folio or, more accurately, of the suspected forgery. But instead she retrieved a turquoise cardboard folder, which she handed to Dracaen. He opened the folder slowly. The single folio seemed radiant, adorned with gold, silver, and azure inks. Though an outside world scholar would understandably mistake the page as a folio from a medieval alchemical manuscript stolen from the university archives, Arjan could tell immediately that it did not fool Dracaen. He bristled and clenched his teeth.

"Where did you attain the inks?" he asked her.

"What do you mean?"

"The inks on this page are clearly a blend of Lapidarian and Dragonsblood, but the calligraphy is sloppy, and the folio itself exhibits no markers of ancient provenance."

"I'm sorry," said Virginia, "but I don't understand."

"This page is an elaborate forgery of an ancestral manuscript. The flourishes in the alpha positions of each line leave no doubt. How long have you trained with the Council?"

Stop being so obnoxious, Dracaen! thought Arjan in vain. *She will leave!*

"I do not belong to a council. I'm a graduate student. As I told the reporter, I found the manuscript amidst historical documents. I know nothing of its provenance."

"Did you work with the original?" asked Dracaen.

"This page *is* the original," replied Virginia.

Perhaps Virginia was being truthful. Though Arjan could not fathom a rationale for doing so, a Scribe in training may well have made and hidden the forgery years ago within the university's archives. Or Genevre herself could have planted it

— though she surely would have told Arjan if that were the case.

"You are lying, Virginia. Something is amiss. The inks and parchment are old, but the inscription itself is recent. I exaggerate only slightly when I say that the ink is barely dry."

"Do you want to purchase this page for the museum or not?" asked Virginia.

"I am not the curator of a museum; that was a ruse to get your attention, just as this forgery is a ruse to get ours," said Dracaen. "I am High Azoth of the Rebel Branch of the Alchemists' Council. If you expect us to evaluate your potential as a Council or Rebel Branch Initiate, I suggest you reveal the truth."

Virginia moved to the edge of her seat and whispered, "I no longer have the original."

"Then who does?" replied Dracaen loudly.

"A Council Scribe named Frank."

"No member of the Alchemists' Council would be named *Frank*."

"He said he was a Lapidarian Scribe. He showed me his pendant and offered to pay me. He brought the supplies. I applied my calligraphic skills. We made two copies — one for me, and one for the library. He took the original. And then he told me that an Elder would contact me shortly to assess my Initiate potential. Then you showed up."

"Then why did you lie to us?"

"You lied to me first. You said you were a museum

curator. How could I know you were the Rebel High Azoth? As soon as you—"

"Fine, fine! Our initial lies matter little now!" exclaimed Dracaen. "We must identify this . . . this . . . *Frank* and retrieve the folio. Describe his appearance."

"Older, pale skin, white hair, piercing blue eyes."

Arjan felt Dracaen surge with rage before he exclaimed, "Fraxinus!"

For the first time since their conjunction, Arjan sympathized with Dracaen. His trusted Azoth seemed to have done something utterly untrustworthy. This apparent revelation shocked Arjan too. What reason would Fraxinus have to secretly confiscate the folio for himself? Even if he planned to use it in some unforeseen manner, why would he have Virginia forge the folio? If Fraxinus doubted Virginia's authenticity as a potential Initiate, he could have retrieved the folio from the library and left Virginia behind. On the other hand, if he believed her to be the next Initiate, he could have brought both her and the folio to Dracaen and thereby won his praise. Nothing of this situation made sense. Unless—

Could Genevre have made plans with Fraxinus without informing Arjan? Did she want Virginia to be considered for the Initiate but, simultaneously, keep the folio out of Dracaen's hands? And with that thought, Arjan was left with three equally disturbing options: either Fraxinus had betrayed the

Joint Coalition, Genevre had deliberately lied to her son, or *both*.

fflaw Dimension — 2016

Of course, Fraxinus denied all charges when Dracaen confronted him. Arjan, who made no attempt whatsoever to appear during their argument, assumed Fraxinus was lying. But when, two days later, Scribe Larix escorted Virginia from Alabama to Flaw dimension, she insisted Fraxinus was most definitely not the librarian in question despite their similar physical features. Though Virginia's insistence displeased Dracaen, he necessarily revoked his accusation. After all, what reason would a potential Initiate have to lie to the High Azoth on behalf of a lower Azoth? The prestige of status within the Rebel Branch hierarchy would be recognizable even to a newcomer. Thus, unable to establish reasonable doubt, Dracaen muttered a half-hearted apology to Fraxinus, bellowed that all Council Scribes must be interrogated for treachery immediately, and called forth Arjan to speak with Virginia while he retreated to develop a contingency plan.

When Arjan suddenly appeared in Dracaen's stead, Virginia jumped.

"Alchemy," said Arjan, by way of explanation.

Virginia nodded. "Mutual conjunction," she said. "I read about Ilex and Melia."

As if on cue, Ravenea appeared at Arjan's side. Expressionless, she addressed Virginia. "In which book did you read of Ilex and Melia — Council or Rebel?"

"What's the difference?"

"What colour was its binding?" Ravenea asked.

"Gold . . . and brown."

"She has described the Council Book," Ravenea said to Fraxinus. "The Rebel Book is gold and blue. Therefore, her tribunal will take place in Council dimension."

Fraxinus nodded. He appeared dismayed, but Arjan presumed his demeanour had more to do with Dracaen's false accusation than Ravenea's justifiable request.

"Come with me," she said to Virginia. Then, turning to Arjan, Ravenea added, "If Dracaen would like to attend the tribunal, bring him to Azothian Chambers tomorrow at noon."

"We will both be there," said Fraxinus.

"We will *all* be there," said Arjan.

Council Dimension — 2016

Virginia stood beside Ravenea, glancing around the room in apparent fascination. Ravenea understood that Azothian Chambers proved irresistibly interesting to new arrivals. The light from the kiln to the left, along with the hundreds of Lapidarian candles lining the edges of water-filled border channels, cast flickering shadows against the colourful Azadirian mosaics adorning each of the four walls: earth, air, water, and fire. Ravenea supposed the everlasting brilliance of the mosaics might enamour Virginia even more than they did the Initiates or outside world scribes, who presumed they would have countless years to observe the space. Virginia, to the contrary, likely believed this day to be her only opportunity. Depending on the outcome of the deliberation, she may never again be invited into Council dimension, let alone into the sacred space of the Elders.

"I recall reading about Azothian Chambers," said Virginia. "But I couldn't picture it. I hadn't imagined such extraordinary opulence."

Ravenea smiled. "Remind me to show you the Scriptorium before you depart." She walked to the head of a long table in the centre of the room. "Have a seat," she instructed. "High Azoth Dracaen and Azoth Fraxinus will arrive shortly. You should relax, prepare yourself."

"How?"

Ravenea did not have a response. She was unfamiliar with such . . . *familiarity* by a potential Initiate towards the Azoth Magen. Then again, Virginia had shown more veneration for the buildings and landscape of Council dimension than she had to Azoths Ruis and Kai. Why should her attitude towards the Azoth Magen be any different?

"How am I supposed to prepare," Virginia said, "when I have no idea what to expect?"

"Your point is sound. None of us knows what to expect. You are the first of your kind."

Virginia laughed loudly — an unusual sound within Azothian Chambers. Ravenea did not know whether the laughter annoyed or delighted her.

"What do you mean *first of my kind*? A Canadian? A graduate student from Scotland? A linguist? A rhetorician? A writer? I can't possibly be the first of my kind on any grounds."

"Usually Council finds its potential Initiates through an elaborate process involving multiple Lapidarian manuscripts, Readers, and Scribes. You are the first to seek us."

"Wasn't that the intention of the Council Book — to lead potential Initiates to you?"

"Yes. But as stated in copious ways in various alchemical manuscripts, including those of the outside world, only those gifted with a combination of skills, patience, and — most significantly — *grace* are able to unlock the encoded language of the alchemists."

"So you're expecting divine intervention?" Virginia asked, glancing towards the ceiling.

"In outside world manuscripts, the divine is typically understood to bestow grace. However, within

Council dimension, the term refers to those whose Quintessence resonates harmoniously with the Lapis. Such resonance resides in the blood — a physical inheritance rather than a divine endowment."

"So, alchemical powers are inherited through the bloodline?"

"All true alchemists are descendants of the original bloodline; however, as with most outside world bloodlines, the passing of generations tends to dilute genetic inheritances. Only a few Council members still carry detectable ancestral blood; most possess a barely perceptible trace. Quintessence, on the other hand, reacts measurably to Lapidarian proximity."

"If my Quintessence . . . resonates, what will I learn here?"

"You will become an Initiate of the Alchemists' Council. We will train you as an alchemist whose skills, when developed, will help to maintain the dimensions."

"If my Quintessence proves unfit for Council, I will train as an outside world alchemist."

"Such efforts would likely prove futile. Most outside world manuscripts contain no accurate alchemical knowledge. Laypeople wrote them, gesturing towards an arcane jumble of inaccurate memories of Council training. Most would-be alchemists were potential outside world scribes who resided within Council dimension temporarily but whom the Elders eventually deemed unsuitable.

Once back in the outside world, out of the proximity of the Lapis, their memories of Lapidarian manuscripts became fragmented. Generally, they spent the remaining years of their lives attempting to recreate the Lapis — which, of course, is an impossibility. They nonetheless claimed success, and their followers attempted to replicate that success for centuries thereafter. A similar distortion of alchemical manuscript memory would likely occur to you."

"And the Council Book? Did it contain the recipe for alchemical success?"

"What do you think?"

Virginia laughed again. "Book or no book, I think I was born to be an alchemist."

"Is that so?"

"The Council won't even need to give me a tree name. Whether by fate or coincidence, *Virginia* was granted to me at birth."

"Indeed," replied Ravenea, thinking to herself of another such given name: *Genevre*.

On this Day of Decision, the Council observed the Procession of Orders. Thus Cedar entered Azothian Chambers beside Tera, with the two other Novillian Scribes — Katsura and Ela — following directly thereafter. Azoth Magen Ravenea had entered first, followed by Azoths Ruis and Kai, then Rowans Esche and Obeche. As Cedar walked directly behind Obeche, nearly stepping on his robes for want of focus, she wondered again if she should so easily have declined Ravenea's offer of a debate for the permanent position of Rowan. Her decision, which she had made a week after her reinstatement, had angered Ruis. *I would have supported your claim!* he told her repeatedly. But his insistence became her main reason for backing Obeche. Ruis had always supported her. Obeche, on the other hand, had repeatedly antagonized her. Though she did not know when or under what circumstances, and given the ongoing dimensional degradation, Cedar reasoned that she would require Obeche's assistance in the future. If she did, he would remember her collegial gesture. *Trade is troth.*

As Cedar settled into her seat between Obeche and Tera, she glanced towards Fraxinus and Arjan. Unlike most of the Council Elders, Cedar would see Dracaen if he chose to reveal himself. Ravenea had asked her specifically to keep an eye on Arjan during the tribunal. She need not have done so. Cedar wanted little else than to observe her son.

Virginia sat in an unadorned chair, arms resting on a small round table. Her position in the centre of the room allowed the best visibility for everyone. Cedar thought back to the last examination she had witnessed here — that of Arjan and Jaden upon their return from Qingdao two years ago.

Thankfully, Virginia did not yet have a pendant for Obeche to drain.

"Virginia Albert," began Ravenea, "I have brought you to Council dimension to determine your suitability as Initiate to the Alchemists' Council. A Joint Coalition of Council and Rebel Branch Elders determined Protocols of Selection during the era of Dissolution. We will question you today and inform you of our decision directly. Our decision is final and resolute. If we determine you unsuitable to the Alchemists' Council, Azoth Fraxinus will escort you to Flaw dimension for a Rebel Branch tribunal. If determined unsuitable to the Rebel Branch, you will return to the outside world. In that event, as difficult as this result may be, you will proceed with your life as if the tribunals had never occurred, as if you had never read the Council Book. Do you understand?"

"Yes, Azoth Magen Ravenea, I understand."

The candidate appeared polite, but unwelcome trepidations continued to grip Cedar. Nonetheless, outright objection would be pointless. According to current protocols, having read and accurately interpreted the Council Book, Virginia had earned the right to request Initiation. Cedar calmed her apprehension by reminding herself that during the tribunal they would test Virginia not only on her interpretation of the text but, more significantly, on the text's interpretation of her. No matter Virginia's ancestral bloodline or Quintessence, Cedar doubted a newcomer would be able to fabricate elaborate lies undetectable to the Elders. After all, the Scribes had taken precautions — they had alchemically enhanced the Council Book to reveal specific formulas only to those worthy to stand trial.

Ravenea took her seat on the Azothian dais, and Ruis stepped into his position as First Inquisitor. He stood in front and slightly to the left of Virginia.

"You admit to having found and read the Council Book," Ruis began. "Why did you not heed its warning?"

"I do not understand the question, Azoth. I saw no warning."

Obeche whispered something inaudible to Esche, who extracted an alchemically replicated copy of the Council Book from a nearby cabinet. He handed the book to Ruis who, in turn, handed it to Virginia.

"Turn to the sixth page. What do you see?"

"Oh — *that* warning," she responded. "*The Alchemists' Council forbids you to read this book.* I had forgotten."

"So, you did read it. Then you chose to ignore it."

Virginia paused, but then answered with a definitive *yes.* Then, when asked to recount what she had read thereafter, she spoke at length. *Lapis, Quintessence, Azoths, Scribes, Scriptorium, pendants, archives, catacomb alembics, Initiate classrooms, residence chambers* — she must have listed three dozen terms and defined them all with accuracy. She understood the hierarchy of Orders and the duties ascribed to each Order; she knew of Aralia and Osmanthus and the Crystalline Wars; she knew of the Rebel Branch and the Flaw in the Stone. But these details, including their associated philosophies and politics, were all discernible elements any reasonably literate person could reiterate after reading the Council Book. What the Elders needed to ascertain with certainty was whether Virginia inherently and intuitively comprehended the Book's ineffable principles — the paradoxical concepts integral to all alchemical texts, the enigmatic elements that required a reader to move beyond text, beyond language, to pass beyond thought, even if only for an infinitesimal moment of time, into what alchemists and outside world mystics alike had dubbed *the cloud of unknowing*.

"Did you find the Council Book *easy* to read?" asked Ruis.

"No."

"Yet you carried on."

"Yes," said Virginia. "I figured I'd have a better chance of eventually understanding the concepts if I kept reading than if I abandoned ship . . . so to speak."

Ravenea nodded and glanced at Cedar, who then stood to indicate she wanted her turn at questions. Ruis yielded the floor and returned to his seat. Cedar smiled at Arjan and then positioned herself directly in front of Virginia.

"Since reading the Council Book," began Cedar, "have you noticed any changes in your life — minor or significant?"

Virginia hesitated, giving Cedar a quizzical look as if she did not quite understand the question. But just as Cedar was about to offer clarification, Virginia nodded. "Yes. Both minor and significant. I thought the changes were just coincidental at first, but then I honed the skill — tested myself each day until I found a means to instigate contact."

Cedar felt a flush of blood. Finally, Virginia had offered something of potential significance. Cedar knew, given their slight shift of postures, that everyone in the room was now focused with rapt attention.

"What changes occurred? And to what sort of *tests* do you refer?"

Virginia sighed loudly, which Cedar found disconcerting. Though she could accept annoyance on the part of a potential Initiate, Cedar certainly could not abide boredom.

"I found the Council Book months ago. My entire life has transformed since then. Choosing just a few incidents as examples is . . . difficult."

Upon hearing that response, Cedar understood that she had again too hastily reached the wrong conclusion about Virginia. The potential Initiate was not bored; she was overwhelmed.

"You said that at first you thought the changes were mere coincidences. Could you choose a few preliminary examples to describe?" requested Cedar.

Virginia closed her eyes, tilted back her head, and wrinkled her nose as if the task of trying to remember was challenging. "Yes. The appointment. I had a medical appointment scheduled — the sort that's booked months in advance. And then a friend invited me to an event that conflicted with the appointment. I wanted to reschedule with the medical office, but that would mean another few month's wait. Right then, I was standing at my desk, leaning forward, with one of my hands resting inadvertently on the Council Book. *Please*, I said aloud, *dissolve this conflict!* And then voilà! Someone from the medical office called and asked if I'd be willing to change my appointment to the following week."

"Who were you hoping would answer your . . . prayer?" Ravenea interjected.

"No one in particular. Universal forces, powers that be, I suppose." She shrugged.

"And then?" asked Cedar.

"Then a few days later, I was holding the Council Book, reading over a complex passage that I hadn't understood the first time. It involved Lapidarian bees — how to distinguish them from outside world bees. Just as I was thinking, *I need to observe one of each bee to ascertain the difference for myself*, I looked up and saw two bees on my windowsill. Still holding the book, I approached them slowly. Neither one moved. I read the passage aloud and watched the bees. One clearly had the blue-green tinge described; the other did not. After a half dozen or so such unintentional incidents, I started the tests."

"Describe these tests," Cedar requested.

"I started holding the Council Book in my hands and asking for . . . *things*. Just little things at first: a feather, a coin, a ring. Then I'd go outside, book in tow, and walk through the streets or parks. Inevitably, within an hour or two, I would find the thing I'd requested. So I began to ask for less trivial, less tangible things: love, healing, wealth. But that didn't work — at least not in any clearly perceivable way. So I returned to reading the text, deciphered esoteric passages, attempted alternative strategies based on new interpretations. But nothing changed."

"Did you abandon the tests at that point?" Cedar asked. Her hands tingled in anticipation of Virginia's answers.

"Yes and no. After a few weeks, I stopped trying to interpret the text. Instead, I summoned the Book itself to assist me. I held it in both hands and asked, *What should I do?* Then I turned to a random passage. And there it was — the answer. *If destiny can be written and rewritten, then destiny can be changed.* Then I realized what I needed to do. I had to write myself into the Book. So I did. I turned to the inside cover and I wrote, *I choose to accept the consequences of my freedom to choose.* And then, over the course of the next few weeks, I wrote in every available space — inside the cover, on the title page, in the margins, between the lines — until my words, my story, existed alongside the original text. And when I finished, I leafed through the pages, admiring what appeared to me like an elaborate gloss, like those in medieval manuscripts of outside world libraries. But then I realized my writing wasn't a gloss. My text was a conjunction — words upon words, I had conjoined my essence with those of the Scribes of the Alchemists' Council. On the final page, I had inscribed a request: that my life — that *I myself* — be transformed. Within minutes, the Book revealed a map that, in turn, led me to a Lapidarian beekeeper. She sold me the honey and candles that I used for the Ritual of Contact. Standing in the mist at sunset under the requisite tree, I expected the ritual to open a portal to Council dimension. It did open a portal, but I emerged beside the lion enclosure at the University of North Alabama. An hour later, I had found the folio."

Ravenea gestured for Cedar to take a seat. She bowed in Ab Uno to each member of the Joint Coalition; all of whom responded reciprocally. She then stood in front of Virginia and addressed her directly.

"As Azoth Magen of the 19th Alchemists' Council, I hereby declare the official admission of Junior Initiate Virginia."

A few years in the outside world can pass in a blink of an eye in Council and Flaw dimensions. But in the last few weeks, Jaden had begun to feel the slow weight of stagnation. She had not left Council dimension since returning from her brief excursion to Santa Fe four years earlier to consult with Genevre and Jinjing. And for the past six months she had worked tirelessly alongside the remaining Initiates to help the Readers, Scribes, and Elders with essential tasks. Earlier war measures had long since given way to perpetual crisis management. *We live in unorthodox times* had become the common refrain. Though dimensional dissolution had slowed substantially over the past two years, the Council had remained unsuccessful in attaining a complete restoration. On the rare occasions that they appeared to have achieved a state of remission, something would occur to remind everyone that their very existence remained tenuous. Yesterday had provided a particularly horrendous illustration.

Ritha, the Senior Initiate to whom Jaden had felt closest since her arrival in Council dimension, had collapsed at the cliff face just as she, Novillian Scribe Katsura, Lapidarian Scribe Wu Tong, and Reader Olivia had been priming for portal transportation to San Antonio. At the moment Katsura finished reciting the portal key, a powerful crackling blaze — that Wu Tong later described as sheet lightning — knocked the Scribes off their feet. Astounded, Ritha stood immobile. Then, according to Olivia, Ritha's knees buckled and she fell to the side, knocking her head against one of the boulders. Wu Tong and Olivia had taken her immediately to the catacombs and assisted her into a healing alembic. Now, still at Ritha's side twenty-four hours later, they glanced at Jaden with disheartened expressions.

"Rowan Obeche has sent me," explained Jaden. "The Elders would like me to report back to them on Ritha's status."

"As yet, she shows no signs of recovery," said Wu Tong.

Jaden felt sickened.

"How is Katsura?" asked Olivia.

"Emotionally shaken but physically fine," said Jaden.

"And the portal?" Wu Tong inquired. "Has anyone succeeded at transport?"

"The Azoths have forbidden transport through the cliff face portal until Elder Council has completed a thorough investigation."

"We should have used the Salix portal," said Olivia. "North American transport—"

"That's what Katsura said," interrupted Jaden. "And then Cedar told her that portal choice wouldn't have made a difference. Based on reports from Keepers of the Book in various American protectorates, the Elders are now testing the theory that the power fluctuation originated in San Antonio rather than at the cliff face. They've temporarily banned travel to several American locations."

Olivia and Wu Tong nodded as if they had expected this outcome. But the news had shocked Jaden. Over the last two years, she had heard rumours of outside world fragmentation. But she assumed the Council would eventually rebalance the elements as they had done for millennia. After hearing about the travel ban, she feared being trapped forever within Council dimension, slowly succumbing to painful dimensional dissolution, melting into the disintegrating landscape.

As she moved slowly back through the narrow catacomb passageways, making her way towards the surface, she kept her head down, her luminescence lantern lighting the path directly in front of her feet. She might otherwise submit to the numbing claustrophobia that the surrounding walls, ceiling, and dim lighting tended to ignite in her even at the best of times. She did not allow herself to look up until she reached the first row of skull carvings. If dimensional cohesion stabilized enough for celebratory rituals to recommence, someday a depiction of her own skull would rest among these generations of alchemists. She amused herself as she progressed through the haunting passageway by imagining Azadirian artisans knitting toques with pompoms for the skulls. Not until passing through the penultimate chamber did she hear the snapping sound. Attempting to determine its origin, Jaden looked towards the row of skulls directly to her right.

Crack!

Jaden watched as a fissure made its way from the forehead of one Council ancestor through the jaw of the one directly above it, gradually expanding to the middle of the ceiling.

Crack!

Jaden turned to watch another, then turned again to watch a third and a fourth. She tried to move forward towards the final chamber and staircase to the surface, but vibrations in the ground slowed her at each step. Bits of rock and dust began falling onto her from above. Clouds of dust billowing through the narrow passageway made her cough. Even as she groped the walls, her fingers entwined in the cavities of nearby skulls for balance and leverage, she assumed the phenomenon to be the sort of earthquake Laurel had described to her — the one that had occurred when she was trapped in Qingdao. Though it had unsettled everyone, the Council had easily remedied its damage. Her fear of being trapped simply made this quake seem worse than its actual dimensional impact. Even amidst the lingering dust, Jaden could see the light filtering down the staircase. All was well above the surface. She needed only pull herself across the final few feet of the chamber and she too would be safe.

Crack!

The sound was thunderous. The skull in whose eye sockets Jaden had laced her fingers for leverage was knocked out of its stone encasement. Jaden herself lurched forward, falling to her knees at the foot of the staircase. Behind her the roar of falling debris thundered. Out of sheer dread, she climbed on hands and knees up the stairs. When she reached the top, she flung herself from the last step onto the thick grass of field. Only then did she breathe again. She rolled over onto her back, sat up, dizzy and wheezing. Smoke appeared to be curling up from the ground in front of her — directly above the catacombs. But when it cleared, she understood that the earth was not smouldering. It had folded inward — a sinkhole of collapsed dirt and mud and rock that had opened crevices large enough to allow the dust from the ruined catacombs to pour through.

Jaden had escaped, but the others had not. The debris had buried Olivia, Wu Tong, and Ritha. At best, they were inescapably trapped; at worst, they were already dead. Or perhaps she should reverse those superlatives — at best, they were dead. In mortified shock, Jaden had not noticed anyone approaching her. When someone put their arms around her, she screamed.

"Jaden! It's me — Cedar!"

She began to sob, rocking in Cedar's embrace.

"We need to move," Cedar said finally. "The ground is not stable here." She stood up and held out a hand to Jaden.

Not until she reached out for Cedar did Jaden notice the skull. Her fingers had remained clenched to it, positioned precisely where they had been just prior to the final blast. She could not move. She sat on the ground, arm extended, observing silently as Cedar pried one finger after the next from the alchemically rendered bone. Finally freed of the ghastly burden, Jaden stood up. Devastated and horrified, she stared at the skull Cedar now cradled in both hands.

"We will take it with us for safekeeping," Cedar said, holding it aloft like a Shakespearean actor's gesture, repeatedly played in the outside world. "When the dimension begins to heal, we may be able to use its lingering Quintessence to reconstruct the catacombs."

"He still had a choice," said Jaden, turning away from Cedar, gazing at the main Council buildings in the distance. "We no longer do."

"Who still had a choice?"

"Hamlet."

"He chose *to be*, just as you did," Cedar assured her.

"I should have turned back. I should have warned them, helped them."

"You would have died."

"I should have died. I should have let the ruins of this world rain down upon me."

"'Conscience does make cowards of us all,'" Cedar quoted, folding an arm around Jaden and guiding her home across the serrated terrain.

"Where are you going? You can't leave now!" Jaden pleaded. "We already lost you once."

Two weeks had passed. In an agreement that Ravenea had brokered within an hour of the catacomb tragedy, miners arrived from Flaw dimension to attempt an excavation. Throughout the first night, the entire Council of alchemists waited for news. Of course, they hoped for the best: *All three survived! The primary alembic chamber held strong!* Inevitably, they imagined the worst: *All three succumbed to the elements.* But as the sun began to rise over the eastern hills, the light merely served to illuminate the dirt and dismay smeared across the miners' faces. They could not provide confirmation of either the best or the worst. They had not managed to excavate more than fifteen feet of debris before reaching a barrier stronger than any they had encountered throughout the dimensions. Though it looked like metal — iron or lead — no one could determine its elemental qualities. Ravenea declared the substance an abomination created in response to the ongoing inability of the Alchemists' Council to maintain elemental balance.

With no Amber Garden for their official grieving, Sadira spontaneously commenced the Song of Mourning, and all alchemists in her vicinity, including Jaden, dropped to their knees. As she contemplated the deaths of Ritha, Wu Tong, and Olivia, Jaden recalculated the dwindling numbers. After multiple dissolutions of conjunctive pairs in the early years of fallout, combined with the three most recent losses, the entire Council now comprised only sixty-eight of the required one hundred and one alchemists. The Senior Initiate had only eight of its twelve members, and the Junior Initiate had only two — Virginia and Javor — both of whom had managed to contact Council after finding a copy of the Council Book, and neither of whom appealed to Jaden even as classmates, let alone colleagues. She no longer knew how the Alchemists' Council could hold even a glimmer of hope for future stability — especially not now that Cedar had announced she needed to leave Council dimension for a while.

Jaden was not ready to risk another devastating loss. In the wake of the catacomb tragedy, Cedar had become Jaden's only source of comfort. Jaden had also been longing to see Arjan, but Ravenea refused to let her visit him in the outside world, let alone in Flaw dimension; and Dracaen refused to enter Council dimension given its erratic dangers. Now, Cedar walked swiftly towards the Quercus portal, Jaden's abandonment imminent.

"I must go, Jaden. I need to consult with Genevre," said Cedar.

"Cedar, no! You cannot risk travel to the United States. Ritha—"

"Jaden!" Cedar turned abruptly and grabbed her arm. "Listen to me. I must consult with Genevre. You need not worry about a portal incident. Genevre, at Kalina's insistence, has temporarily relocated to Canada. She's staying near a protectorate outside . . ."

"Where?"

Cedar let go of Jaden and opened the door to the Quercus portal anteroom.

"Where?" Jaden asked again, stepping over the threshold.

"Vancouver."

"Then let me go with you. I remember the city! I can—"

"No, Jaden. I must speak with Genevre alone. My anger towards her has prevented me for years from doing what is best for the Alchemists' Council. I can delay no longer. At the very least, she may be able to provide insight on the *Osmanthian* folio, whose location remains a mystery despite another search yesterday by Ravenea and Arjan."

"Even the Initiates know that Fraxinus proclaimed the folio worthless and that Dracaen cancelled the search. What could Genevre—"

"Folio or no, Genevre and I have untold topics to discuss. My hope is that, through our discussions, I can convince her to return with me to Council dimension."

Immediately, Jaden felt a pang of anxiety. What if Cedar and Genevre spoke at length about Ilex and Melia? What if they discovered Jaden's deception? In her attempt to exempt Cedar from blame for releasing the bees and, later, to save Cedar the weight of knowing that their release had caused Ilex and Melia to die, Jaden had lied by omission to both Genevre and Cedar. What if, upon learning the truth, Genevre became incensed and refused Cedar's invitation to Council dimension? What if Cedar blamed Jaden? Thus, as Cedar insisted that all would be well, as she stepped into the Quercus portal, as it whisked her away without incident, Jaden found herself wishing never to face the consequences, which meant never seeing Cedar again.

Three days later, having received no word from Cedar, Jaden could not hold back tears as she walked along the channel path towards residence chambers. She had expected to fall onto her bed and cry herself to sleep as she had for the past two nights. Instead, Rowan Obeche intercepted her a few feet from her door.

"Senior Initiate Jaden," Obeche began, pleasantly enough under the circumstances.

Admittedly, since the Fourth Rebellion, Jaden's opinion of Obeche had shifted. During her first few years with the Council, she had dreaded passing Obeche in the corridors, let alone spending time with him; however, more recently she had come to appreciate his logic and candour. Obeche had maintained impeccable calm efficiency amidst the mounting dimensional chaos. His presence and comments at Council meetings somehow produced a comforting effect. Perhaps his promotion to Rowan had soothed his occupational frustrations.

"Yes, Rowan Obeche?"

"You and Laurel—" he began but then stopped. "Are you . . . well?"

"Yes, Rowan Obeche. Novillian Scribe Cedar has not returned from Vancouver, so I am . . . concerned. But I am otherwise fine. Why are you asking me about Senior Initiate Laurel?"

"Given the unorthodox state of current affairs and the need for ongoing caution, the Elders and Magistrates have decided that all Initiates should work in pairs — both in the classroom and during extracurricular laboratory practice, library research, et cetera. Circumstances have also led us to decide that the two Junior Initiates should each work with a Senior Initiate."

Jaden sensed where Obeche was heading, and she frowned in dismay.

"You and Laurel will pair with the Junior Initiates because you two are the least senior of the Senior Initiates."

Though she longed to protest, Jaden knew she had no logical grounds to do so. After all, if not for the circumstances of the Fourth Rebellion and mutual conjunctions, neither Jaden nor Laurel would have yet ascended to Senior Initiate. And until the Council managed to replenish itself back to its standard one hundred and one members, no one would be ascending at all. Instead, years of Council experience determined one's duties in several circumstances, especially regarding the Elder Council and Initiate orders. Besides, the only Senior Initiate Jaden would ever have chosen to work with was Ritha, and she was gone. Jaden closed her eyes in a useless attempt to rid herself of this dreadful image and nodded her consent.

"Let me guess," said Jaden. "You have paired me with Virginia."

"Not I. The Azoth Magen herself has decided you will work with Virginia."

"Long live the Alchemists' Council," responded Jaden, resigned once again to the will and imposition of another.

The golden light of early evening washed over Cedar and Genevre. For five interminably long minutes, they had been sitting silently together on a park bench, the water glistening as the sun caressed the peaks of its gentle waves. Far too much had remained unspoken for far too long. Even Genevre's explanation and earnest apology — which had arrived handwritten on a parchment scroll within a week of Cedar's readmission to Council dimension four years earlier, and which Genevre had undeniably written out of sincere regret — had been unable to expunge the agony Cedar had endured for a century, and it was powerless to resolve its ongoing repercussions.

Intellectually, Cedar could understand Genevre's rationale for hiding Arjan. She also believed Genevre's claim that she had wanted to tell Cedar about their son, but that Saule had insisted on keeping silent. The world of alchemy and alchemists and especially alchemical children had necessitated ongoing secrecy in various contexts at multiple levels. Cedar herself had spent most of her life engaged in keeping secrets for one reason or another. Yet she had been unable to forgive Genevre's primary choice: her decision to lie by omission about the fate of alchemical children — that twins are always born, and that one inevitably dies. When, years ago, Cedar admitted to Genevre that she had looked into the alembic and felt responsible for their daughter's death, Genevre should have admitted that Cedar was not to blame. *That* guilt had been the unbearable component. That guilt had led to her dependence on concealed formulas, to repeated and targeted repression of her own memories, to the fragmentation of her Quintessence, to her inability to heal fully.

Cedar had therefore decided, after returning from Santa Fe to Council dimension, that she should sever emotional ties with Genevre, that what they had left unsaid between them should remain so eternally — no additional words to consider, no insensitive utterances to rail against, no protracted scrolls to interpret, no imposed silences to misconstrue. What hope had she now? What could Genevre say in the disquieting aftermath of ongoing dimensional disintegration to ease Cedar's current pain? What could Cedar ask of Genevre as reparation?

Five additional minutes passed as Cedar's thoughts twisted themselves into tangled knots. And somehow, in that short span of time relative to the preceding four years of turmoil, Cedar recognized with clarity that adjustment was required here and now. She understood that the strained dynamic between them had become hers to shift. Of necessity over the past few years, the Alchemists' Council and the Rebel Branch had crossed the once impenetrable divide in their attempts to repair the dimensions. The least Cedar could do was meet

Genevre halfway across the figurative bridge spanning the distance between them.

"Tell me about him," Cedar said. "What was Arjan like as a child?"

"Circumstances limited my experiences with our son," Genevre explained. "He did not remain with me. Within a month of his birth, Saule took him to live in the outside world with Ilex and Melia. For years, Saule filtered my knowledge of him. When opportunity allowed, she would meet with them — Ilex, Melia, and Arjan — and then she would meet with me and pass along news . . . conversations . . . stories." Cedar thought back to the first time she received news of Arjan, years ago when Sadira had recounted her first contact with him. Sadira had described him as *handsome — beautiful, even — and extraordinarily well spoken*. Now, Genevre was presenting Cedar with the opportunity to learn more about their son. *Yes*, she realized. *Yes*, she wanted to know as much as possible.

"Then tell me a story about him that stands out, one that you enjoyed enough to remember all these years later."

Genevre paused. She smiled and nodded. "Two come to mind above the others — one disturbing, one delightful."

"Disturbing?"

"He almost died — from Lapidarian honey, of all things."

Cedar was startled.

"None of us knew the harm its properties could cause an alchemical child. We later learned that it can completely overwhelm their Quintessence, gradually causing biological functions to cease. Arjan had consumed Lapidarian honey on occasion without incident. But one day he consumed an entire jar. He suffered immeasurably for hours and hours. Saule's description alone captured the intensity and agony. I could barely breathe when I listened. He'd been dying while I'd been examining alchemical manuscripts at the British Library."

Cedar closed her eyes, pressing her lips together.

"Melia nursed him back to health. She saved him."

Cedar nodded, waiting. She did not know how to respond. She too had been absent as their son lay dying. Another several seconds passed in silence.

"And the delightful story?" Cedar asked.

Genevre laughed. "Well!" she began, appearing to relax and gesturing with enthusiasm. "After about a decade of living with Ilex and Melia, Arjan had matured enough to be granted a bit of freedom. At the time, they had been living in Tabriz for a year. Arjan would have appeared to be a boy of five or so. Given their unconventional condition and circumstances, Ilex and Melia were concerned about Arjan playing with other children. But they also realized they couldn't contain a child indoors perpetually. So, they sat him down, gave him basic guidelines on what he was to say and not say to the neighbouring children, and sent him off.

"After a few weeks, he'd all but fallen in love with another boy who lived down the street. They had become inseparable — playing together for hours each day, racing hand-in-hand through the neighbourhood over the course of the entire summer and fall. But eventually, the weather became colder, and they shifted to playing indoors. One fine winter day, Melia came into the kitchen to find several pounds of rice scattered across the floor. She swiftly discovered the two boys crammed inside the large storage basket that had formerly contained the rice.

"*What are you doing?* Melia asked them, pulling the friend out of the basket by his arms. Arjan refused to be excised. In protest, he curled himself into a ball at the bottom of the basket and wouldn't look at her. *Arjan! Get up now!* she insisted. *No! Go away!* he yelled up at her. The other boy, picking stray grains of rice off his shirt, peered up at her quizzically. *I told him it wouldn't work*, he said. *What wouldn't work?* Melia asked. *He said if we curled up together in the basket for a few hours, we'd become one person. You know, like you and Mr. Ilex.*"

Cedar couldn't help but laugh.

"And there you have it. Within a makeshift rice basket alembic, our son's childhood alchemical experiments with the Sacrament of Conjunction both began and promptly ended. A week later, Saule arranged for the family to reside temporarily in Italy."

Cedar had laughed so much she had to wipe away

tears. Once recovered, she asked, "What about your daughter? Did Ilex and Melia also raise Kalina?"

"No," she replied. "But where do I begin that story?"

As Genevre leaned forward to reach for her shawl, the scent of her hair washed over Cedar — sweet, fragrant lemon that stirred in Cedar a yearning to touch her. But the moment passed, and Genevre proceeded to fill the final hours before sunset relaying various accounts of other aspects of her life. Thus Cedar learned of her youth, of her training with the rebels, of her relationship with Dracaen, of their chemical wedding. *I buried my beloved first son and assumed my first daughter was dead*, she explained. The sentence echoed, piercing Cedar. Genevre had lied to her by omission regarding Arjan and his twin, but she herself had survived an equally devastating lie at the hands of a mentor and spouse she had trusted. Story after story, Cedar came to realize that as much as the paths of their lives diverged, they also converged time and again.

After describing in exquisite detail her braiding with Kalina, Genevre told Cedar of a particularly fraught period in her relationship with Ilex and Melia. "They disapproved on ethical grounds. From their perspective, creating alchemical children was morally irresponsible — reprehensible. They refused to speak with me for almost a year," she said as the sun grazed the water's edge at the horizon.

Cedar winced. Ilex and Melia had abandoned Genevre twice: first as an infant and later when they learned of her first created child.

"If not for the extenuating circumstances of the Third Rebellion, Ilex and Melia likely would not have accepted Arjan when the need arose. Such a devastating thought."

"I never knew them well," admitted Cedar. "But I admired Ilex and Melia when they resided in Council dimension. And I am grateful to them for raising our son as their own. He is an extraordinary individual — even conjoined! And he's certainly a talented alchemist."

"Yes," said Genevre. "Like his mothers."

Cedar smiled and reached for Genevre's hand. In that moment, she was thankful to have spent these hours with Genevre. Their conversation had proven not only worthwhile but a definitive step towards healing.

"I apologize, Genevre, for not reaching out to you when I learned of Ilex and Melia's death. But under the circumstances . . ." She could not continue.

Genevre moved her other hand to her amber pendant — one of the outside world, Cedar presumed.

"I understand," Genevre said. "I would never have expected you to. Like you said . . . *under the circumstances*. The circumstances have been complicated, to say the least."

Cedar nodded. "Were you with them when they died?"

"Yes. We were together. They dissolved at the height of the Fourth Rebellion. All that remains of their elemental essence is here." Genevre held her pendant up to the vanishing light. Its amber was the most exquisite Cedar had seen outside the Amber Garden.

"My sympathies, Genevre. Truly," said Cedar. "I should have realized that Ilex and Melia would be affected — even more so than the dimensional fabric — by the other mutual conjunctions. Arjan and Kalina could not have known the repercussions of their actions."

"No. They couldn't have. Neither could Jaden."

"Jaden?"

"Yes. But I don't harbour resentment. She was young. She assumed her action would save the world. It didn't. And now she blames herself. Has she not discussed the matter with you?"

"No. What action? She never met Ilex and Melia, as far as I know."

"No, she hadn't met them. But she released the bees."

"What has that to do with Ilex and Melia?"

"The bees in the apiary — the bees from the manuscripts that disappeared and were later reconstituted in the lavender fields of the main apiary. They had been feeding on Ilex and Melia's blood for years. The powers and effects of blood alchemy move beyond what I understand or can fathom. Through a blood-alchemy ritual, the bees had been alchemically sustaining their conjunctive cohesion. But Jaden released thousands of bees into the outside world, nullifying their blood-alchemy powers in the process. Others stung her, transferring the bloodline into her body. Between the release and the transfer of blood, the conjunction between Ilex and Melia could no longer be sustained. They dissolved in front of me. Jaden has apologized to me profusely. But as you know, the fault is not hers alone."

Cedar burned. The searing pain of sudden, guilt-laden recognition coursed through her. For a century, she had lived with remorse for her assumed role in the death of her daughter. For four years, she had seethed with resentment towards Genevre over her decision to conceal Arjan. For a mere few hours, she had finally breathed relief as understanding and forgiveness of Genevre gradually manifested while she listened to her stories. Now, the repercussions of her own role in the Fourth Rebellion became glaringly transparent to Cedar. Whereas she had once prided herself on her decision to release the bees — on being the one alchemist able to stand up against Council, the one to act on principle, the one to make the apparently right choice for all dimensions — she now recognized the severity of the consequences she had neglected to foresee. Cedar had killed Council's most renowned conjoined couple. Worse, she had killed the parents of Genevre — her friend and alchemical spouse. Worse again, she had killed the two people who had sheltered and raised her son despite their ethical stance against the method of his creation. And, worst of all, she had killed the only parents Arjan had known and loved for his entire life.

Cedar wept. For the first time in her existence, she did not know how to carry on.

Council Dimension — 2018

Two days after her conversation with Obeche, at the beginning of a joint Initiate session on manuscript illuminations, Jaden exchanged a sympathetic look with Laurel before sliding into her seat beside Virginia. Laurel sat across the table from Jaden beside Junior Initiate Javor. She seemed reasonably content, whereas Cercis, sitting beside Zelkova at a Senior Initiate table with Li and Kaede at the next table, appeared visibly annoyed. Jaden wondered whether Cercis was upset because he was no longer paired with Laurel, or because Laurel was paired with Javor. Jaden smiled as she remembered Laurel's comment from the night before. *Javor should have been your partner — an alliterative coupling.* Jaden should have responded, *And no resulting jealousy,* but she had merely shaken her head. Of course, like Cercis pining for Laurel, Jaden would have much preferred to be paired with Arjan, but she had no idea when, if ever, he would return to Council dimension. The weight of dimensional crises had long since buried her hopes of a relationship with him outside work. Still, on occasion, Jaden enjoyed imagining herself intimately connected with him, smiling when her daydream scenario progressed to a picture of Dracaen sitting through an Initiate manuscript lesson.

"I'll endeavour not to be too much of an imposition," said Virginia quietly.

Clever, thought Jaden. Whether false humility or not, the strategy worked. "I was initiated only a few years before you," she responded. "We both have a lot to learn and a lot to accomplish. Who knows where this imposed pairing will lead?"

Virginia smirked and asked, "Are you flirting?"

"What? No!"

"Good, because I'm not interested in a physical relationship."

"Neither am I!" insisted Jaden, slightly too loudly.

Laurel rolled her eyes. "Just wait a few more decades," she said.

"Are you speaking from experience, Senior Initiate Laurel?" asked Virginia.

Laurel laughed. Javor, who had entered Council dimension only a month earlier, was blushing deeply. If Cercis had seen this vivid response, his jealousy would have evaporated. Clearly, Laurel's new scribal partner was too timid to attract her attention outside duty. Jaden realized the Initiate Order had not been this entertaining since the arrival of Arjan. Perhaps, despite her mourning for both the Council dimension and her colleagues, she could manage the occasional grin.

"Initiates!" called Magistrate Linden. "Choose a stylus from the selection within the table alcoves and attach a medium-girth steel-rendered nib as follows." He then illustrated the procedure, which most of the Senior Initiates had mastered years ago.

Virginia attached her nib effortlessly, whereas Javor dropped his three times before Laurel stepped in to assist. Linden then provided instructions on ink preparation, inkwell cleansing, stylus submersion, and linear graphing. Though Jaden had been through similar sessions with Sadira and Nunnera over the years, she realized an hour into Linden's lesson that she felt reasonably content for the first time since the catacomb tragedy. She and Virginia took turns inscribing the letters and accompanying iconography on the parchment scroll. At each interval, Linden provided both explicit instructions and examples — the latter of which were visible via luminescence projector on the white onyx panel of the east wall.

As the inscribed image began to take form, Jaden realized they were inking a laboratory alembic of the sort used in the Initiate classroom — the one the Magistrates operated during lectures and workshops about basic alchemical transmutations. The accompanying text was virtually incomprehensible to Jaden. She could replicate the letters reasonably well, but the words themselves comprised 5th Council script — an ancient alchemical language that Jaden had barely begun to study and upon which *Musurgia Universalis* had no tangible effect. Virginia's skill at inscription appeared to surpass Jaden's: her downstrokes perfectly firm, her point size precise, her embellishments effortless. This observation both intrigued and frustrated Jaden. She resigned herself in that moment to accept that her own ascension through the Orders of Council might terminate at Reader if her scribal abilities remained stunted.

Watching Virginia form her letters, Jaden considered the possibility that Ravenea may have encouraged the pairing so that Virginia could help *her*. She thought then of Arjan and his advanced skill level. She peered at Virginia, wondering about her alchemical origins. Surely Genevre and Cedar would not have created yet another child? Regardless, Jaden became determined to observe Virginia's calligraphic techniques and letter formation judiciously.

"What's wrong?" asked Virginia.

"What? Nothing."

"You're staring at me."

"Just admiring your level of concentration."

"Which you've now broken," Virginia said flatly.

Embarrassed, Jaden temporarily moved her attention across the table to Javor's work, which seemed reassuringly juvenile in both its form and shading. She refrained from shifting her attention away from her own parchment again until Linden requested they all pause and listen. Further observation of Virginia's scribal efforts would necessarily wait until a future lesson.

"The next scribal technique requires you to use skin-to-skin contact with your partner," said Linden. "In the current era, we must all learn to progress through cooperation."

For the love of the dimensions! thought Jaden, debating whether to run from the room.

Linden then called upon Senior Initiate Kaede to assist in illustrating the practice of "membrane concurrence," which involved one person sketching the outline of a letter or object while the other person placed a hand on the wrist of the sketcher. Then, the partners would reverse roles, one person placing a hand on the wrist of the one who is filling in the letter or object with ink. For the illustration, Linden had used a basic alchemical symbol, but he suggested the Initiates attempt something more complex.

"Choose an object whose inking will require at least two colours," said Linden. "To avoid debate or delay, the most senior of the two will choose the design and sketch the outline. Inscribe the object within the alembic."

Jaden opted for a bee — the stripes of which she assumed would be challenging for Virginia to ink without the black accidentally bleeding into the yellow. Besides, bees had been on her mind lately. Despite the bloodline she had apparently inherited thanks to the bees, Jaden had failed to notice a single enhancement to her alchemical skills. *Injected blood can take years to mature*, Kalina had informed her in an apparent attempt at reassurance. Today's feeble scribal endeavours provided additional evidence to support a complete lack of maturity. Any blood-alchemy aptitudes she had anticipated as a result of the bee stings had failed to materialize. Indeed, Jaden doubted whether a single molecule of Lapidarian bee venom or Ilex and Melia's blood circulated within her.

Jaden, stylus in hand, placed the tip of the nib onto the parchment in the centre of the alembic. Virginia lightly clasped Jaden's wrist with her left hand. The sensation startled her — an immediate prickling that, oddly, reminded Jaden of the time she had rubbed Lapidarian honey into a paper cut. At the risk of another rebuke, Jaden glanced at Virginia to assess her expression. Virginia merely raised her eyebrows in the facial equivalent of a shrug and ges-tured for Jaden to continue the sketch. The prickling sensation intensified with each passing minute. By the time she outlined the final wing, the burning seared to the point of pain. When Virginia removed her hand, Jaden inspected her wrist for welts, but she saw only unblemished skin.

Switching positions and reversing roles, Jaden wrapped her hand around Virginia's wrist. Instead of prickling and burning, Jaden felt a soft vibra-tion. Each time Virginia replenished the ink and set the nib onto the bee, the sensation increased in intensity. As Virginia lightly added streaks of blue and green to replicate the Lapidarian tinge on the wings, Jaden marvelled at her ability to keep the stylus steady. Later, the stylus placed back into its holder, their hands in their laps, Jaden and Virginia stared at their mutually created image in amazement. The ink had not bled whatsoever; the bee looked exquisitely realistic.

"How extraordinary!" said Laurel, loudly enough to attract the attention not only of nearby Initiates but also of Linden.

As Linden approached their table, Jaden whispered to Virginia, "Don't mention the burning sensation."

"What burning sensation?" Virginia asked.

Jaden could not tell whether the question was serious or a ruse of agreement.

"Indeed!" exclaimed Linden. "You two have produced an extraordinary illumination! Everyone, gather 'round!"

Within seconds, all the Initiates were standing around the table nodding in admiration, mouths agape in amazement.

"Jaden!" said Zelkova. "If I did not know better, I would have assumed a Novillian Scribe had inscribed that bee!"

"Part the way!"

As the Initiates moved aside, Azoth Magen Ravenea stepped forward. She picked up the sheet of parchment and stared intently at the bee.

"Whose work am I admiring?" she asked.

"The bee is the product of a membrane concurrence between Senior Initiate Jaden and Junior Initiate Virginia," responded Linden.

"Take your seats!" commanded Ravenea to the Initiates still lingering nearby. She then walked to the front of the classroom with the parchment sheet. "Initiate Zelkova, fetch me fire from the kiln."

As Zelkova worked to arrange burning embers into a transfer vessel, Linden collected the sheets from each of the student pairs. After handing the sheets to Ravenea, he slid open a section of the demonstration counter to reveal the stone and steel inset basin. Though the rationale remained unclear, Jaden knew what was about to happen: Ravenea was going to burn each of the parchment sheets, thereby dashing Jaden's hope of keeping her first scribal masterpiece. One after the next, Ravenea held up the sheet and its inscribed image, ascertained the scribal pair, set a corner of the parchment into the flame, watched it burn, and then dropped the fiery remains into the basin. Jaden wondered whether the destruction was a mere precaution against unintentional elemental disruption or Ravenea planned to use the ashes for a specific alchemical procedure. After all, the Initiate images comprised Lapidarian ink.

Ravenea held up the final piece of parchment. She nodded at Jaden and Virginia. "We can all agree on the beauty of this particular illumination," she said admiringly.

Jaden smiled, and the other Initiates nodded.

"But aesthetics," continued Ravenea, "while gratifying to our senses, are a sign of calligraphic rather than alchemical skill. The primary objective of the Alchemists' Council is to maintain elemental balance across dimensional space through manuscript illumination, a task at which we are currently failing miserably. To become a scribal master, an alchemist's inscriptions must be resistant to elemental damage. How are you, as Initiates during one of the most challenging eras of Council history, to help repair the dimension if your work cannot withstand trial by fire? How are you to assist rebalancing the outside world if your illuminations cannot transform into a viable effect?"

Jaden balked. She felt as if she were being rebuked for her pride. She winced as Ravenea held the edge of the sheet to the flame. Like the others before it, the parchment began to burn. But instead of dropping it into the basin, Ravenea maintained her grip. Just as Jaden began to fear Ravenea herself would sustain burns, both the parchment sheet and the flames instantaneously vanished. In their place, in the palm of Ravenea's outstretched hand, was a bee.

All the Initiates, including Jaden, gasped. They stood up, angling for a better view, attempting to determine whether the bee was an alchemical illusion. They needed not wait long for an answer. The bee flew from Ravenea's hand and landed atop a nearby luminescence lantern.

"In this bee, we bear witness to our first glimmer of hope for the future."

Ravenea moved to a position beside the luminescence lantern and extended her hand. The bee walked into her palm and exhibited no resistance as Ravenea carefully moved it into a shallow glass dish.

"Initiates Jaden and Virginia will accompany me to the lavender fields of the main apiary to release our newest resident. The rest of you will spend the remainder of the day honing your scribal skills. This bee alone cannot save us."

After Cedar admitted the truth about the release of the bees, Genevre had backed away — literally, at first. From the beach, Cedar had returned with Genevre to the Sylvia Hotel hoping that they could speak at length. But once they reached the lobby, Genevre insisted on time alone. Instead of returning to Council dimension, Cedar booked her own room at the Sylvia. She then left a note for Genevre suggesting they speak the next day. But in the morning, when she knocked on Genevre's door, she received no answer. Neither did she receive an answer that afternoon or evening. The following day, as Cedar approached the room, a stranger emerged from it. Clearly, Genevre had left without saying goodbye. Their established pattern thereby continued — withdrawal following connection; distance replacing closeness.

Cedar retreated to her hotel room for days, leaving only when hunger insisted. Otherwise, she lay on the bed or stood at the window staring upward or outward, not sure how to proceed. She thought repeatedly of the first time she had met Genevre — her graceful beauty had enamoured Cedar on the day she appeared in the dappled light beneath the cottonwood tree in front of her Santa Fe home. A century had passed since their chemical wedding, since the gestation of their alchemical children, since the death of their daughter, since the birth of Arjan. But the passing of time and the subsequent strengthening of their bond through varying circumstances had made little difference in the face of yet another heartbreaking revelation.

Cedar knew she had no right to expect Genevre to have reacted differently to her disclosure. *I am responsible for the death of Ilex and Melia. Jaden was merely following my directions.* These phrases were mere euphemisms for Cedar's literal revelation: *I killed your parents.* From Genevre's perspective, Cedar had thus wounded her once again — just as she had done years earlier when she abandoned Genevre to the outside world after her first marriage proposal. But from Cedar's perspective, the second betrayal, unlike the first, had been unintentional. Cedar too had been devastated. *I didn't know*, she had pleaded. Genevre had chosen not to listen.

Now, almost a week had passed since her return to Council dimension, and Cedar still teared up when alone in her office or residence chambers. At night, she wept before falling into a restless slumber. She yearned to see Genevre, longed to explain again her sincere regret. *I didn't know! I couldn't have known!* Yet unlike Arjan, Kalina, and Jaden, Cedar could not use the inexperience of youth as a justification for her actions. As a Novillian Scribe, though she knew nothing of their blood-infused connection with Ilex and Melia, she had certainly understood that the release of bees could have negative repercussions. But how could she have known the specific consequences for them, let alone for Jaden? She had released the bees to assist the outside world. She had removed Jaden's pendant to help Jaden and to ensure the Elders saw her as a victim rather than an instigator of Cedar's treachery. *I didn't know!*

Cedar also recognized that her rationale for releasing the bees would mean nothing to Genevre considering the tragic outcome. She fluctuated between hope and despair. She imagined Genevre yelling at her, claiming to want nothing more to do with her, insisting that they permanently sever their friendship, remaining forever in the outside world. But she also imagined Genevre reaching out to her, pulling her into an embrace, acknowledging that all was forgiven, agreeing to move on from here despite the revelation of difficult truths. She pictured them working on manuscripts together late into the night to restore dimensional damage.

But if Cedar were to be honest, she would have to admit that this imagined scenario of reconciliation perpetuated yet another lie by omission, one she had been telling herself for years. Yes, she wanted to continue to work with her. Yes, the Alchemists' Council required their ongoing cooperation. But Cedar wanted more than collegiality, more than scribal comradeship, more than interaction between alchemists. She longed for permission, without guilt or interference or questions of impropriety, without critique by Ruis or Sadira, to fall in love with Genevre, to form a family — one that their mutually created child would anchor.

But Cedar knew simultaneously that this acknowledgement would remain mere fantasy even once enough time had passed for Genevre to accept her apology, even after they had re-established their friendship and collegiality. After all, Arjan was permanently conjoined with Dracaen. And Cedar certainly had no intention of bringing the High Azoth of the Rebel Branch into their little family. Besides, outside her own imagination, Cedar had no reason to believe Genevre had ever harboured reciprocal feelings. If she had wanted to create a family with Cedar, Genevre would not have hidden Arjan from her for so many years. She would have found a means to reveal the truth of her feelings, to help Cedar understand the inherent emotional complexities, to develop a plan together. Thus, to distract herself from the spiralling and increasingly frustrating fantasies about Genevre, Cedar thought instead about work. She focused her intentions on helping Ruis and Sadira save the dimensions, thereby determining once again to abandon her clear and present desires for the sake of the Alchemists' Council.

Cedar stood in the archway watching Sadira, whose back was turned. Though Cedar knew Sadira was speaking with Kalina, she appeared to be talking with herself. If Cedar focused on the subtle shifts in hair colour and texture, she would be able to distinguish each of the conjoined from the other. But imagining Sadira as herself alone comforted Cedar. She thought about their first kiss and yearned again for intimacy.

"Once upon a time, you looked at me with such longing," whispered Ruis. He too had arrived early for the meeting and now stood slightly behind Cedar.

She glanced at him, annoyed. "So you now have the power to assess my level of desire through sheer proximity? Quite the advanced skill even for an Azoth!"

"You were twisting your hair," he responded.

"No!"

"Yes!" he insisted.

"Come in," said Sadira. She had turned towards them. Kalina had retreated, as she always did in the presence of an alchemist who could not see her within Council dimension. "Have a seat," she said, gesturing to the round table in the centre of the room.

"Have you uncovered something of apparent use in a manuscript?" asked Ruis. He glanced at the countertop to his left where multiple scrolls lay unfurled.

"No," Sadira said. "But Ravenea may have. She is the one who requested this meeting."

"In the North Library archives?"

Sadira shrugged and then looked at Cedar. Ruis rolled his eyes. Cedar looked down, not wanting to infer anything further from either of their expressions. Within a minute of waiting, Ruis began tapping his fingers on the table.

"How is Kalina?" Cedar said to break the tension.

"Fine," answered Sadira. "We have finally developed a rhythm that works well for both of us. We've rarely argued in the last few months. And she willingly retreats into the shadows to give me privacy when necessary." She glanced at Cedar once again. Cedar nodded but did not smile.

"Azoth Magen," said Ruis, hands in Ab Uno.

Ravenea had entered the room without Cedar or Sadira noticing. She retrieved one of the scrolls from the side of the room and handed it to Cedar.

"Do you recognize this inscription?" she asked, adjusting her robes before taking a seat.

Ruis leaned towards Cedar to inspect the scroll himself.

"An early rendition of *The Splendour of Prima Materia*," Ruis said.

"Not the content," said Ravenea, "the *inscription* — the scribal hand. Do you recognize the calligraphy? Can you determine the name of the scribe?"

Instead of reading the words, Cedar shifted her focus to the letters. Though neatly aligned and proficiently inked, they were not fully mature. They did indeed look familiar, but she could not readily identify the hand. Magistrates often employed *The Splendour of Prima Materia* during calligraphy classes, so Cedar supposed one of the current Senior Initiates could have rendered it — someone almost ready to ascend to Junior Magistrate status once Council dimension had fully recovered. Cedar recalled the day that Azoth Magen Mundani had announced the official rotation of the *Vitae Aeternae* of the 16th Council. Finally, with the Azoth Magen's pronouncement, she ascended from the Initiate to the Magistrate. Mundani had praised her calligraphic skills and—

Cedar dropped the scroll. "Where did you get this?" she asked. "At least a century must have passed since—"

"Yes and no," said Ravenea. "A few hundred years have passed since you inscribed *this* scroll." She handed Cedar another one. "But the first one I showed you was inscribed last week."

Ruis and Sadira both stood up and peered at the two scrolls over Cedar's shoulder.

"*You* inscribed an identical scroll?" Sadira asked Cedar.

"No."

"She inscribed only *this* one," said Ravenea, pointing to the second scroll.

"And the other?" asked Ruis.

"The other is a copy made at my request as part of an Initiate calligraphy lesson. As you well know, duplicating inscriptions of seasoned Scribes is a time-honoured practice to help Initiates hone their skills."

"Of course, but not usually with such astonishing success," said Ruis.

"Who is the Initiate savant?" asked Sadira. "Who is our future Lapidarian Scribe?"

"*Scribes* — plural. Initiates Jaden and Virginia mutually inscribed the scroll. The salvation of the Alchemists' Council — the fate of Council manuscripts — may literally lie in their hands."

Jaden stood near the cliff face portal with Rowan Obeche. Obeche awaited Dracaen; Jaden awaited Arjan. Though various sections of Council dimension — including the catacombs and Amber Garden — still showed no signs of recovery, the cliff face portal had recently stabilized enough for Dracaen to agree to return. Jaden wanted to believe that the regenerated portal was due in part to the hundreds of bees she and Virginia had inscribed, burned, transmuted, and released into Council dimension over the past month. But, upon hearing Jaden discuss this theory with Virginia, Azoth Magen Ravenea requested that Jaden not leap to conclusions, that she and Virginia had years of dedicated scribal practice ahead of them before a pattern of substantial dimensional change could be deemed the fruits of their labours.

Meanwhile, Ravenea had specifically asked Jaden to take a break from her scribal duties to accompany Obeche to the cliff face and, thereafter, escort Arjan to Azothian Chambers. A few years earlier, Obeche had outright refused Arjan free rein of Council dimension. *He may not be able to control High Azoth Dracaen!* Obeche had warned. Thereafter, he and Jaden had become a team of sorts, dispatched whenever an official visit was warranted. On this occasion, they had not spoken much. Obeche, hands behind his back as he faced away from the cliff face, looked to be contemplating the redwood forest. Jaden tossed small fragments of rock into the nearby pond.

"Ravenea informs me that you have become quite the proficient scribe," said Obeche. He had not shifted his position. To an observer, he would have appeared to be speaking to the trees. "I understand your partnership with Virginia has indeed proven productive."

"Potentially," said Jaden, the splash of a pebble punctuating her comment. "But we are still learning. Beyond inscribing bees, we have yet to understand how our skills might save the dimensions." Her usual pleasant tone had shifted to one that implied dejection.

"That responsibility is not yours alone. We must each contribute."

Jaden glanced towards him. This attempt at encouragement, like many of Obeche's recent interactions with her, seemed uncharacteristically charming. The continual dimensional instability had changed them all. "Years ago, did you suspect Arjan's allegiance to the Rebel Branch? Please be truthful." She stood beside Obeche now, watching a raven pecking at its feathers in one of the tall trees.

"I have always been truthful with you, Jaden. Unlike various other Council members, I have had no reason to lie to you or, indeed, to anyone. Even you must admit now that my early suspicions of Arjan were justified."

"He wanted only what he believed to be best for all dimensions."

"As did I," said Obeche.

"But when you drained his pendant, you didn't read deception."

"No. I read nothing. In retrospect, I assume blood alchemy was at play."

"When you discussed my scribal abilities with Ravenea, did she mention that I am also a blood alchemist? She says my blood has recently matured and that I now need to hone my abilities. Are you suspicious of my intentions?"

"No more so now than in the past," he responded.

Jaden would have requested clarity, but the crackling sound emanating from the solid rock of the cliff face signalled portal activity. They turned and waited. When Arjan emerged, Jaden felt a sense of relief. She smiled. Though now conjoined with Dracaen, Arjan remained for Jaden the alchemist with whom she felt most comfortable. Regardless of his current status, Jaden believed their Initiate days together had bonded them forever.

"Is the High Azoth currently dormant?" Obeche asked Arjan.

"For the foreseeable future," Arjan responded.

"If only we actually *could* see the future," said Jaden. "Even the ancient prophecies appear to be offline."

Arjan smiled and nodded. "Perhaps we should upload everything to outside world digital archives. Given our continual failed attempts at correcting our errors, perhaps deft computer programmers would be of even more value than Council Scribes."

"Don't let Cedar hear you say that!" Jaden said, laughing.

"Enough of the banter," said Obeche, appearing visibly dismayed. "Has Flaw dimension experienced any notable disturbances since your previous visit?"

Jaden would have preferred to chat idly with Arjan on the walk through the forest and across the open field back to the main Council buildings.

However, as had become his habit on such occasions, Obeche insisted on punctuating the conversation with dimensional inquiry.

"None whatsoever. In fact, Flaw dimension appears to have stabilized."

"Ravenea and the Elders will be pleased to hear a full report of your techniques."

"I have no rebel techniques to report," responded Arjan.

Obeche stopped walking and turned towards Arjan. "Dracaen must uphold the Joint Coalition agreement now that the portals have stabilized. The Rebel Branch must share successful procedures with Council for the good of all dimensions."

"If we had an alchemical formula or technique to share, we would do so."

"Then why are you here?" asked Obeche.

Jaden worried momentarily that Obeche would demand Arjan's departure.

"Rebel Branch Elders have concluded that Flaw dimension began to thrive after the catacomb collapse. More recently, during the period corresponding with your portal regeneration, the wrought-iron barrier surrounding the Dragonblood Stone began to rust. Yesterday, the breeze that has animated our wooden chimes for millennia vanished completely. The corridors now stagnate in silence."

"What precisely are you implying, Arjan?" said Obeche.

"We now contend that survival of the Rebel Branch is dependent on the demise of the Alchemists' Council."

"Ruis," said Cedar. She stood in the east doorway of the Scriptorium. Not wanting to startle him, she had spoken his name softly. He remained still, head lowered in observation of the Lapis. He ran a hand along the expanded Flaw. Either he had not heard her call, or he chose to ignore her.

"Ruis," she said again, slightly louder. "What are you doing here?"

He raised his head but did not turn to her. His focus remained on the Lapis. *"One must die so the other may live,"* he quoted, thus echoing the ancient prophecy that Dracaen and Arjan had intoned repeatedly during the most recent Joint Coalition session.

"That idiom applies to alchemical children, not to the Lapis. The rebels understand that the Flaw cannot exist without the Stone. *By destroying the other, we destroy ourselves.*"

"And *that* idiom is nothing more than Rebel Branch propaganda! Dracaen spouts alchemical wisdom to suit his whims. Do you not recognize his pattern? His hypocrisy?"

"The rebels have always sought to increase the Flaw and ensure its permanence, but they have *never* advocated for destruction of the Lapis. Even if we cannot save Council dimension, the Rebel Branch will necessarily maintain the Lapis to harbour the Flaw."

"Harbouring the Flaw is *not* the sacred purpose of the Lapis."

"Clinging to that tenet for generations has brought us to the brink of annihilation. As Arjan has suggested, a fundamental transformation of perspective is now our most viable choice."

He shook his head. "No. I refuse to forsake Council dimension or the Lapis. I refuse to abolish the possibility of re-enacting *Remota Macula*. I am prepared to accept all requisite sacrifices. *To save ourselves, we must enhance the Stone.*"

"Ruis—"

"One additional option has yet to be decreed."

Something was wrong. Though the spatial distance between them was minimal, Cedar's walk across the cold stone floor to reach him seemed interminable. She stood behind him, put a hand on his shoulder, and lowered her forehead to the back of his neck. The familiarity of his scent comforted her. Despite their differences, despite the years that had passed since their physical intimacy, Cedar welcomed his solidity amidst the chaotic fragmentation of her world. He turned to face her then, pulling her into a tight embrace, kissing the top of her head. She looked up at him and kissed him on the lips. Her thoughts raced in the seconds that followed. But her hesitation allowed time for interruption. Obeche coughed. He was standing in the doorway observing them.

"Come in," said Ruis, pulling away from Cedar.

"Perhaps we could wait another hour or so," Obeche replied, not moving.

"No. No more waiting. The time has come."

Only as Obeche drew near did Cedar notice the object he carried in his left hand. Though Obeche's dark robes partially obscured the mahogany box, Cedar immediately recognized its elaborately carved bronze locks. Dread coursed through her.

"No!" she cried. She reached for the box, which Obeche quickly clasped with both hands against his chest. "Give me the box! Be sensible, Obeche! You cannot do this!"

"You must also be sensible, Cedar," Ruis said calmly. "You cannot expect a Rowan to obey the commands of a Novillian Scribe."

"But we can find another way!" she insisted.

"Despite our efforts, Council dimension continues to disintegrate," said Obeche. "Reverberations into the outside world are heightening. We have exhausted our options. Dracaen and Arjan are correct. *One must die so the other may live.* Ruis and I have discussed the matter at length. Our interpretation of that adage is sound."

"No, no, you are wrong!"

"Our decision is no longer up for debate," said Obeche.

"But Dracaen has offered sanctuary to us all. From within Flaw dimension, rebels and alchemists can work together to restore elemental balance while Council dimension heals!"

"Do you no longer know me at all, Cedar? I would rather die than hand the Rebel Branch our power," responded Ruis solemnly. "And I certainly have no intention of living an eternal life in the cold, dark confines of Flaw dimension!"

"Then live in the outside world! We can each choose—"

"We have already made our choice," said Obeche.

Cedar wanted to scream in protest. Yet she knew that Obeche's and Ruis's responses, while obstinate, were reasoned within Council protocols. As a Novillian Scribe, she had no voice to dissuade either an Azoth or a Rowan in this matter, certainly not once they had made their decision. Throughout her Council tenure, Cedar's relationship with Obeche had generally been one of contention. She had assumed such professional rivalry would endure to the end. But the end she had envisioned, time and again, had involved his succumbing to conjunction or Final Ascension. She had never considered *Sangue Morte*. Unbidden and unwelcomed, images of the morbid ritual came to her: blood-stained and graphic illuminations from the most ancient Council manuscripts of the deepest archives.

Tears welled as she watched Obeche open the bronze and mahogany box. It contained a ceremonial knife wrapped in a silk embroidered cloth. The Lapis itself had sharpened the knife's steel blade; potent Elixir infused the coral embedded in its emerald handle. Cedar knew of this knife not only from Senior Initiate lessons but also had witnessed its use by 16th Council Azoth Magen Mundani. She shuddered. Its sole purpose: ritual sacrifice of an Elder.

Obeche intended to enact ceremonial death. In releasing his blood with the Sanguine Blade, he would release his Quintessence, which would return alchemically to the Lapis at an exponentially greater frequency than by pendant relinquishment alone. Obeche would thereby strengthen the Lapis's power within Council dimension by reducing the Flaw in the Stone. But unlike Ailanthus, who had sacrificed himself with a similar purpose through Final Ascension five years earlier, Obeche would not ascend to the One through the act of *Sangue Morte*. He would not be pierced with the Sword of Elixir. He would not turn to dust. Nor would he dissolve into blood, as did the Rebel Branch sacrifice of the Third Rebellion. Instead, by enacting *Sangue Morte*, Obeche would merely bleed out. Killed by his own hand, blood and Quintessence absorbed into the Lapis, he would die not as an alchemist but as a mortal — a human drained of all alchemical substance. His maimed and deceased body would be wrapped in an Azadirian shroud, burned in ritual fires, and returned as ashes in a wooden urn to the outside world for burial in an unmarked grave. Cedar could not abide such desolation, not even for Obeche.

She turned to plead with Ruis. "You are right, of course. As a Novillian Scribe, *I* cannot forbid Obeche from enacting *Sangue Morte*, but as an Azoth *you* can! Please, Ruis, rescind your agreement in the name of the Azoths! Refuse to accept his offer! Forbid his sacrifice outright!"

"I forbade Obeche's offer of sacrifice when he proposed the idea to me three days ago."

Cedar stood motionless, confused. "Then . . . why?" she asked, gesturing towards the box, which now rested on the Lapis.

Ruis placed a hand gently on her cheek, meeting her eyes. "I need you to understand and remember the sincerity of his offer. Had I given my consent, Obeche would have sacrificed himself for the benefit of all — not for the One but for the All, alchemists, rebels, and outside world people alike. His faithfulness to the Alchemists' Council, from the moment he crossed the threshold as an Initiate until now, has been uncompromised and unflinching. Promise me you will forever remember and honour his gesture of faith."

"I promise, Azoth," Cedar said, exhaling in relief. She would not have wished such a death on her most stringent opponent of the Rebel Branch, let alone on a member of the Alchemists' Council with whom she had worked for centuries. She nodded humbly in Ab Uno first to Ruis and then to Obeche. Their ruse with the box had indeed worked to evoke her sympathy and respect. Within these past few minutes, she had irrevocably altered her opinion of Obeche for the better.

Then, as swiftly as relief had flooded in, it vanished when Ruis himself removed the knife from the box. Fleetingly, Cedar feared for her own life, but she then recognized that only an Elder of the Quintessence could enact *Sangue Morte*, and only with the permission of another Elder of the Quintessence. As a Novillian Scribe, rather than an Azoth or Rowan, Cedar could not act as sacrifice. And in that instant of self-reflection, she understood that Azoth Ruis had offered himself as sacrifice and Rowan Obeche had granted consent.

"No!" Cedar screamed. "No!"

She rushed at Ruis, struggled to wrench the knife from his hand. But he was taller and stronger and determined. And Obeche aided him to thwart her efforts. She collapsed, defeated and sobbing, onto the ground. Ruis had spent his entire existence as an alchemist seeking to vanquish the Flaw. He believed in the One. He believed in ultimate Final Ascension. He believed in eternal life for all beings of all dimensions. And he could have succeeded years ago if not for her. Cedar had actively fought against all that had mattered to him. Against his efforts to remove the Flaw, she had sabotaged the *Remota Macula*. Against his efforts to support her ascension to Rowan or Azoth, she had resisted. Against his efforts to love her, she had found someone else to adore. Now, no time remained for her redemption.

"Goodbye, my love," he said.

Cedar could not respond beyond weeping.

"'Bless me now with your fierce tears, I pray,'" he pleaded.

The poem — this revised line in particular — took her back to the latter decades of their union. Before her conjunction, before her betrayal, before her rejection of both Ruis and his ideals, they had oft contemplated their figurative deaths amidst their literal love.

"'Do not go gentle into that good night,'" she sobbed, standing to face him.

"'Rage, rage—'" he began.

He brought the knife to his throat, pushed it in, and pulled it across. As he fell forward, his blood poured over the Lapis into the wound of the Flaw.

Ravenea, Obeche, and Sadira accompanied Cedar to the outside world burial ground. Kalina had agreed to remain in the shadows for the duration. Thanks to Ravenea's activation of a temporary portal, they arrived without incident in the depths of a forest in the Pacific northwest. Obeche had suggested the location after his research revealed that the ashes of the three other Council members known to have enacted *Sangue Morte* also had been brought to this island. The forest was ancient, breathtaking. Thick moss grew not only on the ground and rocks but the trunks of the trees, which towered high above the alchemists standing below. The forest's varied shades and textures of green calmed Cedar. She caressed the smooth urn. Both the urn and many of the trees were cedar, a coincidence that comforted her amidst agonizing grief.

Ravenea leading the way, they walked through the forest to a small creek where Cedrus greeted them. He was an outside world scribe assigned alternately to the Vancouver and Anchorage protectorates. Cedar had met him only once before, forty years earlier when he had come to Council dimension for a few months of training with Jinjing.

We share a namesake, he had said to her upon their first meeting. Today, relieved of protectorate duties, Cedrus would act as their advisor, arranging permissions, escorting the alchemists to the burial site, ensuring their physical intrusion onto the land left no visible trace of their presence.

Cedar had longed to mourn Ruis in the Amber Garden. But even if Ravenea had granted permission under such extenuating circumstances, all that remained of the garden were a few fragments of its border wall — every tree, every bit of amber had turned gelatinous and then melted away long ago. On the day of Ruis's sacrifice, even the few remaining fragments had begun to crumble.

Watching Cedrus and Obeche digging the grave, Cedar breathed in the sights and sounds and scents of the forest. Though the Law Codes obliged the Elders to remove Ruis's mortal ashes from Council dimension, and though Cedar had repeatedly objected, gratitude now moved her to tears. This outside world forest had not been alchemically constructed, but it certainly appeared to have been touched by the One for which Ruis had eternally longed. She gripped fiercely to that thought, content that seemingly flawless beauty would eternally encircle her beloved Ruis. She too would survive, even if necessity meant that she would return to live her final days within this third dimension — to reside where she had been born: inside the outside world *against the dying of the light*.

Arjan crossed the threshold onto the mosaic floor of Azothian Chambers. Even here, cracks were beginning to show. Rowan Obeche stood beside a round table that stood between the Azothian kiln and the tiers of wooden benches. On the table were four Azadirian teacups, small plates, and silver cutlery. Arjan had expected to find Azoth Magen Ravenea and Azoth Kai awaiting Dracaen. But, despite the place settings, Obeche was the only other person in the room.

"Sit," said Obeche, gesturing towards the chair opposite him. "Tea will be brought shortly. In the meantime, I thought we could chat."

Arjan felt Dracaen stir slightly, as if he had been about to emerge from the shadows and resume conscious attention.

"My deepest sympathies for the loss of Azoth Ruis," said Arjan before taking a seat. He bowed his head in Ab Uno. "Though our views differed, I admired him. His determination never wavered. In the end, he made a choice that he believed would revive Council dimension."

"And thus protect all dimensions."

"Has the Lapis shown any sign of recovery?"

"Yes. For the first time since the mutual conjunctions, Lapidarian Quintessence has marginally increased. If it continues to mature at its current rate, we should be able to extract curative properties within a year."

"And in the meantime?"

"We will remain vigilant about our choices."

"Choice is reliant on the Flaw," said Arjan. He placed his hands, fingers interlaced, on the table to the left of his teacup. "Your success may result in our failure."

"The Flaw remains fully intact. Council readily acknowledges that it is a permanent fixture. Our goal is no longer to remove the Flaw in the Stone. The Alchemists' Council and the Rebel Branch must maintain a single objective: to work together to heal the outside world."

Arjan nodded. "Is this afternoon tea your gesture of peace?" he asked.

"No," Obeche responded. "But I am not the one with whom you will be enjoying it. Jaden and Kalina will arrive shortly. Kalina has concluded that your spending a few hours of leisure time with her and Jaden could prove beneficial. Sadira has agreed to the plan and will remain in the shadows. I merely require a preemptive consultation with you regarding your conjunction."

"Would you prefer to speak with Dracaen?"

"No. You will suffice."

Arjan smiled, wondering if the remark was Obeche's attempt at a joke.

"Many years ago," began Obeche, "during the

Ritual of Location that resulted in Council's choice of Sadira as our next Initiate, my nose began to bleed for the first time in my life. I remember standing there, looking into the Albedo pool, watching the drops of blood stain the pristine water and then disappear immediately. The sight simultaneously appalled and intrigued me. My blood had contaminated the waters but then vanished within them. Those waters flow in and out of the Albedo pool through the channels of Council dimension. I marvelled that the waters had accepted my body, but that they considered my blood an intruder to be dissolved. I wondered whether the waters would ever reject an entire body outright, whether the Albedo pool would recognize an unwelcome intruder."

"Are you suggesting I immerse myself to determine my rebel status? Or are you positing that the Council waters would oust Dracaen?" Arjen felt his conjoined partner stir once again.

"Clearly the waters do not reject human bodies, Arjan — whether alchemist or rebel."

"Is there a moral to your story?"

"When I finish, you can decide that for yourself. My story is one of patterns rather than individual incidents." Obeche paused momentarily before proceeding. "The next time my nose bled was a few hours after I read your pendant."

Arjan looked up, curious. "*Drained* my pendant."

"*Accidentally* drained your pendant in unbridled enthusiasm. Regardless, at the time, I thought my nosebleed was a reaction to my own pendant being confiscated."

Arjan's eyes widened. No one had told him this aspect of the incident.

"Azoth Magen Ailanthus altered my pendant's Quintessence as punishment for my alleged crime."

"Eye for an eye."

"So to speak. But I failed to find a connection between the two incidents until I had the benefit of hindsight. You and Sadira have both been mutually conjoined. Dimensional fallout began after the conjunctions. To my knowledge, none of the Council manuscripts predicted the connection between mutual conjunctions and dimensional dissolution, yet we have nonetheless drawn conclusions. We have built the worlds through manuscripts. For years, we have been seeking answers within those pages — the sculpted words, the arcane symbols, the gold-embossed illuminations. But perhaps the manuscripts of the primary dimensions are not our only source of alchemical knowledge."

Arjan shivered. "What are you suggesting, Obeche? Have you found an answer to your dimensional crisis in an outside world manuscript? For years both the Rebel Branch and the Alchemists' Council have maintained that outside world alchemists are little more than charlatans."

"Outside world alchemists believed that the Rebis represented a perfected form."

"If my mutual conjunction with Dracaen is any

indication, even I would have to agree that the outside world alchemists were wrong."

"Were they? As we now understand, the alchemical child is a form of Prima Materia. Outside world alchemists have repeatedly inscribed a flawless conjunction of opposites as the Rebis — an icon of perfection, one even representing the Philosopher's Stone itself on occasion. Having lived for years in Flaw dimension, do you believe pure Prima Materia can exist eternally without degradation? Or that an unblemished Lapis can exist eternally outside the One?"

"What have these philosophical ponderings to do with your nosebleeds, Obeche?"

"Did my body *know* somehow?" asked Obeche. "Was I reacting to a shift in the elements? In Quintessence? Did my blood forecast doom? I had no way of knowing at the time. I have no way of knowing now. But I have recently come to believe that my physical inconveniences may well have been reactions to an alchemical phenomenon."

"Your body sensed that Sadira and I — that is, the impending perfection of our mutual conjunctions — would inadvertently destroy the worlds?"

"Perhaps. Or perhaps my story is one of sheer coincidence. Either way, I believe it provides a lesson."

"Yes?"

"The dimensions cannot sustain multiple mutually conjoined alchemists. Why? Various hypotheses have surfaced, but I surmise it has to do with your physicality — your literal body of elements — and connections among the alchemical, the physical, and the Quintessential in relation to both the Lapis and the Flaw. If the Flaw as imperfection incarnate provides free will, then our choices — *your* choices — must encompass not only the intellectual but also the corporeal. As Azoth Ruis piercingly illustrated, all alchemists are physically connected to the Lapis *and* its Flaw. And I think you, Arjan, a perfected creation of the elements, need to remember the lessons of your body to know what choices you must make on this road to imperfect redemption."

Arjan lowered his head, concentrating. Before responding to Obeche, he needed to be certain Dracaen remained asleep in the shadows. "Kalina and I cannot transfer our perfected bodies far enough beyond the current timeline to make a perceptible impact," explained Arjan. "She can move only to 1814, and I only to 1939. We therefore have no temporal means to hinder the effects of multiple mutual conjunctions of alchemical children within our confined — our current — timeline. To make a difference, we would each need to move hundreds of years beyond *now* and hundreds of years apart from one another. Kalina and I have discussed this problem at length without resolution."

"Nonetheless, I maintain hope that my words today will spur you to an alternative solution."

Obeche had moved Arjan to contemplative silence. Not until Jaden arrived and set a tray of tea, milk, honey, and cake onto the table did Arjan move. He looked up and returned Jaden's smile.

"Enjoy your tea," said Obeche.

"Good afternoon, Rowan Obeche," Jaden said.

As soon as Obeche had departed, Sadira arrived. Though Arjan regretted he would not have time alone with Jaden, he was pleased with the gathering. Not only would he be able to spend time with Jaden but also, as Obeche had suggested, with his sister. No sooner had he thought of her than Kalina emerged.

"Hello, Arjan," she said. "I have missed you."

"And I you," he said, feeling more content than he had in months.

They chatted briefly about nothing in particular. For a few minutes, Arjan managed to forget that Council dimension was crumbling around him. As Kalina poured tea into Jaden's cup, the sight of a crack on the floor intruded on Arjan's respite. When the cups were all filled, Jaden raised hers in a brief toast. Kalina reached for the plate of cake.

"Would you like a piece, Arjan? I made it myself. My specialty: orange-infused honey cake."

"Honey? My body cannot—" He stopped himself and looked at her. *Remember the lessons of your body to know what choices you must make on this road to imperfect redemption.*

"I plan to indulge," Kalina said, passing the cake to Jaden before offering it to Arjan once again. "What better salve for our mutual wounds than Lapidarian honey?"

"Delicious," said Jaden.

Arjan held out his plate, catching Kalina's eyes once again. He could hear Jaden chatting, but he paid no attention to her words. He merely stared at the cake, his fork poised above it, contemplating the repercussions. A few weeks earlier Arjan had refused a piece of toast with honey that Sadira had offered him. He told her that eating Lapidarian honey had almost killed him as a child. What Kalina had offered him now was, for all intents and purposes, poison. What was she thinking?

And then he understood. Kalina knew what she was doing, as must Sadira. If they ingested the honey and if, in turn, it drained their bodies of Quintessence, they could potentially dissolve the mutual conjunctions. They might also die. But their deaths could stop the dimensional fallout. Through willing sacrifice, they could save Council dimension. *Remember the lessons of your body*, Obeche had said. Kalina and Sadira must have spoken with him — attained permission of a Council Elder to proceed with the plan.

Kalina confidently took a bite of the cake, looking directly at Arjan. He realized then that he could not allow her to act alone. She nodded to him, and he too took a bite. Within a few minutes, he had finished his first slice and held out his plate for seconds. When he had finished the second piece, he reached for his cup of tea.

"Please pass the honey, Kalina."

"Are you certain?" she asked.

"Absolutely," he responded.

He stirred a teaspoon of honey into his tea, contemplating the line he and Kalina had together chosen to cross.

Sadira had neither seen nor heard from Kalina in five days. Had their dissolution begun? Had eating the honey had its intended effect? Were she and Kalina about to succumb to the same conjunctive disintegration they had witnessed over the past five years among their colleagues? Sadira had willingly accepted the risk for the sake of Council dimension, but now she trembled, fully recognizing that she could soon die. Or, worse, they could both expire, and suffer the same tragic fate as Ilex and Melia.

If Kalina's absence did indeed mark the beginning of their end, Sadira feared both for herself and Kalina *and* for Dracaen and Arjan. She needed to visit Flaw dimension not only to speak with them but to see whether Kalina would return from the shadows in the presence of the rebels. Yet without Kalina, without her being visibly present to activate a Rebel Branch portal, Sadira had no means to travel unaccompanied to Flaw dimension. She required a Council Elder to send a request for entry to a Rebel Elder. She needed to find Cedar.

A few hours earlier, Fraxinus had summoned Genevre to Flaw dimension. He had sent Scribe Larix to accompany her through the portal at the Santa Fe stronghold. Now Genevre stood beside Fraxinus in an alcove of the cavern pools where Dracaen and Arjan were immersed in an obsidian tub filled with curative salt waters. Sweat beaded their face, which alternated between one and the other every thirty seconds or so. Genevre found the moisture-laden air oppressive. She felt sick with fear. She could barely stand. But she needed to take care of her child. She lowered herself into the water, reaching for Arjan.

"What's wrong with him? Fraxinus! What have you done?"

"I have done nothing other than bring Dracaen and Arjan to the cavern pools in hopes of cooling them down. Their dissolution has begun. The process will take its own course. We can—"

"Arjan could die!"

"He could. So could Dracaen. We will not know until the dissolution is complete. All we can do is ease the pain. We cannot stop the inevitable."

"Then why are they here? Why did you bring them here?"

"I told you—"

"They can't stay here! We must transport them back to Council dimension."

"Why? Has Ravenea developed a cure?"

"No, no, but they conjoined in Council dimension. The dissolution must end in the same dimension it began."

"By inference, the dissolution will *not* occur if they remain here. If we remain—"

"No!" replied Genevre. "If we keep them here, the alchemical disruption will continue, stretching their entwined Quintessence apart. Dracaen and Arjan will suffer immeasurably — they will continue to coexist in perpetual agony that escalates each minute towards unbearable torture, a fate worse than death."

Fraxinus, Larix, and Genevre spent the next hour manoeuvring Dracaen and Arjan from the cavern pools to the portal chamber. Traversing through the narrow passageways of Flaw dimension to the portal took almost twice as long as anticipated. Arjan cried out in pain on multiple occasions. While Fraxinus and Larix supported the weight of Dracaen and Arjan, Genevre reassured startled onlookers that they had the situation under control. But, of course, they did not. Dracaen and Arjan moved closer to dissolution with each step.

Upon reaching the portal, Genevre transported herself to the Santa Fe protectorate where she recruited Gad — Keeper of the Book of the Santa Fe protectorate — to inform Ravenea they required assistance through the conduit access point. A few minutes after Genevre had returned to Flaw dimension, Ravenea arrived. Fraxinus and Larix were able to position Dracaen and Arjan onto a wooden chair set into the centre of the portal mechanism. As Azoth Magen, Ravenea had the powers to transport multiple people through a portal simultaneously. When they emerged into Council dimension at the cliff face, they found Cedar screaming, kneeling on the ground beside Sadira. Genevre immediately grasped the horrific truth: both her children were about to die.

Council Dimension — 2019

Cedar waited with Genevre. They sat together between two low embankments on a bed of soft pine needles. Dappled light filtered through the dense trees swaying in the breeze. They were terrified. On one side of them lay Sadira and Kalina; on the other, Dracaen and Arjan — fallen, unconscious, fading. Cedar and Genevre had both witnessed the dissolution of conjunctive pairings — Genevre of Ilex and Melia, and Cedar of at least a dozen alchemists within Council dimension over the last five years. Genevre had heard the horrific stories. They feared the worst: at any moment, the writhing and wailing would begin. Within the hour, once the conjoined body had become still and silenced again, the elemental separation would continue internally until it reached completion. One essence of each pair would then evaporate. Then, if resilient enough to survive the trauma of the dissolution, the other one would emerge, free of its once-eternal bond. One would survive, drained of the partner's Quintessence, aged by the equivalent of a decade or two, weakened but nevertheless alive. *If resilient enough.*

Perhaps Cedar and Genevre should have anticipated the temporal differences and elemental complexities involved in the dissolution of an alchemically created child. But they purposely refrained from uttering hypotheses aloud. Instead, they offered what comfort they could amidst the agony, taking turns holding a hand of Sadira and Kalina or Arjan and Dracaen.

In bearing witness to these impending deaths, Cedar and Genevre were bound together anew. They staggered under the weight of threatened losses — a lover, a daughter, a spouse, a son. *A daughter. A son.* Knowing the stakes, they understood they must set aside the varied antagonisms they had shared in the past. How could Cedar resent Genevre's attempts to hide her children in the past when, in this moment, they both lay in life-threatening peril? How could Genevre resent Cedar's decision to release the bees when in this moment both a woman and child Cedar loved lay dying amidst fragmented structures of a crumbling dimension? Surely their self-recriminations for this situation were sufficient rebuke for anyone to bear. *If I had not enlivened the manuscript . . . If I had not agreed to the chemical marriage . . . If I had not condoned the mutual conjunctions . . . If I had not allied with the Rebel Branch . . .* If neither had been born, neither would have known death. If neither had lived as an individual with the freedom to choose, neither would have made or regretted her choices.

Through the first hour, Cedar and Genevre waited for their expectations of the dissolution to manifest. But nothing changed — both couples remained conjoined and comatose. Throughout the second hour, Cedar ached to scream merely to fill the silent void. But, of course, she did not. *Steadfast. Steadfast.*

By the third hour, Genevre let go of Arjan's hand and reached for Cedar's. Cedar wavered, eyes watering. In that moment, in that one selfless gesture, in Genevre's acknowledgement that Cedar too felt pain and despair, that she too required comfort, that they were here *together* despite everything that had come before, all was forgiven. All resentment dissolved. Emotions brimming, they permitted themselves brief release from their vigilance, allowed themselves the passing comfort of crying in one another's embrace.

Later, sitting watch again beside Genevre, the wait for the dissolutions became untenable. Cedar strained to focus attentively on Sadira or Arjan, but she could no longer do so. Images from her past pushed their way, uninvited, into her awareness, drawing her attention further and further away from both the couples and Genevre. Waking nightmares invaded one after the next: battle-ravaged survivors of outside world wars; Genevre holding their deceased daughter; Jaden swollen from bee stings; gelatinous, oozing, liquefying amber. A mere few years ago, Cedar had assumed the most tragic spectacle of dimensional disintegration she would live to endure was the dissolving of the Amber Garden. Then, standing witness to the howling remains of the formerly conjoined, she recognized that these horrors had no foreseeable end. Each incident fully garnered her attention; each image seared itself deeper into her memory. Cedar doubted that even evacuation to the outside world could mitigate the persistent pain.

A loud cracking sound abruptly fractured her agonizing visions. Another memory flashed, this one from the outside world — thick ice on a lake breaking apart in the warmth of spring. Genevre had stood up to scan the surrounding forest. Cedar looked back towards the cliff face, seeking a source of the disruption. Had the dimension itself, finally and permanently, begun to sever? The sound reverberated once again, prompting Cedar to stand as well. Were the rocks and trees about to crash down upon them? Finally, on its third iteration, Cedar and Genevre simultaneously understood the source of the sound: Sadira and Kalina.

They were not dissolving; they were not liquefying. They were fragmenting — breaking apart
like the blocks of ice Cedar had remembered. With
each new crack, the sound grew louder. Within minutes, she and Genevre had to cover their ears. Even
then, the noise was thunderous. The final crack
was so loud they both doubled over, legs buckling.
The conjoined body shattered into a multitude of
sharp, thin shards that embedded themselves into
everything they touched, including Cedar's and
Genevre's exposed hands. And then the shards vanished — utterly and completely vanished. Sadira
and Kalina simply were gone.

"No!" Cedar screamed, pounding her fists on
the ground.

Genevre wailed, collapsing.

"Arjan!" cried Cedar, helping Genevre to
stand. They both rushed to his side. Within seconds, their son's conjoined body began to alternate
faces: a few seconds revealing Arjan, a few seconds
revealing Dracaen. Genevre lay a hand on Arjan's
shoulder, Cedar on his hand. Eventually, the fluctuation between faces became so rapid in its shift
between one and the other that physical distinc-
tion was literally blurred. A low humming noise
began. Soft at first, it increased exponentially in
volume by the second. Cedar and Genevre were
on their knees, bent forward with their hands over
their ears and heads touching the ground when
the vibration reached its shuddering climax and

promptly ceased. They slowly raised their heads, stood up, and turned to face Arjan and Dracaen. They expected nothing. They expected vanishing shards, as with Sadira and Kalina. But once again their expectations were upturned.

Arjan had survived. He stood alone, arms open, inviting his mothers' embrace.

Genevre could not move. She was lying in a bed in a familiar room: guest quarters within Council residence chambers. Years ago, she had resided in such a room for months on end. *Years ago.* How many years? How many hours? How had she arrived here today? How long had she been here? She could not remember. She felt numb, empty, barely alive. She waited for death to arrive and release her — not into the One but into nothing. *Nothing.* What had been the point of her choices? *Nothing.* Of her intentions? *Nothing.* Of her life? *Nothing.* Of her child's life?

Everything. Everything!

Kalina! she screamed.

She could not hear herself. Could anyone hear her? The walls that she sensed were closing in around her were also absorbing her voice. Or she was dreaming — a perpetual, voiceless nightmare. Awake or asleep, she could not tell the difference. Minutes, hours, days passed. Or no time at all. Uncertainty persisted.

But then she had seen Arjan. He had simply stood, tall and silent between two trees. A dream? Yes. A dream, one vivid in its details. Along with the branches of the trees, his hair fluttered in the wind. He stretched his arms to reach the trees, brushing his hands against the foliage. He then held out his hands to her. She stared, confused and then comprehending. In one hand, he held a sprig of cedar; in the other, juniper. She placed her hands into his and then stepped forward, welcomed into his embrace.

Now, awake, sitting up in her bed, Genevre moved continually between utter devastation for the loss of Kalina and unrestrained joy for the return of Arjan.

Cedar had known loss. She had lost many a friend and colleague through conjunction or ascension or even erasure. But over hundreds of years as an alchemist, she had forgotten the agony of death. And now, as if to make up for lost time, death haunted her, beckoned her. Like the personified figure of medieval literature of the outside world, Death hunted with its scythe, cutting down those whom she had loved with no thought whatsoever to her.

Though she had always doubted the validity of Final Ascension, the alchemical transformation of the Azoth Magen to dust provided a visual representation of possibility — of the chance, however slim, that the end of the current life was the beginning of the next. But what of Ruis? Would she have loved him more fiercely if she had known his life would be extinguished forever? At least he had turned to ash; at least his ashes had returned to the world from which he had originated. But what of Kalina? And what of Sadira? What, even, of Dracaen? They were all merely *gone*. They were nowhere.

Nowhere.

At the memorial ceremony, rebels had cried for Dracaen and Kalina. Alchemists had cried for Sadira. But Cedar had sat stunned, silent, tearless. She had not even been able to speak in tribute to her beloved Sadira. She had already done so once before. She could not do so again, especially not when she had refused Sadira's numerous attempts to spend time with her since her resurrection within Kalina. Despite Sadira's reassurances, Cedar had never been able to overcome the discomfort of believing Kalina could observe anything Sadira said or did. No one understood the guilt of that decision — of rejecting love for what seemed like logical reasons at the time. *At the time.* No time remained. Nothing remained. Now she sat alone on the one remaining segment of the wall that once protected the Amber Garden. She could not change her mind. She could not reciprocate the love Sadira had offered because Death had already stepped in where she had feared to tread. Now she was alone in her agony.

"Cedar."

She looked up.

"Genevre."

"May I join you?"

"Yes."

They cried, side by side, clinging to each other beside the faltering remnant of a dying world until their myriad tears had salted the earth.

X

ꜰʟᴀᴡ Dimension — 2020

Cedar, Genevre, Fraxinus, and Arjan made their way silently through the dimly lit pathways of the Flaw dimension archives. They had walked directly from Council's North Library into the Flaw's archives through a rift spontaneously torn between dimensions. Though inexplicable, they assumed it to be temporary — such had been the case with three other rifts that had opened, lasting approximately two days each. If this rift followed the established pattern, Cedar and Genevre had another twenty hours before they would lose direct access, necessitating a return to Council dimension by way of the cliff face portal conduit.

Of course, Wardens of both the Alchemists' Council and the Rebel Branch guarded the rift, but Cedar and Genevre had permission to move freely between the libraries and archives of both dimensions to facilitate research and consultation. The last thing either the Alchemists' Council or the Rebel Branch needed now was for a rift to open between either of the two primary dimensions and the outside world. Therefore, although their relationship remained laced with distrust, Ravenea and Fraxinus — as Azoth Magen and High Azoth, respectively — had renewed the Joint Coalition vow to cooperate in an effort to protect the outside world. Under continually shifting circumstances and dimensional structures, they had begun to approve even the most unorthodox of approaches. Today was no exception. Fraxinus, having discovered that he could no longer access the secreted libraries without Dracaen, required Genevre to reactivate the bloodlocks.

Years earlier, when Genevre first discovered and opened the door-not-door to the ancient archival libraries, Dracaen had thereafter been able to come and go from them without incident. Fraxinus had regularly accompanied Dracaen. Indeed, on many an occasion, Dracaen had left Fraxinus and other Rebel Elders unattended in the library to consult the archives and transcribe specific manuscripts. But since Dracaen's dissolution three months ago, the door had remained locked to Fraxinus, which led him to conclude that his access had somehow been linked to Dracaen and, in turn, Dracaen's relationship with Genevre. Today, they would test a few theories. Genevre would open the primary door once again. Then Fraxinus and Cedar would each attempt to access the libraries through the reopened door. Fraxinus, as High Azoth of Flaw dimension, would make the first attempt, and Cedar, as chemical spouse of Genevre, would make the second. Arjan would supervise as a neutral party.

When they reached the door-not-door, Genevre retrieved a small blade from a pocket of her robes and incised her left index finger just enough for the blood to begin to flow. When she pressed her blood-covered fingertip against the door, it opened immediately. Fraxinus smiled and nodded. He stepped forward, but she stopped him.

"Wait. We agreed: Let me enter and close the door. Then you may attempt to enter."

As Genevre crossed the threshold, closed the door behind her, and gazed around the room at the shelves of manuscripts, she remembered how nervous and excited she had been all those years ago when she first stepped into this library. She longed to progress alone through the multiple libraries to reach the tenth, the one still housing the *Osmanthian Codex* — all but its one missing folio. But today's tasks precluded such indulgence. They were here to unlock the libraries and then, at Ravenea's insistence, to discuss *Turba Philosophorum 1881*. So Genevre merely turned her gaze to the door to see who, if anyone, would enter. She assumed the others were speaking with one another, but she could not hear their voices. A full two minutes passed before the door opened again. Carrying the manuscript, Cedar stepped into the room.

She whispered to Genevre, "Fraxinus is upset."

"I assumed he would be," she responded.

Cedar held the door open for Fraxinus and Arjan to follow.

"This predicament makes no sense," complained Fraxinus, sucking on his cut finger. "The High Azoth should have access to *all* Rebel Branch materials. Dracaen certainly did!"

"On the day Dracaen originally entered the libraries, I resided in Flaw dimension. He was my High Azoth and, later, my alchemical spouse," said Genevre. "Now, I neither live in Flaw dimension nor am I married to you."

"Indeed," responded Fraxinus grudgingly, looking at Cedar. "If chemical marriage were not a factor, your own access today would make no sense."

Genevre purposely refrained from looking at Cedar. They certainly were not about to admit to Fraxinus that Genevre had inoculated Cedar with her blood.

"Dimensional rules are no longer predictable," said Arjan. "Alchemical laws that functioned generations ago — or even a week ago — may no longer be viable. We cannot assume that something that works today will work tomorrow. We may never know why Dracaen could enter but you cannot, Fraxinus. We know only that Genevre and Cedar currently can."

Fraxinus pushed the first door shut and walked across the floor of the library towards the second. "Follow me!" he insisted. He then let loose an angry grunt of frustration when the second door likewise refused to yield to his touch.

"Let me try," said Cedar. She pressed a still-bloodied finger against the door, which immediately opened.

With Cedar in the lead, they made their way, door by door, to the sixth archival library, whereupon Fraxinus indicated they should take seats around a centre table. Once they were all seated, he slammed his hands on the table, declaring that the situation made no sense to him. "How am I to conduct research without access to the libraries?"

"Fear not, Fraxinus. I can accompany you," said Genevre.

Fraxinus glared at her and then turned to Cedar. "In the meantime, onward. Why is *Turba Philosophorum 1881* of such importance? What has it to do with the secreted libraries?"

"For one thing," began Cedar, "it indicates that the manuscripts in these libraries belong to both the Alchemists' Council and the Rebel Branch. Like the *Osmanthian Codex*, we believe it was once housed here — that High Azoth Magen Makala presumably hid it amidst her various treasures, to be awakened when time or circumstance necessitated." She gestured outward to encompass the innumerable manuscripts. "We cannot know what else awaits us."

Cedar then recounted the day she had first observed *Turba Philosophorum 1881*. She placed the manuscript on the table and opened it to folio 16, which revealed the illumination of Makala. She pointed out the message she had received about Ravenea and her twin and explained the conclusions she had reached regarding the multicoloured pebbles and the alembic. Finally, she explained what she had learned by reading through the entire manuscript more recently. In particular, she had discovered the origin of the secreted libraries and their books, many of which the rebels had stolen from Council during the Second Rebellion.

Fraxinus understandably refrained from railing against Cedar's accusation of theft. What would be the point? Like everyone at the table, he knew that none of the remaining Council Elders would suggest relocating ancient manuscripts from Flaw to Council dimension given the potential disintegration of Council libraries. Indeed, Fraxinus likely expected Ravenea soon to request that Council manuscripts be transferred for indefinite storage within Flaw dimension. Thus, his only response was one of silent gesture. He pulled *Turba Philosophorum 1881* towards him and stared at it for quite some time, peering at the lettering of the mysterious message.

"Did Ravenea speak of her twin?" Fraxinus asked.

"She said he was transported to a future timeline without her."

Fraxinus nodded and continued to inspect the message.

"Do you recognize the hand?" asked Genevre.

"No," said Fraxinus.

"Fraxinus, today is not the time to withhold information. We have agreed to cooperate. If you recognize the calligraphy or scribe, you must—"

"I swear upon the three dimensions, I do not recognize the handwriting. The flourishes on a few of the letters seem familiar. That is all."

"Familiar?"

"They are similar to those on the forged folio brought to us by Initiate Virginia. However, as I am certain Arjan will confirm, the calligraphy is not of the same hand."

Arjan, observing the manuscript for himself, agreed. "Fraxinus is correct. Only a few flourishes match those of the forgery."

"What do you make of these particular illuminations?" Cedar asked.

She opened the manuscript to a two-paged illustration comprising three panels, apparently representing the three dimensions. The following folio depicted a globe within a triangle; atop the globe was a black-haired man wearing turquoise robes and holding a gilded sceptre. Above his head was a single word: *Jakanil*.

"The Champion of Dimensions," said Fraxinus.

"Ravenea concurs," said Cedar. "But what are we to infer? How are we to proceed?"

Over the next few hours, they listened as Cedar described or read aloud various passages from *Turba Philosophorum 1881*. They discussed, and they debated; they followed hypotheses, and they thwarted conclusions. And though they had no definitive answers by the end of their session, Fraxinus agreed that the manuscript warranted further investigation.

"We may have had the answers all along," said Genevre. "We have been focused on the *Osmanthian Codex* and its missing folio because of its focus on alchemical children. But High Azoth Magen Makala ensured her message and that of the primordial ancestors was spread across various manuscripts, including in *Turba Philosophorum 1881*."

"Though I continue to doubt whether we will find answers in *any* manuscript," said Arjan, "I agree we need to understand the more obscure terms in this one — beginning with *Jakanil*."

"I concur," replied Fraxinus. "But I advise caution. Cedar contends this manuscript holds the dimensional key because of its revealed message. But we have no idea who sent the message or why. *Turba Philosophorum 1881*, like various other manuscripts, could offer us nothing."

Having arranged a subsequent meeting time, they walked in silence back through the series of libraries and the narrow passageways of the deepest archives until they reached the dimensional rift. Through the glow, they could see into the main consultation room of the North Library.

Obeche and Jaden were seated at a table awaiting them. When he noticed them approach, Obeche stood, nodding to indicate that all was well from his perspective.

"I will remain here with Fraxinus," said Arjan.

"Are you certain?" asked Genevre, gesturing discreetly towards Jaden.

"I will visit soon."

Cedar nodded, held *Turba Philosophorum 1881* tightly against her, and stepped through the rift. Genevre bid farewell to Arjan and turned to follow Cedar. But the rift sparked brightly and loudly, causing everyone to back away. When the sparking ceased, Genevre could see only Obeche and Jaden. They appeared startled and confused.

"Where is she?" asked Arjan. "Where's Cedar?"

Genevre stared through the rift. Then, after a loud sound akin to thunder, the rift vanished. Genevre felt terror flood through her. She turned and ran down the corridor to the lift, Arjan and Fraxinus immediately behind her. Upon reaching the Flaw dimension portal conduit, Genevre and Arjan transported themselves back to Council dimension. When they emerged at the cliff face, Ravenea awaited them. Twenty minutes had passed since Cedar had stepped into the rift.

"Is Cedar here?" asked Genevre. She could barely breathe.

"No," said Ravenea. "She had extended a hand from within the rift, which Jaden had clasped to help her through. But then the rift sparked and, along with Cedar, vanished."

"And the manuscript?" asked Arjan.

"It had dropped onto the floor when the rift closed. Obeche has it now."

"The manuscript is the least of our concerns!" Genevre exclaimed.

"Unless it's the key to getting her back," said Arjan. "I lied by omission to Fraxinus."

Genevre slowed her breath and stared at him.

"I did recognize the calligraphy in *Turba Philosophorum 1881* — specifically in the message revealed to Cedar," Arjan continued. "I saw a sample of near-identical script during my recent visit with Jaden on a few of her practice scrolls. The message to Cedar is the co-writing of Jaden and Initiate Virginia. Somehow, some*time*, they mutually inscribed that message."

Council Dimension — 2020

Having worked meticulously for over two months translating and interpreting *Turba Philosophorum 1881*, Ravenea and Genevre reported that they had finally developed a hypothesis — one aimed at rematerializing Cedar. According to an esoteric phrase on folio 34 verso, *the Alchemical One transfused with the Ancestral Blood of Two* can be ritually transported throughout the current timeline by way of a fourth-dimension temporal rift. If Ravenea and Genevre's interpretation was correct, then Jaden — an alchemist inoculated with the blood of Ilex and Melia — should be able to catapult into the past. Moreover, since Jaden was the last person to have touched Cedar within the current timeline, her dimensional resonance should function as a beacon during the ritual, enabling the alchemical equivalent of echolocation.

To retrieve Cedar, Jaden needed to reconnect with her at the precise point where and when they first met: the Vancouver Art Gallery café in 2013. However, this time, instead of Cedar bringing Jaden to Council dimension, Jaden would bring Cedar. This meeting and shifting of roles would align Cedar's Quintessence with Jaden's and, thereby, with the Quintessence of the Lapis. In effect, together they would recreate a conjunction of opposites — the primary principle of alchemy that exists eternally through time and space.

"You understand, within seconds of the temporary conjunction, your current memories will be erased," said Genevre. "For all intents and purposes, for the duration of first contact with Cedar, you will be *that* Jaden — the person you were on the day you became Initiate Jaden."

"Yes," Jaden replied. "I understand."

"If all goes as planned," Genevre continued, "you will separate into two selves the moment you and Cedar enter the portal. The one *you* will remain with Cedar to be brought into Council dimension as the 2013 Initiate. The other you will bring Cedar to us, moments from now in 2020. But if something goes wrong, if the blood alchemy cannot separate you or cannot sustain Cedar, you will either live your entire experience again, minute by minute, without memory of doing so before, up until this hour, or you will return here without Cedar."

"Yes, I understand," Jaden repeated. Thus, by the Protocol of Agreement, she had sealed her consent.

"If the separation has failed, we will know within minutes. We will work to determine a means to send messages back to our former selves. We will learn. Eventually, we will make a new choice, a minor adjustment, and we will move forward. In time — one day in one timeline — you and Cedar together will return to us."

"The choice is mine. I choose the risk."

Within the hour, Jaden had moved through the time portal. She materialized just outside the gift shop of the Vancouver Art Gallery. She walked quickly upstairs to the café, scanning the crowded tables for her former self. Approaching from behind, Jaden reached out and placed a hand on the other Jaden's shoulder. They conjoined instantaneously, and she forgot who she had been before this moment.

Flash. Vancouver Art Gallery.

Cedar: *You are Jaden, Junior Initiate of the Alchemists' Council. The Scribes have named you. The*

Readers have read you. The Word of the Book is the Word Eternal.

Flash. Council dimension. Jaden stood alone.

"Why isn't it working?" cried Jaden, exasperated. "I walk in. I find Cedar. I speak with her, but then she's gone. Or I'm gone. I'm gone from there and return here without her."

Genevre shook her head. "I don't know what to say, Jaden. We've tried five times. Either we've misinterpreted the text, or you've misremembered the scenario."

"But I remember the original meeting. I replayed it repeatedly during my first year on Council. The words Cedar says to me now are the same words she said the first time."

Ravenea, Arjan, Genevre, and Jaden were sitting in the main courtyard on stone benches under the willow tree. The tree's rustling green leaves in that moment brought hope to Jaden even in her frustration, even in Cedar's absence, even amidst their multiple failures. Though a minor element, the vibrant leaves on the tree were evidence of the dimensional potential — several signs of which she had observed since *Sangue Morte*. If the willow tree could flourish amidst dimensional decay, she, Arjan, and two powerful blood alchemists could find a means to rescue Cedar from dimensional obscurity.

"I remain convinced that the inscription that appeared to Cedar in *Turba Philosophorum 1881* provides the answer," said Arjan. "That manuscript is ancient. But, like the partnership of Virginia and Jaden, the inscription itself is relatively new. They must inscribe the same message to Cedar again. And they must do so *before* we send Jaden back through the fourth dimensional portal. I am certain that inscription is key." He looked pleadingly at Jaden. "If you two are able to make bees come to life through your mutual inscriptions, surely you can make a mere message appear!"

"Arjan, we've been trying! I've been meeting with Virginia daily for weeks. We've tried every sort of parchment — including the most precious gold and cinnabar weaves. We've used every type of ink — various blends of Lapidarian and Dragonsblood. We even managed to succeed at scriptural levitation — the words, literally, floated above the page. But we've not managed to move a message from a parchment sheet to a manuscript. And even if we could achieve such transference, what good would that do us now? We need the inscription to appear in Cedar's past, not in our present!"

"Maybe that's the problem?" said Arjan. "Maybe you need to *be* in the past."

"Attempt the inscription in 2013?"

"Not necessarily in 2013. Any time prior to Cedar receiving the message could work. You need only develop and inscribe an ink that will become visible in the future. We could adjust the inks to manifest their visibility with age — a year, two years, two decades — in 2014."

"Yes," agreed Ravenea. "That could work, especially if we were to match the inks' resonance with Cedar's."

"But Virginia would have to accompany her," Genevre reminded them.

"What if you were to inoculate her with your blood — or mine?" Jaden asked.

"No. Even if our blood were to affect Virginia the way Ilex and Melia's blood affected you, it would need time to mature — as it does within a developing alchemical child or, in your case, as it did after the bees injected you."

"What if we *both* went? What if *I* were to transport Virginia?" asked Arjan. "Could you perform a blood-alchemy bonding ritual of some type to allow for accompanying transport?"

"Possibly," said Genevre. "But your time travel matured when you accidentally moved between 2014 and 1939."

"Then we will go to 2014, a few months before Cedar reads the manuscript."

"No, that won't work, either. Subsequent travel for an alchemical child is limited to the earliest point on the child's timeline. You would have to go to 1939," said Ravenea.

"Meanwhile, I've now matured in 2013 in the café," said Jaden.

"No. Jaden's time-travel abilities are different than that of alchemical children. A fourth-dimension portal is not— Wait!" cried Genevre. "We . . . at the time . . . back in Qingdao during the original time transmutation, we wondered whether Arjan had transferred Jaden *back* in time — if that was the reason we were able to see her. Since she travelled alongside Arjan to 1939 already, Jaden may be able to do so again. She could go back with Arjan and Virginia to *that* point and revise the manuscript."

"Of course!" exclaimed Arjan. "Jaden *had* to be in Qingdao for the time transmutation to work. Since she had been present in 1939, she also had to be there in 2014. We can manipulate that connection to solve our current timeline dilemma."

"Yes," said Ravenea. "Yes. We must try. But we will require a third for the portal triangulation. One person for each dimension: one in Council dimension, one in the outside world, and one in Flaw dimension."

"That leaves us no choice," said Genevre. "We will have to inform Fraxinus."

Council Dimension — 2020

Though a mere seven years had passed, the day Jaden had first met Cedar seemed an alchemist's lifetime ago. As Jaden waited in the portal chamber for Arjan, Virginia, and Genevre, she thought also of her early days in the Initiate, the hours she had spent watching the Scribes, the months she had spent longing *someday* to be able to revise manuscripts herself. At the time, she had envisioned inscribing her own destiny — when she would ascend, with whom she would conjoin. Cedar had rightly cautioned her against such Law Code violations, assuring her that by the time Jaden herself became a Scribe, she would have learned to honour proscriptions against self-interested revisions. Perhaps Cedar was correct; perhaps, once Council dimension healed, Jaden would eventually honour Law Code prohibitions. Cedar certainly had been right on numerous occasions over the years of their acquaintance. But for now, Jaden remained a mere Senior Initiate. To ascend through the rotations from the Initiate order to Junior Magistrate, then Senior Magistrate, then Reader, and *then* to Lapidarian Scribe would take at least another two hundred years.

To accomplish that feat, she would have to survive. To become an official Council Scribe in the future, she must inscribe manuscripts unofficially, unlawfully today. The Scribes of the Law Codes had not considered mutual conjunction or alchemical children or bloodline transfusions or transmutations of time. Jaden and the others must take utmost care. They could make only the most minor of manuscript revisions without causing untold ripple effects throughout the dimensions. The agreement was firm in the vow they pledged to Ravenea: they would aim to return to the Council only what the dimensional rift had unjustly taken.

She smiled thinking of her first scribal infraction with Arjan — the day in the North Library when she had inscribed her name into the excised space under the Kalina tree in *Sapientiae Aeternae 1818*. If not for that early act of inked rebellion, Jaden may never have mentioned the marginal gloss in *Serpens Chymicum 1414* to Ravenea.

You will be my saviour, and in saving me, you will save the Alchemists' Council.

"Tell me the truth, Jaden," Ravenea had requested firmly a few weeks ago. "Have you and Virginia been making unlawful manuscript inscriptions?"

"No, Azoth Magen. I swear upon the Lapis!"

"Have you — you, on your own — *ever* written *anything* into a Council manuscript without permission?" asked Ravenea.

Jaden paused, swallowed, and looked up guiltily at Ravenea. "Yes. Yes, I have. Once," she admitted.

"Tell me *everything*. Recite every detail leading up to that inscription."

Jaden's recollection of her connection with Kalina finally proved to be the required key. The following afternoon, Ravenea had brought Jaden the missing and integral piece of the puzzle.

"I have consulted the Records of Essence. *Cruentus* — the word you and Sadira believed that Kalina inscribed into *Serpens Chymicum 1414* — comprises the blood of Ilex and Melia. As you know, their blood now resides in you."

"But Kalina left me the note — the one that led me to *Sapientiae Aeternae 1818*. And Sadira told me that Kalina inscribed the word *cruentus* using Dragonblood-infused ink. She wouldn't have . . . lied to me . . . would she?"

"What reason would Sadira have for lying?" asked Ravenea.

"To gain my trust, she may have told me what she believed I wanted to hear."

"Perhaps. Or perhaps Kalina told Sadira only what she wanted her to hear."

Jaden nodded. "And what about the other note, the marginal gloss in *Tabula Rasa* — the volume on Protocols of Erasure that led me to *Serpens Chymicum*?"

"According to a spectral analysis of both inks and alchemical essence, Arjan inscribed the gloss in *Tabula Rasa 3669*. During her Council tenure, Kalina's quintessential bloodline connections both to Arjan and Meliex would have drawn her to both *Tabula Rasa* and *Serpens Chymicum*. She then used *Sapientiae Aeternae* as an instrument to connect with you."

"What does all of this mean?" asked Jaden.

"It means that when you return to 1939 to inscribe the message to Cedar in *Turba Philosophorum*, you must also inscribe the word *cruentus* in *Serpens Chymicum*, and Arjan must inscribe the note in

Tabula Rasa. All must be both as it was and, therefore, as it will be."

Arjan, Virginia, and Genevre arrived. Genevre had collected the required texts and objects. To allow for the possibility of an error in chronology, they would aim to rematerialize on a day two months prior to the day of the original breach in Qingdao. Genevre would hold position at the Quercus portal in Council dimension, Ravenea at a temporary portal near the Qingdao protectorate, and Fraxinus at the portal nearest the secreted archives in Flaw dimension. Jaden, Arjan, and Virginia would use the Quercus portal as a catalyst — *our time machine*, as Arjan had laughingly referred to it. If all aspects of the ritual succeeded, Jaden, Arjan, and Virginia would appear in 1939 within the Rebel Branch archives immediately outside the door-not-door that Genevre had long ago opened with her blood.

"Try your own blood first," Genevre said to Jaden. "Like me, you literally carry forth Ilex and Melia's blood. The doors should respond accordingly. But if they don't, if they refuse to open to you in the past, try my blood." She handed Jaden a small opaque flask with a ruby lid. "By 1939, my blood had already unlocked the doors for the High Azoth. They remained unlocked for the Azoths until Dracaen's death. But the libraries will perceive you as an intruder from the Council; the doors may purposely lock you out. The flask contains more than enough of my blood to open all the locks once again."

Jaden tucked the flask into a pocket of her satchel alongside other required elements.

"And here," Genevre continued, "is a note from current Ravenea to past Ravenea. In Council dimension, after you are done with *Serpens Chymicum 1414*, leave the note where a Keeper of the Book will find it in the North Library. It instructs future Ravenea to insert the note for Cedar regarding *Turba Philosophorum 1881* into the scroll after the Fourth Rebellion. She will not know *why* she must do so, but we already know that she does."

"Do you have the portal keys?" Arjan asked, joining Jaden and Virginia on the platform.

"Yes."

"All three?"

"Yes, Arjan!" Jaden assured him.

"And the key to the Qingdao protectorate?" asked Virginia.

"Yes!"

"And the key to *Serpens Chymicum 1414*?" asked Arjan.

"Yes, I have *all* the keys — literal and figurative! Let's go!" Jaden said. She then looked at Genevre. "Ready?"

"Ready." Genevre nodded.

Virginia put an arm around Arjan's waist and leaned her head against his. Their identical expressions, hair colour, and skin tone made Jaden pause and smile — in the outside world, her two friends would be mistaken as siblings.

"One, two, three . . ." said Jaden, putting everything else from her mind.

Jaden, Arjan, and Genevre each pressed the blood-infused, alchemically sustained button on their synchronized timepieces and counted to three again. When the button on Jaden's timepiece turned purple, indicating Ravenea's response from the outside world, she nodded to Genevre, who indicated a simultaneous response from Fraxinus. Then, as Jaden began to recite the portal key, Genevre began to recite the transmutation chant. Once Jaden and the others arrived at the door-not-door, they would have only one hour to find and adjust the specific manuscript before Genevre's subsequent chant would begin. At that point, they would need to be positioned on a Flaw dimension portal platform where Arjan, simultaneously with the chants of the others, would recite a rebel portal key for their journey from Flaw dimension to Qingdao.

More so than usual, the transport was nauseating. Upon arrival, Jaden doubled over, retching. She needed time to recover before she extracted the thin ruby blade from its case and, assuming she would require more than a finger-prick's worth of blood, incised a paper-thin cut along the back of her left hand. She winced. Blood ran. She put away the blade, touched the fingers of her other hand to the blood, and pressed her hand against the door. She felt an intense vibration, but the lock remained firm.

"Try Genevre's blood," suggested Virginia.

"Wait!" said Arjan. "Let *me* try."

"What? Why?" asked Jaden. "We have Genevre's—"

But Arjan had already cut his finger and pressed it against the door. Nothing happened — not even an additional vibration. He looked disappointed.

"You're not *one born of three*," said Virginia.

"What?" asked Jaden.

"Nothing, sorry — something Ravenea mentioned about Genevre. It doesn't matter now. We're wasting time. Use Genevre's blood."

Jaden extracted the flask, removed the ruby lid, and tipped a drop onto one finger.

"She said you have more than enough — no need to scrimp," said Arjan.

"No need to waste it, either," cautioned Virginia.

"The door vibrated with my own blood. I doubt I will require more than a drop of hers."

Jaden was right. Pressing a mere drop of Genevre's blood against the spot she had already marked with her own triggered the door to open. She and Arjan, with Virginia directly behind them, ran across the first library to the door on its far side. Blood to door, door to door, they entered and crossed the increasingly large libraries one after the next.

The sixth library — their intended destination — was so immensely vast that Jaden feared half their limited time would expire merely in proceeding from the entrance to the specific manuscript location. As Arjan finally pulled *Turba Philosophorum 1881* from its position, Jaden checked her timepiece. Eighteen minutes had elapsed.

They found a table on which to open the manuscript and prepare the ink. Before leaving Council dimension, they had assembled the ingredients; however, due to transmutation effects with the chronological sequence of events, they had not yet mixed the time-sensitive ink, which Ravenea and Genevre had concocted to manifest visibility in seventy-five years. Arjan pulled blending bowls and an inkwell from his satchel. Virginia began uncorking containers of ink. A drop of Lapidarian indigo accidentally fell onto the table from one of the vials. Jaden thought back to Magistrate Linden's calligraphy lessons, none of which had taught her the skills she required today. Instead, Genevre had provided the vital training in one three-hour session. They had all practised repeatedly; nonetheless, Jaden's hands were now shaking. She could not afford another mistake, not one that could have consequences throughout dimensional space and time. Twenty-three minutes had elapsed.

Jaden unwrapped the powdered blood. This blood was a cured and dried mixture that included both her own and Cedar's, which Ravenea had supplied from Azothian Records of Essence. Jaden's was bloodline-infused and had already moved through the timeline between 1939 and 2014; Cedar's would act as catalyst in the future. In theory, the correct mixture of ink and blood, combined with Ravenea's 5th Council blood-alchemy time-transmutation chant, would allow a message that Jaden inscribed today — in 1939 in Flaw dimension — to remain invisible until Cedar opened the manuscript herself in 2014 in Council dimension. Over the next ten minutes, Jaden measured and poured, scattered and stirred, until a flickering blue flame indicated the transposition ink was ready for inscription. Thirty-three minutes had elapsed.

"Here it is," said Arjan. He pointed to an illumination of Makala.

"Are you sure?" asked Virginia. "Are you certain this is the right one?"

"Yes, look at the words surrounding her image."

On the ornamental ribbon encircling her, the phrases *Azoth Magen Makala* and *High Azoth Makala* each appeared three times. Jaden dipped the nib into the flaming ink. Virginia placed her hand on Jaden's as Jaden pressed nib to page. One precise letter after the next — lettering that they could not see since the ink's visibility would take seventy-five years to manifest — they slowly, carefully inscribed the message into the blank space beneath the image: *Ravenea is an alchemical child. Her twin also survived.*

The moment Jaden lifted the pen after inscribing the final period, the remaining ink in the bowl vanished. The message that Genevre had repeated to her, the message Cedar had already received in their original timeline, was the only message Jaden could inscribe. Though she did not fully understand them, indissoluble rules of interdimensional time travel evidently existed.

Arjan did not move until Jaden wiped the pen and set it into its case. He and Virginia then placed the supplies back into the satchels. Virginia suggested she carry Jaden's satchel so that Jaden could freely carry the manuscript.

Once certain the ink had dried, Jaden secured the manuscript in her arms, and they raced down a narrow corridor into the main archives. Though Jaden had no knowledge of Flaw dimension geography and thus no idea where the nearest portal was located, Arjan did. In his conjoined tenure with Dracaen, he had learned all that he could about the intricacies of Flaw dimension, had spent the hours exploring the ancient pathways and corridors.

Fraxinus had suggested this specific date because he knew no one would be in the archives or wandering the corridors. The entire Rebel Branch, including the miners and other workers, were attending a tactical session regarding the advent of the outside world war. Despite the looming deadline, they were all invigorated as they stepped off the lift.

They arrived at the chosen portal, safe and unseen. At precisely the one-hour mark, Arjan recited the portal key; simultaneously, back in 2020, Fraxinus would be reciting the alchemical chant. Emerging on the street in Qingdao near the Rebel stronghold, they walked quickly to the Council protectorate.

"Should we knock?" asked Jaden.

"Fraxinus was not wrong about the tactical session," said Virginia. "Why would Jinjing be wrong about being called back to the North Library on this day?"

"Agreed," said Arjan. "Just use the key."

Once inside, they went upstairs to the manuscript library. The room looked almost identical to the one in which Jaden and Arjan had worked in 2014.

"We need the marker number," he reminded Virginia.

"15.23.8," she recited.

"Here," Jaden said, having scanned the shelves. She readjusted a few of the larger, heavier manuscripts to make room for the relatively small *Turba Philosophorum 1881*.

"Don't worry," Virginia reassured her. "Ravenea said this section is rarely accessed."

Shortly thereafter, they returned together back to the Qingdao portal. When they next materialized, they were standing at Council dimension's cliff face. A crescent moon and stars were visible in the sky, but the grounds were suitably dark for Jaden and Arjan to traverse the distance between the cliff face and the main Council buildings unnoticed. Virginia would remain out of sight within the forest to await their return.

Jaden and Arjan made their way through back corridors to the North Library. A slightly younger-looking Linden staffed the main desk; he barely paid them attention as they moved, robe hoods raised, from the entrance into the stacks. Having memorized its location marker, they quickly located *Tabula Rasa 3669*. Jaden found the requisite passage and the words *erratum imperceptus*, beside which Arjan then inscribed *Serpens Chymicum 1414, folio 44 verso*. Once the ink had dried and they had reshelved the manuscript, Arjan kept watch while Jaden retrieved *Serpens Chymicum 1414*. Sitting at a table partially obscured from view of the main desk, Jaden used the prepared key to unlock the manuscript and turned to folio 44 verso. She recognized the image: a vibrant green dragon atop a bright red circle.

Once again, she removed the ruby blade from its container and reopened the recently incised wound on the back of her hand. Wincing in pain, she set down the blade, withdrew a stylus, checked the nib, dipped the pen into the incision, and inscribed a single word in her own blood under the circle of the dragon — the word to which Kalina would be quintessentially drawn; the word that would lead Kalina to *Sapientiae Aeternae 1818*; the word that would later lead Jaden to the manuscript and back to Kalina; the word that Sadira would claim Kalina had inscribed; the word that would, thereby, form a bond of trust among the three of them; the word that would weave its way through dimensional time to this moment of inscription; the word inscribed with blood of an incision that would, in turn, allow Jaden to save both herself and Cedar: *cruentus*.

Council Dimension — 2020

"Yes, I understand," Jaden repeated. Thus, by the Protocol of Agreement, she had once again sealed her consent. "The choice is mine. I choose the risk."

Within the hour, Jaden travelled through the time portal. She materialized just outside the gift shop of the Vancouver Art Gallery. She walked quickly upstairs to the café, scanning the crowded tables for her former self. Approaching from behind, Jaden reached out and placed a hand on her shoulder. They conjoined instantaneously, and she forgot who she had been before this moment.

Flash. Vancouver Art Gallery.

Cedar: *How long have you had that scar?*

Flash. Council dimension. Jaden stood beside Cedar.

How long *had* she had that scar — the scar Cedar had healed on the day she and Jaden first met? Now she held two memories of the first meeting. When Cedar originally asked her the question, she had not responded. She had been *unable* to answer. Now, she wondered whether the time shift had distorted her memory. She held out her hand to Ravenea.

"The me that met with Cedar this time was the me *after* the 1939 revisions of *Turba Philosophorum 1881* and *Serpens Chymicum 1414*. But the original me — the me that first met with Cedar on my day of Council Initiation — already had this scar. How can that be?"

"Do you not remember another scar? One that Cedar originally healed?"

"I remember a scar. But I thought I'd had it for years. Yet I have no memory of getting it — of being cut on my hand prior to making my own incision in 1939."

"Perhaps your two selves overlapped in that one moment of time," suggested Ravenea. "Perhaps your younger self saw the scarred hand of your older self. Then your younger brain compensated, convinced you that the scar had always been present."

"Perhaps," said Jaden, not completely satisfied.

"If logic makes no sense, then, like all alchemists, you must accept the paradox," said Ravenea. "Duality is the foundation of the primary dimensions — the presence and the absence, the light and the dark, the One and the Other, the Flaw and the Lapis, the scarred and the pristine."

Genevre walked into the room before Jaden could pursue the matter further.

"We have a potential problem," she announced.

"With Cedar?" asked Ravenea.

"No. Cedar is fine — resting. She asked to speak with you later. The problem is that Arjan cannot find the blood."

"What blood?" asked Jaden.

"The flask of my blood that I gave you to open the library doors."

"I . . . I assumed Arjan or Virginia—" began Jaden.

"Virginia says you were the one who accessed the flask."

"Yes, but we put the flask into the satchel with the other supplies after we'd finished. At least, I think we put it into the satchel. We were so focused—"

"Are you suggesting that a flask of Genevre's blood was left in 1939?" asked Ravenea. "Do you understand the repercussions?"

"Yes, Magistrate. I'm sorry . . . I don't know what happened," said Jaden. "Maybe when we were mixing the inks—"

"If you left that flask in the archival library in 1939, Dracaen may well have found it!" said Ravenea. "That could explain his varied attempts to create alchemical children."

"Yes, it could," said Genevre. "But let's think this through. If Dracaen had found it, if he had realized it belonged to me, he would have needed to use the entire flask on his first attempt. And we would have known. We would have known if he had succeeded.

He would never have agreed to conjoin with Arjan if he had already created another alchemical child."

"On the other hand," said Ravenea, "Dracaen or Fraxinus or some other Rebel Elder may have used it for a blood-alchemy ritual that we cannot even fathom."

"Or maybe it slid under a bookcase never to be seen again," offered Jaden. She knew her hypothesis to be unlikely. But Jaden needed assurance that a mistake in the distant past was not about to compromise her future.

"What did you see when you were trapped in the void between dimensions?" asked Genevre.

"Nothing," responded Cedar. "I was conscious of existing within a . . . chasm, a void. But I saw absolutely nothing. I was weightless, floating, but without *feeling* anything — no water, no air against my skin. Nothing. Just . . . *me*, my mind, my thoughts."

"So you couldn't move?"

"I felt no need to move. I felt no . . . body. It wasn't like—"

"Yes?"

"It wasn't like being trapped within Saule. I didn't feel *trapped*. I simply felt . . . relaxed. I remember wondering briefly if I had died, and then I began calculating my age. Three hundred and forty-seven.

And I realized that for more than three centuries, I had managed to proceed through life with relative normalcy, even within Council dimension. Then, within a span of a few years, I became trapped in another body and, finally, left to exist without one."

"The entire time, you could sense nothing whatsoever?" asked Genevre.

"Eventually, after some . . . time . . . I sensed *Turba Philosophorum 1881*."

"You could see the manuscript? But it remained with us, in Council dimension."

"I couldn't see it. I couldn't touch it. Its essence surrounded me, encapsulated in a single word: *Jakanil*."

"Yes. *Jakanil*. Ravenea and I finally agreed on a potential interpretation of that word during your absence."

"What did you determine?"

"*Jaka* is an ancient form of *haca* meaning *one*, and *nil*, as in various outside world languages, means *nothing*. We believe Makala chose the oxymoron intentionally to misdirect those without means to understand alchemical paradoxes. It means *one thing, no thing*."

"It's a reference to the Prima Materia from which all and nothing were created," replied Cedar.

Genevre understood in that moment that the seemingly impossible was, in fact, probable. "Years ago, when Arjan was an immature alchemical child in Qingdao, we believed him to *be* the Prima Materia responsible for the time transmutation's success. Ravenea believes Arjan still represents Prima Materia, but not because of his timeline abilities. She posits that he is the Champion of Dimensions — the one who can save Council dimension."

"No, he can't. And neither can Jaden. For years, thanks to Lapidarian prophecies, I believed Jaden would save me, but I had not understood how or why. In consultation with Saule, I even inscribed manuscript lacunae to ensure Jaden's Initiation to Council. With Arjan's assistance, she did indeed save me from the void. Perhaps someday she will save the Council, but no one can save our dimension. We must choose instead to abandon it, which is the *Jakanil* ritual I now believe we must ask Arjan to perform."

"Cedar, you—"

"*Without one, the other cannot exist.* For centuries, that alchemical paradox was my primary directive. But in the void, various personal beliefs and Council tenets were twisted, turned upside down, released. The Flaw requires the Lapis, and vice versa. But the Rebel Branch does not require the Alchemists' Council."

"What are you saying?"

"I absolutely *know* now, that to save ourselves, we must leave Council dimension, closing its gates behind us. We must return to live in the outside world. My time in the void convinced me that we have only one choice left if Council dimension is ever to heal: we must renounce the myth of ascending to the One; we must forsake the Council illusions that can no longer sustain us; we must leave behind the Lapis to allow the Flaw to root; we must abandon this world for others to find and explore."

"The one and the nothing is all that was and all that will be," recited Genevre.

She held aloft *Turba Philosophorum 1881* and read from folio 50 verso. Many of Makala's varied riddles and their complex diction had puzzled both her and Ravenea for months. But now, thanks to Cedar's time in the void and understanding gained therein, they had agreed upon a critical interpretation. Genevre stood to Ravenea's left, Cedar to her right. Arjan sat on the Azothian dais in front of them. The other thirty-three remaining Council members and three Keepers of the Book knelt on the mosaic floor to witness and grant their concurrence. On this day, having reached mutual agreement after manifold days of various Meetings of Decision, they would together vow to accept the Words of Commencement and, thus, the initiation of *Jakanil.*

"As *Turba Philosophorum 1881* clarifies, Prima Materia cannot be confined," declared Ravenea. "No one and nothing — including mutual conjunction — can contain an alchemical child once birthed from the sacred alembic. Sadira could not contain

Kalina. And Dracaen could not contain you, Arjan. As Prima Materia, you must be free from the perfected bond of the Rebis — free to choose, free to create, free to extinguish, free to renew."

"How did I survive when Kalina did not?" Arjan asked. He had already asked Genevre this question, but all in attendance were required to witness and accept Ravenea's response.

"As Makala would say, evolution breeds exception," said Ravenea. *"He will be the exception*, she told me repeatedly — the Champion of Dimensions. But I did not fully comprehend the implications of *Chimera Veritas*. And, until recently, the wisdom of *Turba Philosophorum 1881* remained hidden from us all. The former outlines the means to enact mutual conjunction; the latter outlines its repercussions. Neither text is complete on its own." Ravenea opened both manuscripts to the illumination of the young man in turquoise robes with the gilded sceptre. "You, Arjan, are the exception. You are the Champion of Dimensions."

"This image could be of anyone with similar features to mine. My existence was no more an exception than Kalina's."

"We posit two theories regarding your survival," said Genevre. "Either or both could be the factor or factors that made you uniquely suitable for the intended transmutation."

"Tell me," said Arjan.

"The first," said Genevre, "is your pendant cord.

An Azadirian metalworker in Qingdao alchemically altered the cord's silver. Thanks to its elemental structure, you may have spontaneously entered the quintessential void it produced while Dracaen succumbed to dissolution."

"The second," said Cedar, "is us — Genevre and me. Our genetics and histories, like those of everyone, are distinctive. But ours evolved separately and conjoined together to encode *you*: our creation, our alchemy, our child. Without our crossing paths — forging eternal bonds — you would not exist as *you*. Life. Existence. Desire. Love. All so utterly simple in theory, yet so astoundingly complex in their variations."

"You are the seed, the kernel, the stone," Ravenea said to Arjan. "You are both the Lapis and the Flaw. With us, you will behold an ending. With us, you will create a new beginning through the Ritual of Renewal. But first we must fulfill *Jakanil*. And to begin the process, you must choose to die once again."

"Again?" asked Arjan.

"You died during the dissolution with Dracaen," Ravenea explained. "You were reborn from the alchemical flames. Now you must die in the presence of your creators and abandon the world in which you were forged. Only then will the dimension begin to restore itself anew through the rebirth of the Alchemical Tree."

Arjan held out his hands — one to Genevre and one to Cedar.

"Only one born of three can make the invisible visible," recited Ravenea. "Genevre awakened the *Osmanthian Codex*. Extinguishing this iteration of Council dimension and reawakening together in the outside world requires one *conjoined* with three — four essences, four elements to bind as the fifth: Quintessence."

"Who will be our fourth?" asked Arjan.

"I advise balance," said Ravenea. "Since you, Cedar, and Genevre each have ties with both the Council and Rebel Branch, so should your chosen fourth. This conjunction will ensure balance between the ideals and requirements of both the collective and individual."

"Jaden," suggested Cedar.

"No," said Ravenea. "She and Arjan were both initiated to Council. Genevre maintains her quintessential connection with the outside world. For equanimity between Council dimension and the outside world, Arjan requires the fourth to align, like Genevre, not only to both Council and Flaw dimensions but primarily to the outside world."

"Jinjing," said Cedar, Arjan, and Genevre at once.

"Do you accept this nomination, Jinjing?" asked Ravenea.

"I do, Ravenea," answered Jinjing.

Ravenea paused and moved her hands into the second position of Ab Uno. The others followed suit, heads up, eyes watching.

"In the name of the Azoth Magen of the 19th

Council of Alchemists," proclaimed Ravenea. "I hereby declare that Cedar, Arjan, Genevre, and Jinjing will comprise *Jakanil*, thereby enacting the Quatrain of Quintessence. In you four together lies our greatest potential. Let the Phases of Death and Renewal begin!"

ꬵlaw Dimension — 2020

The Elders — rebels and alchemists alike — held certain Law Codes inviolable. No matter their differing views on matters of the One or the Flaw or the advent of *Jakanil*, they all agreed that manuscripts were sacred. No manuscript, including *Chimera Veritas* and the *Osmanthian Codex*, should be purposely extracted from a primary dimension — not without severe extenuating circumstances, not without deliberation. Now, after three full days of intense debates over the manuscripts in Azothian Chambers, the Joint Coalition reconvened on the fourth day in Flaw dimension. High Azoth Fraxinus presided. Ravenea sat immediately to his right, Genevre and Arjan to his left. Elders from both the Rebel Branch and the Alchemists' Council filled the remaining seats along the sides of the Grand Table. Alchemists and rebels from all other orders were seated on wooden benches along the walls of the room. Cedar doubted a shift of location would lead to resolution. All she could hope was that the vote, when taken later that day, would not result in a tie.

"We cannot know what the future holds!" said Fraxinus, thus repeating his primary sentiment from the previous debates. "The Elders of the Alchemists' Council can choose to abandon Council dimension, but you cannot make ultimatums about Rebel Branch manuscripts."

"The manuscripts in question are not yours, Fraxinus," replied Ravenea. "Be grateful that we are asking for only a few and not the thousands the Rebel Branch stole from the Alchemists' Council generations ago."

"And all but one of the archival manuscripts remains in pristine condition," he said, glancing at Genevre, "because the Flaw dimension libraries are *safe*. Hence, our proposal to house *all* Council's manuscripts within our libraries. During your . . . absence from Council dimension, rebel Scribes and Readers would be able to continue to seek answers in myriad manuscripts."

"You already possess more than enough manuscripts to keep your Scribes and Readers busy. The other Council manuscripts will remain safely locked within Council dimension as it heals. We ask only for the few manuscripts, currently within possession of the Rebel Branch, that we know pose extraordinary danger to the worlds."

"The *Osmanthian Codex* is *ours*."

"No, Fraxinus," interjected Genevre. "I awakened the *Osmanthian Codex*; thus, it belongs to me. I agree with Ravenea. We cannot risk future alchemists — whether those of the Council or the Rebel Branch — making the same mistakes that we did in our recent past."

"In destroying alchemical manuscripts, you would be setting a dangerous precedent!" bellowed Fraxinus.

"The greater danger is to continue to house the manuscripts within reach of power-hungry alchemists. If we leave *Chimera Veritas* and the *Osmanthian Codex* in the Rebel Branch archives, the possibility remains that alchemical children will be created and that those children could affect the timeline. We must put an end to this cycle *now!*"

After two additional hours of debates that continually circled back to variations of these primary points, a vote was finally called. Fortunately, Ravenea had prevailed in gaining equal support for her position from both Council and Rebel Elders. With all votes cast but one, the room stood at a tie. Under other circumstances, Obeche's vote would not have seemed so crucial. But he had been randomly selected as the Final Vote.

"What say you?" Fraxinus asked Obeche.

Cedar watched him intently. He caught her eyes. *Trade is troth.*

"My choice aligns with Azoth Magen Ravenea," responded Obeche.

Fraxinus slammed his fists onto the table.

Thus, two days before the remaining thirty-six members of the Alchemists' Council would systematically forsake their dimension, the Joint Coalition opted to excise from the primary dimensions the *Osmanthian Codex*, *Chimera Veritas*, and *Turba Philosophorum 1881*, each of which prideful ancestors had inscribed and covetous descendants had abused.

Santa Fe — 2020

Jaden thought back to the first time she had seen Arjan — that day, years ago, when Sadira had ushered him into the Initiate classroom. He had seemed so suave, so self-assured, so unlike her. Beforehand, on good days, Jaden had felt ambiguous about her relatively new life with the Alchemists' Council. She had felt trapped, powerless, despite the virtually eternal power a seat on Council seemed to promise. On bad days, she had longed for escape from Council dimension, occasionally even from life itself. And then, there he was. Arjan had walked into the Initiate classroom and into her life. Little by little, he had become for her a reason to persevere. He represented hope where none had previously existed. Working with him, she had come to recognize her own value: her ingenuity and integrity.

The fire crackled. The table at which they sat awaiting their meal seemed to Jaden precariously positioned — the heat emanating from the fireplace a bit too intense for her comfort. Her mouth likewise burned, not from the fire but from the spices in the appetizer. To anyone else in the restaurant, she and Arjan would look like a couple on a date. For one night, they were two ordinary people, spending time with each other, on vacation from their day-to-day responsibilities. No one watching them knew that — mere days ago — alchemical bloodline descendants had anointed Arjan to embody the *Jakanil* in his conjunction with others. No one knew that — mere days from now — he would represent the Prima Materia in a ritual meant to seal one world in order to mitigate the destruction of others.

"You seem a world away," he observed.

"Just lost in my thoughts."

"About me?"

She blushed, embarrassed. But, with relief, she doubted her face could turn any redder than it already felt from the heat of the fire.

"I don't have a penny for them — your thoughts — but would you believe I can turn this salt into gold?" He clinked his knife against the mill.

"I believe you could turn this water to wine," she said, tapping her glass.

He nodded and smiled in appreciation of her wit. "So, you think me a messiah?"

"If the robes fit."

He laughed. "Actually, I find these outside world clothes rather binding. Perhaps you could help me remove them." He paused, and Jaden met his gaze. "Of course, restaurant etiquette would require us to wait until we vacate the premises."

"Do messiahs generally engage in carnal pleasure prior to ritual sacrifice?"

"I hesitate to speak on behalf of all messiahs. But as Arjan — Champion of Dimensions — I will say I've been wanting to kiss you since we first spilled ink on a manuscript."

Jaden almost tipped over her water as she reached across the table for Arjan's hand.

Rathtrevor Beach, British Columbia — 2020

Arjan stood amidst borders. Like the illuminations of the Champion of Dimensions, he wielded a sceptre. Dimensions, elements, geography, and time intersected here on the beach between forest and ocean, between day and night. At this liminal point, he would die and be reborn. Slain yet not dead, alive yet not born, Arjan represented the essence of Prima Materia, able to transmute his very being and all that it embodied. He pushed his heels into the moist, supple sand.

His dark hair hung loose, cascading over his shoulders. He wore a knee-length white cotton cloth fastened around his waist. The sun rested on the horizon, beginning its descent out of sight, the moon already visible. Skeletons of burnt trees from a scorched land stood within his sightline. Seaweed floated in the waters before him. To his right, holding the alchemical sulphur: Ravenea, Obeche, and Genevre; to his left, holding the alchemical mercury: Jaden, Jinjing, and Cedar. The sweet fragrance of roses wafted. The salt waves of the ocean teasingly licked his feet. He spotted an eagle feather and reached towards it. But, just then, his skin began to crackle, as if desiccated from beneath its surface, transforming from the sleek softness Jaden had caressed earlier to something akin to reptilian scales. The infusion had begun.

Seemingly random lines of black against his skin appeared first — like ink infused with obsidian from the deep caverns of Flaw dimension. The lines gradually joined with one another to form sketches of familiar shapes: flowers, bees, trees, plants, and planets. One after the next, such images appeared along his arms. Within minutes, the black outlines traversed his entire body. He became parchment to an invisible pen, then canvas to an unseen brush as the colours bled in. The flowers became purple and red and pink; the bees yellow and black; the trees tan and rust and amber; the plants, shades of verdant green. An innocent onlooker — of whom there were none at this late hour — would deem him covered in extensive and elaborate tattoos. But the alchemists knew the truth: the text was about to consume the body.

Jinjing held the Manuscript of Infusion. Its folios were sewn together with a spiral of thin copper wire, its pages not parchment but bark of arbutus trees. Jaden turned each page as Genevre and Cedar alternately read aloud its text. Obeche raised his face to the sky, moving his hands through the air above his head. Ravenea lowered herself to the ground, palms down, hands sinking into the sand. Arjan began to whirl — twirling and twirling, his feet burrowing into the moist sand. His body moved so quickly that it defied gravity, the multiple colours inked into his skin blurring into a cyclonic spectral. Finally, abruptly, the whirlwind collapsed. The colours that now comprised Arjan himself fell as grains of sand to the beach, swiftly dispersed in the landing and retreat of a crashing wave.

Jaden cried out, dropping to her knees beside Ravenea. She gathered a handful of sand, but Cedar convinced her to let it go. As the water washed the granular remains of Arjan from her hands, Jaden wept. No one could convince her in that moment that Arjan would rematerialize.

"When?" Jaden demanded. "Where?"

Ravenea need not reply. The transmutation had already begun. The individual grains burst from the sand and water, concentrated into a ribbon of colour that swirled in rapid contortions through the air at the shoreline. A sudden, bright flash across the expanse of sky and ocean caused all alchemists who watched to recoil, temporarily blinded. But then, upon opening their eyes and refocusing, they smiled.

Arjan once again stood before them — naked, and as suave as always.

"The world has been primed," he said. "In the wake of this symbolic death and rebirth, together we can begin our move towards Renewal."

Santa Fe — 2020

Cedar lifted a small copper bowl from the tray and set it on the table.

"Try one," she said to Genevre, gesturing towards the sweets in the bowl.

"What are they?"

"Spheres of cardamom nougat."

"Did you make them?" asked Genevre.

"No."

"What's in them?"

"Sugar . . . cream . . . egg . . . cardamom. Cinnamon, probably."

Genevre nodded. She reached for a small piece and held it to her lips. The scent of the cardamom enticed her. She watched Cedar pouring the coffee. A drop of dark liquid fell to the tray as she moved the pot between the two cups. The taste and texture flooded her senses — soft, supple sweetness against her teeth and tongue. She closed her eyes to savour the moment.

"Pistachios," said Genevre.

"Pistachios?"

"The nougat also contains pistachios."

"Right." Cedar nodded. "I had forgotten."

They consumed sips of tea and bites of nougat in speechless observation of one another — hands to cups, cups to lips, fingers to nougat, nougat to mouths, tongues to nougat-sticky fingertips. Several minutes passed before Genevre stood up, breaking the illusion and silence.

"I have something for you," she said. From behind a book on a nearby shelf, Genevre retrieved a rectangular package wrapped in paper inlaid with a symmetrical design of gold and silver. She handed it to Cedar.

Cedar stared. "The paper is exquisite." She carefully unwrapped the gift, removed the box's lid, and withdrew a black cloth bag, which she tipped forward, releasing its contents into her palm: two small golden spoons.

"I don't understand."

"What better means to stir honey into our tea?" said Genevre. "In our studio."

"Our studio?"

"Do you not remember our fantasy studio?"

Cedar smiled. "I do."

"I made the spoons with you in mind. I finally managed to transmute base metal into gold."

Cedar blushed, laughing. She placed the spoons onto the table and stood up, taking a step towards Genevre.

"I have an idea," Genevre said. She moved from the table to the door.

"Studio shopping at this hour?"

"No," Genevre laughed. "Follow me."

They walked along the streets of Santa Fe. Genevre ran ahead. Cedar raced to catch up. She reached for Genevre's hand. Genevre stopped and turned to her. A light breeze brushed past them in the moonlit alcove of juniper.

"What are we doing?" Cedar asked.

Genevre pulled Cedar towards her, holding her close. Cedar felt bathed in the sweet-lemon fragrance of Genevre's hair.

"Mutual regeneration," said Genevre.

"But the catacomb alembics no longer—"

Genevre held up a fragment of Dragonblood Stone. "Fraxinus has provided me permanent access to Flaw dimension. His motive remains unclear. Most likely he hopes to keep me as an ally. But tonight, we need not concern ourselves with anyone else's agenda."

"Rebels would nonetheless question our presence in Flaw dimension."

"Fraxinus, along with all the rebel Elders, surely remains immersed in the archival libraries, confirming their catalogue holdings. We will immerse ourselves in the cavern pools."

Within the hour, they were traversing the dimly lit, uncomfortably cool passageways of Flaw dimension. But, soon enough, the damp chill of the upper passages gave way to the warm comforting moisture of the lower caverns. As they crossed the threshold into a large grotto, the empty darkness brightened into swaths of colourful light emanating from the pools.

"This one," suggested Genevre, having surveyed the options and chosen the only one made of crystalline blue obsidian.

Genevre undressed and stood beside Cedar. Cedar smiled. She lay her own clothes over a nearby stone partition. Together they stepped into the warm waters. They lay on their sides, facing each other, heads against soft cushions, bodies submerged.

"I don't know the words for mutual generation in Flaw dimension," said Cedar.

"I do," said Genevre. "But once I chant them, the alchemical powers of the pool will subsume us. We will then be unconscious, immobile until the regeneration is complete."

"Wait, then. I want some time first. With you. With us. Conscious. Able to move."

Genevre kissed Cedar's forehead, her cheeks, her lips. Under the water, they embraced each other. She gently pushed Cedar onto her back and shifted position, moving one of her legs between Cedar's. Their breasts touched. Cedar pulled Genevre closer.

The luminescence of the cavern pool began to

change colour. The waters were calling to them, unwilling to wait.

"When you recite the chant, I want you inside me," said Cedar.

They moved through the water, side by side once again.

"Earth and Air," Genevre began. She reached for Cedar. "Fire and Water." And Cedar reached for her. "From the Flaw to the Scribe." She moved inside Cedar. "From the Scribe to the Reader." And Cedar moved inside her.

Her mouth brushing Cedar's, Genevre recited the ritual chant in its entirety. Their physical movements mirrored the rhythms of the text — word by word, line by line, embodying the alchemy of transformation. The maroon and amber hues of the cavern pool changed to bright red and vivid orange. Cedar and Genevre gasped, entwined in their embrace, suspended in time, healing the wounds of their labours.

Qingdao Protectorate — 2020

"The three remaining protectorate libraries must be maintained for future alchemists that we cannot currently foresee," Jinjing said, by way of explanation for the armful of scrolls she held. "Of course, you may prefer to assist in London or Santa Fe. But

I want you to know . . . I *need* you to know that, provided everything progresses as intended with the Ritual of Renewal, you would be welcome to live here with me."

She released the scrolls from her arms onto a table and began their reorganization.

"Your generosity astounds me. *You* astound me," Obeche responded. "But what will we do together when our ages catch up to us?"

"Were you not listening to Ravenea? Tomorrow's final ritual should ensure our Quintessence remains strong even after we have sealed the portals, even outside Lapidarian proximity. After all, our daily tasks will no longer require its expenditure. Elemental balance will no longer rest solely in the hands of the alchemists."

"I no longer know how to live in this world."

She placed a hand on his arm. "Then let me teach you."

Council Dimension – 2020

Inside the fragmented remains of the deteriorated Amber Garden, Jinjing, Arjan, Genevre, and Cedar moved silently into position: north, south, east, west; water, air, fire, earth. Each a direction, each an element — together the chosen four; together the hallowed square. Four were to create the fifth: the nascent Quintessence that would begin the final transmutation of the Alchemists' Council. If all progressed as planned, they would plant and cultivate a new Alchemical Tree — one whose roots, branches, and leaves would stabilize Council dimension.

One by one, they walked from their respective corners to the centre of the garden. Where the original amber tree had once stood, all that remained was a circle of barren ground — dry, russet-toned, emptied of life. Arms up, they clasped hands and positioned themselves so their feet touched one another's around the circle. Four squared became one ring. Eyes closed and faces towards the sky, they waited until the wind stirred the dust at their feet.

Cedar released her grip on Genevre and Arjan. She knelt to the ground and removed from her pocket the gift Genevre had offered her as a marriage pledge. "In the name of earth, as symbolized by this copper coin given to me by my beloved Genevre, I present to you the mineral from which the Tree of Renewal will be conceived." Cedar kissed the ground, dug a shallow hole, and set the coin therein. She returned to her position in the circle.

Jinjing stepped forward next. "In the name of water, as symbolized by this flask of honey-sweetened milk, I present to you the elixir from which the Tree of Renewal will be nourished." She tilted the flask, wetting the ground, then moved back into the circle.

Arjan smiled as he knelt. "In the name of air, as symbolized by this feather my conjoined partner

Dracaen once gave to my mother, Genevre, I present to you the breath with which the Tree of Renewal will disperse its Quintessence to all who require sustenance." Beside the coin, he gently pushed the feather into the milk-dampened ground. He then returned once again to the circle.

Genevre moved forward to the centre. "In the name of fire, as symbolized by this amber pendant formed from my tears and the flesh of my parents, Ilex and Melia, I present to you the spark with which the Tree of Renewal will inspire all to create anew." She set the pendant atop the coin. Then she stood and returned to the circle with Arjan, Jinjing, and Cedar.

"When floundering in despair," said Cedar, "welcome the extended hand."

"When lost in darkness," said Jinjing, "accept the burning flame."

"When resting in comfort," said Arjan, "wipe the fallen tears."

"When bathed in love," said Genevre, "walk the chosen path."

Eyes open, heads upright, they released their hands, walked silently back to their corners, and bowed in Ab Uno towards the circle. They then walked about the garden to greet the other alchemists and rebels who had gathered to watch the spectacle. When the sun began to set, when the rays of light warmed their faces, everyone congregated once again around the centre circle.

Jaden nodded to Obeche, who stood directly across from her holding Jinjing's hand. When the sun had descended just far enough towards the horizon, the amber pendant and copper coin glinted. The earth shook; the feather fluttered; the milk's moisture seeped away. The ground and its sacred objects blazed in flame, and a ribbon of leaves — emerald green and glistening gold — arose, twisting, flowing, growing, until it stood, solid and majestic. Branches extended, buds sprouted, blossoms released their fragrance. Petals floated overhead on the breeze. Where absence had reigned, the Alchemical Tree of Quintessence now thrived.

"The outside world calls us," said Cedar to Genevre.

Hand in hand, they walked out of the garden.

London, Waterloo Station — 2020

"Do you imagine me naïve?" asked Ravenea.

"On occasion," responded Fraxinus.

"On multiple *past* occasions, I grant you. But I have matured since then."

"Not nearly enough, clearly. In opting to encourage the destruction of the *Osmanthian Codex*, you have not only disrespected your ancestors but severed a link to their blood."

"Their blood runs through us all. The manuscript did not preserve our ancestors. It merely perpetuated their mythology — outdated words and rituals destined to be misinterpreted and misused time and again. We have sealed Council dimension. Alchemists will write new texts, inscribe their own future, as citizens of the outside world."

"In rejecting our past, you compromised our future — *your* future. Surely you can sense the resonance. When the gates were locked, our three nines began. Your days are numbered."

"Time will tell."

Fraxinus huffed. "What specifically did you do with *Osmanthian Codex*?"

"We excised it along with the others."

"Did you retain its ashes?"

"You misunderstand, Fraxinus. We did not burn the manuscripts. The Alchemists' Council, even in the worst of times, is not in the habit of burning books. We used the blood of Osmanthus — purged from multiple folios of the *Osmanthian Codex* — to open two breaches. Through one, we sent the *Osmanthian Codex*, *Chimera Veritas*, and *Turba Philosophorum 1881* into a void wherein they will be suspended for eternity. Through the other, we sent hundreds of Lapidarian manuscripts to an alternate point on the timeline."

"You sent sacred manuscripts into a future timeline?"

"No. We relegated them to the past."

Fraxinus stared, unbelieving. "When? Where? To Council dimension archives?"

"No. To a cave in the outside world."

"What?!"

"Well, more of a cavern, within a protected rock formation. Ten thousand years ago."

Fraxinus could not respond.

"Jaden suggested it — indirectly. *How did the outside world develop its alchemical lore? How did they know of the Rebis?* she asked. Of course, we would never choose to intentionally distort the past. But the more we theorized together, the more we recognized that outside world alchemy has always already had mythical origins. You know the sort — alchemy as a gift from the heavens, original manuscripts that appeared as if from nowhere at all. We asked ourselves how such divine manifestation could be possible in their world. And that's when we realized *we* could provide the outside world with the basic principles of alchemical knowledge. And with that knowledge, they themselves could learn to maintain the elemental balance of their world."

"But that is not what happened. We know they misunderstood alchemical knowledge."

"As have we all," said Ravenea.

"You have deprived us of our birthright and endangered the outside world."

"No, Fraxinus. We have ensured that the people of the outside world have access to alchemical texts, to the knowledge and possibility of transformation.

They can now — today — choose to reinterpret, to rewrite, to recreate those texts. They can choose to change. Or they can choose to stagnate. They can choose to create. Or they can choose to destroy. As the ancestors offered to the primary dimensions, we have offered to the world."

"The entire Alchemists' Council has broken its sacred vow."

"No. We have merely chosen to change its words."

Nanaimo, British Columbia — 2020

Cedar and Genevre stood on the apartment balcony looking out towards the mountain in the distance and down at the cars on the street. Snow fell in large feathery flakes. A seagull flew by, only a few feet from the railing, startling Genevre.

"I don't like it here," she said. "This city is too small. And cold. And damp."

"You said you wanted to be near Jaden and Arjan," replied Cedar. "They've chosen to live on this island."

"I *do* want to be here for Jaden and Arjan. But I prefer Santa Fe."

"We can go back if you want. I'd go with you — wherever you'd like."

Genevre kissed her lightly on the lips. "Thank you, but no. We agreed. We'll stay here. Besides, I may prefer the climate and landscape of Santa Fe, but given all that happened there, I have no desire to return for more than occasional visits."

"Perhaps you should ask Fraxinus to open a portal between here and Flaw dimension," Cedar said. "The statue in front of Nanaimo's downtown library seems ideal in that regard. Tell him that, in return, you'll visit with him each month to open the door-not-door."

Genevre shook her head and smiled. "Let's go inside," she said, taking Cedar's hand. "The snow is pretty, but it's too cold for me."

A while later, sitting on the sofa, the heat from the fireplace warming the room, Cedar asked the questions she had avoided during the weeks they had spent transitioning into their new home and landscape. "Do you think our plan will work? Do you think, left alone to take root, the Alchemical Tree can flourish? That without our interference, it will grow to support and stabilize Council dimension?"

"I don't know. But I think we made the right choices — to leave, to reside in the outside world close to Jaden and Arjan, to live with one another like regular people."

"Ha!" Cedar laughed. "We will *never* be regular people! It's *far* too late!"

Genevre smiled and nodded. "Fine. We can be *irregular* people, like all former alchemists who used to control the elements but now can barely keep themselves warm."

"I'm perfectly comfortable here," said Cedar. "But I nonetheless hope that someday we can return together to Council dimension."

"Ravenea or Fraxinus will send word soon enough."

"That prediction presumes Fraxinus will keep his word to Ravenea."

"He will," insisted Genevre. "Despite everything, I have faith in him. Besides, what choice does Fraxinus have now other than to work with Ravenea towards the stability of all three dimensions? Meanwhile, you, Jaden, Arjan, and I have residual Quintessence and each other for support."

Cedar lifted her wine glass for a toast. "To the plan! To dimensional stability!"

"To change! To growth!" responded Genevre.

"Long live the Quintessence!"

"Long live the Alchemical Tree!"

EPILOGUE
ffLaw Dimension — Dusk of the 5th Council

A s had become her weekly habit over the past century, High Azoth Makala contented herself on this otherwise unremarkable day by engaging the time turrets in each of the ten obscured libraries of Flaw dimension. She presently stood at the bronze-gilded railing on the second floor of the sixth library about to engage the turret. Bent slightly over the barrier, she could observe the main reading tables on the lower landing, as well as extensive bookcases holding innumerable manuscripts on the floors directly above and below. Each of the obscured libraries housed a timeline vantage point, but this one allowed a particularly unobstructed and impressive view. She never tired of positioning herself at its edge and admiring such a remarkable portion of her greatest accomplishment. Over the centuries, presiding as both Azoth Magen and High Azoth, Makala had made numerous and substantial contributions to both the Alchemists' Council and the Rebel Branch — not the least of which was the indisputably practical and powerful 5th Council script and dialogue. But her greatest accomplishment had been the confiscation of alchemical manuscripts of the Second Rebellion and the series of secreted repositories in which to hide them.

During the first century of her reign, Makala had charged several dedicated Scribes with three primary tasks: first, to replicate the most valuable of manuscripts, thereby mitigating the negative impact of loss or damage to the originals; second, to create feigned simulacra, thereby substantially increasing the prospect that unwelcome intruders would be misled in their historical and alchemical pursuits; and, third, to create the alchemical equivalent of an optical illusion, thus making the already impressive manuscript collection appear manifestly grander. Now, only Makala remained to distinguish the originals from the forgeries, the tangible from illusory. She sighed. She knew her remaining time with both alchemists and rebels had begun to diminish. Her elemental essence had started to fragment, her alchemical cohesion to separate. Such was the eventual fate of every alchemical child, whether conjoined or not. Indeed, such was the eventual fate of every alchemist, of every alchemical creation. Even for the most powerful of alchemists, eternity was a misnomer outside ultimate conjunction with the One.

How many years remained for Makala to locate the bloodline alchemist who would open the libraries for her son who, in turn, would open the manuscripts for her daughter? Her hope had begun to fade that her children together could resolve the impenetrable alchemical mystery that had eluded all alchemists since Aralia and Osmanthus: the conjunction of concord and discord, of perpetual harmony among beings who continuously assert individual choice.

Makala grasped the inlaid emerald knob atop the fourth obelisk of the railing and twisted it one rotation to the left. Immediately, dimensional unity within the library noticeably shifted and, a few seconds later, resettled. Every aspect of the room appeared virtually the same as it had only moments ago, but Makala understood by the citrine tinge on the airborne dust that she was now observing a time outside her own. Though she remained standing at her vantage point in her own library's timeline, the room into which she looked existed at a random point in the future. Seeing nothing amiss, she twisted the knob again. Here too, in the next time shift, all remained the same as it had before. As usual, after only twenty of her intended sixty rotations, she was lulled into expecting to see an identical room in the next time shift. She almost lost her balance when she noticed a young woman standing directly beneath her in the middle of the first-floor landing.

Makala watched her glance around the room, its magnificence seemingly impressing her. But the woman did not linger in the sixth library; instead, she moved across the landing, past the manuscript tables, and through the door to the seventh. Makala was stunned. Finally, she had crossed paths with an alchemist who had done the virtually impossible: unlocked the doors of the obscured libraries — something even her own children were alchemically unequipped to do given temporal shifts and blood-line transposition.

Makala raced from her position on the second floor down to the lower landing and through the entrance to the seventh library. Of course, having left the time turret, Makala had simultaneously abandoned the means to see into the future. Therefore, as she raced through the seventh, eighth, and ninth libraries, finally crossing the threshold into the tenth, she did so in her own timeline. Though she had of necessity lost track of the woman, Makala held hope that if she sat in the requisite turret chair in the tenth library and turned the knob on the left armrest twenty full rotations, she would see the woman again within *her* timeline. Her theory proved correct.

The woman had long dark hair with a white streak at her temple. She stood in front of the room's sole manuscript, turning its pages slowly. She appeared perplexed, thoughtful. Suddenly, the woman shuddered visibly. She then removed a piece of crystal from within her robes, sliced open a wound on her finger, held it above the manuscript, and released a large drop of blood onto the first folio. Gradually an inscription appeared. Makala smiled. The Draconian prophecy Osmanthus had inscribed eons ago had materialized. This woman was the *one born of three*.

The ability not only to unlock the libraries but enliven the *Osmanthian Codex* meant that this woman of the future carried the blood of the ancients. Makala had, after all, sealed the doors and inscribed the prophecy with originary blood salvaged from the cinders of *Materia Liberi* — the manuscript she had burned in front of Savar. Like Makala herself, this woman of the future carried the blood of the Prima Materia — the ancestral blood of Aralia and Osmanthus.

Makala looked up as a man walked into the room, startling the woman.

"Congratulations," he said.

As Makala listened to their conversation, she realized that the man was High Azoth and the woman was an outside world scribe. Eventually, he commanded the woman to leave the room, but she refused. He explained — justifiably so — that the manuscript needed to mature, and the woman appeared to believe him, acquiescing. Yet, before leaving, she asked him to translate the inscription that had already manifested on the first folio. He glanced at the words, appeared elated, and called the manuscript *our greatest potential.* Makala laughed.

"What do the words say?" the woman asked him.

"Roughly . . ." replied the High Azoth. Then he paused, seemingly for dramatic effect. "*Formula for the Conception of the Alchemical Child.*"

Makala clasped her hands together in joy.

After watching the High Azoth lead the woman out of the room, she remained seated, contemplating, for several more minutes. Finally, generations into the future, someone had awakened the *Osmanthian Codex* just as Osmanthus had intended. Makala could now relax into her final days, knowing the Rebel Branch would indeed gain access to ancestral knowledge in the future, knowing that the bloodline of her father would be perpetuated, that alchemical children would be born and bred once again, that the Alchemical Tree would flourish.

Contemplating these future children, she then thought back to her own. Though her twins had left her centuries ago, never to return, she had vowed at their birth to love them both equally. As she had planned centuries earlier, only her son would reside with the rebels. Thus, only her son would have access to this manuscript. Without the help of her brother, her daughter would never attain the alchemical secrets of the *Osmanthian Codex.* She wanted to know — needed to know — if Fraxinus had shared the manuscript secrets with Ravenea.

Makala made a spontaneous and unorthodox decision in that moment of need. Against the well-established protocols that her ancestors set forth, she opted to purposely search for him. If he had ascended to Azoth within Flaw dimension, he would know that someone had activated the manuscript. More pertinent, he would seek its knowledge, engage in its study within its dedicated room. So, she pushed back against the chair and rotated the knob to the left, then again, and again. At each time shift, she paused and surveyed the room. The manuscript appeared alternately opened or closed, but on none of the subsequent forty-three rotations did she see anyone — not the High Azoth, not the one born of three, and certainly not either of her alchemical children. Finally, on the seventy-fourth rotation — one short of the point at which she had promised herself she would desist — her desired outcome manifested.

"Fraxinus!" she called.

He heard her, turned, and stared open-mouthed.

"Mother? How can it be!" he asked, astounded. "Have you crossed through time?"

"No. I've not *crossed*. This chair is a time turret — a point in my time from which I can covertly observe the future. You are able to see and hear me only because you yourself once crossed from my timeline into your own."

He moved towards her, reaching his hands

through the invisible barrier separating dimensional time. Their alchemical bond allowed for a temporary breach through which they could touch before the rift crackled and sparked, causing Fraxinus to jolt quickly to the side. Only then did Makala notice that the *Osmanthian Codex*, which had previously rested on a stand on the table, was gone.

"The *Codex*!" she exclaimed. "Have you taken it elsewhere?"

He turned towards the table. "No."

"But I observed a woman enliven it — years ago, I presume, within your timeline. And for many years thereafter it resided here. On every rotation —"

"Yes, it did reside here until quite recently."

"What is her name — the name of the woman who enlivened it?"

"Genevre. An outside world scribe with superior alchemical pedigree. She's a daughter of Ilex and Melia who, as it turns out, were both direct descendants of the primordial bloodline. You may even recall Melia's grandfather, Vetasah."

"Vetasah?"

"Reader Vetasah of the 3rd Alchemists' Council — the first alchemist born of the bloodline to abandon Council for an outside world lover."

"Vetasah! Of course!"

"Thereafter, he became the first to propagate biologically rather than alchemically. He taught his children and grandchildren all that he knew of blood alchemy. But that is a story for another day."

"The repercussions!" exclaimed Makala. "He should have been sanctioned rather than left to perpetrate his unorthodox perversions!"

"If the Council had taken such action against him in your time, the *Osmanthian Codex* would have remained sealed in mine. We should be offering him our gratitude for providing us a descendant who allowed rebels of *this* timeline to regain ancestral knowledge."

"Yes, I suppose you are correct. Needless to say, I have always intended for you and Ravenea to gain access to your ancestral powers. When was it activated? And where is it now?"

"Genevre enlivened it more than one hundred and forty years ago. A few weeks ago, against my advice, the Alchemists' Council opted to relegate it to a dimensional void. For all intents and purposes, the *Osmanthian Codex* is currently inaccessible."

"Impossible!"

He explained everything to her then — all that he knew of the events leading to the manuscript's relocation. She listened for over an hour, shocked but enraptured.

"Oh, Fraxinus! Your bloodline power is intrinsically linked to that manuscript. And what of Ravenea? If the other one—"

"The other one? Are you suggesting the *Osmanthian Codex* has a duplicate?"

"No! Not a duplicate, but—"

"Do not spare me the truth, Mother! These

shelves are full of duplicates and triplicates, more replications than I have been able to count! I have been exploring the obscured libraries since the day Genevre unlocked its doors."

"Did she unlock the door for you today?"

"In a manner of speaking," he said bluntly. "You were saying . . . the *Codex*—"

"Duplicates exist of *other* manuscripts. But the *Osmanthian Codex* is unique. Its ink comprises blood of Osmanthus and original Lapidarian Elixir. It can be *transcribed* with Lapidarian or Dragonsblood ink, but its true alchemical powers are bound to the original. Once the original is removed from the dimension, all transcribed folios simultaneously will begin to dissolve."

"Fascinating."

"Fraxinus, you are a direct descendant of Osmanthus. With the *Osmanthian Codex* virtually destroyed in your timeline, your own powers may likewise begin to dissolve. The three nines will begin if they have not done so already. Ravenea—"

"They have indeed begun. But I feel perfectly fine."

"You may *appear* fine, but eventually you'll be unable to halt the repercussions of the manuscript's relocation. You must return to your original time-line — *my* timeline. Come home!"

"What would happen to an extracted folio?" Fraxinus asked, ignoring her plea.

"An extracted folio? What are you—"

"If someone had extracted — torn out — a folio from the *Osmanthian Codex* prior to the manuscript's dimensional relocation, what would have become of it when the *Codex* itself was transferred into the void? Would it too begin to dissolve, like the transcriptions?"

Makala laughed, perplexed and unnerved. "A loophole! I doubt the possibility of such blasphemous defacement would ever have occurred to my father. It certainly never occurred to me. Does such a folio exist?"

"Indeed, it does. Shortly after the manuscript matured, Genevre confiscated one of its folios in defiance of High Azoth Dracaen."

"Are you suggesting the outside world scribe possesses not only the blood of Vetasah in her veins but also holds the only remaining blood of Osmanthus from the *Codex* in her hands? Fraxinus, listen to me! You must do as I ask. You and Ravenea—"

"Fear not, Mother. I subsequently attained the folio for myself. Perhaps in preserving that page, Genevre inadvertently preserved my life — and the lives of untold others. I must find a means to express my gratitude."

"Fraxinus! For the sake of the dimensions, return to this timeline with the folio. Together, we can determine a means to locate the *Codex* and retrieve it from the void."

"I have neither interest in nor intention to return to your timeline. My *home* is here."

"Then you must attain the other one — the other manuscript."

"Which other manuscript? You said—"

"Listen to me! Go now to the ninth library! Bring back the volume that resides between *MS 15.4.9* and *MS 15.5.9*."

Fraxinus stood still, observing her intently. He then smiled, laughing quietly.

"Fraxinus, I am serious! Locate and retrieve the requisite manuscript!"

Makala felt helpless. She was unable to move from the chair to retrieve the manuscript within her own timeline — not without potentially losing sight of Fraxinus forever. She had expended thousands of rotations over the past century to find one intersection of time together.

"As High Azoth of the 5th Council Rebel Branch *and* as your mother, I insist you retrieve the manuscript! Now!"

Fraxinus nodded his consent, left without speaking, and returned a mere but interminable five minutes later. He carried the large but aesthetically unremarkable manuscript.

"Listen to me carefully, Fraxinus. You must safeguard this manuscript — ensure that it is hidden from prying eyes of both rebels and alchemists. Conceal it discreetly within Flaw dimension. Preserve it from the fate of the *Osmanthian Codex*. Tell no one, other than Ravenea, of its existence or whereabouts. If this manuscript is never found, neither it nor its blood alchemy can ever be vanquished."

He looked down at the closed manuscript. "I have already peered into this manuscript, Mother. I see no reason to inform Ravenea."

"Of course you cannot *see* a reason. The pages *appear* empty. But its current state is illusory. Like the *Osmanthian Codex*, it must first be enlivened. You are holding the original *Aralian Codex*. If Genevre—"

"Really? The original? The one and only *Aralian Codex*?"

"The manuscript is inscribed with the blood of Aralia — my mother, your grandmother. Corylus carried it through the dimensions into our timeline. If Genevre were to gain access to the *Aralian Codex*, enliven its blood alchemy for herself, her powers would be unlimited — much stronger even than my own. Or yours, or Ravenea's. But the *Aralian Codex* may well ensure the alchemical supremacy of both you and your sister!"

Fraxinus smiled, laughing as he had before.

"Pledge your vow to me, Fraxinus! Pledge that you will hide the manuscript from others and reveal its whereabouts only to your closest kin."

"In the presence of High Azoth Magen Makala, I hereby pledge my vow to reveal the whereabouts of the *Aralian Codex* only to my closest kin."

"You have remained a faithful son and brother through time and dimensions."

"No, Mother. Like the manuscript itself, my appearance has deceived you. In truth, I have not remained faithful to either of you. Removed from Council dimension, Ravenea herself will begin dissolution, just as I always intended. Of course, her demise took longer than expected, and the three nines could take years rather than days. But, like all alchemical twins, as you well know, one must eventually die. She is to be the one."

"What? No! You can help her. Take her the manuscript. Its blood-alchemy rituals—"

"I see no personal benefit to that plan."

"Fraxinus, Ravenea is your sister!"

"Your hypocrisy is unbecoming. Self-preservation has spurred my steps — like mother, like son. The actions I have taken over the centuries were to assist *me*, not you or my sister."

"My goal was the preservation of *all* alchemical children, including the three of us!"

"Yet you chose to wield victory over your own twin brother and then to hide the *Osmanthian* and *Aralian Codices* from your children, even though the blood alchemy revealed therein could have helped us immeasurably throughout our potentially eternal lives. You opted to maintain power in secrecy until the advent of your own Final Ascension."

"I hid the manuscripts to keep them and the most potent primordial bloodline rituals safe until the means to enliven them revealed itself. I inscribed and followed ancestral prophecies and protocols. I have only now crossed paths with you again. The moment I learned the *Osmanthian Codex* had been not only activated but vanquished, I provided you the location coordinates of the *Aralian Codex*. My only request is, as it has always been, that you share knowledge of its existence with your sister! Together you two can—"

"Are you certain that only one original exists for each of the two ancestral codices?"

"Yes. I told you—"

"And, as with the *Osmanthian Codex*, only the blood of one born to a mutually conjoined pair of the primordial bloodline — a pair impregnated alchemically through sexual liaisons with a third party — can activate the *Aralian Codex*?"

"The prophecy speaks only of the primordial bloodline and the requirement of one born of three. Whether or not the child must be born to a mutually conjoined pair is irrelevant—"

"No need to elaborate. I toy with you, Mother. I already know the answer."

"Fraxinus! You needn't locate another one born of three. All you require is a sample of Genevre's blood. Surely, you and your sister can devise a plan to attain her blood without requiring her permission or raising suspicion. The *Aralian Codex* may well hold the secrets to—"

"Do you presume me naïve? The very day I learned the *Osmanthian Codex* had been activated was the day I began searching for the *Aralian*. Do

431

you honestly think when I initially found it, I would simply decide to leave it untouched? That I would not conceive of a means to activate it as soon as possible without informing Genevre?"

"What are you saying?"

"Decades passed, of course. I required time to search. Fortunately, the High Azoth provided me ample opportunity on my own in the libraries — who better to help him research than his most trusted Azoth? Sixty-five years after Genevre had activated the *Osmanthian Codex*, I happened upon both the *Aralian Codex* and a means to access Genevre's blood. In fact, she provided it willingly when I offered to mix the inks for her braiding ceremony with Kalina, her alchemical child — *Blood of the Mother with Ink of the Stone*. A few days later, I activated the *Aralian Codex*. Over a century has passed since then."

"Fraxinus . . . no."

"Among its myriad secrets and ancient alchemical formulas, I discovered a few of specific interest to my self-preservation. Would you like to hear them?"

Makala stared at him, her breath becoming laboured.

"Alchemical children," he continued, "who travel forward in time and subsequently conjoin in the alternate, future timeline, fall victim to a slow degradation that results in a truncated lifespan. Fortunate coincidence had spared me from being called to conjunction until then. And upon learning this detail, I thereafter worked to ensure my name would never appear as a candidate for conjunctive partnership. Being an Azoth of the Rebel Branch had its scribal advantages."

"*Had?* Has your High Azoth seen fit to excise you from Flaw dimension?"

"Circumstances have shifted. I *am* the High Azoth and, as it happens, Keeper of All the Books." He gestured first outward to the room and then towards himself.

"What happened to the High Azoth I saw with Genevre?"

"Death by strategic planning. You see, Mother, the *Aralian Codex* also warns that any alchemist who mutually conjoins with an alchemical child will spark a destructive ripple effect through the dimensions. The effect is hastened exponentially with each additional such conjoined couple existing at the same time as the first pair. Under what I dubbed the Treaty of Fair Warning — an entirely made-up edict that I convinced Ravenea we were obligated to follow — I provided my dear sister with just enough advice to ensure she would seek and provide me with the information I required to pursue my goal: ascension to High Azoth of the Rebel Branch. Dracaen is the one who was naïve — he should have chosen someone other than me as his primary advisor and trusted confidant."

"Redeem yourself, Fraxinus! Leave here and

take the manuscript to Ravenea. Its alchemical formulas may yet be able to save you both!"

"I cannot. Doing so would break the vow you yourself insisted I make on this very day. As promised, I am to reveal the *Aralian Codex* only to my closest kin."

"Yes, to Ravenea! To your twin! She *is* your closest kin!"

"No, Ravenea may be my twin, but she is not the one to whom I am closest."

"No one is closer to you than your own kin!"

"Finally, we have reached a point on which we can agree. I have a daughter."

Makala froze, confused. Then she whispered, "Fraxinus, no . . ."

"Time and again," he continued, seemingly delighted, "High Azoth Dracaen attempted to create another alchemical child — to replicate the success he had achieved with Genevre. But he failed repeatedly. He believed he shared an ancestor with Ilex and Melia. Perhaps he did, but they did not share the ancestor that mattered: Vetasah. Dracaen simply could not accept that Genevre was the key to all. I, on the other hand, had reached that conclusion shortly after Dracaen's first failure. But I too had been partially misled. *She* was not the key per se.

"The creation — the survival — of an alchemical child did not require Genevre herself. According to the *Aralian Codex*, creation merely required her blood; that is, *the sanguine Quintessence of one born of three*. Another could stand in her place for the marriage rites, provided Genevre's primordial and prophesied blood infused the sacred vessel. You can appreciate the paradox here. I *had* a few drops of her blood, but I had already used them to activate the very manuscript in which I later discovered I required her blood to create an alchemical child."

"What is your daughter's name?"

"Though Genevre trusted me — confided in me, even — I could not simply request another sample of her blood without raising suspicion. And I certainly could not request her direct assistance. She would never again deign to enter another chemical marriage with a Rebel Branch Azoth. But then the most extraordinary miracle occurred."

Makala waited, shaking. "Fraxinus! What is her name?"

"Rest assured, Mother, she cannot be erased or manipulated through your manuscripts."

"Why would I even attempt to erase or manipulate my own grandchild? I merely wish to recognize her should we ever cross paths among the timelines."

"You are reaching the end of your tenure. You will never meet her."

"Trade is troth, Fraxinus. I gave you my blood. I ask for her name."

"Virginia."

"And what is this . . . miracle . . . that led to the creation of Virginia?"

"One day, in 1939, as I made my way across the landing of the sixth obscured library, I stumbled upon something — literally, I stumbled upon it: a small opaque flask with a ruby lid stained with blood. The properties of the blood were unmistakable. I immediately recognized it as belonging to Genevre. And the vial itself contained just enough of her blood to create for myself one pair of alchemical twins. That is, I created one enduring alchemical child: one created not only of Genevre's blood, but of mine — a descendant of the primordial ancestors. As it happened, thanks to a time transmutation Genevre orchestrated, Virginia herself left me the blood with which I created her. I had described this scenario and the flask to her so many times over the years that she recognized it when she had it in her hands.

"Over eighty years have passed since I found the blood, almost fifty since the conception. I knew Council would welcome my child once she appeared old enough to join the Initiate. All I had to do was ensure she found the right book at the right time. And all she had to do was gain access to the primary dimensions, which she managed by convincing Dracaen that someone of my appearance had stolen his precious *Osmanthian* folio. Her intellect and alchemical powers have already proven astonishing."

"Perhaps I could assist—"

"I require no further assistance, Mother. Piece by piece, over hundreds of years, I have been assembling the game. The players assumed each of their choices — for better or worse — had been made freely. But all along I have been encouraging the moves, rewriting and manipulating the rules that would lead me to victory. Even the previous Azoth Magen inadvertently provided me with key components. To make my next move, I need neither you nor Ravenea. My faith resides in my daughter, an alchemical child forged from the blood of Genevre, Vetasah, and me — a second, and completely unique, *one born of three*."

Makala did not respond.

"For years, I have honed my creation. Of late, I have been training her to be the leader she was meant to become. To answer your earlier question, Virginia supplied the blood to unlock the library doors for me today. Together, our blood-alchemy powers may well be limitless. Within the decade, she will escort me to the newly restabilized Council dimension. Our first order of business will be, in a manner of speaking, to change the locks."

"No."

"Yes. At that very moment, the nascent era of Dissolution will reach a premature end." He paused, smiling. "Long live Virginia, Azoth Magen of the 1st Council of Alchemists in the era of Fraxinus!"

He turned and walked out of the library, his future and that of the dimensions firmly secured in his hands.

ACKNOWLEDGEMENTS

So, here we are, six years later, at the end of Book Three. As in the acknowledgements of Books One and Two, I'd like to thank almost everyone I've ever met — all the family, friends, and colleagues who helped me progress to this point in my writing career. You know who you are (or, alternatively, you can look back into the previous acknowledgements and dedications to remind yourselves).

But, alas, "By Fraxinus!" as Kenneth would say, a few additional folks have stood out over Book Three's progress. Kenneth Duggan — you're one of them (despite the lack of an invitation to your Nanaimo birthday). In all seriousness, what a pleasure it has been over this past year to have you as a colleague at VIU and, even more so, as a friend at the cliff face portal. Thanks especially for your enthusiasm regarding the first two books and all the lively commentary thereon that inspired me as I worked on Book Three. Posting the shot of the owl puzzle with the missing bee was a delightful high point.

A sincere thanks, once again, to all my other colleagues and friends at VIU for your ongoing support and encouragement. Thank you, also, to my international colleagues and friends; in particular, on this occasion, I'd like to thank Cynthia Burkhead from the University of North Alabama for hosting the *Slayage Conference on the Whedonverses* in 2018. Where would Dracaen and Arjan have met Virginia if not for you and UNA's delightful campus?

Working over the years with the people at ECW Press has been an ongoing delight. Not only do I appreciate the dedication and professionalism of everyone with whom I've worked through the publication process, but I also admire ECW's commitment to engage personally with its authors. On that note, I must mention David Caron and Jessica Albert in particular: thank you for the work, walks, meals, and engaging conversations during World Fantasy Con in San Antonio and beyond! Speaking of World Fantasy Con, both Jess and Jen Albert contributed their dedication, professionalism, generosity, and joyous wit to our Los Angeles book promotion — thereby making WFC 2019 one of the highlights not only of my year but of the entire *Alchemists' Council* journey. Thank you also to Jack David for the chat over drinks in Victoria, and to

Crissy Calhoun for three books' worth of exquisite copy edits. Rest assured, Crissy, I will never again use the words "gasp" or "suddenly" without thinking of you and these books.

And to my primary editor, Jen Hale . . . what can I possibly say to express my appreciation? Back in 2014, when you informed me that *The Alchemists' Council* had been accepted for publication, you made manifest my childhood dream to become a writer. In doing so, you changed my life. For instigating and encouraging that alchemical transmutation, I will forever hold you in my heart. Your editorial advice has been stellar at every stage of the process. And as challenging as I found the revisions to implement at times — especially with Book Three, Chapter Five — I know that your suggestions and influence over the years helped to strengthen not only the books but also me. Like Cedar, Genevre, Jinjing, and Arjan, together we chose to change the words and move forward with good intentions. With love and sincere gratitude, thank you "Editor Jen" — *Long live our Alchemical Tree!*

CYNTHEA MASSON works in the English Department at Vancouver Island University where she teaches various writing and literature courses. *The Alchemists' Council* series is anchored in concepts of medieval alchemy, many of which evolved from her postdoctoral research on alchemical manuscripts at the British Library. The series' first two books won Independent Publisher Book Awards for Fantasy: Gold in 2017 for *The Alchemists' Council* and Bronze in 2019 for *The Flaw in the Stone*. She has published and presented academic works in both medieval and television studies; she is a co-editor of the book *Reading Joss Whedon*.